CARO

CARO

A Novel
by
Bernard Packer

E. P. DUTTON & CO., INC. | NEW YORK | 1975

LIBRARY OF CONGRESS CATALOGING IN PUBLICATION DATA

Packer, Bernard J
  Caro.

  I. Title.
PZ4.P117Car   [PS3566.A316]   813'.5'4   75-11858

Published simultaneously in Canada by Clarke, Irwin & Company
Limited, Toronto and Vancouver
ISBN: 0-525-07650-6

Designed by Dorothea von Elbe

For Richard Gross,
who kept the faith,
and Juris Jurjevics,
who found it.

Part One

Part One

1

Trinidad sank on the west as the *Blythe* veered toward the Río Verde delta. The island blurred into a charcoal smudge on the horizon and Jack Ritter watched the gulls swoop down for the slop he dumped into the wake. Tonight the gulls would dine on garbanzo soup, squash, whitefish and Swedish pancakes with lingonberry jam. The *Blythe,* a creaking freighter under the Norwegian flag, was not noted for its cuisine.

Ritter dropped his garbage pail and climbed over the tarpaulins covering the coiled manila lines. He rested his back against a rusty winch. The end of the supper shift meant a cigarette and he blew his first puff into a warm breeze. Mists were rolling in from all points and the rain clouds over the coast were splayed with pink membranes. It was, Ritter thought, the moment Rubén Darío had captured in his "Symphony in Grey Minor," though few of the seamen around him seemed to be savoring it. The Scandinavian deckhands were occupying their bench to starboard, discussing the body and flavor of Australian beer, while the Latinos from the engine room were on their bench, to port, boasting about what they would do when they docked in Puerto Acero the next night. Ritter glanced over at Henry Carr, the ship's carpenter, and wondered whether this man might be appreciating the spectacular sunset. Carr was at his usual niche, sitting on a mooring bitt with pipe in mouth, and obviously not engrossed by the book in his lap. Every ship had its loner, a man touched with mystery, and the carpenter filled that position on the *Blythe*.

"Hey, Jack!" Rodolfo Piñedo called to Ritter from the Latin bench. "You gonna' fickyfick in Puerto Acero tomorrow night? Last time you went with two girls."

Piñedo leered, outlining a lush figure with his palms. Ritter waved him off and shouted back, "That's because I'm young and vigorous, Piño, so I don't run surveys on what other people do. I believe your own apparatus doesn't snap to attention any more so you get your charge by hearing what the young aces are up to."

Piño's friends roared and the Gallego rose to defend himself: "Ace? You, F.B.I.? I'm twice as old as you and twice the man you are. Tomorrow night we'll ask all the girls at the Club Moderno. Back in Russia, when I was with the Blue Legion, I melted the snow over a two-kilometer area whenever I made love."

"And when you opened your mouth to talk," Ritter said, "you melted it over a five-kilometer area."

Piño's friends cackled again but the Gallego ignored them and jabbed his thumb into his solar plexus. "I am so potent, F.B.I., that a Colombiana once whispered to me, 'Gracias, su merced.' Do you know what that signifies, Gringo? 'Su merced' means 'your grace,' and that means they are yours, body and soul, and might return the fee. They might even work for you."

"That's Piño's ambition," Antonio, the wiper, cut in. "To be a pimp."

The Gallego stopped to scowl at Antonio as if he were the class dunce who had just interrupted a brilliant lecture. Then he cleared his throat and raised a didactic finger. Before he even spoke, a new idea occurred to him and he grinned

4

lewdly. The Gallego's features tended to dissolve and re-group in honor of each fresh thought in his head. Another tack was on him: humor.

"Have I told you gentlemen the joke about the Venezuelan immigration official and the Colombian artiste?"

All the Latins groaned and protested. Piño had an endless store of rotten jokes: jokes for all nations, races, religions, trades and situations. They were invariably hissed but derision only provoked Piño into launching a barrage in the same category till one drew a laugh. Tonight they squelched him. He clapped his hands for silence but his shipmates continued to hiss and simulate the act of vomiting and kept making the Roman thumbs down sign. For a few seconds Piño was help-less but then shrewdly extricated himself from this humilia-tion by fixing on Carr. Instantly his rubber face became grave and he brought his finger to his lips. "Shhh. Shhh. Quiet, you scum. We've been disturbing the carpenter with all our braying. We have no right to make this racket out here as if we owned the poop."

Piño abruptly shuffled over to the mooring bitts and draped his arm over Carr's shoulder. "I'm sorry, Henry. We didn't mean to annoy. Sometimes I get excited and forget where I am. You'll pardon us?"

Carr was startled by the intrusion. He had been oblivious to both the Scandinavians arguing about beer and the Latin merriment. He shrugged off the Gallego's arm and said, "You weren't bothering me. I didn't even hear you."

"Yes, carpenter. But when a profound man like you is with a book, the fools should be quiet and respectful. In-stead, I storm around here like a clown."

Carr sniffed. "I wasn't reading, Piño. I was in a fog. You go on about what you were doing."

"O.K., Enrique. But I'll try to stop those monkeys over there from rattling their cages."

The Gallego turned back toward his mates from the engine room, imploring them to hold down the noise. That inspired them to raise their voices and show Piñedo that they did not quite share his awe of the English carpenter.

Jack Ritter lit another cigarette and smiled at the complexity of all these petty undercurrents. As a messboy he was lowest in the pecking order and could sit back and observe all the crude nuances. He was worried because he enjoyed it out here. To his chagrin, he was a happy man lately: the sun was toasting him, his guitar was coming along, the chin-ups were filling him out, there was time to read, and his logbook was bulging with portentous reflections on the state of the cosmos. Best of all, tomorrow night he was scheduled for some "sympathy" from Lupe at the Club Moderno. Free love off a whore; much more important at this stage than the games of upward mobility back in Philadelphia.

He still felt that he should be more concerned. If this kept up he would never mature or grow deeper. Mr. Ritter, the recently minted social studies teacher, had thrown a highly cathartic hook to the mouth of a large, loutish juvenile delinquent, bruising his knuckles and ending his teaching career in the process. Two days later he declared a moratorium on his commitment to contemporary social problems. He had too many problems of his own to work out first. He took a bus to New York to catch a ship, to write and see the world. He went to sea to suffer and instead he just plain liked it on the *Blythe*.

Strangely, it was easier to break into the movies than catch the legendary tramp steamer. The Coast Guard gave no papers until the union promised a job, and the union offered no job until the Coast Guard issued papers. It was a closed circuit, which helped to explain why most American merchant vessels looked like floating old age homes.

He finally relinquished his fanciful ideas about sailing on an American ship and began hanging around the Scandinavian Seaman's Center in Brooklyn. The Scandinavians, at least, let outsiders sign on after all their card-carrying members had gotten first crack during the daily job calls. But

6

shipping was tight all over. His savings went and he found himself slipping into a bleak halfworld, where men spent the night sleeping on the long subway ride out to Coney Island or in Times Square movie houses. At Lower East Side employment agencies, he bought dishwashing jobs for eighty cents and made the car wash shape-ups to collect the quarter paid for showing up. This had been dragging on for over a month when Rodolfo Piñedo approached him in the Brooklyn hiring hall, poked him in the ribs and said, "You have a philosophy book in your back pocket, muchacho. Where do you think you are? Athens?"

"It doesn't look like Athens," Ritter answered in Spanish, for lack of greater inspiration.

"You look like an old sea dog, muchacho. You Scandinavians start out when you're fourteen."

"That's funny. I'm not Scandinavian and I'm trying to sign on my first ship."

"First ship?" The Spaniard's face underwent three transitions. "A novice? Excellent. We can sign on a ship together and become great comrades. It's been a long time since I had a great friend. I appoint you my friend. How old are you, chaval?"

"Twenty-three," Ritter answered.

"Twenty-three? A puppy. You're lucky you latched onto me. I'm a man of wide experience and I can teach you everything I know. You must be Polish or some strange thing like that. You look like a Pole I used to know."

"Close, hombre. Close. I'm from Philadelphia, U.S.A."

An evil grin creased his cheeks. "So? A Yankee is seeking a berth on a foreign ship? You're probably a spy and you'll be writing reports on our activities. And where did you learn Spanish, Mr. Hoover? At the F.B.I. espionage institute?"

"Not quite. I studied for a year in Mexico."

"Coño!" Piño spluttered. "Mexico? A magnificent country. You imperialists are lucky you didn't conquer the entire land. Then you'd have to travel all the way down to Gua-

7

temala to get your heroin and abortions. I spent two years in jail in Durango.''

From that day on he was Piño's ward and they went to the job calls together. Piño guided him to grim Baptist missions where macaroni and meatloaf dinners were served for the price of a cold shower and a fiery sermon, and took him to back alley kitchens where immigrant women dished out seventy-cent suppers to men with false passports. The Greeks and Sicilians would squint at Ritter, and Piño whispered, ''It's that damn innocent face of yours that makes everybody so nervous, F.B.I. You look like you wear red, white and blue undershorts.''

Yet Piño also made them nervous. He entered those clandestine kitchens like a Crusader returning from the Holy Land: bellowing, pinching all the female behinds within range, insisting on sticking his nose into the pot and sampling the stew before ordering, and perhaps adding a pinch of pepper or a garlic clove. Wherever he went, Piño was what was happening.

The Gallego had two chances to sign on ships and twice he turned them down because of his determination to stick with his new compañero. Naturally, Ritter had to wonder whether his self-appointed mentor might be just a little queer, but as the days passed he became ashamed of those suspicions. He could only excuse himself by remembering that this was, as the literary supplements proclaimed, the post-Freudian period, and nobody was allowed to be naïve in the year 1960. Piño was all for the ladies. Unfortunately, the ladies failed to reciprocate and so he was constantly making a fool of himself, as when they finally received their cards to sign on the *Blythe* together. They took the subway over to the doctor's office on Rector Street and Piño leered so wildly at a model in a short skirt that the girl rose and gave him an obscene finger sign before slipping out of the subway car. Fifteen minutes later he came close to igniting a riot in the doctor's office. The officious nurse had drawn blood from their arms and then pointed at the examining table. "O.K., boys. Drop your pants and the doctor will see you in a few minutes."

"What do you mean—drop my pants?" Piño demanded to know.

"Just what I said. You'll have to drop your pants if the doctor is to check your rectum and genitals."

"Such emotion you put in your voice when you say those words, madam."

"Look, sailor," she snapped at Piño. "Over the course of the years I've seen thousands of those things on a daily basis and I'm not impressed any more."

"Good. If you stay here while I drop my trousers, I'll restore your faith in mankind."

"You're sick," the nurse said calmly.

A maniacal gleam lit his eyes. "I can also be very sweet, my dear."

The Gallego shrugged as she slammed the door behind her. His day was not over. They reached the *Blythe* too late for supper and, after dumping their gear, they entered a gloomy diner at the foot of the pier. Ritter, with long experience at greasy spoons, ordered the simplest item possible—a grilled cheese sandwich. But Piño only grimaced at the splotched menu and continued picking at his temple, scratching his chin and running his fingers through his graying hair. Finally he gave up and turned to his partner. "Why don't they print these autopsies in a Christian language, F.B.I.? 'Salisbury Steak'? You speak this language. What vile deed is known as 'Salisbury Steak'?"

"Hamburger, usually. With some kind of brown goop on it."

"Hambuergesa? You see? This land is a citadel of deceptions. Even dead Duke Salisbury is compromised by your capitalistic manipulations. Like the woman I took out in Atlantic City. Three nights I couldn't touch her because she told me she was a virgin. Hech! Maybe her left ear was still virgin."

"You ready, Mac?" the impatient waiter asked.

Piño smiled up brightly. "Yes, your honor. The Salisbury and a glass of . . . how about your Cabernet Sauvignon?"

The counterman wiped his hands on his apron and then readjusted his cap. "Are you kidding, buddy? This ain't no bar."

Piño winced at him incredulously. "Who said it was a bar. I only want some red wine to wash down the donkey meat I can smell all the way from the kitchen."

"Tough. We ain't got no license to serve wine."

Piño tapped Ritter as if he had uncovered significant evidence. "Did you hear that, F.B.I. You call this a democracy but everybody needs a license. It's pure bluff."

Latent patriotism bristled in the counterman. He drew his shoulders back. By now all the customers were listening. "Look, buddy. If you don't like it here you can take the next boat back to whatever shithole you come from."

The Gallego smiled up at him suavely. "Thank you. This is a great honor. To be served our supper by the Minister of Immigration."

"You can't serve no wine with no license," said the counterman. "This is New Jersey, buddy."

Piño nudged Ritter with his elbow. "What a nation you spy for, F.B.I. You dump your wheat in the ocean and you can spit through this bread here. You have one thousand universities and your president is an idiot. And your waiters don't even have enough imagination to keep a bottle of wine under the counter for emergencies like me."

Piñedo stepped up his activities once he was established on the *Blythe*. He initiated rumors, defended the weak, protested all injustices, proposed improvements in all systems, and bought, sold, bartered and volunteered for all the dirty jobs so he might later grumble that he was being persecuted. The Swedes and Norwegians from the deck crew despised him. There was talk of forming a committee to settle the Spaniard down but that project was dropped the day Piño manifested inordinate strength across the shoulders. On a dollar bet with Antonio, the Gallego climbed hand over hand, legs dangling loosely, thirty feet up the port shroud, almost to the yardarm. He hung there by one arm, grunting and scratching his ribcage like a chimp. When he came down the rusty, twisted wires, his palms looked like bloody roadmaps, but he was too happy collecting his dollar to complain.

Perhaps Piño's most irritating trait was his generosity. He was constantly proving his friendship by concrete acts. Piño had decided that Bergen, the short Norwegian *jungmann,* was too frail for his duties, and would run over to help Bergen with heavy loads, infuriating the boy, who wanted to make it on his own. The latest victim of this unsolicited aid was the carpenter. Henry Carr had threatened to hit the Gallego with a wrench unless he kept his distance, but Piño persisted in doing him favors, sneaking off at night to straighten up the carpenter's shop, or bringing back bottles of whiskey from shore and leaving them on Carr's bunk. Piño also persisted in spreading the story that Carr had once been much more than a ship's carpenter. Just last evening, during the poker game in the dayroom, Piñedo had almost gone for Antonio's throat when the Panamanian wiper scoffed at his claims for the Englishman. The other poker players grabbed him and made him sit back down, but Piño was not through. He said, "You can laugh, Antonio, because you are a roach, incapable of lifting yourself over the rim of the toilet bowl to peer out and recognize quality. You don't want to recognize it. What are we? We're chaff. We're destined to end up as bums sleeping in our own vomit in back alleys. And that's what we deserve for the way we've wasted our lives. But Carr? Carr is a gentleman. Carr has an education. Carr has a profession. You can see it from his chin, his table manners, the way he holds his pipe."

Antonio giggled and said, "Piño's in love with the carpenter," and then bent double with glee.

The Gallego's face darkened. For the first time since Ritter

11

met him, Rodolfo Piñedo looked intelligent and completely lucid. He shook his head sadly. "It must be terrible to be like you, Antonio—to live in a small, dirty world without standards. The carpenter is here because of an unkind destiny. He deserves better. Carr should have a home in the country, a wife, children, dogs to greet him when he returns at night."

Antonio thought this even more hilarious and they had to slap him on the back to relieve his coughing fit.

"Look at you," Piño said. "You're nothing. You're so backward you can't even speak your own language properly. Carr is an Englishman and he speaks a purer Castilian than all you yapping monkeys. He has conversed with me and his Spanish is worthy of a bishop!" With that, Piño kicked over the card table and stormed out of the dayroom.

Ritter smiled, recalling the fracas. With his back against the winch and the dusk around him, he stared at the carpenter. Carr had not turned one page in his book and his pipe had gone out. Absorbed by the dim coastline, the man seemed oblivious to all the commotion as the Scandinavians rearranged the benches and helped the steward set up the screen and projector for the movie. *The Naked Spur,* with Robert Ryan and James Stewart, had been featured for five nights running and Ritter had the dialogue almost memorized. According to his routine, he was supposed to go down to his cabin for an hour of scales on the guitar, three sets of push-ups, ten pages of Kierkegaard and at least a one-page entry in his diary. Ritter decided to have a last cigarette before going down to his fetid cabin and all the self-development.

He studied Carr again, now just a deeper shadow in the darkness. Piño might have been correct about his archaic, formal Spanish but he was way off on the Englishman part. This carpenter was a ringer. He spoke a Spanish with Sephardic traces and there was a giveaway lilt to his impeccable English. Of course he looked English— which was to say he looked like any white man from San

Francisco to the Urals. There was even something off-key about this spurious universality. His head could have been modeled in clay for a museum bust of European man and, with those old scars running across his back and torso, he looked as though he had survived a major industrial accident and been subjected to an intensive conditioning course so that he came off as a lean, tan athlete. A hell of a role.

It was both annoying and irrefutable. Henry Carr was the only man on this ship—officers included—with a brain to his name, and the carpenter displayed no inclination for philosophizing with a messboy. It had nothing to do with the caste system. Carr had little small talk for anybody. He spent most of his time in his cabin, reading, and Piño, of all aboard, was the only man who managed to extract a few consecutive paragraphs from him in Spanish.

Ritter stood up. He had come out to sea to meet characters like this and they certainly were not going to come to him. He walked around the movie screen and sat down on the other mooring bitt next to Carr. His cigarette went sailing into the darkness and he glanced at the older man.

"Mind if I sit down here, carpenter?"

"Couldn't help it much if I did. We get one seat per bottom around here."

"Going into town tomorrow night?"

"I hadn't planned on it," Carr said without bothering to look at him.

"Fascinating place, Puerto Acero. Cadillacs and Mercedes-Benz zooming around. You see Indians coming into town with bows and arrows on their backs."

"Picturesque."

"Women from all over the world, carpenter. Cubans. Even a few French girls."

Carr sighed. To Jack Ritter it sound like the noise a man might make as he wondered when his ordeal would be over. He ignored the wheeze and continued. "Some of the crew have been telling me you've never been off the ship down

13

here. They said this was your seventh trip to Puerto Acero and you've never been ashore.''

''I suppose that's right. I hadn't been counting.''

''It's my third trip,'' said Ritter. A long silence ensued. Obviously if he did not do the talking, no talking would be done. ''You know, carpenter, last night there was an argument about you in the dayroom. Piño was claiming that you spoke Spanish like a bishop, and I thought that was kind of amusing.''

''You did?''

''Sure. I've listened to your Spanish carefully. You never commit the errors of a man who learned a language in school but of somebody born into a special dialect—in your case, Ladino. Once I caught you saying 'bebienda' instead of 'bebida.' That's pure Ladino.''

Carr knocked his pipe against the hollow metal bitt under him and blew the loose ashes into the wind. ''Don't you think you're wasting your talents as a messboy, Mr. Ritter? With your ear you should be a professor of linguistics or serving with one of your country's espionage agencies.''

Ritter chuckled, detecting an almost friendly tone. ''That's what Piño's always accusing me of. I'll probably go back to school and get my Ph.D. after I put in a few years at sea. Meanwhile I have this compulsive curiosity. I have to verify all my observations.''

''Lots of idle curiosity, eh?''

''That's right. From the lilt to your English I had you figured for a German.''

''German, now? Well, I guess that's all right. A member of the master race.''

''Your English is too perfect, carpenter. A bit too clipped and polished. It's so perfect it isn't spoken in any county of England. It's as though a Martian had decided to master the language.''

A quick flash of amusement crossed the carpenter's face and then the somberness returned to his eyes. He slowly

14

packed the bowl of his pipe, staring out at the deep blacks of the shoreline as they approached the mouth of the Río Verde. Ritter, imagining that he had struck an amiable chord, said, "And you're still going to stay on this damn hot boat tomorrow night? I don't see how you can stand the heat when it's tied up at the dock—"

"Look, boy," Carr interrupted. "I have sensed that you've wanted to somehow pounce on me before this. You are obviously a young intellectual out here to see the world, and I assume you think you can get some words of wisdom from me. So, some words of wisdom. On this ship, or anywhere you go in this world, mind your own fucking business. Is that clear? Mind your own fucking business."

"I'm sorry, carpenter. I didn't mean to—"

"That's quite all right," Carr cut him off. "Apologies are accepted. Good evening, Mr. Ritter."

The steward switched on the movie's soundtrack and the music of the American Wild West exploded over the Río Verde delta and floated out to the jungles of Santa Cruz. Henry Carr watched the messboy retreat in humiliation and confusion, circle around the screen to avoid the beam from the projector, and open the door to go below. The carpenter struck a match and sucked the flames into his pipebowl till the ashes glowed. He hadn't wanted to be that brutal with the American boy, but it was necessary. The boy was a *kavka*, a black daw—a bird of ill omen. At least this would curtail more forays into his privacy. He had nothing to spare for a callow student. There was no way he would sit out here and explore the meaning of existence with a ruddy boy.

The spectators watching *Naked Spur* laughed and Carr wondered how they could be delighted with the same film for five consecutive nights. They were fortunate, he thought, and let them be. There should be more joy in this world. Any sort of joy. A man of good will would not begrudge one second

15

of happiness to a tarantula. If this crew could sail under this darkness and derive some relief from self with nothing more than those simple images on the screen, they were to be congratulated. Henry Carr was not about to prance in front of them and whine, "Look at me. My face has been ripped away, and yet you can all laugh."

They needed to laugh. And who needed his self-pity? Who could use it? Obviously, it was bearable. When things became unbearable, a man committed suicide. These sailors had put in a hard day chipping rust under a hot sun and needed to relax. Their carpenter was not going to burden them with his particular afflictions. He was calm. The English had provided him with a serene, Celtic profile, more appealing than the original. The English plastic surgeons were excellent. Traditional excellence. After all, it was an Englishman, Joseph Carpue, who reintroduced the "Indian Nose" method to the Occident, reviving the Tagliacozzi technique. They were so proud of their handiwork. The stranger in his mirror was infinitely preferable to the shredded pulp pulled out of the ruins in London. How often had he thought this thought? How often had he sensed it forming in his mind only to reject it and find it forming anyway?

They were leaving the muddy delta and turning into the main channel. Another evening had been endured. Another night had passed without an English carpenter slipping into the waters.

2

Ritter checked the day's quota for his journal and experienced the usual disappointment. What sounded so resonant in his mind had curdled on paper. He disregarded the dubious ethics involved in editing what was supposed to be a spontaneous logbook and began making corrections.

Puerto Acero,
Santa Cruz
July 19, 1960

This whorehouse music gets to you. It floats across the moon-drenched harbor, carried by the beams and lapping waves, and—thin as it is—it fills. The music comes from Panama Street, the string of bars and brothels curling into the foothills ringing Puerto Acero, and by the time the lyrics reach the docks they have been purified of meaning. It is true misery to sit here when I could be at the Club Moderno right now.

The *Blythe* is tied up at the AmCruz Company dock. It's been nine days since our last port of call

and everybody is itchy. The Norwegians are hurting for their juice and are apt to sneak into your
cabin and drink your aftershave lotion, and all the
Latin lovers are poring over cock novels from "La
Colección Venus." One notices that the girlie magazines in the head tend to have pages stuck
together.

I finished the morning's dishes in record time
because I wanted to be up on deck when the Indian
canoes came out. By nine the sun was already high
and the *Blythe* surrounded by swamp and jungle.
This is my second attempt to paint the immense desolation of these *llanos,* and I am still
unable to satisfy myself that I've conveyed the
emptiness that fills you as you stare at this wild
savanna. A man would sink in seconds in those
marshes. Scorpions nestle under the lavender blos-
soms. Puma and kinkajou peer out through the *balata*
plants and cancerous snarls of vines.

Ocelots scamper through the branches as the
Blythe sounds its horn rounding a curve in the
river. Given a month to accomplish the mission,
the foliage, creepers and palm groves would choke
this stream and reclaim the riverbed for the plain,
but the Río Verde has a force of its own and
sweeps along mossy tree trunks all the way down to
the mouth of the Caribbean delta.

Heat and noise are in constant attendance. The
heron and crane conduct random maneuvers and
squadrons of scarlet-necked marabou fly to the east
while flights of yellow wren arrive from the west.
We are the intruders here. The occasional crocodile
on the marshy banks seems unimpressed by our
passage.

Just as living was becoming intolerable, and you
thought your skin would blister, that you would

have to throw yourself in the muddy river or go up in smoke, the sky grew viscous and murmured. It mysteriously congealed into a gray porridge, and the clouds pouring out of the mountains of the Cumaná Cordillera cracked under a whip of lightning. Sheets of harsh water slash down, pounding and pinging on the metal decks, draining away millions of splattered insects, and flooding them over the side. The sudden torrential downpour is as oppressive as the heat it alleviates.

The storm started out ferocious and then rose to higher and higher crescendos of intensity, as if nature were some mad conductor straining for codas to obliterate the auditorium. And it is over just like that. A giant spigot turns in the sky. The sun burns through the dark, widens, and repossesses the horizon. As the *Blythe* passes under the trees in the narrower stretches, the Insect Kingdom attempts to overpower the ship, dropping down legions of black and red ants, centipedes, florid caterpillars, and tenacious bloodsucking *zancudos*. They do their worst until the next cloudburst washes them over the side.

We were waiting for the girls to come out. With satellites in orbit around the earth, here are these tattooed bucks, with blowguns and darts, peering at us from the bushes. Civilized hamlets dotted the higher ground and occasionally we saw a lonely villa perched in the hills. But the natives are sealed in a time fault on those banks. They squat in the doorways of their thatched grass huts, next to unambitious plots of yucca and cassava and corn, run their dwarfed cattle and let the twentieth century, as represented by the cargo ships, go sliding down the river. They want very little from us, just cigarettes and pots and bottles, and maybe a few rags.

A whoop went up from the men on the prow as we reached the confluence of the Río Blanco and the main channel. A canoe darted out of the rushes with four girls, all naked, all about fourteen or fifteen years old. The bucks, we knew, hid in the bush and only ventured out if the sailors lowered a rope ladder and tried to tempt the women aboard. Other canoes appeared and up on the bridge Captain Erlander began blowing the whistle, warning them to steer clear of our sluggish ship. The river pilot was shaking his fist and shouting that there was a federal law against molesting the aborigines and we would all spend ten years at hard labor if we tried to lower a ladder.

Captain Erlander frantically blew the ship's horn but the girls continued paddling toward us and then Antonio, the wiper, went berserk as two of the girls in the canoe rose and cupped their breasts up at us. Antonio dashed below to his cabin. Seconds later he was back on deck with a carton of Luckies in a plastic bag. Even the dull Swedes cheered as he threw it toward the girls with a mighty heave. (European men throw awkwardly, with a pronounced hitch. Almost any kid off an American sandlot can outdistance a strong European.)

The race was on. The *Blythe* had left the girls astern and we ran aft to watch the contest. From another village on the near shore a low, sleek *piragua* had come flashing into action. Two bucks were stroking smoothly, matching their muscles against the girls' advantage of being so much closer to the prize. The *piragua* slashed ahead like a famished shark while the girls struggled courageously, with an incredible show of will. We were cheering and rooting for the girls, our eyes popping in admiration of their bobbling tits.

20

It was hopeless. They were losing. For every yard they covered the two huskies in the *piragua* advanced three. The girls churned up a storm with one final burst of fury and energy but it was no use. With a gesture of dismay they retired from the race, heads bent, their soft shoulders drooping. We booed and cursed. Then, out of nowhere, a dinky rowboat, powered by an outboard motor, entered the scene. The two aces in the canoe doubled their stroke and took off in a flurry of arms, shoulders and paddles; and we immediately switched allegiances, howling and screaming for the two men to defeat the smug bastard with the outboard. They were so much closer and seemed to be winning. Their prize was only ten yards away when the *mestizo* with the outboard cut smoothly in front of them, casually scooped the cigarettes from the water and shot off with an arrogant sweep that almost capsized the *piragua* in its wake.

We groaned in disappointment but the groans were transformed into laughter as we saw Piño, midships, kicking up his heels, flailing his arms and blowing kisses down to another Indian girl in a canoe. She was calling, *"Ropa! Ropa!"* her small breasts trembling with the exertion.

We ran midships to egg Piño on and Antonio shouted, "She wants your clothes, Gallego. Throw her your clothes. Be generous, Gallego."

Piño quickly unbuttoned his shirt, tied it into a knot, and flipped it over the side. He blew her another kiss and roared, "That was for the mother that dropped you, my darling."

Antonio was poking him in the ribs. "The pants, hombre, the pants. She'll need the pants for the shirt, won't she? You want her to have a matching combination, don't you?"

Piño was blinking rapidly, his face a map of confusion. We were bellowing in his ears and the Gallego suddenly unzipped his trousers, yanked them down, lost his balance and almost toppled through the chains as he did so. He was balls naked. The Norwegians roared with laughter and the Latins clicked their heels, Gypsy style, clapping their palms, and shouting, "Olé! Olé! Viva España! Olé!"

"It's a magnificent thought," Piño announced. "My workpants on her soft bottom."

With a kiss to his trousers he tossed them into the breeze. They were suspended there for a second in a capricious crosscurrent and then floated lazily downward and settled into the water. "May you lower them only for me," Piño called down to the girl.

She hurried her stroke to retrieve the pants before they sank and Piño grabbed his long hose and flapped it at her. He thumped on his hairless chest like Tarzan and roared, "Adiós, mi vida! I'll be back with this. You'll be the last love of my life, you little savage. We'll have an idyll in the jungle, you bitch."

We turned the curve in the river and she was out of sight. Piño's chest heaved in resignation and he sniffed at me and removed a cigarette from my shirt pocket, sniffed it again as he lit it.

"That's what I need, F.B.I. That's what an old fart like me needs before I pickle myself in alcohol—to roll around in the bushes with a soft little cat like that. I'm sick of the women that I can have now. I'm sick of their eyes and voices. But you could never understand, Jack. You're too young and full of yourself yet."

First Mate Johansen was shaking his fist at us

from the bridge. He raised his megaphone and growled in English: "You men! Get the hell back to work down there. Piñedo! Go below and put some clothes on, *feefan!* This is not the Turkish Navy."

The Gallego tossed his head, as though the world were filled with narrow-minded people abusing their positions of authority, and shuffled off, his sandals flopping across the metal deck. The crew retrieved their hammers and scrapers and returned to their chipping in the shade of the lifeboat platform. Carr was still sitting there, a few feet away. The carpenter had not joined in any of the rushing around but he had broken into laughter when Piño tossed his pants over the side.

Why I will never know, but I decided to bait the aloof sonofabitch again. I recited in German with my schoolboy accent: *"Der Schiffer im kleinen Schiffle, Ergreift es mit wildem Weh."*

"What's that supposed to be?" Carr asked.

I nodded toward the retreating Gallego. *"Und das hat mit ihrem Singen die Lorelei getan."*

"German, Mr. Ritter?"

"C'mon, carpenter. Even with my accent you should be able to recognize the *Lorelei.*"

"I thought you were speaking to me in Arabic. I thought that was from *Sinbad the Sailor.*"

"Sorry about that. I'll practice."

"You do that," Carr said with a tone of mocking encouragement. "There are many things you should practice."

The carpenter picked up his tool kit and headed for the fo'c'sle. Carr had put me down again but there was no venom in him today. Last night I felt like a fool, bugging the man with my smart-ass philology and linguistics. Still, I think the car-

penter respects me for the way I stood up to Svensen, the O.S., when we almost had a fistfight this
morning.

The sun set early this evening but there has been
no perceptible lowering of the temperature. If anything, these muggy nights are worse than the blaz-
ing afternoons. Piño was the first to finish supper
and make for shore. Lord knows what the man is
up to by now. Holding off like this and fulfilling
my daily quota for the logbook, I am gambling on
my ''sympathy'' with Lupe. Consider the alterna-
tives: If I get to the Club Moderno too early (and
thus get her relatively clean, before anybody else
has had her tonight) she might tell me that first she
has to fulfill her quota, and I'll have to wait. If I
get there too late, she might be tired and tell me to
skip it, or even try to charge me like a regular customer and spoil the whole triumph. One never
knows for sure how to play these deals.

Thoughts for the day:

1. Today, as we crept up the Río Verde, through
this cosmic emptiness, I wanted to think enormous
thoughts and none were available.

2. Upon reading a chapter from *Orgías de Buda-
pest* an implacable erection sprouted and plagued
me for the rest of the afternoon. Hypothesis: You
have not really learned a language until you can be
excited by its pornography. Research should be carried on by the appropriate institutions.

3. Everybody in Santa Cruz babbles about economic development but this is still a wonderfully
screwed-up country. Most of the clocks are broken
and the timetables are pious hopes. As you walk
down the street the men measure you for violence
and the women measure you for sex. You light
your cigarettes with thick wooden match sticks,

sling solid, resonant coins on the counter, there are
no mothers' clubs, justice is reasonably priced, and
the bars have no locks on the doors.

Ritter thickened the period on his last sentence and en-
larged the speck into an ominous black dot. He considered
adding another postscript about the carpenter and then decided against it. Carr regarded him as a nosy young snot and
maybe he was a nosy young snot. That was that. He would
leave the man alone. He sniffed at his armpits and checked
his beard. If Lupe was offering "sympathy," the least he
could do was reciprocate with a romantically smooth cheek
and a fragrant armpit.

Fifteen minutes later, after a quick shave and shower, Ritter locked his cabin door behind him. Some of his shipmates
had the habit of returning early, drunk and broke, and became desperate when they could not find the Sparks to ask
him for a few more dollars off the book. Their only recourse
was to examine their neighbor's wardrobe and see which of
his suits could best be bartered off for a bottle.

The *Blythe* was painfully quiet without the vibrations of
the engines and deserted, except for the watchman up on
deck and the roaches scurrying about underfoot. The only
light in the passageway came from the open door of the carpenter's cabin. Ritter hesitated and then continued down the
corridor.

Carr was stretched out on his narrow bunk, dressed in his
off-time khaki clothes. He glanced up from the Bible he was
reading. With old-fashioned rimless spectacles on his nose,
he looked older, professorial.

"May I come in?" Ritter asked.

Carr laid his Bible aside and nodded. He pushed the stool
out so they could both share the ashtray. Ritter scanned the
walls as he sat down. They were blank, with none of the
cheesecake calendars, souvenirs, bar snapshots or silk ban-

danas that gave most of the cabins the aspect of fraternity dens. The only specific piece of furniture was a cluttered bookcase containing what Ritter regarded as incredibly dry texts: Buber, Heidegger . . . mostly thick volumes in German.

"See anything you want to borrow?" Carr asked, amused.

"I didn't want to bother you, carpenter. I just wanted to apologize for coming on so strong with my bullshit last night. That was pretty crass of me."

"It's not a good policy, Mr. Ritter, but I wouldn't blow it out of proportion."

Carr reached for his Bible again and Ritter saw that he had been dismissed. He refused to take the hint. "Don't you have anything better to do in a place like Puerto Acero than read the Good Book? You should go into town and catch the other side's viewpoint."

"I've already had the other side's viewpoint."

"Well, why don't you refresh your acquaintanceship? There's something so dreary about you holing up in this cabin with all that life out there. I mean, I know that you've probably seen most of the world and its fleshpots but you could at least go into town and get a good meal. You've got to be fed up with the fishballs and tomato goop."

Carr smiled, not patronizingly. It was at some private joke. He removed the pipe from his mouth. "I can't understand this concern for my welfare, Mr. Ritter. You act toward me like some kind of solicitous nephew."

"Well, you called it last night, carpenter. It's humiliating for a guy as vain and egotistical as I am to be cut dead by the only man on this ship with a brain to his name. Before going to sea I envisioned deep philosophical discussions on the bow, listening to old sea wolves tell me about Shanghai in the twenties. And all I end up with is Piño jabbering about Francisco Franco, and the Norskies arguing about which country makes the best beer."

26

"Forgive me for not leaping enthusiastically at the chance to be your comrade, Mr. Ritter."

"Oh, man. You depress the hell out of me, Carr. I'm going ashore now and, when I hit the Club Moderno, I'll be seeing you sitting back here, gloom incarnate, playing the role of the Flying Dutchman, Lazarus and fifteen other pariahs. Why the hell don't you come to shore and have a drink with me? We can swap war stories. Piño tells me you were all fucked up in World War Two and I have two frost-bitten toes from Korea and a lively imagination. We can go to the Club Moderno and drink toasts to World War Three. If you're feeling morbid I can assure you Puerto Acero is a great place to feel miserable. We can go look at all the thir-teen-year-old prostitutes at the Club Montparnasse and sniff all the dead cats up the alleys. C'mon, man. I'll sport you to a few drinks."

"That's a very generous offer," Carr said, "considering that I make about four times as much salary as you do."

"Good enough," Ritter said cheerfully. "Then I'll let you buy the drinks. And afterwards we can go over to the Danu-bio Azul and get some good Continental cooking."

"The Danubio Azul?"

"Sure. There are a couple of other restaurants, like the Chink place, but the Danubio Azul is the only decent spot in town. Very good egg and garlic soup, and Wienerschnitzels. All washed down with tall steins of dark beer."

Ritter was startled as the carpenter's face turned ashen. Carr laughed—an eerie, inhuman sound.

"So, you want to take me to the Club Moderno and the Danubio Azul?"

"That was the general idea," Ritter answered quietly. "Though I don't see what's so hilarious about it."

"It could be very amusing," Carr said, rising and snap-ping his Bible shut. "Wait for me out in the passageway. I'll have to wash up if we're going out on the town."

3

They crossed the grim stretch of railroad tracks that separated the docks from Barrio Flores. Most of the houses in this neighborhood had running water and a few of the streets were paved, but it was still safer to walk down the middle of the road than along the cracked, uneven sidewalks. Open gutters assaulted the nostrils at every corner and there were few street lights, yet life in Barrio Flores was infinitely more comfortable than on La Colina—the clusters of floorless, windowless shacks clinging to the hills behind the red light district.

The gas lamps from the public square and the electric lamps from Avenida Reforma spread their haze over Barrio Flores and then the area was dark except for the glow from the brilliantly advertised brothels of La Zona. In the shadows crept pets and livestock—cats copulating under rain barrels and scratching it out for domination of the rickety fences, while pigs and goats disputed shares in the garbage dumped in the backyard trenches.

It was after eleven, but Barrio Flores never retired this early. The impudent could stare through screened windows at nutskinned old men on hammocks and fat housewives, in slips and brassieres, relaxing on low beds, their puffy thighs

28

exposed to slowly turning fans. Some families were just finishing their evening cocido, munching at their dishes of
boiled beef and vegetables. In other cottages the tables were
cleared, the men playing dominoes and drinking chica, while
the women and children slept in their mosquito nets. Radios
screeched, bringing news and music from distant Concepción. Surrounded by this jungle, the families of Barrio Flores
were secure and sheltered, protected by their wooden saints
and their crucifixes, the prints of the Adoration and the Passion blessing their plaster walls. They chose not to see the
sailors passing their opened shutters. It was a part of life. For
nearly four hundred years the men who came down this river
had used the women of Puerto Acero.

The carpenter and the messboy both paused to listen to the
music emanating from the pulpería on the corner. El Nuevo
Amanecer was open for business. Inside, squat brown
women were shopping for tinned meats and sacks of rice and
beans under sputtering neon tubes. A corrugated iron roof
slanted off from the grocery and three walls of screens had
been mounted to create an outdoor café. Carr looked at the
group of farmers clustered around the high wooden steps.
The campesinos were enjoying the singing and four-stringed
cuatro of an old ragged Negro while a sinewy black child
danced barefoot in the sand, rattling an accompaniment with
two red maracas.

"Mind if we go in for a while, Mr. Ritter?"

"Don't mind at all. I enjoy this folk music myself."

The swarthy, mustached campesinos parted to let the
sailors join them and nodded cordially. It was not often that
sailors entered the New Dawn pulpería. Usually they just
stopped, listened for a few seconds with blank faces, and
continued on toward La Zona.

Ritter signaled the waitress for two beers as they sat down.
The black boy in the circle was about nine years old. His body
seemed made out of raw rubber as he rolled his shoulders,
rattled his gourds and shuffled his feet to the thumping beat of

29

the cuatro. The blind man's bony fingers pinched and tortured the metal strings with the audacious confidence of a half century's acquaintance. Ritter's smile widened. The troubadour was slightly too gamy for any tourist poster. Filthy corduroy leggings were held up by a piece of rope, and his ragged sport shirt was knotted at the waist. The getup was completed with dark glasses, a straw hat, shower clogs, and a silver medallion resting over his sunken chest. His chanting was flat and nasal and there were pitifully few coins in the battered cup at his feet.

All around them the llaneros and farmers began clapping and stamping their feet in a crude counterpoint. Ritter could catch little more than the gist of the lyrics. It was the ballad of Blanca Flor and Filomena, a tale of lust and infanticide from medieval Spain. The Negro slapped at his warped, ancient cuatro, tossing his head with every chord, and repeated the verses with the harshness of gravel in his toothless mouth. Joining in the clapping, Jack Ritter glanced sideways to see whether Carr was appreciating this great music. The carpenter was straining to blink back tears. Carr felt the eyes on him and straightened up.

The song ended and the portly campesinos applauded, but only a few tossed coins into the cup. Others beamed at Carr, touched that their music had moved a foreigner so deeply. Carr searched through his pockets and came up with three dollars. He crumpled them into a wad and dropped them in the cup. Rising, he spoke in Spanish: "Would you play that ballad for us again, grandfather? But not with so much grace and style. Otherwise the angels will sequester you for their celestial orchestra."

The llaneros mumbled in approbation. This foreign mariner spoke their language like a professor from Salamanca. The blind guitarist clamped his instrument under one arm and held a hand to his ear. With a hideous grin he said, "I didn't hear you drop anything into my cup, stranger. My cuatro has a very rare defect. It becomes untuned after every song and requires the ring of good solid coins as a pitchfork.''

"I suppose that paper is an improper pitchfork,'' Carr said. "In my ignorance I dropped in three American dollars, so I guess I'd better take them back and try a few Cruceño coins.''

The crowd in the pulpería laughed at this rally. The Negro protested amiably. "No, chico, no. We forgive your ignorance. Paper can perform miracles for this cuatro. For three dollars it can produce the whole opera *Carmen* with two encores.''

"Sing the same ballad,'' Carr ordered. "I always wanted to sleep with my sister-in-law.''

The campesinos roared again but their laughter was cut off as the blind singer smacked the wooden panels of his cuatro and the child automatically shook his gourds and scuffed through the sand. The llaneros joined in, accentuating the driving beat with hardened palms and heavy feet.

Henry Carr, the English carpenter, repressed a shudder. This music poured right through him and it was as if he had fallen over the lip of a chasm and tumbled into the past. This ballad took him back over thirty years, a long train ride, a student spending the summer with distant relatives in Salonika, a picnic with exotic foods, and a jovial uncle strumming a guitar as his wife nagged him and tried to grab the instrument away. "No, Gabriel. Don't teach him those disgusting songs. He's only been here a month and you've already taught him all those terrible songs. His family will never forgive you.''

They were all dead now. That whole community in Salonika had disappeared. This version was different, the accent was different, but thirty-five years later he was hearing the story of how the Moorish king married Blanca Flor, and then raped her younger sister, Filomena, and came home to a broth prepared with the flesh of his miscarried son. He was

31

hearing the voices of the dead and slaughtered from the mouth of this black man on another continent. Now he was sure the American boy was a black daw. The closing verse, that the troubadour kept repeating with higher and higher pitch, seemed to vault across the centuries and make the world whole, and terrible.

> Mothers with daughters
> Marry them in your own land
> For I bore two
> And fate decreed
> One die desecrated
> And the other of love.

The black had put so much of himself into the song that his audience was silent as he concluded. They all seemed affected by the mood and the expression on the carpenter's face. It was not until the more realistic child thrust the cup at Carr that they cheered and applauded, and congratulated the old man with shouts of "Viva! Viva Florencio Negrón."

Carr placed more dollars in the child's cup. "Your grandfather carries the secrets of the ages in his voice and fingers, boy. He should be preserved in marble and cast in bronze."

"Three more dollars from the foreigner," the youngster shouted gleefully, and all the campesinos chuckled.

From his sitting position Florencio Negrón bowed at the waist. "We are only here to serve you, generous stranger. Come around again when you have surplus money. Florencio Negrón will be here every night for many years to come, God willing."

"God willing," Carr repeated.

Ritter paid the waitress and then they had to shake hands with each of the campesinos before they could make their way to the screen door and leave the pulpería. They walked down the dim alley and Ritter said, "Very warm and simple people. That was a fine moment."

32

"Quite nice."

"That music was great," Jack Ritter said enthusiastically. "Did you catch all the words, carpenter? I followed the general drift but I still have trouble with this Cruceño accent. These people are worse than the Puerto Ricans, dropping all the d's and changing the 'r' to 'l.' A lot of it went right by me."

"An old Spanish romance, Mr. Ritter. All about family troubles."

Ritter had grasped enough to laugh at the cryptic explanation as they climbed the last hill leading to La Zona. Henry Carr was also amused, amused at his recent lapse. Surely a rational man had to scoff at the chill that had curled in the nape of his neck as he listened to that ballad. It was too late, too inane to be stirred by music now, even the music of the loved long in their graves. Music? *The Meadow Lands* was a great song; *Lili Marlene* was moving. The Republic had the stirring songs but Franco had the tanks and the petroleum.

They headed up Panama Street and Ritter savored the hilarious vulgarity of the marquees and neon signs. These dives had expropriated the prestigious names from all the joytime streets in the world. For five blocks a man could appease his cravings at dinky little cat houses—the Moulin Rouge, the Seven Seas, Club Manhattan, Texas Bar, Club 21, Club Montparnasse—and at the far end was the most pretentious establishment on the strip—El Club Moderno. And it wasn't only on Panama Street that the businessmen of Puerto Acero borrowed the resonant names from the outside world. The alley of tailor shops and used clothes booths near Plaza Paez was known as Saville Row and the creaking bleachers and rough baseball diamond in back of the municipal cemetery was called Yankee Stadium.

They both winced at the shouts of "Carr! Enrique! F.B.I.! Coño!"

Piño was charging at them, crashing up a side alley, bang-

33

ing into beer cases and garbage cans. The Gallego was wind-milling his arms in delight at finding his two compañeros. His hair was disheveled and his shirt was hanging out of his trousers. With a heavy hand he pawed at both of them. "Carr! Enrique! What a miracle. You've finally left the ship. This is a fine deed you've done, F.B.I., extracting Enrique from his cabin, our carpintero, reading every evening like you were going to graduate from night school next year."

"Phew," Ritter moaned. "You smell like you've slept in a vat of rotgut, Gallego."

"You just have a delicate nose, Gringo." He grabbed their arms and hurried them along. "Come over to the Club Tango with me. I invite you both. All drinks and food will be paid for by Rodolfo Piñedo. They have this giantess at the Club Tango, carpintero—Graciela. Graciela's only fifteen years old but she's already two meters tall. The manager told me she suffers from a glandular condition and should be dying soon, so I'd like to get her before she passes on."

Ritter disengaged the grip. "Thanks for the invitation but we're heading for the Club Moderno."

"Ah hah!" the Gallego bellowed. "The Club Moderno? First class. Wait till you see the women there, Enrique. There's one, Aurora, who could make a eunuch grow another prick, and this other, Soledad, could straighten out a cork-screw. Our first trip down here she was already in her fourth month and she was still the most luscious woman in the bar. Not beautiful, really, but formidable. Abundant, imperious, strong hips, white skin, black hair, blue eyes, legs like a center forward. It shows you what a squalid age we live in. In an age with more respect for human values, a woman like Soledad would be the mistress to an archbishop, not a com-mon whore in this backwater port."

It was Carr's turn to remove his arm from Piño's grip, but the Gallego did not skip a beat in his monologue. "The last time I was down here I wanted to go with Soledad. I offered her three times the normal price and she refused to go with me, said I was a clown. I was going to try for her again to-night, but the taxi driver told me she was too pregnant to accept customers any more. And that today there was some kind of trouble, some incident with her. Tell me—up till what month is it safe for a woman to have relations? If one is very gentle with her. You're a doctor, Enrique."

Carr struck a wooden match and applied the flame to his pipe. "Whoever told you that trashy lie, Piño?"

The Gallego wagged an admonishing finger and snorted with the cynicism of a man with inside information.

"No, no, Enrique. None of that. No false modesty. Did you know, F.B.I., that our Enrique is a doctor—that he once performed an operation on another ship before he signed on the *Blythe?* First Mate Johansen told me the whole story. Four years ago, on the *Gustav Jansen,* they were hit by a hurricane. A boom swung loose from its moorings and smashed the second cook's arm. No helicopter could get through the storm to take him to a hospital ashore, and the second cook was screaming so horribly the officers decided to cut off his arm. They were all prepared to saw it off when Enrique entered the cabin, pushed them aside and set the bone. There had been no need to amputate the arm. How do you like that, F.B.I.? Our Enrique is a doctor."

"Johansen exaggerated," Carr said. "If any of those mates had done their advanced first aid, they could have set that bone themselves."

"Don't lie, Enrique. Don't lie. You're among friends. You don't have to hide anything from us. You see, Jack, you can never tell who you'll meet on these ships. You can meet ex-judges, musicians, fine men. And a surgeon here! It's a great thing to be a doctor, Enrique, to alleviate pain. You understand pain, Enrique. I've seen how your old scars glow in the sun. There is nothing like physical suffering. Everywhere I go people are somber and tell me they are unhappy. They complain they are suffering. I always want to stick a needle in them for one minute. When I pull it out they'll dance in

35

the streets and be happy for the rest of the day. In Russia, when I was with the Blue Legion, I suffered. It was so cold I used to hope my best friend from my own village would die so I could inherit his fur-lined boots.''

Carr smiled. Piño, encouraged, quickly ran five steps ahead and turned around to walk backwards so he could face the victims of his harangue.

"You understand those matters, Enrique. I'd love to be like you: cold, hard, self-sufficient. I'd love to have that temperament. You're brilliant. I'll bet you that you haven't done a stupid thing in twenty years, and I do twenty stupid things a day. You too, F.B.I. You could be brilliant, too, if you weren't so dumb. And me, I'm almost an old man and I'm still a fool. Today I went and threw my best work trousers into the river because a little Indian girl wiggled her pussy at me. I'm so dumb, and I was so excited, I even forgot I had eighty dollars in my trouser pockets.''

"Eighty dollars," Piño moaned. "Eighty goddam dollars. That's four hundred cruceños. I could have screwed the mayor's wife tonight for four hundred cruceños.''

They reached the swinging doors of the Club Moderno and Jack Ritter said, "This is the place, carpenter. I hope you don't mind me dragging you all the way down here but this is the joint where I have my girl.''

Carr looked at the crowded dance floor, the full tables and the congestion at the bar.

"Seems very adequate. Very lively.''

It might have been the blinking green neon sign overhead, but Ritter thought that the carpenter had turned pale again, with the same ashen look that had crossed his face in the cabin. Piño led the way and the trio from the *Blythe* plunged into the smoky din of the brothel. There was just one table open, next to a pack of seamen off the Italian freighter docked near the *Blythe*.

A tango from the jukebox was being amplified into a scratchy blare by three wall speakers. Ritter chuckled at the

36

way self-interest was messing up the teamwork out on the dance floor. The paying customers wanted to tango Apache style—promenade ferociously, dip their partners to the floor, whip off a few intricate steps while the resisting girls were there on business and would only consent to let themselves be mauled and tugged around with a minimum expense of energy. For one cruceño a dance they were not about to become Ginger Rogers.

Piño squirmed impatiently and snapped his fingers at the disdainful waiters. Half of them were clustered in the back, arguing with a group of girls who gave the odd impression of being lobbyists holding a caucus in the hallway. The Club Moderno was packed with miners down from the Cerro de Hierro diggings, also Portuguese and Italian immigrants easily identified by their sports shirts and pointed shoes. A conclave of Svenskas and Norskies from the *Blythe* occupied the long front table. They spotted Carr and immediately went into consultation. None had ever seen the carpenter off the ship before. They peered over their shoulders suspiciously and then their heads went together.

"Remember," Piño said. "All drinks are on me. It is a privilege, and an honor, to buy drinks for a man like Dr. Henry Carr."

"Great," Ritter said. "We'll order champagne. To celebrate dragging Henry off the ship."

Piño grimaced. "For you? I wouldn't spend five cents to get you a suck on the bar rag. But in honor of Dr. Enrique's leaving the ship we could even order champagne."

"I wish you wouldn't spread all that bullshit around," Carr murmured calmly. "I can really do without it."

"Nonsense, Enrique. Maybe I can embarrass you into leaving the *Blythe*. A man like you shouldn't associate with the scum like us. You should practice your profession. Whatever you did, the past is the past. How about a woman, Enrique? I know you deserve better, but the Club Moderno does have a reputation for hygiene."

37

Carr shook his head no.

"Oh, c'mon," Piño said cajolingly. "After a year and more on the *Blythe,* you can relax your standards. My treat, Enrique. I want you to have a good time for once." Piño pointed to the crowd of women. "There's good stuff over there, imported items from Cuba and Colombia and Argentina, besides the stock of Cruceñas. And the petite blonde is French, specializes in la mineta."

Jack Ritter was embarrassed for both himself and Carr as the Gallego babbled on about women and Japanese girls with twitchers and the whores in the storefront windows of Amsterdam. A sneering waiter finally appeared and Piño interrupted his lecture on prostitution to beam up at the man and say, "So nice of you to join us. We thought you might be attending your mother's wedding. How about a bottle of your finest champagne?"

"Don't be an idiot," Carr snapped at the Gallego. "Three beers, waiter."

It took another five minutes for the waiter to return with their beers and Piño used the time to complain about how expensive Puerto Acero was—a midget bottle of beer cost more in the Club Moderno than it would in a New York cabaret and, with all the oil money around Santa Cruz, Puerto Acero was probably the most expensive town in the most expensive country in the world. When the waiter arrived Piño handed him a one hundred cruceño note over Carr's objections, and told the waiter, "Start subtracting from here, and all these men's drinks are on my bill. They must not pay for one thing. The simple-looking one is the future chief of the F.B.I. and the other man is a great physician."

Carr winced as Piño grabbed his beer bottle and, with the dramatic turn of a bullfighter, launched himself toward the women arguing in the back. To Ritter the Spaniard could pass for a muscular Groucho Marx without mustache, as he slouched across the dance floor, ducking and weaving to avoid the flailing elbows and kicking heels of all the dancers bobbing up and down in the din of the raucous mambo. The deadpan miners, in their white ducks and guayaveras, shook with gusto and rolled their shoulders; while the pouting whores endured their dance partners with brittle smiles, eyes vacant.

Ritter sipped at his beer and glanced sideways at the older man. Henry Carr was bored by all this. And worse, he looked ill—as if the smoke and hot racket of the Club were getting to him. Ritter felt like a fool. He had annoyed this man, cajoled him from his cabin to this dreary hole, and now Carr looked about ready to vomit.

He raised his glass in a mock toast. "You know I'm really feeling low about having brought you. I knew this place was raunchy but I didn't realize how much until I saw you sitting there, sucking on your pipe."

"It's fine for what it's supposed to be."

"Sure. You're looking like a bemused anthropologist and I feel like I took my father to a strip joint and he was bored."

"I've had a good evening so far, Jack. By coming out I heard that music, which, as you saw, touched me very deeply. I thank you for that. The ballads took me back a long way."

"Well, I'm glad you got at least that much out of it. I'd hate the night to be a total loss for you."

Jack saw Lupe waving to him from the bar. She had just come through the turnstile that blocked the hall to the back rooms and was powdering her nose. She was slim and had a light, understated prettiness. Without her silver spiked heels and Sadie Thompson red dress, an optimist might take her for a librarian.

"That's my steady," said Ritter. "Claims she loves me."

"Congratulations. She's very attractive."

"You don't mind if I take off for a while, do you? I should only be an hour or so. I don't think Lupe can donate too much free time during working hours."

"Go right along. I wouldn't want to cramp your style, Jack. Give the lady my regards."

"I won't be too long. Thanks."

39

Ritter sensed an irritating tension in the Club. The argument between the whores had grown more heated and even the big Zambo bouncer had joined in, along with most of the waiters. Their shouting was louder than the listless bolero on the jukebox.

Lupe slipped into his arms and pecked him on the cheek. He felt suddenly relieved. With both Carr's and Piño's eyes on him, her greeting was all he could have hoped for. They stepped into the rhythms of music. Lupe was making him the cool and casual man for the evening, just as she could have made him look like a fool in front of his friends.

"Have a good trip, marinero?"

"Sure. I even rigged a sail so we'd get down here quicker. Miss me, guapa?"

"Sometimes. When I thought about you," she said, and giggled.

Lupe suddenly turned him so she could examine the rear of the club. "Who's that man at your table, Jack? Is he a friend off your ship?"

"No. He's my father. I told him about the wonderful girl I met in Puerto Acero, how I wanted to marry and take her back to our mansion in Philadelphia, so he's accompanied me down here to inspect you and give the family seal of approval."

"Clown!" He straightened up as she pinched his back. Her lips puckered and she became the crafty customer eying the bananas. "He is very striking, Jack. Very distinguished. I like my men well bronzed, with gray hair. Is he an officer?"

"No. He helps me in the kitchen."

"Liar," she laughed. "You have every right to be jealous. He's much better looking than you are."

"Well, would you rather go with him than me?" Ritter asked in a sulking tone, and only half in jest. "He can probably use it more than I can. This is the first time he's been off the ship in over a year."

40

"Doesn't he like women?"

"I never asked him."

"Is he one of those?" She put her index finger to her left nostril, apparently the sign for queer in Santa Cruz.

"I'd say not. I don't think he thinks about sex. He seems to have other problems on his mind."

"Maybe I'll find out later," she murmured. "I'm feeling generous tonight."

The bolero petered off into a static fox trot but they could hardly hear the music over the competition from the debate in the corner. The bouncer slapped one girl as all the whores and waiters were jabbering at him and one another.

"What the hell's happening over there?" Jack asked. "Are you girls calling a strike?"

"Maybe," Lupe answered, with no reaction to the sarcasm in his question. "A terrible thing happened yesterday and everybody is angry at the proprietor. Many of the girls wanted to walk out unless Señor Arnstedt makes some kind of reparations to Soledad. She won't even see him, though, and keeps threatening to kill him."

"Well," he said, taking her hand and leading her toward the bar to buy drinks to take back to the room. "We'd better go before you decide to join the strike. That would be a hell of a note after the way I've been looking forward to this."

Lupe had been assigned other quarters, a considerable improvement over her old room. A baby-blue washbasin, with a hose and nozzle spray, had replaced the tin bucket in the corner, and instead of a roll of toilet paper, there were fresh Turkish towels draped over the bedrail. Best yet, the walls were uncluttered. Her ex-roommate, back in number six, papered the walls with rotogravure clippings of film stars and world figures. The last time down he had been inhibited by the stern visages of Joseph Stalin and Joan Crawford. That merciless gallery had been reduced to an aquarella of the Holy Mother and a listing papier-mâché figure of San Benito. San Benito had a reputation for tippling in Santa Cruz.

41

Stripping down to his shorts, Jack heard a woman crying beyond the partition to the next room. Lupe undressed quickly with no show, stepping out of her red dress and flinging it over a chair, then tossing aside her black panties with the same casualness. He kissed her and, as he stretched out next to her, she suddenly curled around, ready to do him an unsolicited favor. He did not want that. He wanted to kiss her lips. He forced her back down, entered her, and her legs locked high around his back, her hazel eyes wide, then narrowing.

Lupe muttered rasping noises in her Indian dialect. The mysterious syllables were as exciting as the thin girlish thighs pressing at him. He bit her lips, blotting from his mind the terror, the bourgeois terror, of disease, and the fact that she was a whore and had used these lips to service a thousand drunken sailors. He was using her too. He was inside this frail pathetic Indian girl and using the soft shanks in his palms to dream about other women. He could hear the noon bells pealing at S.C.S.U., see all the college girls who had denied him: arrogant coeds rushing off, their strong pink legs under blue skirts, innocent white sweaters pointing at him. But Lupe was better, kinder.

The woman was still whimpering beyond the partition. Other voices consoled her. More arguments and shouting from somewhere else down the hall, and joropo music seeping in from the bar, a band taking over from the jukebox. No way to maintain a steady sexual rhythm with that clickity-clickity joropo music fouling up his beat. Another group cursing up a storm out in the hallway, a woman threatening to kill some sonofabitch. Doors slamming. There was no respect for a man's basic needs around here.

Lupe grabbed his hair and tugged his head back down. He must pay attention to business. More bawling in the adjacent room, shriller crying. Damn emotional Latins! More slamming of doors and shouts in the hallway. He did Lupe the

42

favor of thinking only of her. Her face was blurring. She became a child with soft features, eyes cloudy, and he sensed it happening, Lupe coming, with one enormous exertion, bringing him with her in a welter of groans.

Minutes passed before she pushed him away, saying, "You're very nice, Jack."

"You're nicer. I assure you."

They shared their last beer and Ritter studied the roaches crossing the dim plaster maps of the ceiling. They were like monsters wandering over forgotten lands. No way to keep the roaches out, not even in the tightly sealed and sprayed duplexes he'd seen in the American village in La Loma.

There was more action in the corridor—a door slamming, and the smack of a fist against bare flesh. Ritter slipped out of bed and unbolted the lock. He peeped through a slit in the door. It was Piño out there, the Gallego at the top of his form, scuffling with a hefty brunette in a black half slip.

"Jack!" Piño pleaded. "F.B.I., come and help me."

The brunette swung her shoe at Piño's ear and screamed, "Pervert. Degenerate. For a stinking fifty cruceños."

Piño ducked away from her shoe and had his arms crossed over his head. "Jack! Come out and help. This woman's crazy. She'll kill me."

Ritter waved him off. Nobody was going to accuse him of being a Yankee who interfered in people's internal affairs. He watched the Gallego attempt a new tack. Starting with a conciliatory grin, Rodolfo drew himself erect but was still shorter than the splendid panting beast that had him cornered. Clearing his throat, he projected dignity. "Aurora," he said firmly. "Please try and be reasonable. You're making a scene."

"Scene? Gallego de mierda!" Her shoe came down in a whizzing arc but Piño ducked under her arms and scampered up the corridor with Aurora chasing after him, three chambermaids scurrying out of their way.

Ritter smiled as he shut the door and snapped the bolt. Piño seemed to be getting his money's worth of entertainment.

"Who was it out there?" Lupe asked when he returned to bed.

"Just a compadre from the ship. Having a spat with a girl called Aurora."

"Aurora has a terrible temper," Lupe said. "Even Ezequiel Cardenas is afraid of her. He slaps almost all of us but never goes near Aurora."

A sudden sharp wail from the next room tore right through Ritter's chest and he twisted in irritation. The whimpering in there had become unbearable.

"What the hell is that?" he asked, reaching for a cigarette. "They've been bawling and moaning over there for hours."

"Soledad," Lupe explained. "She's refused to take an injection to calm herself. Soledad is very stubborn."

"They having a wake in there? I've never heard so much wailing and sniffling."

"No. The wake is tomorrow," Lupe answered flatly. "Soledad lost her baby. Everyone predicts there will be lots of trouble afterward. Soledad has a ferocious temper —worse than Aurora's. I saw her almost scratch a man's eyes out on Avenida Reforma once. Soledad promised to kill Señor Arnstedt after the wake."

"That the owner, the European?"

"Yes. He was very unfair. All the girls agree. That's why they were all out there in the bar talking about a strike until he compensates Soledad. Soledad was in her last month. She was crazy to have another baby. I told her she was crazy. Don't you think so?"

"Sure," Ritter agreed with a shrug.

"She already has two boys at home; she doesn't need any more. But Soledad is very determined and Señor Arnstedt was very unjust. In all the other clubs on Panama Street, when a girl is pregnant the owner lets them stay in while they

44

have the baby. It's the rule. They're only supposed to charge the regular room rent every week. That's the policy at the Club Tango and at the Club Lido and all the other good clubs. You keep your room. But Señor Arnsted told Soledad she would have to get out because he was making no profit on her bed and it depressed the customers to see a pregnant woman sitting around. So Soledad said it was the unwritten rule she could stay. But Señor Arnstedt told her to go home to Cali and have the baby in her own house. And Soledad replied that her mother maintained a decent home and nobody knew about Puerto Acero and everybody in Cali believed she was a secretary in Concepción. Then Señor Arnstedt ordered her out. Soledad refused to leave and they had a horrible fight. Soledad screamed that she would tell everybody in La Zona he was an unnatural man and had begged her to let him use positions condemned by the Church—you know, on his knees. And Señor Arnstedt called her a liar and smacked her. She slapped him back and he began shaking her and shaking her, and then Soledad fell to the floor, moaning and holding her belly.''

"That's quite a story.''

"It was horrible,'' Lupe assured him. "The whole day. We called a taxi and the taxi was over twenty minutes late arriving, and when we reached the dispensary there was no doctor on duty.''

"No doctor?''

"No doctor at all. Dr. Gomez and Dr. Lopez were out directing the malaria sprayers and Dr. Lobos was supposed to be on duty but nobody could find him. We sent people to the Danubio Azul to look for him but Lobos had disappeared. The nurses tried to help but the baby was coming out the wrong way and Soledad was screaming so terribly we all cried with her.''

"Jesus, that's enough of the clinical details. How long did the baby survive?''

"Three days. But it couldn't eat. It refused all food. The

45

velorio is tomorrow night. Do you want to come to the velorio, Jacquito? There'll be lots of free drinks and all the girls
from the entire street are invited.''

"Sounds like a gala occasion. I'd like to attend, but the
Blythe sails at eight tomorrow night."

Lupe blew a smoke ring at the ceiling and said, "That's a
shame. It should be a very nice wake. Soledad baptized her
daughter 'Alma.' Padre Garibay baptized the baby even
though she was already dead and said Alma would not have
to spend centuries and centuries in purgatory. He assured
Soledad that Alma had died innocent so she'll go directly to
heaven. Do you think she'll go to heaven, Jack? Because
she's pure and untouched? A baby conceived in this place?''

"I'm sure she'll go to heaven. If I were God I'd definitely
let her in.''

Twenty minutes later Ritter was back in the uproar of the
club. The strike threat seemed to have been called off and
another hundred thirsty men had crowded in, bringing in the
smell of axle grease and petroleum and iron ore and sweat.
Mexican mariachis were yodeling on the jukebox and the
dance floor looked like an oversubscribed snakepit.

Piño grabbed him as he passed the bar. The Gallego was
brandishing a beer bottle and holding a dishrag to a cut near
his temple.

"Ah hah, F.B.I. You were back there a long time, chaval.
What were you doing—playing poker? You saw my beauty.
Wasn't she magnificent?''

"Looked like she threw a good right cross.''

"Aurora's strong. Solid. I tried this little Japanese trick on
her and she said, 'What the hell are you doing?' And pof!
She hit me. Pof! And another. I could really go for Aurora
if I hadn't fallen for that little savage on the river today.''

"Sure, Piño. Good man." He patted the excited Gallego
on the back. "Look. I'm going over and talk to the carpenter. He's been drinking all alone ever since we left him.''

"Of course. We are two putrid egotists to desert him this

46

way. You go there and remind Enrique that all his drinks are on me."

"Sure. Behave yourself."

Ritter shrugged off the Gallego's grip and circled the crowded dance floor. They had turned up the volume for a quick paso doble but the carpenter at the rear table seemed unmoved by the strains of "El Beso en España." A couple had barged in and taken over the other chair: a fat Italian cook with a squinting Cruceña on his lap. The cook was still in his apron and soup-stained jacket, locked in a long, wet kiss with his girl while his hand worked inside her unbuttoned blouse. Carr seemed oblivious to all this passion in his vicinity. He was staring across the dance floor and Ritter glanced backward to note that he was fixed on the owner of the Club Moderno. The proprietor was table hopping, playing the host for his boisterous customers.

"Sorry to have run off for so long," Ritter said, grabbing a loose chair from the next table.

"That's quite all right. I was far from bored."

"But you do look kind of sick. All green around the gills. This joint getting to you, carpenter?"

"It might be a little too much excitement for one evening," Carr agreed in a voice that trailed off till the last word was barely audible.

Ritter pointed out the owner. "You see that guy over there? The boss? That's a real cock-sucking bastard from what I've just been told."

"How so?"

"Lupe told me this story—"

"Your girl?"

"Yeah. While I was back there this broad was bawling her ass off in the next room, and Lupe said how the ace there had clobbered the woman in an argument. She was pregnant and it caused her to miscarry."

"That's strange. From here I'd take him for a very amiable gentleman. Not the kind to slap around pregnant women."

47

"I don't know, man. I only know what Lupe told me."

"She was probably lying, Ritter. Prostitutes are congenital liars. I'm sure the man would give you a completely different version of what happened."

Ritter studied the owner of the Club Moderno as the man made his way around the room. He seemed to have a quip for every table, shifting nimbly from language to language like a tourist guide. He exuded joviality as he distributed his cards, pinched his girls, slapped his patrons on the back, snapped his fingers at the waiters to signal free drinks for selected favorites. Yet the guy reminded Ritter of a certain type of troublesome customer he had had to serve while waiting tables back in college—tall, sallow, highstrung men capable of outnagging their wives, always bickering, and who always seemed to send their dinners back to the kitchen.

"It looks like you'll get your chance to hear his version right now, Carr. Here he comes."

Arnstedt swooped down on their table in mock horror. "What's this, boys? You're splitting a bottle of beer? How's the Club Moderno to make any money at this rate? If you're broke, tell me and I'll have the waiter bring a quart on the house. Gratis. But no sharing. Sharing is against the rules of the Moderno."

This with no sense of chiding. The proprietor was merely kidding his customers.

"We're not broke," Ritter explained. "We just couldn't get any service from your slow-ass waiters."

"Well, we'll fix that right away. And how about our chicas? Have you been to the rooms yet? Look how wonderfully those two are getting along." Arnstedt beamed at the couple sharing their table: the fat cook was still submerged in a moist kiss and they were lost to the world, though only four feet away. "They're getting along fine, aren't they?"

Both Ritter and Carr wore faces rigid with scorn but that only seemed to provoke Arnstedt into more babbling. "You, young man, I've seen in here before. But you, sir, are new to us. You must be one of the officers from the *Blythe*. Norwegian?''

"English," Carr said. "Carpenter."

Arnstedt flattened his lower lip and nodded as though congratulating Carr for his rank and nationality.

"But about the chicas here, gentlemen. You can feel perfectly secure with them. Clean, all of them. I pay a high fee to one of the public health doctors to check them out not once, but twice a week." He leaned forward, resting his hands on the table, close enough to make them blanch under his whiskey breath. "Confidentially, I wouldn't have you go near most of the girls in La Zona. The Montparnasse. The Texas Bar . . . Entire crews have left port dripping. I'm proud to state I run the cleanest club on Panama Street."

Neither Ritter nor Carr made any comment. After an embarrassing pause Arnstedt extracted two cards from his vest pocket. "Will you boys still be in port tomorrow?"

"Most of the day," Ritter answered.

"Excellent." Arnstedt placed two cards in front of them. "Then try us for lunch. If you feel like a good homecooked meal, my wife operates the best restaurant in Puerto Acero—El Danubio Azul. Viennese cuisine. Latin American dishes. Or American favorites such as fried chicken and hotcakes. I might mention that we run the only restaurant in town that uses bottled water for absolutely everything. Many of the other establishments—I won't mention them by name—attempt to deceive you with bottles on the table, but they fill them from the tap. Entire crews have left here with the runs. Now I ask you—what's the good of that?"

"Very little," Ritter was forced to answer.

"We're a bit expensive," Arnstedt confessed. "Everything in this town is imported by ship or airplane."

"I can see that," Carr agreed. "The town is so isolated. So far from the regular trade routes."

Winking picaresquely, Arnstedt slyly deposited another

49

card in front of the girl and the Italian cook who were still clamped in a ferocious embrace. He straightened up and gave one more wink. "Take it easy, boys. Enjoy yourselves."

They listened to him repeat his litany at the next table, this time in fluent but atrocious Italian.

"Well," Ritter said, "aside from being an unctious, obnoxious cocksucker, the guy's a real Dale Carnegie."

"Quite charming," said Carr, softly.

"Shall we be going? I'd say the joys of the Club Moderno had just about run their course. Unless you feel like taking a woman. My girl, Lupe, told me she sympathizes with you greatly, thinks you're quite distinguished looking."

In lieu of an answer Carr rose and Ritter hoped he hadn't offended the man by offering him seconds on his woman.

They were about to push through the swinging doors when a scuffle erupted near the jukebox. A band of Italian sailors and Cruceño miners were arguing over a spilled bottle. Piño had somehow inserted himself between the two factions and was trying to act as mediator. Holding the more pugnacious types back, he shouted, "Tell me who is right. Tell me who is right here. I am for whoever is right."

Achieving accord with a glance Carr and Ritter went out to the turmoil of Panama Street. It was past two in the morning, yet La Zona was teeming: shoeshine boys, lottery sellers, pickpockets, drunken sailors, strolling musicians, and the old whores too ugly for the clubs. Music blared from every joint, joropos and rock and roll blending into an earshattering pandemonium in the twisting lane. Under the neon signs the carpenter's face changed colors, his gray hair pink, then green. Ritter wondered what had happened to the man. He seemed to be in a drunken daze, eyes glossy, and nearly staggering. Twice he almost bumped into musicians plucking at their cuatros. Ritter was tempted to steady the man by the elbow when Carr abruptly stopped, drew his shoulders back, sucked in air and, with visible effort, recovered himself.

50

The pulpería was shut tight and the black troubadour gone. Ritter whistled the tango that had been playing when they entered the Club Moderno: ''Y el mundo sigue andando . . .'' The world spins on. Their shoes made sucking noises in the mud. After the bedlam of La Zona they were back in the quiet, grim land of work where men needed their sleep. The radios were off and the kerosene lamps and light bulbs extinguished. Night sounds seeped through the open shutters, mosquitos buzzing at screens, the coughing of the old and sick, the wails of infants.

"It's always the same, isn't it?" Ritter mused out loud. "You shave and you shower and the music sounds so great. But no matter how fine a time you have, the end of the night leaves you with a sour taste in your mouth. Like, I really enjoyed myself tonight and all of a sudden everything becomes so shitty."

Carr did not reply, and the messboy felt the obligation to keep on talking, to explain.

"I still feel sort of sorry about dragging you out of your cabin, carpenter. I have this confession to make. I wanted to observe how you'd act on land. That's my weird hobby, creating situations and observing how people react. Like, I'll invite out two guys who I know will detest each other and just sit back and watch the flack. But you did exactly what I thought you'd do, Carr—nothing. You play such a cool role on the ship, and I had to check that out, but you were just as cool on shore. Like I have this uncle back in Philly. Uncle Burt. Big deal. Big entrepreneur and very big with the Republican Party. Always flying around the country to make speeches. I was always sure, though, even when I was a kid, that Burt was a royal phony. Besides being an ass and blowhard. It took me about twenty years to prove it. When I was going to college in L.A., Burt came through town and called me up to take me out to dinner. So I took him to this strip joint on Sunset Boulevard afterward, just to catch his act.

51

And Burt did exactly what I predicted he'd do. He made a total slob of himself. Spent around eighty bucks just for drinks with this twatty, snotty B-girl, got stewed, took her to a motel for another 'C' note, and he slipped me an extra fifty not to mention any of this to my Aunt Joan when I got back to Philly. As if I had to be bribed to hold my tongue. So I—"

The punch came out of nowhere, exploded on Jack Ritter's nose, then inside his skull. He was down and it hurt too much for him to lose consciousness. Electric snakes and meteors danced insanely, spun in erratic orbits, slowed, revolved again, and the galaxies gradually faded, concentrated into bright nova. The novas drifted outward, toward oblivion, and went out one by one till a single brilliant dot of light remained. It duplicated itself as his eyes teared.

His mouth was full of blood. Even though stunned, he twitched in irritation as a trickle of blood ran the wrong way down his cheek and dripped on his ear.

A dog wandered over to inspect him. It sniffed, rejected his odor and trotted away.

The moon came into focus again. He blinked his tears away and checked his wrist watch. His mind was clearing. He had probably been sprawled in the mud for a minute.

Rising, he made the mistake of brushing off his knees. His hands and back were matted with mud. A tooth felt loose. Glancing down, he saw his shirt was splattered with blood. He sniffed.

The carpenter was sitting on a trash can. In the dull glow of the moon Carr was misery incarnate, like some grotesque take-off on a Rodin statue. Ritter walked toward him and wondered what he was supposed to do now. By all normal standards he should slug the guy, tear into this bastard for throwing that sneak punch.

Carr was oblivious to the messboy standing over him. Ritter sensed it would be stupid to swing at this man. The blow had been like a hand coming out of the sky to quash blas-

52

phemy. He shook his head. Perhaps it was too much abnegation, or he was too much under Piño's spell, but if a man like Carr had bashed him, he probably deserved it.

"Is there something I can do, carpenter?"

"Fuck off."

Ritter turned and headed down the alley. Clucking chickens scattered from his path. He wiped the dried blood from his nose off on his shoulder. He hated chickens. His father had gone broke twice on chickens. A fever and three thousand died overnight. He was ten and he had gone out to help his father shovel the rotting poultry onto dump trucks. There had been a bonfire, spluttering with the stink of burning feathers.

The Cruceño watchmen playing dominoes on the number four hatch laughed and nudged each other as the filthy, blood-smeared sailor came up the gangplank, yanking at the slack ropes for support. Another brawl in La Zona. There were always riots on Panama Street. Whenever the oilmen, thieves, miners and seamen mixed on a busy night there was trouble. The police were less than useless. They had the habit of waiting for fifteen minutes after an emergency call and then showing up to collect the bodies. So far three sailors had come down the dock looking as if they had been in a brawl, and two had left with their suitcases, jumping ship.

Ritter went below to the mess. A drunken oaf had spilled the tray of lunchmeats and then stomped all over the cheese and bologna, and tracked stains down the passageway. Another drunken slob had left the coffee percolating. Inside the bottom was a steaming cinder of charred grinds. With a moan of disgust, Ritter snapped off the burner. It would take him hours to clean up this mess and he had a grinding headache. His eyes were swollen; he felt as though he were going blind. Down the passageway a pack of drunks were arguing in Svensen's cabin. Bottles and glasses crashed to the floor.

53

In the washroom he stripped off his ruined clothes and dumped them into a bucket of hot water. The glob of green paste they used for soap on the ship produced a murky film of suds; he stirred the brew with a toilet plunger. A wreck of a face stared back at him from the mirror. The carpenter threw a pretty good hook for a man his age.

He showered and scrubbed the dried blood off his neck and ear. It had not been a three star evening for Jack Ritter. His head was splitting and he felt disgusted with his performance. With all of his cleverness and linguistics and bullshit and yakking he had provoked a dignified man like Carr into taking a swing at him. Who the hell knew what that man thought about when he sat on that bitt every night? But Jack Ritter had to kick his little ball into another man's private yard.

It was impossible to sleep with all of the racket in Svensen's cabin. All the shouting. The real drinkers never drank on shore. The dedicated brought their liquor back to the ship and squabbled till dawn. Ritter chain-smoked on his bunk and listened to all the banging around.

He finally slept. It might have been for minutes or hours. When his eyes opened again, the river mists and the dull gloss of dawn were on the portholes. Carr was standing in the doorway, looking almost ghostly.

"Sorry to wake you, Jack."

A second passed before that statement registered. Ritter remembered that he was two hundred miles up the Río Verde River. And that the man posed in the doorway had punched him in the nose a few hours ago. The sudden sharp throb in his nose reaffirmed that recollection. Carr was incongruously attired in a gray business suit, button-down shirt and necktie, and was holding a brown leather valise. He looked like a dapper professor off for vacation. Incredible.

"Mind if I come in?"

"I don't know," Ritter muttered dubiously.

54

The carpenter entered anyway and sat down on the wooden bench across from the bunk. "How is the nose?"

"I don't know. It may survive. In a new form."

"From here I'd say it isn't broken. I'll check it before I go."

"Thanks . . . I don't think you scored a direct hit. At least my loose tooth would indicate you were slightly off target."

"I'm truly sorry about that, kid. Snapping on you that way."

"Yeah," Ritter mumbled. "You were pissed off at things in general, and I just happened to be in the vicinity."

Carr chuckled bitterly. "No. In a way you've just made my life very difficult. Could I ask you a question? Are you planning on making another trip down here?"

Ritter scratched his head, perplexed as to why the carpenter should be impeccably dressed at five thirty in the morning.

"No, I hadn't planned on it. I'd been thinking about signing off in Brooklyn and taking a freighter. For Europe."

"Well . . ." Carr shrugged in resignation. "I don't have any right to—not after the way I hauled off on you, but I was going to ask you for a favor." The shrug deepened.

"Well, go ahead, man. Speak up."

"I'll be staying on here in Puerto Acero for a while and there were a few things I needed. I'd hoped to give you some money and have you bring them in on the next trip: medical instruments, a few texts. Drugs."

Ritter tossed his head back and smiled. So the Gallego had called it. This man was a doctor. "Can't you get that stuff here? From Concepción?"

"I've just been to the public dispensary in town and talked to the young doctor on duty."

"You've had a busy time of it."

"Problems," Carr said. "Certification. Residence. Valida-

55

tion exams. And to obtain any medical supplies there are customs, permits, an incredible amount of red tape. The youngster at the dispensary told me that if I tried to order those items from Concepción, only four hundred kilometers away, they would cost me three times as much and might take months to arrive. And half might be stolen en route. In a country like this you can't trust the public services. Everything must be done on a personal basis."

Ritter puffed on his cigarette, taking perverse pleasure in this reversal of positions. Carr was definitely pleading with him. In a dignified fashion, of course. But the man was pleading. He repressed a smile. He had already formulated his answer but decided to punish Carr with at least ten seconds of silence.

"Well, if it's that important I can make one more round trip. None of my affairs are that pressing. I guess Europe will still be there in three months."

"It's important. You'd be doing me a huge favor. A favor I don't deserve after the way I slugged you. An apology isn't enough, Jack. When you return I'll try to give you a full explanation."

Ritter snorted, touching the bridge of his nose. "I used to be very proud of this thing. You've altered my profile. But if you can't get dueling scars from Heidelberg any more, a broken nose will have to do."

Carr laid two envelopes on the stool next to Ritter's bunk. "Here's money and a letter to an old friend of mine in Manhattan. Several items on the list may only be secured by licensed physicians. Dr. Slavik will purchase them and turn them over to you."

Ritter checked through the contents of the first envelope. There were two sheets, written longhand in what looked like Polish or Yugoslavian, and a list of instruments and medicines. He examined the second and his eyes widened at the sheath of hundred dollar bills. "Hey, carpenter! There must be about two thousand here."

"I know. I've taken all my money on the book. Captain Erlander and the Sparks were not happy about being rousted in the middle of the night but it couldn't be helped."

"And how do you know I'll be back? At a messboy's salary on a Norwegian freighter, this here is several years' wages for me."

With a wave of the arm Carr dismissed the objection. He reached for his valise and stood up. "I envy you, Jack. Envy your purity. I don't mean that to be patronizing. I'll see you in two months."

The farewells were concluded with mock salutes and Dr. Carr closed the door. Ritter heard him clanging up the metal stairs, and then the slam of the screen door leading to the deck. He flopped down on his bunk and examined the contents of the envelope again. Twenty-one hundred dollars. A lot of loot and yet it was nothing. Carr was quite right. He had a much higher price. He was a curious sucker for flattery. For a little pat on the rear he was losing months of his life and fouling up his plans for Europe.

Ritter slipped the two envelopes under his pillow and curled into a position for sleep. He knew he should get up and start to clean out that mess in the galley, but his lids were too heavy. He patted the pillow. The O.S. would call in twenty minutes. Meanwhile he'd have twenty minutes of unadulterated and perfect sleep.

His cabin door banged open and Piño burst into the room. "F.B.I.! Sorry to wake you. I've come to say 'adiós.' In case we don't meet again."

"What the fuck is this?" Ritter snarled, sitting up with an agonized jerk. "Suddenly my cabin is Grand Central Station."

The Gallego was dressed in a maroon cardigan, unpressed khaki trousers and scuffed sneakers. He had a duffle bag slung over one shoulder and his expensive German camera hanging from a strap around his neck.

"Adiós, F.B.I. I've signed off. I went to get my money

57

and the Sparks was very angry. He said the next man who woke him would be thrown overboard.''

"What the hell are you jumping off in this dump for? You can't get a ship out of here. Why don't you wait till we get back to Brooklyn?''

"No more ships, compadre.'' Piño dropped his duffle bag. "I am through with Western civilization. Remember that girl on the river this morning? The pretty savage?''

"Cut the shit, man.''

"It's not shit. I'm going to steal a boat and go search her out. That's all I need, F.B.I. All I want. A simple girl. A hectare of corn. Some fish from the river. Tranquillity and love.''

"You're out of your fucking mind, you nutty bastard. You go messing around down there and those Indians will shoot fifteen arrows up your ass.''

"Hach! That's where you're mistaken,'' Piño said smugly. "I know the Indians. They're good people. Not like us. They take you in.''

"How about immigration?'' Ritter sat up. "Will immigration let you sign off?''

"I spit on immigration. I spit on governments, taxes, maps, boundaries, armies and priests. Why should I ask an immigration official for permission to take a canoe up the river? He didn't put the river here. God put the river here. This is between me and God.''

Rising, Ritter extended his hand. "You're nuts but good luck, Gallego. It's been great knowing you.''

Piño spread his arms wide. "Vamos, hombre. Don't be a dead Yankee iceberg. Vamos. Un abrazo.''

They embraced and pounded each other on the back, each trying to pound harder. Piño pushed him away and picked up his duffle bag, slinging it over his shoulder with the time-honored gesture of the departing traveler. "Say farewell to Enrique for me, chaval. I went to his cabin but he has disappeared.''

58

"Sure. Good luck, Piño."

"And to you, F.B.I. You're a good boy, for a Yankee. If you sail down here again look for me on the banks. I'll wave to you from my hut. *Ciao!*"

The Gallego gave him one last goofy wink before slamming the door shut. Ritter shook his head in admiration and bewilderment. Just like that. Just like that the Gallego had stormed into his life and then blasted out like a man hurrying to catch a train. Things were happening too fast around here. If this kept up he and Captain Erlander would have to take the *Blythe* back to Brooklyn by themselves.

Shrugging, he stretched out on his bunk for one more cigarette. It was too late to sleep. In ten minutes the O.S. would be knocking on his door for the six o'clock call and he would have to go and clean up that mess. He blew a smoke ring and wondered which of them was worse off—a brilliant guy like Carr who held it all in and writhed inside his own skin, or a happy-go-lucky schmuck like Piño who let it all out, bounced from catastrophe to catastrophe, and always climbed out of the mud with a big shit-eating grin on his face. Or, perhaps, worse off was a guy like himself—Jack Ritter, drifting through life as a mere observer.

4

Henry Carr followed the mulatta secretary into the dingy lobby of the AmCruz offices. Through the screened windows the overhead cranes were dumping load after load of reddish-brown ore into the holds of the *Irridenta*. Puffs of pink smoke and powder rose above the deck with every thunderous drop and scores of railroad cars filled with the red ore stretched kilometers down the tracks and sidings.

This mulatta was familiar. She was from Trinidad, spoke English. A driving downpour had apprehended her on the ramp once, a hundred yards from shelter, and her flimsy white dress had become drenched, completely transparent. The stevedores and crewmen rushed over to admire her measured, stately progress toward the lobby and she had not hurried for fear of shaking. She had pretended not to hear their indecent calls, Carr remembered.

He left his valise by the water cooler and marched into the main office with her as might a major stockholder in the concern. English was indicated in this situation. "Good morning, Señorita. Mr. Jones said I might use your reproduction equipment."

The secretary blinked in confusion. She knew of no Mr. Jones, but there were so many Canadians and Gringos and foreigners coming in for the dam and the steel mill that she could not possibly keep track of them all. She pointed to the manager's glass-enclosed cubicle.

"Mr. Anderson won't be in until ten thirty, sir. Maybe you can use his typewriter."

Carr installed himself behind Mr. Anderson's desk and rummaged through the contents of the top drawer. Apparently Mr. Anderson was a very disorganized chap. From this spot check it appeared that Manager Anderson did little more in Puerto Acero than scribble, doodle, play cards, and read *Confidential* magazine.

There was one white, virginal, immaculate sheet of bonded paper. He clamped it into the Olivetti and admired its pristine emptiness. Who was he now? From which university had he matriculated? Doctor Henry Carr (rich, resonant, reassuring) graduated from the—Nothing in England. Edinburgh. Edinburgh, of course; Edinburgh emanated all of the oak-paneled sobriety, dry sherry aroma and guaranteed tonnage of the Anglo-Saxon institution, and was yet untainted by the syndrome. It was echt-British without being excruciatingly so. If the prefect of Puerto Acero had any background at all, Edinburgh would evoke overtones of Liston and Simpson, Napier, Bonnie Charlie, clashes between Saxon bowmen and Thanes, and perhaps Bruce's tenacious spider. The spider should strike a favorable chord. A bush bureaucrat invariably conceives of himself as frustrated, and unrecognized, coping valiantly with the sloth of his bungling superiors in the capital.

Henry Carr would be a Scot for a while. "Scots wa' ha' wi' Wallace bled." How nice. The members of the ancillary nationalities failed to appreciate the advantages of their dualism: to be Flemish rather than French; Austrian not German; Ukrainian instead of Russian; Canadian and not American. They enjoyed all the benefits of the hermetic identity, accrued the protective aura of the known quantity, the mantle of cohesiveness, and were exonerated from the stigmas of the

61

master races, the onus of their arrogance, the obligation to comply with a stereotype.

Should this be in Latin? His Latin was mislaid. Two decades in disuse and it had seeped out through the uncemented fontanels. On his deathbed he might babble Virgil but at this crucial juncture the Latin chose to recede like a penis in cold water. Yet, as a Britisher, he must muddle through.

Given a proper parchment, a fine brush, proper ink, he could forge a medical degree from any university in the world but none of these materials was available. Moreover, what would a disgraced, outcast ex-doctor be likely to cart around with him as proof of his true identity, folded in his wallet, to be taken out once a year, like the faded snapshot of a family wiped out in an accident, too pain-provoking to be in plain view, and yet too cherished to be thrown away. Certainly not his framed degree. Not if he had been wandering the earth for eight years as a sailor. No. He would be carrying a . . .

Notification of Matriculation

Just the notification. Excellent. A mere form letter, naturally. The degree, the parchment, would be forthcoming subsequently, cost money. And it was quite plausible that a shady character like this Dr. Henry Carr might carry this form around all these years, a shabby little reminder of past glories, his one proof of a vanished life. He took out a yellow pad and began to scribble.

It took him a half an hour to compose the two hundred-word draft of quasi-legal, pseudo-academic poppycock. He typed out his creation and the final copy was stunningly pretty on the white paper. To attest to his competence, he made space below for four signatures. Typing carefully, he invoked Dr. Liston Roberts, M.S., D.D.M. of the Edinburgh Royal Infirmary; Dr. Samuel Guthrie, M.D., D.S., of the Royal College of Physicians; Dr. Alexander Symes, M.D., D.L.M., of the Society of Surgeons of Scotland; and Dr. Fleming Brundage, M.D., British Medical Association, National Examining Board.

Carr scribbled the four names with his left hand and then examined his handiwork. Something was lacking. He held the crisp sheet up to the light. Too naked, not busy enough. A few seals and emblems would enhance it immeasurably.

Manager Anderson had a rack of five stamps: oval, rectangular, elliptical, circular. Carr pressed each one lightly in the ink pad and then pounded each corner of his document. He inspected the faint impressions. Much better. They were superb. The indecipherable imprints were imbued with all of the power of eroded hieroglyphics, as informative as wind-worn Etruscan inscriptions. Still, the credulence must be striken to the second or third power. A proper fugitive carried only a carbon copy.

Carr left the cubicle and walked over to the copy machine. He sensed the secretary's eyes on his back. She was suddenly intrigued. He glanced back at her, concentrated on the good-looking knees below her short, tight skirt, and forced her to turn back around in her swivel chair.

The AmCruz machine was quite defective and produced a wonderfully murky copy of the original. The secretary was still doing totals in the ledger, her back turned, and he used the moment to quickly tear up the original, then dip his finger into a paper cup of yesterday's coffee and add stains to wrinkle and shrivel his blurred forgery.

"Thank you kindly, young lady," Carr called across the office. "When Mr. Anderson comes in please tell him that Dr. Carr was asking for him."

She nodded suspiciously and watched as the stranger took a drink from the water cooler and gathered up his valise and overcoat. The screen door clapped shut behind and she shrugged. At least he looked like a doctor. He had gray hair like old Dr. Apolinario, and Dr. Mendicuti.

Outside, the heat attacked Henry Carr like a personal enemy. It was not yet nine and the valley had become one vast sauna bath. He put on his dark glasses and stared at the sweat glistening on the backs of the shirtless stevedores. This afternoon he would purchase the loose white trousers and white jacket, the sensible attire of the natives here.

But first his certificate needed more aging and curing. He struck a match and ran it lightly over the surface of the copy. It needed more tanning, maturation, years of friction and wear in a sweaty billfold. He crumpled the copy into a ball, squeezed tightly, and then slowly and carefully unpeeled it. He flattened it out between his palms, patted it gently, smoothed it out, and then repeated the process. It took him fifteen minutes of abuse to give the sheet a proper sheen of antiquity, a legitimate maze of dogears and creases. If all went well it would simply fall apart on the prefect's desk and require Scotch tape to put it back together. He smiled: Wolf Karol, the con man. History had made these puerile games unavoidable. The university that had conferred his medical degree many years ago was not likely to send a transcript to Santa Cruz. He was a non-person. An un-person. The Charles University might even deny he existed.

Carr carried his valise through Barrio Flores. The mongrels and goats peered at him with somber eyes along the way. The heat was their enemy, too, and they lacked the vigor to resent him. He passed a group of women lined up by a public spigot. They were gossiping and giggling, many with their hair in curlers and covered by bright kerchiefs. He wondered how those women could manage those tubs and tins of water, carrying them to their homes, while they gaped at him and wondered how the foreigner could wear a suit and necktie in this heat, and carry a heavy suitcase up the hill. A pert black girl wolf-whistled at him and her compañeras screamed with glee, and then hid their mouths and averted their gaze when he nodded back at them.

The lowered awnings on Avenida Reforma afforded him some shade. Unappetizing fruits and vegetables were piled high on the open stalls. Flies swarmed over the flanks of raw beef suspended from hooks. The flies made no troublesome

64

distinctions—they were equally at home on horse manure in the street and on the evening's roast. Carr noticed the amused disdain in the merchants' eyes as he passed them. Only Indians recently arrived from the hills carried their own bags in Santa Cruz.

He crossed Plaza Paez. The wide central square was ringed by more elegant shops, and baroque and colonial structures predating the War of Independence. One modern edifice, next to the unfinished Cathedral of San Benito, shattered the architectural harmony. The municipal center, a cubistic glass and concrete affair, parodied the Niemeyer School in Brazil, borrowing his ideas and not his genius for the squat contraption. At the central fountain he paused to admire his new town. A moldy Bolívar, El Libertador, pointed his sword to the south, and a bird-stained, mounted General San Martín pointed his pike to the north. The plaza was defended by four rusting antique mortars and pyramids of green cannon balls.

According to the plaque on the front door, Municipal Center office hours were from nine to one, and three to seven, but the receptionist at the desk informed Carr that Jefe Civil Señor Mendoza did not usually arrive until eleven, and it would be better for him to return later. Carr ignored the advice and sat on the bench reserved for petitioners. A tattered, back-dated *Selecciones del Reader's Digest* was on the table to his left, and he sensed that by just sitting there, still and complete, he was making the receptionist nervous. She smiled at him finally, revealing four gold teeth. A pity. She might have been an attractive girl except for the pomade on her hair, the gold teeth, and the hairy calves. The lobby was also sadly run down. The Center could be no more than five years old, but it reeked of unwashed bodies, ammonia, garlic, poverty. Cigarette butts littered the tiled floor. Carr glanced upward. Deep fissures were visible in the ceiling. Maintenance and repair were not Cruceño fortes.

Jefe Civil Mendoza did not put in his appearance until eleven thirty. A stout little peacock, he bustled into the lobby with a briefcase under his arm—obviously displeased to find an occupant on the petitioner's bench—and hurried on into his office. The temperature rose as the minutes ticked on. Eyeing the clock, the receptionist nodded at Carr in sympathy as another hour went by. It was past one when her buzzer rang and she received instructions to usher the petitioner to the Jefe's chambers. Carr understood. The Arabs ruled Spain for seven centuries and had imparted their Levantine grace.

Jefe Civil Mendoza stressed the importance of his position by not looking up. He was poring over a report on his desk, tapping at vital items with his pen, while the sailor sweltered quietly in front of his spacious desk. A minute dragged by before he snapped the report shut, quite decisively, and glanced up at the petitioner.

"You may sit down."

"Thank you, your excellency."

Mendoza nodded appreciatively, at being answered in his native tongue.

"You are a mariner, no? Officer?"

"Carpenter. Off the *Blythe*."

Mendoza frowned. A mere carpenter. The Jefe toyed with the Parker Pen from his Christmas desk set.

"You cannot be a distressed seaman as yet. The *Blythe* is still docked. It does not take on a pilot till seven this evening."

"Which is precisely what I've come to see you about, your excellency. I seek your permission to stay on here in Puerto Acero."

"Then you've been wasting your time waiting for me, sailor. That's a matter for immigration. Immigration is on the third floor."

"And immigration would automatically say no."

"Exactly," Mendoza said with a broad smile. "We have enough riffraff here already. And it is not my custom to circumvent the procedures of our Immigration Department."

"I'm afraid that my case is a bit complex, your excellency. A special case requiring your intervention."

Mendoza stirred in his swivel chair and shrugged complacently. "You believe yours is a special case? You think you're the first mariner who has ever entered my office? Let me tell you what your situation is: You've found a responsive girl, no? Up in La Zona, no? She intimates that she wishes you to stay with her, jump ship, be her compañero . . ." Mendoza closed his eyes, and pinched the bridge of his nose. "I strongly advise against it. We've been through this before: a few nights of passion, the inevitable quarrels, you call her a dirty whore, and you're out on the streets. Then you become a public charge and we either throw you in jail or your company agent has to provide you with food and lodgings until we can put you on the next ship out. I am sorry, señor mariner. We have had too many unfortunate experiences. Just four months ago we had one case. A seaman, a Greek, garroted his fallen angel with her own nylon stocking. And you don't look like a pimp, my friend. You look like a solid, honest working man. Forget this woman. There are more in every port."

"That's not quite my situation," Carr said after a pause. "No woman is involved. I'm seeking to live and work in your city for a considerable period. And practice my profession once again."

"Profession?"

Carr took out his pipe and pouch and began to pack the bowl. He examined the Jefe's high-ceilinged office, the symbols of authority: the red, yellow and green banner of the Republic of Santa Cruz, a photo of Jefe Mendoza receiving an abrazo from the President at a political convention, and a colored photo of the Jefe, la señora Mendoza, and three little Mendozas at the entrance to Disneyland, California.

"Before I went to sea, years back, I was a medical doctor. In Great Britain."

Jefe Mendoza straightened up. This interview had suddenly taken on serious dimensions. He extended his hand. "Your passport."

Thumbing through the British passport for stateless persons, Mendoza grimaced at the profusion of stamps: Dakar, Port Said, Valparaiso, Lourenço Marques, Capetown . . .

"Almost too many, no? You're quite the traveler, mister."

"So was Magellen, your excellency."

"And where did you learn your Spanish?" It was an accusation.

"I spent several years in Spain, in the late thirties," Carr answered, using the truth when the truth was useful.

Mendoza opened the passport again. "It mentions nothing about a doctor in here. Under occupation it lists laborer, seaman."

"True, your excellency. At the time I left England I was none too anxious to publicize the fact."

"There are, of course, documents to substantiate this rather grand claim."

Carr took out his wallet, removed the mimeographed copy of his Notification of Matriculation. Mendoza snatched it up. The Jefe Civil snapped it open officiously, spread it flat on his green desk pad, and deepened the tear as he smoothed the worn and withered credential with his palm. This document warranted the closest possible scrutiny. Mendoza put on his ebony-framed glasses and scanned the certificate with his pen, underlining the word "Magna" with his Parker Pen, and affixing periods to the signatures. After a moment of reflection he refolded the certificate and slid it across the green desk mat toward his petitioner.

"I congratulate you, my friend. Over the years innumerable swindlers and poseurs have sat in that chair and regaled me with the wildest stories but you have positively the biggest balls of any man who has ever entered my office."

"Unfortunately, your excellency, I came to you with a true story."

"A highly entertaining one, at least. A carpenter off a freighter marches into my office, and calmly proclaims that he is a doctor. And as proof he offers up this flimsy piece of toilet paper. Where do you think you are, *Mister* Englishman? This is not the Congo or the Gold Coast. You are in the Republic of Santa Cruz. We have been independent for one hundred and thirty-four years. Our capital, Concepción, boasts one of the great universities of the Americas, founded fifty years before you English established Harvard, and at that university we have a renowned medical faculty, staffed by professors who specialized at the Sorbonne, in the United States, at the most prestigious institutions of Germany. And yet you have the audacity to—"

Carr raised his hand. "If you would pardon me, your excellency. I in no way seek to denigrate either your nation or your educational system. The Central University of Santa Cruz is highly regarded in Europe. Several of its distinguished members have even held chairs at Edinburgh. But here, here in Puerto Acero, what do we see, Señor Mendoza? Concepción has the excellent doctors. We can fill the telephone book with doctors in Concepción. But here? Last night I conversed with two of your young physicians at the public health clinic. They frankly admit they are swamped by their burden. And they are all there is, except for a few graybeards, thirty years behind the times. I've walked through your barrios, Señor Mendoza, seen the conditions. What do you have in the barrios? A few scabrous midwives. Perhaps some bone setters converting simple sprains into crippled limbs. Fortune tellers and faith healers prescribing death. And the campesino, ten kilometers from the city? The campesino has nothing. I would stay here and minister to your poor."

Jefe Civil Mendoza smiled sardonically. "Oh? How pretty. How kind of you. Our own Dr. Schweitzer has arrived. Come here to bestow his blessings upon the savages.

69

And perhaps dabble in our politics? And perhaps stir up troubles? And criticize our social system? And our faith? And perhaps attract a host of newspaper reporters for self-serving publicity?''

"None of that, Señor Mendoza. None of that. Perhaps I'm just an excellent surgeon who made a mess of his life. And a man who is tired of running from himself. And running from crimes which were, perhaps, not so terrible.''

Mendoza slouched in the swivel chair. A peculiar intimacy had been achieved; the rapport and the fascination of the persecutor and the harried who have come to a mutual understanding of terms. Mendoza slumped, assuming the posture of the state prosecutor who is about to hear the long-awaited confession. "That would interest me, Mr. . . .'' He flipped through the passport again. "Dr. . . . Carr. That would interest me greatly. I would like to know what you find so attractive about Puerto Acero. Perhaps it is our insufferable heat. Or the fevers in our marshes. Or tell us what prevents you from practicing your profession in your native land.''

Carr nodded. He had worried that the lurid tale he had concocted might reek too much of sensationalism. But over the last five minutes, he had concluded that this provincial prefect had the type of facile mind that abhorred the grayness of reality and responded best to bold slashes in black and white. For the next hour he told Jefe Mendoza the story of Dr. Henry Carr, a brilliant and wealthy young physician catering to London high society, an excellent surgeon with a weakness for women and the good life, a married man with two children and an expensive mistress, so expensive that young Dr. Carr began to engage in illicit activities, abortions, the sale of drugs to Negro jazz musicians and titled daughters of the British aristocracy. Jefe Mendoza was so intrigued by this portrait of the decadence of the British elite that he rang his receptionist and had her serve them both coffee. After she departed, Carr continued the story of the young surgeon's downfall—a patient dying from complications after an abortion, the investigation, expulsion from the medical association, the revelation of his sale of opium and cocaine to entertainers, the trial, jumping bail, slipping onto a ship in Liverpool rather than await the court's certain verdict. Then, years at sea, contemplating suicide and the ruins of his life. "Let me add, your excellency," Carr said, finishing off, "that this has been no sudden decision . . . no whim. I've been pondering this these many years. My life on the ships has not been unbearably hard but I've seen misery all over the globe: children suffering in Haiti, Calcutta, Africa, on the streets of your very own city. I've come to realize that I've been coddling myself, luxuriating in remorse. My crime—and scientifically there was none, the complications were caused by the patient's lying to me—was nothing compared to the waste of these last twelve years. If you don't accept me here, Señor Mendoza, then I will go elsewhere. But I'm determined to be a useful man once again."

With his head back, resting against the carved woodwork of his vice-regal swivel chair, Jefe Civil Mendoza puffed on his cigar and mulled over his decision. Finally he sat up.

"I'm afraid you'll have to go elsewhere, Mister. You present yourself, in your own words, as a man of dubious moral character. On the strength of this incredible slip of paper, and your rather astounding tale, how can I possibly entrust the health and well-being of my people to you? One solution might be to send this certificate to the Ministry of Public Health in Concepción. If they choose to validate it, then we might be able to afford you the opportunity to redeem yourself."

Carr sniffed bleakly. "You know full well how long that might take, sir. Months. Months as it goes from wire basket to wire basket."

"My hands are tied, Mr. English Doctor."

"Then let me untie them for you, your excellency. Let us

71

put this on a different basis. Let us establish a personal bond between us.''

Carr extracted a white envelope from his jacket pocket. He opened it and tapped out the corners of ten hundred-dollar bills, and placed the envelope on the desk mat.

Mendoza frowned. He fingered the envelope. ''And what is this supposed to mean, Mister?''

''Exactly what I said, sir. This can constitute a personal and inviolable bond between us.''

''I gather this is a crude attempt to bribe me.''

''Not at all. It's exactly what I said it was. This will be my bond. This will be my guarantee against incompetence or malpractice. You may administer this sum personally and, at the first complaint against me, forfeit this quantity to the victim, or his family. And I'd hoped it might cover any administrative costs.''

Mendoza glanced at the envelope. ''One thousand American dollars.''

''One thousand dollars. And when you're completely satisfied that I am what I say I am, you may return my bond . . . minus the administrative costs.''

''This still smells like a cheap attempt to bribe me.''

''I reiterate that I merely seek the opportunity to prove myself, Jefe Civil. You, and you alone, can give me that chance.'' He touched the certificate on Mendoza's desk. ''And you may send this along to the Ministry of Public Health in Concepción for validation. Though I'd much prefer to have it hanging in my surgery . . . till I can send to London for my framed Latin degrees and permanent papers.''

A full thirty seconds passed with the two men staring into each other's eyes before Mendoza said: ''It would be better to keep this until they arrive. You'll need it in your office. Meanwhile I'll have one of my assistants type up and sign a local temporary permit.''

Carr muffled a smile.

72

Mendoza's aide had been understandably reluctant about signing the paper. If there were any repercussions, the Jefe would obviously lie, disclaim all responsibility and complain about the recklessness of underlings. Mendoza himself probably chose to half believe the story, the convenient half that sweetened his bank account while enhancing his self-image as a dedicated public servant snipping roughshod through red tape.

Carr touched at his billfold and stared at his reflection in the front window of the Danubio Azul. It was three o'clock. His operating funds were much depleted since morning. He had signed off the *Blythe* with five thousand dollars and three were already gone, plus one hundred for the first month's rent on his cottage. Expensive, but it was a commodious, whitewashed place, with running water and solid furniture. He would not be ashamed to invite Señor Arnstedt to this home. A cottage on a prominent hill. From his porch he could take in the sweep of the river, the docks and warehouses of the AmCruz Corporation, the bungalows of Barrio Flores, the hovels of La Colina, and the ten or fifteen mansions belonging to the plutocrats of La Loma.

The windows of El Danubio Azul looked too much like the demonstration table in a pathology lecture. Lobsters in brackish tanks glided over azure and crimson coral, lustrous pebbles, porcelain cornucopias. A quartered wild boar roasted on the spokes of an asador, ribs exposed to the glowing coals of a brick hearth. Carr opened the door and merry bells tinkled overhead. It was cooler inside, quaintly atmospheric, with flasks of hot peppers and vinegar, red and white checked spreads on every table, racks of mugs and vases, and pale china lining the varnished walls. Reproductions of red-jacketed hunters galloping after foxes through idyllic forests. They had even managed to salvage a few choice pieces of the Jablonic Bijouterie, which produced a pang. Stolen family heirlooms on the shelf of a South American café. He could

73

picture Bela methodically stuffing her husband's swathing cotton into each glass figurine, wrapping them in newspapers, and tying the bundles tightly with twine as the Red Army rumbled through Moravia.

The waitress was serving Carr his side order of fried bananas when Bela Arnstedt came in from the kitchen. He heard the exotic rattling and clicking of the strings of beads strung across the kitchen door. Bela stepped into his life again. As with Emil, last night, there was no physiological reaction, no dramatic gasps or twinges, no wavering in the systolic or diastolic flux. Least of all was there any ominous background music.

The proprietress of El Danubio Azul fidgeted with her skirts and then punched the cash register. She began to total the day's receipts, examining each check, running her fingers down the additions, and impaling the checks on an upraised spike. Carr was disappointed. She had once loomed so enormously in his mind, dominated it like a vast oceanic Hecate; had festered in his mind like a giant witch. Now she was reduced to mere human proportions. Another man would see only a formidable woman in her early forties, a sensual mouth, cunning green eyes, auburn hair, freckles on a handsome face. Perhaps a proper Etonian would find her irresistible with a birch rod in her hands. But it was over. Bela was only a woman—a few feet away—to be struck or fondled. Cut.

Bela opened a ledger next to the cash register and wrote in a few figures. It was ironic. The attractive sow behind the counter would not, of course, remember that her childhood ambition had been to own a café. All of the sincere, undernourished, and unrecognized artists, writers, and composers of Prague would use it as a refuge: Czechs, Germans, Slovaks, Jews. All would be welcome to the free coffee and free beer and though Wolf Karol was insincere and wealthy—so wealthy he could summer abroad in England—he would also be entitled to her largesse.

74

Only he would remember. A cigarette flicked into the slow waters of the Vltava as a younger Bela pressed against him saying, "You're too capricious, Wolf. You're either too silly or too gloomy."

"No one is ever too gloomy, Bela. Even Christ on the Cross was frivolous in his agony. He had time for gestures for the masses, and famous last words."

"Now you're being silly again. You never speak to me seriously like Emil does. Emil will tell me everything on his mind and speak to me for hours."

"It shouldn't take that long."

"If that's the way you speak about your best friend, what do you say about me?"

"I have nothing to say about you, dear. I have nothing to say about anyone. I said all I have to say three years ago and have been repeating myself ever since."

The Vltava flowed through Prague under its thirteen bridges, past the stately Radice, and Bela stared up at him accusingly. "Yes. You particularly don't wish to speak about me with your father. He would shrivel up and die. Dr. Karol! The grand philosopher. But all of his precious liberalism disappears when it comes to his son marrying a gentile. What word do you people use—shicksa?"

Young Wolf Karol laughed. "I can't even use my father as an excuse. He likes you very much and has intimated that you would make an excellent wife. It's me, Bela. It's all me. I do not wish to marry you. I intend to be a genius of sorts and have no time for baby trams in the vestibule. Of course I would love to live with you for a while. That would be very nice, to live with you."

"For how long, Wolf?"

"For one year, three months, six days, and two hours."

She pinched his wrist and moaned, "I'm ready to cry and you're laughing."

"I'm not laughing, Bela. I'm deadly serious. Someone has to be great and it might as well be me. I intend to shave off

75

the atavistic hair, slice away the ripe scalp, trephine through the skull, and plunge my scalpels into the darkest of hemispheres. I'll snip away my patients' psychoses and pincer out their fantasies and I'll place them under my microscope and say, 'Look what you were imagining, you swine! Aren't you ashamed?' "

"You are so terribly silly, Wolf. You sound more like a would-be poet than a gifted surgeon."

"But why not, my Bela. Chekhov was a doctor. Pío Baroja, a doctor. Somerset Maugham. Marañón. Claude Bernard came to Paris as a dramatist. I'll develop the Karol technique for resectioning, restructuring, and purging the afflicted mind, and then deliver my paper to the medical congress in austere Alexandrines. I can do anything, Bela. I can do everything, in fact . . ."

Carr rose as the proprietress approached his table, tucking a roll of bills into her apron pocket. She motioned for him to remain seated and with a cordial smile took a chair across from him with all of the self-assurance of a comely woman who knows she will be welcome.

"Did you enjoy your lunch, sir?"

It had been so abrupt. His heart had thumped as her eyes took him in. For just one second he imagined that she could see right through him and his English mask, and twenty years of attrition.

"It was fine, madam. Very spicy."

"Oh? You're not an American? I took you for an American."

"English, madam. Off the *Blythe*."

Bela rose slightly to smooth her skirts under her. It was such a familiar gesture. Except for the flowery tropical dress and deep tan, she might have been her mother in 1938.

"Then you'll be sailing shortly. In a few hours. Captain Erlander and the officers usually lunch here."

"The *Blythe* will sail but I won't. I've been thinking of staying on for a while."

76

"Consuelo!" Bela snapped her fingers at the waitress dozing open-mouthed in the rear booth. "Consuelo! Dos cafés, por favor."

The waitress hurried to prepare two demitasses and Bela turned to him again. Her face was strong. The woman exuded vitality. She had always been stronger than Emil.

"You'll be going up to the mines then, sir? We've been having a great many new engineers coming in. This entire region has become very active since the mines opened."

"No. I believe I'll be here in town, Señora Arnstedt."

"You know my name?"

"Well. Your husband gave me this card last night. He told me that this was the only restaurant in town. And after finishing this delicious almuerzo I'm inclined to agree with him."

Bela laughed, a throaty full sound.

"You were at the Club? You don't look like the type of man for Panama Street. I had taken you for a gentleman."

"I was taken there by some friends. The Moderno looked like the best of a bad lot."

Consuelo placed filter pots of thick black coffee between them and Bela reached over to offer him a cigarette. "Then you'll probably be working at the offices on the dock. With Mr. Anderson. And living in the American compound."

"No. Not really. You see, I'm a physician. And I've been planning on opening an office here. On the hill. I've already rented a cottage. A very comfortable place on Los Olivos.

"A doctor?" The proprietress of El Danubio Azul bloomed with genuine enthusiasm. "That's wonderful. That's precisely what we need more of in Puerto Acero. Whenever the children have something I generally go to Dr. Baker in the American settlement. There are only five doctors—six if you count Dr. Baker—in the entire region. And there should be twenty. The poor boys at the government clinic are terribly overworked . . . and terribly inexperienced."

"Oh?"

"Yes. Dr. Lopez is very conscientious but I wouldn't trust the other two youngsters."

Carr scraped the last stain of carmel custard from his dish. "Well, I hope to take some of the pressure off them. There seems to be room for more."

"You already have a cook, no? The local help is very economical."

"Not as yet. It'll probably take me a few days to settle down."

"Then we'll be expecting you here, doctor. For la cena. And you might think about coming over to our home for dinner one evening. I'm sure that Emil would be delighted to speak with you. He's so starved for contacts with the outside world. He says that's what he most misses in Puerto Acero—stimulating conversation."

"I'm not too adroit at that."

"But much better than I, I'm sure, Doctor. My husband says I'm not even a good listener."

He reached for his check and she rapped his hand reprovingly. "Please. Today you're invited. The first meal you're the guest of the Danubio Azul."

Resting in his chinchorro, the hammock enveloped in thick mosquito nets, Carr traced the mark with his fingers. No boil or corruption swelled over the spot. In times past the superstitious might have cleansed the skin with fire.

He had been unable to sleep through the heat of the late afternoon siesta. Tomorrow he would take the paddle steamer downriver to Ciudad San Martín, the state capital, and purchase the basic items for his office with the temporary permit, and perhaps an appropriate black leather case for house calls. He would hang a sign from his porch and invite one and all to drop by with their cysts, fevers, fistulas, and carcinomas. Bring only a chicken or a sack of turnips. They would be converted into hard currency. Henry Carr had very

78

simple wants. All he required was one properly equipped operating room and privacy.

Carr tossed in his gauze cocoon. This had to be a nightmare, just a bizarre variation on his obsession. The threads of divergent lives could not be rewoven in this arbitrary fashion. Decades had gone by, there were five continents and three billion people on the planet, and yet he had been caught up in this strange snarl. In a few moments the watchman would knock on his cabin door. In thirty minutes, after the bread and cheese and a hot cup of coffee, he would trudge up to the foc's'le with the others, help the bosun distribute the paint and brushes to the young boys standing under a dark sky, a harsh spray blowing from a barren coast. Were all those years in lonely cabins merely a trance inspired by too much study at his desk, the map on the wall, the pale pinks and greens of vast colonial empires? The gray sky was not over the Atlantic. It rolled over autumn marshes and in the distance there were barley fields, the river, bleak November clouds reflected in gray eddies . . . The mind was such an unreliable instrument. He could not recall what he ate for breakfast yesterday and could still hear Emil's strident speech, words spoken decades ago.

"Hitler, whether or not we approve of his tactics, has been the salvation of Germany, Wolf. And with Germany stable the rest of us may breathe easier. With a powerful Germany there will be no further encroachments from the Communist East. Hitler is the bulwark of the West."

"If you say so, Emil. You're our political expert."

Young Dr. Karol did not bother to contradict his companion. Both were very English that day, resplendent in their wool jackets and red caps, leather vests, knickers and high rubber boots. They smoked pipes and lunched on a dry knoll as their retriever scuffed at the autumn straw.

"Your chief fear is his Jewish policy?"

"I would say so, Dr. Brenner. I find it much more reasonable to worry about myself than the Hottentots of Africa. As you well know, I am an agnostic and I happen to have no great love for the majority of my compatriots. If and when I marry and have children I have no intention of raising them in my grandfather's faith. And my grandfather's arrogance makes me ill. But with the laws that your Chancellor Hitler has passed in Germany, I would be subject to their every provision."

"Exactly! Then you'll have to consider the contradictions inherent in your father's course of action. And in his public declarations. He must define himself, Wolf. Is he German? Czech? Jewish? He was acclaimed as an ornament of the German community, teaches in the German tract at the University. Yet he is a Czech nationalist. Which we both know is ridiculous. This state is a fiction. With the revival of a Czech state we may as well revive the Hapsburg dynasty, restore all of Palestine to the Zionists, give the United States back to the Redskins. Then your father salts his lecture on ophthalmology with anti-clerical anecdotes. He has been attacked by the Catholic press. Attacked by the Jewish press. None of this is necessary, Wolf. For a while he was the only professor of Jewish derivation whose expulsion was not demanded by the German *Studentenschaft*. They ignored his background in the light of his accomplishments. 'All must go but Doctor Karol.' They demonstrated against every single one but your father. And then he goes and participates in a Zionist subscription campaign. For a library in Haifa. Haifa! Of all places. Why not in Timbuctu? If only he could be more discreet. He does not weigh the gravity of his actions against the international ferment. Germany will annex the Sudetenland. France is mobilizing. The Hungarians will rip at our soft underbelly. The Poles eye the northern border. The Slovaks will break away and the democracies will not defend this fiction. When Germany repossesses its own, the jackals will come in for the leavings. But your father cannot keep his mouth closed. You see all the contradictions, don't you, Wolf? My father is infuriated with him. He says that it is perverse, masochistic that your father should suddenly, after forty years, play the Jew when the world is collapsing . . ."

The argument continued over dinner that evening, old Dr. Karol intervening only to be witty and play the jovial patriarch for his twin daughters, Naomi and Ruth, his winter wheat. The girls giggled at his every sally. Dr. Karol waited fifteen years after Wolf to have the twins, accepted them in exchange for a beloved wife who did not return from the hospital. All were astonished by the old fellow's energy, lecturing at the university, maintaining a practice, publishing philosophical essays.

"I hope you boys didn't argue this way while you were hunting. Politics should never be discussed with shotguns in your hands. Politics is for cafés and meeting halls. And when it's a meeting hall you should always serve the beverages in paper cups. That way, the worst you can get is a folding chair on the head."

"It's impossible to argue with your son," Emil said. "He already knows everything. This afternoon he told me he was going to Spain, to serve in the medical corps."

Dr. Karol blanched but his tone was calm, sarcastic, as he glanced at his son. "Spain, eh? On whose side will you serve?"

"I haven't decided yet. I'll flip a coin when I get there."

"He's going to fight for the Republic," Naomi announced proudly.

"For the Communists," Emil said.

"This is true, Wolf?" Dr. Karol asked.

"It's the place to be, at the moment."

"Ho-ho," Dr. Karol chortled. "So, it's as I always suspected. Beneath that callow cynicism and carefully cultivated façade of misanthropy lurks a sloppy sentimentalist."

"That I always knew," Emil said. "But I didn't suspect the sentimentalist was a Communist."

"Don't be simplistic," snapped Wolf Karol. "I spit on the

81

Communists. I'm going to Spain because the Republic needs trained physicians. And because I wish to do something rewarding before I become successful.''

Young. So painfully young. He twisted in his hammock. He had been dreaming about Spain, the one good year in his life, and the buzz of distant music snipped off the spool from the past. Every man was entitled to one good year and Barcelona had been Wolf Karol's year of pure glory: the child prodigy of the operating room, the tall young Czech surgeon, admired by his older colleagues and lucky with the nurses. All the camaraderie and all the sense of community from fighting in a doomed cause. And the music. Pity the poor land that has beautiful music.

Henry Carr checked his wristwatch. It was almost eight. The *Blythe* would be sailing. Bela Arnstedt was expecting the English doctor at the Danubio Azul. Fine. He would not go. If she were disappointed by his failure to appear, she would be that much more pleased when he dropped by tomorrow. He wanted to be alone tonight, to stroll about Avenida Reforma, sip a coffee, at a sidewalk café, familiarize himself with his theater of operations.

The neighbors on the hill observed Carr from their screened porches as he left his cottage. Dona Felicia, proprietress of most of the homes on Los Olivos, had already informed them that he was a suspicious character. He had given his name as Dr. Henry Carr, an obvious alias, and during the negotiations had not behaved like an honest man. He had arrived in a taxi, with only one suitcase, and instead of trying to bargain on the rent, he had paid her first asking price plus a month's guarantee. An honest man, sure of his rights, would have stalked out three times and secured Los Olivos for half of what she demanded. And then he had signed the inventory list, assuming responsibility for all the household effects without making any check whatsoever. An honest man would have at least complained about the cracked kitchen sink or the torn screens, but this so-called Dr. Carr said he was completely satisfied. Obviously he was a refugee or fugitive, up to no good.

Panama Street was relatively deserted as Carr paused at the entrance to the Club Moderno. A ceremony was taking place inside. The ladies were in matronly dresses, and no drinks were being served at the bar. The guests were procuring their refreshments from a tastefully decorated table, covered with trays of empanadas and sandwiches, bouquets of flowers, baskets of fruit and nuts, and a silver punch bowl. A quintet of harps, cuatros and guitars was supplying a dispirited waltz for several couples shuffling in slow motion. Only the trade seemed to be present: girls from other clubs, bouncers, pimps and scowling hoods in chauffeur uniforms. They were acting with unusual decorum.

Carr pushed through the doors, gathering that this was an engagement party for one of the dames and some worthy caballero. On a festive occasion, such as this, it would be appropriate to approach Señor Arnstedt and congratulate him on the splendid cuisine at his restaurant.

Carr served himself from the punchbowl. Several of the bucks had noticed his intrusion but instead of challenging it they had placed a bar over the front door to prevent the entrance of more outsiders. He sipped at the sweet punch and was struck by the fact that this fiesta had an incongruous tone. It was somber yet hysterically gay, like a birthday party celebrated in a gallows chamber.

The women gathered in the far corner separated and he had the answer. It was a wake. Six empty cases of Coca-Cola had been stacked to form an altar, another box on top. The white tablecloth only partially covered the cases. He walked over to examine the display. From the size of the casket, lined with red and green wrapping paper, he guessed it was a wooden beer crate. The infant was swathed in a white gown and nestled in a cloud of cotton wool sprinkled with silver eye-dust cosmetic. Paper golden wings sprouted from the shoulders, and a gold paper crown was perched on the tiny, hairless head. The casket was surrounded by pastel candles and, wisely, two bronze chalices of burning incense. But, in the heat and moistness of these lowlands, the flesh was already swelling with a pale glow. The smoking incense failed to cover the faint smell of decay.

Behind him a gaunt chauffeur was reciting in faltering Latin:

"Et quo quisque fere studio divinetus adhaerat ant quibus in rebus multum sumus ante morati . . . . atque in caratione fuit contenta magis mens in sommis . . ."

Which was true, Carr thought. But the grotesque sincerity and quoting of pagans only intensified the parody mass. The black chauffeur's jacket was his cassock, the black cap reversed on his skull, the metal license and visor resting over the occipital ridge. He leavened a novena with snatches from Caesar's *Gallic Wars*. The staccato bark of his incantations prevailed over the plinking guitars and harps. This sallow, haggard chauffeur had materialized from a lost El Greco canvas.

The mother was crying by the door to the ladies' room. She was being consoled by her compañeras, and the big girl, who had chased Piño into the bar last night, was supplying her with napkins to dry the tears. She had cried past the point of dignity. Deep-brown half moons curled under her eyes and black strands of mussed hair hung over her swollen cheeks.

The quintet rested. Pedro Alfarez clapped his hands over his head, drawing attention to himself. "Soledad! Soledad! Stop these silly tears. This is a fiesta. Everyone is to be happy. Tonight a pure and unspoiled soul rises to paradise."

Alfarez was a fat black bandit with white frizzled hair, notorious along the docks. When the *Blythe* came in, Pedro was the first on board with offers to barter monkeys, parrots, or absinthe for marijuana, pistols, and shirts. Pedro called to the women by the latrine. "Vamos, Soledad. Vamos, chica. Your little girl, Alma, is dead. Alma is much better off. People like us shouldn't have babies. Look at all the misery she is spared by dying now. Alma died clean. She flies straight to the arms of the Blessed Mother while we are condemned to fifty thousand years in the Inferno. They will be sticking pitchforks up our asses while Alma sings sweetly by the right hand of our Lord, Jesu Cristo."

Soledad stormed toward them, pushing the drunks out of her way. "And what do I care, Alfarez? Everything is over for Alma. She leaves this unfeeling world. But Arnstedt! I'm going to kill that shit-eater. Cut off his balls. Drop his eggs on Alma's grave as an offering."

The crowd around them mumbled, concurring in her plan. Alfarez took her under his arm. "Good, Soledad. It's a good idea. We'll help you. But this is a party. You have to do things right at a party. You have all these guests. All of your faithful friends contributed to give Alma a proper farewell. Tonight she'll be singing with the cherubim and seraphim by the golden throne. And you are here, using this language, before she is even in the ground."

Pedro clapped his palms over his head. "Let us sing for our unknown Alma. Let us form a chorus and praise her spotless soul. Let us sing for her mother, the most beautiful courtesan of La Zona. We will sing the traditional chants of our noble and eternal race, the great people of Santa Cruz, the music cherished by our ancestors and which will be cherished by our progeny."

Carr was swept along as they divided into choruses. He did not resist. Ceremony and ritual were instinctive here. The simplest among them could mount a coronation.

Alfarez conducted Soledad to the position of honor by the gay casket. He snapped his black fingers for silence.

Pedro pointed to the quintet, putting them at the ready. His arms rose majestically toward the ceiling. Suddenly he was the maestro of orchestra and choir.

> "The Angels have a duty and love
> to take our part in heaven above . . ."

Carr joined them as they repeated the verse. He clasped hands with the chambermaid to his right and the whore to his left and sang verse after verse with equal fervor as they circled the altar.

Pedro signaled for them to sway in the other direction and the quintet changed key and tempo, as their voices rose.

> "Don't cry, mother don't cry.
> Accept this consolation.
> The daughter of your loins,
> Tonight enjoys salvation."

The chorus dissolved and the guests in the Club Moderno applauded each other warmly, congratulating themselves on their success, and toasting their own performance. Soledad responded with racking sobs and the women rushed to her. Alfarez had more verses. He motioned to the harpist for an accompaniment and minced into a cha cha cha.

Carr refilled his glass of punch and sat down at an empty table. He stared at the weeping woman and hoped that the tramp was not serious, was merely spouting to let off steam. Because Emil's life was sacrosanct. No overwrought trollop was going to touch him. The woman might, or might not, be serious. These were Latin realms and all endeavors had to be preceded by florid proclamations. It was conceivable that she could work herself into a sufficient frenzy to fly at Emil, blindly indifferent to consequences, or with an eye cocked to her public.

Italians from the *Irridenta* were pounding on the front

door. They wished to join the party, but none of the revelers would let them share in the gaiety. The good behavior was disappearing along with the sandwiches and punch. Whiskey was being served, and through the sultry heat, the cheap toilet water and sentiments of grief, these smugglers and bouncers took advantage of being hosted by Panama Street whores. The quintet was providing a slow bolero and many of the couples on the dance floor were kissing, while elsewhere breasts were being fondled, skirts rising, drinks spilling.

Alma's wake verged on turning into an orgy when the Moderno's bouncers came out of the office. The guests mumbled, "Ezequiel, Ezequiel Cardenas," and the music stopped. Carr refrained from smiling, though there was something ludicrous in their postures. The three bouncers stood there with the wide-footed stance and scowls of Western bandits. Their thumbs were hooked into their belts as they intimidated the mourners with fixed stares. The largest, an enormous Zambo, held up his arms and the dancers separated. Ezequiel glowered, enjoying himself.

"All right, everybody! Señor Arnstedt sends his regards. He says he hopes everybody has had a good time but the velorio is over. The Club opens for business at eleven and all the girls must be on the benches and all the dregs, who are not customers, must get out. And you girls will have to clean up this mess."

"Tell that cowardly faggot to come down here," Soledad shouted, "and I'll put a knife in him!"

"Soledad. Chica, chica," Ezequiel complained, "What's this knife? Has Señor Arnstedt not been reasonable with you? He gave you five hundred cruceños and let you use the Club during working hours for the velorio. Do you believe that any other club owner on the Street would let you use his establishment for a private party on a business night? They would have told you to go celebrate in the shithouse. You fail to appreciate his generosity."

Soledad stood up to him, her hands on her round hips. "There would have been no party but for your boss. My daughter, Alma, would still be safe in my womb, waiting another month to enter this rotten world. So tell your precious Arnstedt not to walk alone at night. I might be waiting behind a tree. Tell him to look three times and spit before he crosses the street. And tell him to watch his boys carefully. I might take one of his blondes in exchange for my dark angel."

"Ach!" Ezequiel snorted. "You talk a lot of shit, Soledad! All you whores shoot off your mouths. Next week you'll be in some other club and next month you'll have the seed of some other prick blooming in your belly. When everything heals up, you drop around and see me, Soledad. I personally will console you."

Soledad rushed at her tormentor. Carr found her admirable. She was hideous in her grief, a panther scratching at the Zambo's cheeks, spitting in his face, kicking at his shins. Cardenas held her off easily, his thick hands locked about her wrists. He was amused by her fury. His lips parted. There was the bully's sensual exultation from humiliating a woman before an appreciative audience. Carr saw that none of these men was going to help her. Neither was he. The Zambo was too large. Soledad bit at the Zambo's finger and Cardenas had had enough. He heaved her into the crowd, almost toppling three of the women.

"O.K.! O.K.!" Cardenas pointed to the swinging doors. "Everybody out but the employees! Everybody out! You girls. Clean up this mess and get ready for business." The Zambo beamed at Pedro Alfarez. "Pedro! Get your ass out of here. We'll have to ventilate this place for an hour before we let a respectable customer enter the premises. Señor Arnstedt said he wanted everybody out by eleven." They grumbled but they complied, filing slowly past the Zambo and his two helpers.

Cardenas stared down at Carr. The stranger looked like a

legitimate customer with money in his pocket. Cardenas winked at him, indicating that he was exempted. The barking had been only for the scum. Henry Carr went over to help Pedro Alfarez snuff out the candles on the altar, then took the other handle on the beercase casket. Alfarez's smile revealed great white teeth. He would have made a magnificent overseer in a Byzantine seraglio.

On the street the hired mourners were in attendance. Most of Soledad's friends were obliged to desert her. The girls kissed Soledad on the cheek, and distributed free kisses to the men, as if the warm open-mouthed kisses were the only means of shedding the unbearable sentiments. The men started to disperse after the obligatory kiss to Soledad. Everyone had to hug and embrace and shake hands with everyone else. All women had to be pecked on the cheek at least. No one could be missed or slighted.

They placed the casket on the khaki army stretcher and Carr and Pedro lifted it from the pavement. Behind them the lloronas wailed, the signal for the procession to begin. They marched slowly and the shriveled hags shrieked and howled. They passed the garishly lit clubs and the customers gazed at the cortege from their bar stools. Some came to the doors to watch silently. The wandering trios stepped off the curb to let them pass and the drunken torch bearers held aloft flaming poles, illuminating the swarms of mosquitoes swirling over the narrow street. A pack of sailors at the corner whistled at the chauffeur weaving beside the stretcher, praying in his unique Latin. One sudden lurch and he would knock the casket over. He had exhausted his repertoire of litanies, could only wring his hands solemnly over the flower-strewn beercase and monotonously repeat, "Carthage must be destroyed."

Las lloronas, eerie in black hoods and capes, scratched their cheeks and punched at their breasts. They chilled the night with their wailing. "Alma now rises. Alma ascends to the House of God. To the Halls of the Eternal. Hear us, San

Pedro. Alma Cumare rises to the bosom of our Lady. Baptized moribund. Baptized on Sunday, buried on Tuesday. Baptized on Sunday, buried on Tuesday. Baptized moribund.''

It was an arduous climb up the hill to the pauper's cemetery, made more difficult by the weeping and stumbling. The athletic field stretched below, and Carr could see the lights he had left burning in Los Olivos. No point in Puerto Acero was too far from any other. The irregular topography heightened the sense of closeness, created an optical illusion of proximity, as the entire city was visible from any of ten different hills.

There was no discernible pattern in the cemetery. Chunks of rock were scattered among the pale trees, enclosed by a low stone wall. The floodlights were on in the stadium below. Two teams were engaged in a baseball game and the hundreds of spectators were booing and hissing. Pedro Alfarez fitted the lid over the beercase and the lloronas sighed, then conjured up one mighty, final wail as the casket was lowered into the shallow pit. Carr shuddered. Those three shrunken crones had produced that infernal cry, like the mindless shriek of legions of bats swarming through mountain caves. A long silence followed.

Carr picked up one of the spades and, with Pedro Alfarez, began throwing fresh dirt over the lid. As they shoveled, the torch bearers planted their burning branches in a circle around them, one by one kissed Soledad on the cheek and departed. The chauffeur had also wearied of his sacredotal functions. He made the sign of the Cross over them three times and repeated in dire tones, ''Ascend to your maker, Alma Cumare. Ascend to your maker.'' Then he returned to his, ''Carthage must be destroyed,'' as he stumbled toward the gate, and La Zona.

They patted the dirt smooth over Alma's grave and Alfarez helped Carr adjust the stone, face upwards. It read:

Alma Cumare
Thursday to Sunday
Well loved

Pedro kissed Soledad's hand and gave her one more passionate embrace before he turned away, tears streaming down his black cheeks and glistening in the torchlight. He staggered off, his own torch held high.

Carr rose and brushed the dirt from his knees. He withdrew from the circle of torches and sat down on a low gravestone. It was disrespectful but he had to have a smoke. He struck a match and applied it to his first local cigarette. The flame touched the tobacco and he coughed. The Cruceño cigarette attacked like a phalanx of needles in the throat.

From his perch he could see the athletic field below, beyond the stone fence. There was a swing, the sharp crack of a bat, and spectators cheering. A player in a white uniform was being chased by two players in gray uniforms.

The lloronas were rubbing fresh dirt into their bleeding cheeks, frothing at the lips with their self-induced hysteria. Their wailing sent another chill up his spine. Soledad was gazing at him. He motioned gently for her to come to him and she rose from the grave and brushed the dirt from her knees.

With the circle of the torches outlining her strong thighs through the silk dress, she looked like a lovely Hungarian vampire coming to devour him. She took his cigarette and inhaled deeply, one last sob escaping her as she sat down on the stone by his side. Grief could be such a devastating cosmetic for a woman. It was a potent aphrodisiac for a man. He could not remember when he'd last felt this tenderness.

She accepted a fresh cigarette, lighting it from his. There was another crack of the stick and hundreds of spectators rose from their benches, roared and screamed as the players scampered across the field. When the cheering faded Soledad said,

"Thank you for helping with the casket. The others were too drunk. They might have spilled it."

"I had to speak with you, Soledad."

"About what?"

"Señor Arnstedt."

She stiffened and drew away from him. "Are you one of his friends? If you are, do what you have to do now, because otherwise I'll get him."

"I am no friend of his, Soledad. I just wouldn't want you to hurt him and get yourself in trouble."

"Have you ever heard of anything filthier? Of hitting a pregnant woman, and throwing her to the floor?"

Carr smoothed her wrist. "Unfortunately, I have."

She pulled her hand away. "I'm going to cut his balls off."

"So what? That's not enough," Carr said calmly.

"I'm going to kill him. He deserves to die."

"Deserves what, Soledad? Precisely what? Peace? Rest? To think no more? That might be a blessing to the man. Look at this graveyard, woman. The just and the unjust sleep here alike. Every one of those spectators shouting down there will enjoy the same sleep one day. Of what do you deprive a man when you kill him? Of a treasure he no longer knows he's lost. Of ten years of life . . . and perhaps spare him the sicknesses of old age. No, Soledad. When your hate is strong, killing is hardly enough."

Soledad Cumare examined this stranger. He seemed so calm, as solid as the stone they were sitting on, and suddenly she sensed his intensity. She examined his face in the shadows of the flickering lights. This was a man to be afraid of, yet she almost enjoyed the small tingle of fear that curled through her heart.

"Are you Argentinian? Your Spanish sounds Argentinian."

He shook his head no. "I can help you. And I'd like you

to help me. I have a proposition. How would you like to live with me?''

He noted the sudden sobriety of her expression and could almost read her thoughts. She had no money, no place to stay. He looked reliable. Before she even opened her mouth he could hear the reservations coming:

"Would you pay all my expenses?''

"Within reason.''

"Every month I send one hundred dollars to maintain my mother and children in Cali. Could you afford to do that, every month?''

"Most likely.''

"I don't even know what you do for a living,'' she said accusingly.

"I'm a surgeon, Soledad. And I can teach you many things—train you to be a nurse. I can teach you a skill, how to handle instruments in an operating room. It's a valuable skill, and if something happened you would never have to go back to La Zona.''

A worried look crossed her face and she shook her head.

"What?'' Carr said.

"I can't be a woman to you for many weeks yet.''

He reached out and stroked her hair. "I don't even know whether I'm a man. I haven't been with a woman for years.''

Soledad suddenly lunged at him, covered his lips with her open mouth, her arms hard around his neck. When she released him she whispered, "I'll make you a man again. Do you have a room in town?''

"I've rented a cottage, a pretty house, on Los Olivos over there. Come home now and I'll put up another hammock for you. You can rest. And let Alma go in peace.''

Carr rose and walked over to the grave. He scattered a handful of paper and silver cruceños over the fresh dirt and the lloronas scrambled to scoop them up, raising the pitch of their whining at the sight of the generous fee.

Soledad was awaiting him with the dim floodlights of the baseball field shimmering behind her, tracing the fullness of her body through the translucent dress. She gave him a quick kiss on the cheek and then placed her arm around his waist as they walked down the rocky path. Carr smiled. He was insane, of course, and yet that hardly mattered. He was coming alive again after so much emptiness. A woman's hip pressing against him and he had plans, projects, details to work out. He wondered what his father would have said of this strange evening.

Soledad suddenly paused and looked up at him. "Here I am going to live with you, Mister, and I don't even know your name."

"It's Carr. Enrique Carr."

She squeezed his hand. "You seem like a very kind man, Enrique."

Part Two

5

Emil Arnstedt paused with the forkful of *Rotkohl* suspended under his lips. He slipped it into his mouth and spoke as he chewed: "Klaus, here, took odds with various concepts in my preface. It was Klaus's contention, and with his inadequate medical background he has no right to make this type of analogy, but . . . I'd like to throw out his theory to you, Dr. Carr. For your view. Views which I have found invaluable to a degree I could not have foreseen."

"Go ahead, Emil. I'm always receptive," Carr said and nodded at the young student blushing behind the fruit bowls and candelabra. Cousin Klaus was a sensitive boy and considered himself censured. His position in the Arnstedt mansion was equivocal: he was the poor relative taken on as a tutor for the Arnstedt boys, and yet he could not be treated too shoddily because he knew too much about his Uncle Emil. Klaus was in his third year at medical school and would stay on in Puerto Acero until the latest strike was over at the Central University.

Emil frowned at his dependent again. "Klaus here, indiscriminately leaping disciplines, compared Germany's attempt to rid itself of its Jewish cancer, with all of its concomitant dislocations, to the dire and unforeseen effects resulting from the extirpation of the thyroid gland in the nineteenth century, with the attendant onset of cachexia, cretinism, and the progressive degeneration of the entire system. In other words, Henry, Klaus agrees that the Jews were our goiter, a cluster of strategically located nodules, strangling our full development. But then he flees the consequences of his insights and asserts that by the rash and unrealistic therapy we did irreparable damage to our entire system."

Carr picked at his *Rehbraten* and nodded his congratulations to his hostess. Bela had trained her Cruceña cooks to prepare all the specialties of home and hearth. The dinner table was fatuously laden with trays of *Rehbraten mit Rotkohl, Kartoffelpuffer mit Preiselbeeren,* and a heaping bowl of pickles. From the sideboard they were menaced by a chafing dish with mounds of *Eirkuchen,* a sweet omelet for dessert.

Bela had effectively deployed the candelabra to favor her bare shoulders, and her rich dinner was flavored with an unsubtle Mosel from the Arnstedt bodega. Carr sipped at the Mosel and nodded encouragingly at the tutor. "I'd say the boy has something there, Emil. It's a worthwhile hypothesis. That's very good, Klaus."

"It runs in the family," Arnstedt cut in. "We Arnstedts have always had this flair for the incisive correlation of apparently unrelated data. And what has most pleased me, Doctor, in the progress of my own work, is that so much of what I wrote five years ago, contained in the rough drafts of my first few chapters, has already been substantiated by the onrush of events. Every newspaper, every pertinent article, sustains what I put down with only my intuition to guide me. It's been difficult, Henry, but piece by piece we form a cohesive picture."

Bela dumped another load of the leprous red cabbage on the doctor's plate. She believed he was much too gaunt. "Emil spends at least four hundred cruceños a month for periodicals, Henry. You will not believe this but we pay almost one hundred dollars a month to obtain the *Times* of New York, the *Times* of London, *Le Monde*, the *Allgemeine Zeitung*, the—"

"Bela!" Emil snapped. "Bela, please. I'm talking to Henry." He reached across the table to refill his guest's goblet. "And, as you can well imagine, there is no greater satisfaction for a theory maker than to have his theories verified by events. Take, for example, my chapter three. In three I wrote that the Jew is an ideological hermaphrodite, an elusive chameleon, or that his Jewishness was more vital in him than any contemporary dogma or doctrine. This Jew may be a rabid socialist or, at the other end of the prism, a bourgeois magnate, but he will always identify more closely with his brethren, even nationals of another state, representatives of another class, than he will with his gentile peers at the next desk. And look how events in this post-war world have justified this observation. Who stole the secrets of the atom bomb from the American laboratories? Naturally, a pack of Jews. But! But, can we infer from this that the International Jew is automatically Red? Can we? Of course not. For it is this same Jew who operates a clandestine boot-making shop in Kharkov and deals in illegal currency in Kiev, who is the bane of the Marxist system. This same Jew opposes Apartheid in South Africa, aligns himself with the black savage to topple the white regime. And so this Jew defines himself, Doctor, by his opposition to the status quo, whatever that status quo might be. He thrives as an intellectual termite, gnawing at the structure of the state that shelters him, at variance, always, with the eternal values and destiny of his state, whichever that state might be."

Arnstedt coughed and cleared his throat, simultaneously raising a finger to silence Klaus, who wished to interject a point. Emil pinched his thumb against his index finger, assuring Klaus that he would receive his turn. "Now, Henry. Examine the first Marxist schism under the fresh lens of my thesis. Trotsky, the cosmopolitan Jew, craves his world revolution immediately. Eternal Folklands do not exist in the Trotsky world vision. Stalin, the provincial Georgian, the Russian, realizes that it is his primary duty to create the powerful national state and to achieve the aspirations of Pan-Slavism . . . Ah, Henry. Every new fact I uncover supports me. Klaus, here, has informed me that throughout his studies of the literature of the Spanish Golden Age the most acerbic critics of Spanish society were the Jews. Is this not true, Klaus?''

Klaus perked up. He had been called upon to recite so he chewed his mouthful of venison hastily. ''That's correct, Dr. Carr. The two novels that most deride all Spanish values: the code of chivalry, knightly honor, the priesthood, the cloistering of women—both were Jewish products. *La Celestina* and *Lazarillo de Tormes*. They both greatly exaggerated the social ills of the Spanish nation and were extremely pessimistic.''

''You see, Doctor. And this is precisely what Hitler perceived so clearly, aside from his many blind spots—that our Jews were useless for, if not inimical to, any national crusade. Not because of any ideological commitment but because of their very nature, their adherence to their own cause.''

Carr let the maid take his plate and responded coolly to Bela's twinkle. Her flutter had become cloying lately, messages from beyond the candlelight, slack-lipped, overt, indiscreet. He returned to his host. ''Cause? That's not too clear, Emil. They certainly don't try to proselytize.''

Arnstedt drew himself up triumphantly. ''Secure converts? Why bother. They have already proselytized the entire Occident. What is Christianity but a Jewish heresy by which a rebellious tribe from an insignificant province toppled the mighty Roman Empire. They sacrificed one of their hysterical rabbis on the common symbol of degradation and set the slaves and vermin of the slums against their patrician masters. The Jews and malaria destroyed the Roman hege-

100

mcny, Dr. Carr, undermined an orderly world, plunged Europe into seven hundred years of darkness. Hitler, dear Henry, for all his faults, had a manicly lucid sense of human nature. He understood that the raison d'être, the motive force, of the Jew is—to be Jewish, to preempt the stage, be noticed, even if that attention comes in the form of a whip. Take the formation of the State of Israel. Why not a chunk of Africa, Dr. Carr? More fertile. Not disputed. Not on the crossroads of the world. But no. Impossible. The Jew must plunge into the midst of his enemies, irrigate the desert while wearing a hair shirt, evoke admiration, fury, sympathy, hatred. Hitler understood this. It would have been better all around had he been able to ship them to Madagascar, as planned. Madagascar would have solved our mutual problems.''

"Madagascar would have done it," Carr agreed. "No doubt about that. But I don't know what your problem was.''

Bela Arnstedt glistened with pride, as if her guest had just scored a telling shot in a tennis match and had her inept husband on the run. Even Klaus, a *parvenu* in matters of intrigue, was attuned to these waves. But Emil was too engrossed with his *Realpolitik* to worry about his wife's defection. Emil reached for the basket of fruit.

"This, Dr. Carr, was the problem." Emil selected a tomato. "This is France; soft, delightful, squishy to its rotten core, seeking to contain us by a series of alliances with the Balkan states." He moved the flask of green Mosel to a position above the tomato. "This, Henry, is Germany; betrayed by the Jews and socialists in World War One, burning with energy." He placed a long yellow banana under the bottle. "Italy! Our ally, but more of a liability than an asset." The hand went into the basket and a green pear was placed next to the wine. "Poland." The hands scattered a series of nuts and grapes under the pear. "Czechoslovakia, Dr. Carr. And the Balkans." The large tray of red cabbage was pulled to the east of the pear. "Russia." The massive heaps of red cabbage ominously overshadowed the fruit and nuts but were counterbalanced by the shimmering spire of green wine.

The black maids continued clearing away the dishes as Arnstedt expounded on the juxtaposition of cabbage and walnuts. He employed his fork as a pointer and used the toothpicks as vectors for the centrifugal thrust of the *Drang nach Osten*. Arnstedt tinkled the fork against his goblet to recapture Klaus's straying attention. "Hitler had no quarrel with England. He regarded you as fellow Anglo Saxons. The cardinal question of Europe then, as now, was who would dominate the East, the *Ostland*." The supple fingers circled over the fruit and nuts. Emil had the hands of a pianist.

"Every great nation has its destiny, Dr. Carr. Britannia ruled the waves. France? Napoleon! Spain its century. Even little Portugal had its hour. The United States conquered its west and now dominates the world. Only Germany, of all the great nations and peoples, had been cheated. Our destiny was in the East. Either Germany or Russia would rule the Balkans. Either Germany or Russia would be the other great world power in this century, balancing the U.S. This was why Hitler had to handle the Jews. They had lived among us for more than one thousand years, but would they have participated in our crusade? Of course not. They controlled a disproportionate share of our commerce, banks, industry, academia, press; they did not support the basic interests of the German nation. An age of glory was impossible with the Jews infecting every facet of our national life. A similar house cleaning was the prelude to the Spanish age of glory, Henry. You were aware of that, weren't you?"

"I knew that the Spanish burned a few Jews at the stake, but I wasn't aware that they did anything on a massive scale. Like your camps."

"That's a fascinating chapter of history, Henry—the Diaspora, the expulsion of the Jews from Spain. It grieves me that not *one* of Hitler's advisers had the sensitivity to put a book on the expulsion in his hands. One *diktat:* All Jews in transit by March fifteenth. Hep! Hep! Hep! And the matter is resolved. You were raised in Gibraltar, Doctor. Surely you would agree that if the inept Spaniards could do it then the infinitely more effective German mechanism would have performed much better, extruded our alien pus and avoided the excesses of the camps.''

"Possibly, Emil. But why? Why bother? Spain had its miserable hour and has been stunted ever since. I've read the novels Klaus mentioned. They tell a different story. Right during the apogee of Spanish power, food was the preoccupation of the common man. The bureaucrats, the nobles, the elite thrived, conquering on four continents, and the masses groaned in misery. There was plenty of gold and no wheat.'' The same held true for the British Empire.

Arnstedt dismissed this with a wave of the arm. "And rightly so. Biological man dies but those epochs of glory enrich the heritage of every Spaniard. They enhance him, are the wellsprings of his pride. And a man can be great only as part of a great society. Little nations produce little men. Nicaragua can spawn only Nicaraguans. Germany, which has contributed so much, was denied the breathing space for her fullest realization.''

"And so the camps, Emil?''

"I never condoned them. With an expulsion we could have pursued our goals while simultaneously maintaining the façade of decency that the modern state requires in the implementation of its policies. With the camps we allowed unsavory elements to infiltrate the echelons of government—in many cases, mediocrities who were obsessed with the Jewish situation to the exclusion of our broader aims.''

"That's quite an admission for you,'' said Carr.

"I'll go that far, Doctor. And no further. Every movement has its seamy aspects and the victors will harp on the misdeeds of the vanquished. Only the Americans have dropped an atom bomb and it was you British who invented the concentration camp in the Boer War. And you who first fired machine guns into crowds of peaceful demonstrators in India. Germany lost, Dr. Carr, and so Germany is the whipping boy. All power and greatness are born in blood, Doctor. Take the Americans. I deal with the Americans in my chapter seventeen. I would call them hypocrites but they are too ignorant for hypocrisy. I would describe the Americans as a species of neotenics, creatures who have successfully adapted to their environment during an extended larval period and never advanced to a higher state. The Americans oppose conquest. Of course! They secured their *Lebensraum* in the last century by annexing half of Mexico. Genocide? They went about it unscientifically, romantically, piecemeal, decimating their aborigines, burning their villages, herding them into reservations—just as the Argentinians herded their Indians into Patagonia so they might perish of the cold. The Americans decry our racist doctrine, but look what they do with their loyal, politically insignificant black minority when we had to face an influential, disloyal—''

"Why this perpetual 'we,' Emil? You told me you were born in Prague, that you only served in the German Medical Corps under duress."

Arnstedt glanced sideways at Klaus. "That was a rhetorical question, Doctor. A man can only be what he chooses to be. Klaus, here, was born in Concepción, here in Santa Cruz. The great majority of the Germans have assimilated, and others no. Klaus is of the third generation and he chooses to regard himself as European, and not Cruceño. Do you find his attitude praiseworthy?"

Carr turned to the tutor, giving Klaus leeway to speak. He brightened. "In all earnestness, Dr. Carr. I cannot take pride in my Cruceño passport. How can I be proud of this country when we have only one author, one composer, one artist, and we are famous mainly for the violence of our revolutions, our lack of punctuality."

Carr lit a cigarette and balanced the lingering sweetness of his coffee with the astringent Cruceño tobacco. Emil had digressed and was off on a tirade about the impending elections and the sniping from the balconies in Concepción, but Carr was hearing the voice of old Dr. Brenner, Emil's father, decades back, citing his statistics on the ratio of German and Czech clerks in Sudenten post offices, the discrimination of the civil promotion lists and the outrageous pro-Czech bias in the location of new schools. The tone carried across the continents and infected the fluent Spanish his son was speaking.

Bela signaled with her cigarette and, as he reached across the table with his lighter, Carr noted that she consciously strained her décolletage to display the deeper shadows of her breasts. Her face was blatantly sensual.

"Gracias, Enrique. Es usted muy amable."

"Por nada, mi amor."

She smiled at the flirtatious "mi amor."

Bela Arnstedt was quite taken with the English abortionist. This was his fifth dinner with the Arnstedts during his two months in Puerto Acero. Over cocktails she had apologized for wearing the same dress again. He had exhausted her wardrobe. She was again sheathed in the emerald taffeta frock that had been so touchingly inappropriate his first evening at this table. The woman was out of trim for the rigors of seductions and affairs. Bela had become tropical, with no nuances, no reservations. She averted her eyes or stared imperiously into his. She was so obvious. Klaus was on to her. The maids and cooks were enthralled.

With a toss of her chin she indicated that they must be tolerant of her husband, still haranguing Klaus about the coming elections, and then she called across the table, "Do the peasant women ever offer themselves to you, Dr. Carr?"

"I beg your pardon, Señora Arnstedt?"

She wagged her finger at him. "Don't feign such shock with me, Henry. I know what the women of this region are like. The peasant women bring you baskets of fruit and chickens to pay your fees. They're also practical. Haven't any ever offered . . . direct payment?"

105

"You know that I'm bound by my professional ethics not to gabble about that sort of thing."

"Of course you are, Henry. But with that face of an *enfant terrible* you have, I wouldn't trust you alone for a minute with all of these Indian women. They lift their skirts so easily. Fortunately, Soledad is there to protect you from them."

"Yes. She does a rather effective job of managing the office."

Bela refilled their cordial snifters and glanced at him. "Is it true that ex-prostitutes are very prudish in their intimacies?" She was being brutal, taunting him about Soledad this way.

"I couldn't say, Señora. My sampling has not been extensive enough to give any weight to the opinions I might have formed."

"You're so terse, Henry. So diffident. Are all English doctors as terse as you are?"

"I couldn't say. I'm not a spokesman for the entire association. In fact I'm not even a member any more."

"You know, you've been a godsend to us, Henry. To both of us. Emil's been so starved for companionship. I think I've adjusted to the rawness of this place much better than he has. Emil, of course, has his work. But before you arrived, that was all he had. He would come from the Club and then lock himself in his study and work for hours, snipping up his newspapers and arranging his index cards. And, I'll admit, it was lonely for me. I had the restaurant and my circle of friends over in the American settlement. But, since you've arrived, Emil has been so much easier, now that he has an intellectual equal, a man with a background and education."

"What are you telling the man there?" Arnstedt called across the table, turning away from Klaus.

"I was telling Henry that he was a godsend and that you had been much easier to get along with since he came to Puerto Acero."

"Yes, and I think you've monopolized him enough. Dr.

Carr, would you care for another cordial? We can have them out on the galería, where it is cooler.''

"I wouldn't mind," Carr agreed amiably.

"Good. Bela could you please retire into la sala, with Klaus, for a while? I don't wish to deprive you of Henry's company but I have some matters I need to discuss with him privately.''

Arnstedt gave instructions to the maid to serve two more coffees and Curaçaos and Bela winked as they rose from the dinner table. This had become the established routine: cocktails, dinner in the spacious comedor with Emil pontificating, and cordials on the galería with Emil synthesizing his theses.

Carr slumped into the cushioned rocking chair, startling the lizards on the mosiac tiles. They scurried back into the cracked masonry of the Moorish fountains as he rested his feet on the stucco railing. It had become his second home in Puerto Acero. Emil's patio was placid in the evening, designed for reflection. His friend had prospered in the Americas. There were more expensive homes in the American compound but up here on La Loma only Jefe Mendoza and the Turk, Medina could boast of larger mansions.

He thanked the maid as she left the tray. He took a cigar from the can on the wicker table to his left. Raising it to his nose, as though he knew something of tobaccos, he recalled Emil's lecture on the subject: the soil possessed all of the conditions for cultivation of a top Havana leaf, but the Cruceños had much to learn about maturing, selection, curing. Emil was informed on every conceivable topic, from geological strata in the delta region to the local magic.

Carr bit off the nib of the cigar and dropped it into the ashtray. This was all too easy. Emil had been much too anxious to take the English abortionist into his confidence. Even if he were merely Henry Carr and not a walking cadaver, there was something queasy about the friendship of the seedy expatriates—the "Swiss" brothel owner and the "English" physician cozily chatting in this courtyard in the middle of the jungle, commenting with the sweep of a Spengler and a Toynbee on the affairs of the outside world. Once he had caught Emil gazing at him oddly, but the man still seemed to suspect nothing. Or else he had attributed his suspicions to paranoia. But surely it was illogical of Emil not to give more importance to his friend's choice of women. Emil expressed concern and yet received in his home a man shacked up with a whore who had sworn to do him in. One did not know who was toying with whom on this patio.

He glanced up as he heard shuffling on the galería. Arnstedt had put on his slippers. Bela always chided her husband for such informality, but Emil scoffed at these objections, insisting that Dr. Carr loosen his tie and roll up his shirtsleeves.

Easing into the chair next to Carr, Emil reached for a cigar and said, "A new shipment. Cuban. I'm stocking up on these. Within another year they will be embargoed because of the Communists."

"I suppose so."

Arnstedt bit off the nib and spit it onto the patio. "You know, Henry, I don't wish to bore you with a repetition but Bela was quite right. You have been my salvation. I was stifling here. You can't conceive of what it was for me, functioning at ten percent of my capacity. Bela? A woman has no use for abstractions. Sometimes they ring true with observations on daily life, but they have no gravity, no entry to the immanent, the ineffable. Klaus? Poff! A clever youngster. I even tried the American village. But it was too much for me, all those drunken engineers with their loud wives demonstrating their garbage disposal units."

"How about among the Cruceños, Emil? You belong to the Ateneo Club."

Arnstedt winced. "The Ateneo, the Ateneo. If the Athenians but knew. The atmosphere is fetid. At times I hesitate to include Latin America in the Occident. There is no mentality quite so vague and shallow as the Latin American. To the

108

caballeros of the Ateneo a deep discussion is one in which they conclusively prove that the United States is responsible for all their backwardness. I have a theory, Henry, not actually my own—I've come across it several times—that the fact that the Church gathered to its bosom the most promising minds in each generation, century after century, siphoning off the brightest for the priesthood, played havoc with the Latin gene pool. It altered the configuration of the intellectual pyramid, broadening the base to the detriment of the apex, so that one would record on a bell-shaped curve, or curve of Gaus, proportionately fewer intelligent Latins per random hundred than among other Caucasian groups. This would help account for the stagnation of this region, Henry. The Indians of this river basin were inferior Indians. The Spanish conquistadores discovered no temples here, none of the imposing structures of the Incas or Aztecs."

"Everything is explained by race?" asked Carr.

"Almost everything. Race will be the drama of the coming century. The brown, black and yellow masses of the planet against us. They were the victors. During our internal strife, they threw off our civilizing yoke. The Jews grabbed Palestine, and the Mongolian Slavs penetrated Central Europe. The inbreeding and isolation of a circumscribed gene pool in the ghettos might also go far to explain the peculiar power of the Jew. I had a friend, a Jewish friend, who gave me many insights into their peculiar and special powers.

"We discussed this very obvious phenomenon that among any random one hundred Jews one would encounter a high percentage of active, aggressive intellectuals. As he explained it, the Jews were the only group in the history of mankind that prized—to the exclusion of all other virtues—quickness of mind, shrewdness, sharpness. This was the quality most appreciated in their offspring. In the ghettos, the apple of the eye was the smart one, not the handsome or athletic or noble son. The Jew despised the Don Juan ideal of the Latin man, despised the ideal of the warrior, was con-

109

temptuous of the northern drunkard, mocked the concepts of inherited nobility, breeding, gentility, and spawned for little scholars . . .''

Carr did not flinch. His body seemed to grow heavier, denser, as it responded to the melodrama inherent in this quiet chat in the lush courtyard. He searched for guile behind the tirade but there was nothing in Emil's mien or tone to convey baiting. Emil was merely citing one Wolf Karol, dredging him out of the silt of twenty years—quoting him. Emil was paying homage to his long dead school chum, far from the dingy beer hall and somber afternoons where Wolf had railed about his family. There was a bizarre satisfaction in having one's words remembered like that, paraphrased on another continent. Emil was quoting him almost verbatim now, translating him from German to English.

''—but such a narrow concentration on one faculty, such excessive specialization, could not fail to engender compensatory debilitations. After generations of selection, and given the molding of their peculiar family life, the Jew tended to produce highly Oedipal hypersensitive neurotics . . . oral, slightly hysterical, with sadomasochistic inclinations. You can find this strain running through the false Messiahs of the sixteenth century and later on through Heine, Proust, Freud, Kafka and many others.''

''How about all the furriers and vulgar merchants?'' interrupted Carr. ''How do they fit into this picture?''

''Ach, Henry! I could run off like this for hours but I didn't bring you out here for this. I have something much more important. I'm extremely concerned. We will have to thrash this out.''

Emil dropped his stance of lecturer with rapt andience. He was pressing at his guest now as might a doctor with a stern creditor, sincerity and appeal in his posture. Carr let the smoke drift through his lips into the static air of the patio. ''What is it, Emil? Nothing serious I hope.''

''I'm still concerned about your opinion of me, Doctor.

That sales talk in the Club Moderno. My callous references to prostitutes. You could have formed an irrevocably low opinion of me, considered me crass, common.''

Carr started to protest.

"No, no, Henry. Let me finish. I could understand why. But you can't imagine the strain we've lived under. We've been suspicious of every stranger. We kept our Emil and Bela but used assumed surnames. I could not practice my profession for fear of detection. It has been a fearful strain, and I have become the owner of a brothel. Your contempt for me—''

"Emil, I—''

"Please. You don't have to deny it. It's a contemptible life I lead. But the circumstances . . . and the money. I don't deny that—I wanted my sons to have something when they return to Europe. I don't want them to lose themselves and go down the drain here in Santa Cruz. And I'll need lots of money to publish a large edition of my collected works. The Jews, or their sympathizers, control publishing in almost every nation of the Western world. I will have to finance the publication of my own works and overcome great difficulties in their dissemination and distribution.''

Carr had to grab his host's arm to cut off the flagellation. "Look, Emil. There's no need for this. You're not obliged to give me excuses for anything. None of us are living as we wish to or where we want to. There isn't a white man in Puerto Acero who wouldn't be elsewhere if he could help it. You've undoubtedly heard the rumors as to why I'm here and I wish I could refute them. But . . . they're substantially factual. So let's have no—''

"Ach,'' Arnstedt interrupted, "I've heard them. Mendoza's secretary has spread the story over the entire town. And so what? One accident should not ruin a man's life. A man should be judged by the totality of his works, not by one aberration. Some of us have things in our past, things. . . . But look how you do now, Doctor. You've been here only

111

two months and they love you. The peasants worship you, Henry. I've seen them line up in front of your shack. Most of them have never trusted the old doctors or the lads at the government clinic. They would rather die on their straw pallets than submit to an operation from them. And yet they trust *you*. While I . . . I have been here for ten years and I operate the Club Moderno. And that also troubles me . . . Soledad.''

Carr shifted impatiently on the rocking chair. ''Oh, come on, Arnstedt. We've been through this fifty times and I've already told you she's gotten over it. Let's not stir it up again. I'm tired of the subject.''

''But I must, Henry. Of all the women in La Zona to move in with you. She hates me! She still swears that I hit her. I know when you go home from here at night and get in bed with her, she still speaks against me.''

''I've told you she's gotten over it,'' Carr said calmly. ''Look. The night I came over here, I'll admit that my curiosity had been aroused. Bela invited me, and Soledad had painted you as some sort of monster. I wanted to see the monster in his lair. And then I informed you that a girl by the name of Soledad had moved in with me, and I enjoyed your consternation. But we seem to have hit it off, Arnstedt. This place would be much drearier for me without your home to come to. And I was honest enough to tell you that I was expressly forbidden to come here by my little mistress and I had to tell her to hold her tongue or pack her kit. She's settled down now, Emil. You know how women are. They blow off steam, and they settle down.''

''But I've never had the chance to explain, Henry. You say she tells you this cock and bull story that paints me as a beast, and you've never heard my side of it. I was never going to throw her into the streets. I only asked her to leave for Cali and have the child in her own home. I was going to pay her fare and expenses, but she insisted on staying. And you can't have a pregnant woman running around a nightclub. You're a man of the world, Henry. A sailor or miner doesn't want to see a pregnant woman on his night out. It depresses him. I offered to install her in the Alcazar Hotel, behind the Club Lido, and still she refused to leave, and began to spout these filthy lies and make accusations in front of the other girls. But I never struck her. I only jostled her.''

Carr reassured his host with one hand and recovered the cordial with the other. "Let no more be said about it, Emil. From what the nurses at the clinic said about the position of the baby, it's miraculous that the child survived even two days. If you jostled her, it precipitated what was bound to be a miscarriage anyway. And second of all, I recognize that Soledad's a provoking woman. I've slapped her a few times myself. And I've told her that you're the only friend I have in Puerto Acero and that if she doesn't like it, she knows that she can pack it up. With all of the consolation in La Zona, I don't intend to put up with a nag or let her limit my associations. I only took her in because she seemed forlorn, but she'll damn well conform to my tastes."

"I don't want it that way," Arnstedt said earnestly. "I'd like to make peace with her. I feel her presence at our table and I don't want her to come between us."

"She won't, Emil. Don't worry. I assure you she won't."

"Well. Bela suggested that we send her a few dresses and a bottle of perfume. As a peace offering . . . And maybe you could bring her for dinner one night, if you wished to elevate her status . . . to formal mistress. But I don't want to poke or pry there, Henry. I realize how complex these relationships can be."

Carr chuckled and drew his shoulders up. "I don't know. That might well do the trick. Soledad's essentially a simple girl. She'll see that your heart's in the right place." He glanced at his wristwatch. "And I guess I'd better be running now. It's late for a man who has to have his eyes wide open tomorrow morning. We're scheduled for another thyroidectomy at the clinic."

113

Emil suddenly looked up at the square patch of sky over the patio. "Sometime I'd like to come down and watch you, Henry. You can imagine that I feel a certain nostalgia."

"Oh, I don't know. The clinic isn't equipped for anything too interesting. Not for a man with your background. It's really shocking for a town this size. That's why I'm striving so hard to get my own mobile unit. When I get it, you'll be the first to know."

Arnstedt pushed himself up from his rocking chair. "No time for a game of chess, Doctor? You surely must want revenge for Tuesday night's debacle."

"Wish I had. What's our series now, Emil? Nine to seven, your favor?"

"Ten to seven, my favor. Just a minute, Henry. I'll call Bela." Emil flicked cigar ashes into her prized potted plant, and went to the partially opened French doors. "Bela! Bela! Come out, dearest. Henry must go home early. He has an operation early tomorrow."

The goodnights were said in the marbled vestibule. Bela pressed the neatly wrapped bundle of dresses and the decanter of perfume into the doctor's hands. The decanter was covered with baby-blue tissue paper and tied with a scarlet ribbon. Her voice was humid with concern. "Good perfume is hard to come by, Henry. Most of the women on La Loma buy these cheap imitations from Concepción and they go rancid with the heat. You can't trust the labels. Many of the stores purchase the flasks and labels from famous Parisian brands and then fill them with simply horrible local colognes."

He brought his lips across her cheek. "I'm sure she will appreciate this, Bela."

He felt Emil's arm draping over his shoulder. "Henry, do you ever do any hunting?"

"I used to, a little. Nothing much to brag about."

"Fine! We have prime hunting in the highlands here. Boar. Puma. Deer. How about Sunday? The superstitious

114

peasants won't go near the ruins because they say they're haunted. But the only thing it's haunted by is puma. Jerry Anderson has a magnificent head mounted over his fireplace and I've sworn to get one for mine.''

''Sounds fine.''

''I hate to ask, but could we use your jeep? We could go by horseback but it's not wise to take horses into that puma country.''

''Surely. Sunday's fine. I'll switch with Baker at the mine. If you provide the rifles, I'll provide the jeep.''

''Did you come with the jeep tonight?'' Bela asked.

''No, I walked.''

''Walked? Bela. He walked!'' Arnstedt exclaimed as if the three-kilometer stroll constituted an arduous trek.

''Wait a minute. Ezequiel is on duty tonight but I'll get Klaus to drive you home in the Lincoln.''

''That's all right, Emil. No need to drag poor Klaus out at this hour. After all I ate of that delicious meal, I can use the exercise.'' He received one more kiss on the cheek from his hostess, and one more solid thump on the back from Emil, before they released him.

The lock clicked and Carr paused in the shadows of the solarium. He could hear the arguing through the French doors. They had reverted to German. Bela Arnstedt was aghast at her husband's temerity. This Dr. Carr was shifty and devious. One could look right into this Englishman's eyes and never know what he was thinking. Her husband was a fool to confide this way to a total stranger. Could he not be more circumspect? Was it necessary to blurt out every single detail of their pasts? One word too much, one phrase too strong, and Carr might inform on them.

Nonsense, Emil replied. Henry was not that kind of man. Besides, Carr was in no position to report anyone. His own situation was precarious enough without his looking for trouble. She was just a nag, never content to let well enough alone.

As he walked down the path to the exit, Carr smiled. It was impossible to tell whether Bela were suspicious of him or if she were merely throwing up a smoke screen to cover her flirting. The guard at the gate flashed his red lantern in Carr's face and, recognizing him, motioned him on with a "Muy buenas, Dr. Enrique."

Ezequiel was on tonight, their lumbering Zambo. The oligarchs of La Loma could not sleep securely without a guard to protect their villas. Members of the household staffs alternated at the district's gate and no car could pass through the privileged quarter of town without an inspection. No pedestrian entered without first accounting as to identity and destination. The wealthy of La Loma had much to fear. It would come. All these villas had their cupboards stocked with carbines, pistols, canned food, and tins of water. The more luxurious caches contained grenades and heavy automatic weapons. As Emil said, since the death of Dictator Morales the ruling class existed in a state of endemic siege.

Carr took the long way home. The mongrels of Barrio Flores no longer barked at his heels. The dogs accepted him, but Dr. Carr and his housekeeper were still the subject of much controversy. People were defining themselves by their view of Henry Carr and his whore. The powerful damas of La Loma chose to accept the romantic myth that he had once been a society physician in London, and had signed off his ship in Puerto Acero out of infatuation for the ravishing prostitute Soledad. Pedro Alfarez reported that there had already been several fist fights in La Zona between defenders and detractors. Pedro had appointed himself handyman and seemed to be conducting polls to furnish his new boss with the prevailing opinion in all strata. The wretched of La Colina, the peasants from the surrounding countryside, "loved" the new man. It was Soledad and Mustafa Medina they resented. After all, poor as they were, they brought their bagged turtles, jaychoughs cured in arsenic, their stuffed monkeys, their varnished straw hats, wild ducks, bags of fruits, mangos, av-

116

ocados, yams, and coconuts to pay his fees, and it was Soledad who ran his finances and sneered at their offerings. And, worse, they knew it was Mustafa Medina who was eventually making all the profit. Poor as they were, they left a splendid cornucopia on Carr's front porch. Then Medina drove up the hill in his pickup truck and robbed Dr. Enrique, fingering his Turkish chin and making those aggressively low offers. Why, they asked, did Dr. Enrique not bargain and fight for his rights, demand more cash from that bandit Medina? Dr. Enrique should have it out with him and not let that exploiting Turk make off with a whole truckload of produce and handicraft for a measly forty or fifty cruceños. The doctor might be a good man, but he did not have to be a fool.

The proper ladies of Barrio Flores said it was inimical to morality for an educated professional to be living with a tramp. Soledad might flounce around in her white smock and pretend she was some kind of nurse, but everyone knew about her previous trade and they would still be going to the government dispensary if the doctors there were not so young, and the lines were not so long. It was shocking. Sometimes, to get in to see the English doctor, they had to sit on the benches in front of Los Olivos, right next to putas from La Zona, and Soledad was so snippy that she greeted her old friends effusively but snubbed the decent women, and ostentatiously made dates to meet her friends for tea at the Café Juno.

But the men of Barrio Flores had told their wives to shut up, according to Pedro. Had not many of the couples in Barrio Flores lived together for years before paying five cruceños for a civil license or visiting Father Garibay? This Englishman had been touched by a misfortune, but if he were not competent the Americans would not have hired him to relieve Dr. Baker two days a week at the mines.

It had begun to disturb Carr. He had not the slightest intention of affecting the lives of these people and yet they were all reacting to his presence, taking positions. The very first

117

week two colleagues had dropped by to extend him a semi-official welcome. They were delighted, of course, to have him aboard, another to share in the onerous burdens, another hand on the rope to pull the great barge of progress from the muck of ignorance and sickness. They reminisced about the old days, when Puerto Acero was only a scattering of huts and a trading post with a fishing pier. Jefe Mendoza had vouched for his qualifications and he could count, they assured him, on their closest cooperation so long as (they hinted) he did not attempt to siphon off any of their well-to-do patients from Avenida Bolívar, or La Loma.

Then the three boys at the government clinic had invited him to participate in a thyroidectomy, and once the woman was wheeled in he learned that he was to wield the scalpel, as none wished the blame for leaving the woman mute or dead, and none felt competent to cut through the ghastly blue nodules at her throat. They submitted him to a test they could not pass themselves and were ready to denounce him to the Ministry of Internal Security in Concepción. When he finished they were no longer his examining board but his students. So strange that he had actually forgotten he was a technical virtuoso. A man could stray from the roots of his being. In Spain, and during the Blitz in London, he had performed several thousand operations in a welter of blood, sirens, ambulances and bombs. It was all a dream now. Any past would do.

Afterward, he had been modest with the three youngsters, endeavoring in no way to deprecate their training. Within a week they came out with it, all of it. Their Central University in Concepción was a porquería—a mess. Soledad mixed the drinks that night and the young men outdid each other in unburdening their woes. There were no entrance exams and every year thousands enrolled and only handfuls graduated. The first year was wasted in weeding out dullards and then many professional students took eight or nine years to finish the five-year course while dawdling in cafés arguing politics. Politics tainted everything. The law school had been on strike and they had missed two semesters because they could not cross the picket lines. After the last coup many of the better professors had been dismissed and replaced by men of the correct political complexion, but undistinguished in their fields.

Now the youngsters had been sent out here by the Ministry and, among themselves, had to confess that they could not cope with Puerto Acero. The dispensary was not properly equipped and they simply were not trained for many of the operations that diagnoses revealed as imperative. It would be an invaluable experience for them to consult with a man of his caliber.

Consult? He had taken over. And he had brought Soledad with him to train as an anesthetist. His first crisis. The five practical nurses threatened to resign if that woman entered their clinic. Dr. Lopez told them that they might do just that if their self-righteous hypocrisy was going to deprive him of the opportunity to "consult" with an eminent surgeon like Dr. Carr. The practical nurses stayed on. Jobs were hard to come by.

Carr shook his head at his own guile. After years of dead-ness, this had been such an explosion of energy. He had been cold, methodical, efficient. He had even made an ally out of poor Father Garibay. The old padre came snooping around on a courtesy call and then spoke of his sordid difficulties. The North Americans, through Caritas, had generously provided his parish with powdered milk for the undernourished chil-dren. Sad to say, many of their drunken fathers either sold those packages or drank it themselves, hot, in the morning, to cure their hangovers. He had already consulted with Doc-tors Apolinario and Mendicuti and both replied that nothing could alter human nature. Then he consulted with the young doctors at the clinic and they said it would be a long process, requiring re-education. But there was no time. Their ribs showed today. The children cried. Could Dr. Carr recommend a solution?

Yes. Meat extract. In powdered form. It was a highly nourishing substance and had a repulsive, calcinaceous taste that made adults gag but that didn't matter to a famished infant. Not too much should be used, as it could form caked accretions in the abdominal organs. He would draw up a chart with the proper proportions to make it safe for infants and nauseating for their fathers.

The priest found that to be an engaging remedy. Padre Garibay was a lonely man and Carr found it shamefully easy to put him in his pocket: a few games of chess at the Café Juno, a few conversations about Teilhard du Chardin, an interest expressed in the Avignon schism, an offer to attend to his more destitute parishioners free of charge—if only the good Padre would send them with a card. Garibay suddenly could be counted as one of his staunchest supporters.

There was one man left in town who might be dangerous. Remberto Davila, the editor of *La Tribuna*, had invited him to the Ateneo for a late evening drink and probed him, hoping for some sort of outburst. Davila was too intelligent to be put off with murky references. He might have as easily asked Davila why he had chosen to bury himself here in Puerto Acero and given up a promising career in the capital, but it was Davila who asked all the questions.

"You're going to visit the Indians again this week, Doctor?"

"Most likely."

"That's most interesting. Why do you bother to visit the Indians?"

"Probably because they can use my help."

Davila was a tall man, emaciated, totally bald, with a thin gray moustache. He smiled up at the ceiling, without cynicism, and yet was obviously amused by the response. "That's intriguing, Doctor. Those Indians have needed help

120

for the last five thousand years and we Europeans have been here for four hundred, and no one has ever noticed it before. You arrive, a complete stranger, and almost immediately start to visit them once a week and give free medicine. Don't you find that unusual, Dr. Carr?''

"Call it my social conscience. I believe you have one also.''

"It's my trade. The entire city, minus the illiterate sixty percent, is aware of my social conscience. It doesn't impel me to make an uncomfortable trip fifty kilometers up a perilous tributary every week. It obliges me to sit in my air-conditioned office and write stirring editorials. Would you object to me accompanying you on your next excursion, Doctor? And taking some photos? I'd like to write a feature article on your ministrations to the Indians. It's been quite a while since the dailies in Concepción used my byline.''

"I'd mind very much. And if you attempted to follow me I'd tell one of my friends out there to stick a spear in you.''

It was said in jest.

Davila laughed sardonically. He had to wave off the bartender, who approached to see if they needed another round. "I believe you would, Dr. Carr. And I thought you would react this way. It's fascinating watching you. A benevolent cyclone has descended upon us to labor for us sixteen hours a day, cure our poor and give free medicine to our Indians, paid for out of meager honorariums. And he wishes no publicity. I don't know what you are doing here but it is fascinating watching you dash about. By the way—what are you doing here?''

"Practicing medicine. Making a living.''

Davila took another sip from his highball and then dabbed a paper napkin against his lips. "A splendid living, no doubt. You know . . . it's very extraordinary, but you have made a very excellent impression on us. The llaneros don't take to outsiders but they take to you. Most unusual.''

Carr pushed the dish of guava paste toward the journalist.

"I'm not particularly trying to win any popularity contest, but I'm not adverse to having your good opinion."

"I am envious. I lived here for two years before being accorded any degree of acceptance and I am a Cruceño, born in Concepción. You have been here for less than two months and, do you know, you were already proposed for membership in the Ateneo? Pepe Sierra nominated you and Dr. Apolinario protested, citing the rumors about England. He was shouted down, hissed. They shouted down Dr. Mendicuti and Dr. Apolinario, and suspended the two years' residence requirements so you may join as soon as you've lived here six months."

"I'm very grateful to hear that."

Davila chuckled. "Frankly, I don't think you care, and that's probably why they nominated you. I've learned much about my own people by the way they've reacted to you. If you had just come and given so freely of yourself, as you give to the Indians and to the poor at your cabin, they would despise you. The men would shit on you. Saints and social workers tend to turn the average Cruceño's stomach. But a generous man like you, who has also installed in his cottage, if you will pardon the indiscretion . . . a . . . ."

"Woman of the streets?" offered Carr.

"Yes. That they find admirable, masculine. Soledad is the symbol of your humanity. And they like your language. My people attach much importance to the way a man expresses himself."

"Probably too much. And not enough to substance."

"That's human too. And that's all we care about. The man in his moment. You know, Dr. Carr, we had a dictator here for twenty-seven years—Morales. The Europeans and the North Americans always asked me how could a man like Morales last for twenty-seven years. And I have always replied that it was because the great majority of our men secretly admired Morales. Even as they cursed and told obscene jokes about him, they lived through him. Morales was a terrible creature: cunning, depraved, an egomaniac. But he liked to drink and fondle children and play the guitar. He negotiated outrageous contracts with the American oil companies and stuffed millions in his pockets, but since most of us would have done the same, we applauded his astuteness and boasted that our dictator was stealing more than Trujillo. Morales had fifteen-year-old girls brought to his chambers. However, as most of our workers would like to get their hands on such virgins, they made jokes about his virility. Everything Morales said and did was wrong. Everything his opponents said was right. But the opposition—the merchants, the liberals—all looked like stuffed capons. Morales looked like a king. It was not until economic development permitted enough peacocks to evolve so they could demand their own likeness in the Presidential mansion that we were able to get rid of Morales. Essentially we remain the same, Dr. Carr. We have the façade of parliamentary government and still have no respect for rules, laws, the written word. We value the *man,* that is all.''

"Whose side, Davila, were you on?''

"My own. But it did not matter. I was tortured. Cigar butts pressed under my armpits. The experience has greatly influenced my editorial style. You've noticed its vague tenor.'' Davila picked up his glass.

"I think *La Tribuna* is a rather adequate paper for a town this size.''

"There is one matter here that disturbs us, Dr. Carr. People comment upon your association with the Arnstedts.''

"Do they?''

"The Arnstedts are not well regarded. Emil Arnstedt was only admitted to the Ateneo because he made substantial contributions to building our library. But their contempt for us is only too apparent. People ask how you can have dinner at his home every week?''

123

"Perhaps I like the cooking."

Davila laughed and rocked back his chair. "I have a theory, Doctor. Would you like to hear my theory?"

"No."

"You wouldn't like to hear my theory? It's very interesting."

"No. I don't care to react to your theories."

Davila snapped his fingers at the bartender and then lowered his voice. "I can tell you one thing. When the Arnstedts arrived here after World War Two they let it be known that they were Swiss. Amusing, no? Swiss?"

"What's that to me?"

"Nothing at all perhaps. Has Arnstedt shown you his manuscript? He wanted my august opinion on the first two thousand pages. I managed to struggle through the first twenty. The man is an unregenerate Nazi."

"If that concerns you, why haven't you denounced him?"

"It doesn't concern you, Dr. Carr?"

"The war's been over a long time. I'm really not too keen on the idea of digging up a lot of old bones and sniffing at them again. All of us in Puerto Acero, all the outsiders, were once something different, a long time ago and in a land far away. You also."

"That intrigues me." Davila touched his lips. "You don't mind if I write to a few friends in London, and have them investigate who Dr. Henry Carr was, a long time ago, in a land far away?"

"I'd mind very much."

"It doesn't matter. I intend to do it anyway. But don't worry, Dr. Carr. Whatever I learn, I shall continue to be your friend. It's too fascinating observing you, Doctor."

Davila he would have to watch out for. His legs had grown stiff with the long climb and he decided to smoke one more cigarette on the screened porch before going inside. Tomorrow would be a full day: another thyroidectomy in the morning and the *Blythe* was scheduled to dock in the afternoon. The tropics had provided him with another hideously beautiful night to impinge on his thoughts. Across the river a faint white patina glowed in the treetops. Up above a hyaline clarity captured every star in its course. It had been an audacious decision to build a town on this bend of the river four centuries ago, to plant a flag in this quicksand.

Soledad was asleep. He undressed in the darkness and checked the button on her alarm clock. The clock had been one of her few contributions to the household effects and it did not function properly. But she became very peevish when he suggested buying another, as if that would diminish her share in the common goods. She insisted that it had at least six months' more service to it.

She stirred. He would have preferred to keep the chinchorro, but his criolla mistress regarded hammocks as declassé. No one slept in a hammock in the technicolor films she saw at the Teatro Atlas. A bed signified culture.

He slipped the mosquito net aside and pulled the warm sheet over her legs. The woman had a magnificent body. She complained that she was too heavy but that was only false modesty.

Soledad turned over and laid her arm across his chest. She had been feigning sleep and now she was going to simulate some anger for him.

"Why are you so late, Enrique? I've been waiting up for hours."

"I told you not to wait up. Emil always has a great deal to say. They were very concerned tonight. The Arnstedts want to make peace with you, Soledad. They've given me some dresses and a bottle of perfume for you. French. The next time I go there, they want me to bring you along."

She drew away from him and said, "How can you be so false, Enrique? How can you sit there and eat and talk with them? You're falser than any woman I've ever known. I've

125

never met anyone as cynical as you are. You don't believe in anything and yet you'll sit there for hours arguing about religion with Padre Garibay."

"So? I do Padre Garibay a lot of good. I restore the man. He comes alive for our arguments."

"And Arnstedt? How can you go to the house and laugh and eat the food of a man you intend to kill?"

Carr kissed her hand lightly and then returned it to his chest. "I've never said that I intended to kill Emil. We're going hunting on Sunday. We're going to shoot for puma at the Jesuit ruins."

Soledad twisted against him in excitement and said exactly what he knew she would say before the words came out of her mouth. "Then that's your chance, Enrique! Don't you see? A hunting accident. You could put a bullet in him and be done with it."

"Really?"

"Jefe Mendoza would make an investigation and the case would be over."

"I'm sure it would."

"Enrique!" she groaned. "This is your opportunity. What you want to do to him is too impossible. Something will occur first."

"Who are you, little Soledad, to decide what's impossible? What's impossible for one million men, the next man does every night . . . absentmindedly. Tomorrow the *Blythe* will be back and the boy will have many of the things—"

"How do you know?" she cut him off. "You're so ingenuous, Enrique. You're so wise and yet you still live in dreams like a child. Your friend probably spent all your money on women in the biggest nightclubs in New York, and you'll never see him again."

"Prepare supper for three tomorrow night."

"And if he shows up, so what? We've only saved two hundred dollars for your clinic. And we wouldn't even have that if the Americans hadn't given you two days a week at their mine. You said thirty thousand dollars, Enrique. I think you're crazy. It will take us twenty years at this rate.''

He rolled over and supported his chin on his palms. He had sought a capable and compliant helper but this woman did not exactly meet those specifications. ''Why now, Soledad? Why must you weaken on me now? I predict that we'll be ready in less than a year. The American boy had a letter for a friend of mine in New York, a famous doctor. And that doctor will be going to many charitable institutions, to the United Nations, to get one of them to donate a mobile operating unit.''

Soledad sat up. She took her cigarette case from the nightstand and flicked without success at her lighter. Then a glow illuminated her pale oval face. The fire died and he reached for her breast. She shrugged his hand away. ''We can still do as I suggesed, Enrique. We could go to Concepción and bring my sons there. Then you'd no longer have to send all that money to Cali. You could make much, much more in Concepción and then, when you were ready, you could invite Arnstedt there.''

''Of course. I could probably do well in Hawaii and, once I had everything arranged, I could invite him to Honolulu.''

''But in Concepción we could live like normal people and—''

''We'll go there when it's over, Soledad.''

She abruptly turned her back to him, tugging the sheets with her. He rested as she puffed noisily at her cigarette, knowing that she would be back shortly with a few more remarks.

''It would still be easier for all of us if you shoot him on Sunday. There would be no danger for you. Everybody hates him, Enrique. Everybody likes you. It would be over. We could go away.''

''After we're finished, woman. Don't complicate things now.''

''Death is enough for him.''

"Is it? I hardly think so. There was a curse my people had. 'May he have one hundred estates; and in each mansion one hundred rooms; and in each room one hundred beds; and may he spend a day of agony on each bed." Carr glanced at her. "And that's what I intend to arrange for my friend."

Soledad clamped her hand over his mouth to silence the curse and her eyes filled with tears.

She touched him and he was ready for her. Soledad smiled triumphantly and forced him down, mounted him with her soft breasts pressing against his cheeks and then her lips came down on his. He might dominate her during the day— play the stern and demanding professor to her petulant and resisting pupil—but on this bed she was in command. That first night they made love, tears had filled his eyes. He had forgotten what it was like to be inside a woman. Three years on English hospital beds. Four years in a Communist prison. Eight years of wandering the earth, dry, a ghost shunning women as if they were of alien substance, and then this richness, this fierce lushness. He moved deeply into her loins and blessed her.

6

The AmCruz wharf was littered with wooden sleds, torn slings and sacks of potash, and crowded with dockworkers and customs officials as the Norwegians threw the last loop over the bitts and the *Blythe* shuddered to a dead stop. Ritter spotted Carr below, behind the wheel of a jeep. His compadre had gone criollo—loose white ducks and white jacket and a jaunty Panama hat. Carr blended into the scene better than the inspectors in their green neo-fascist uniforms. Two guards were attempting to hold back the pack of vendors and whiskey hawkers straining to get aboard and do some trading.

The gangplank was lowered and the deckhands hollered for everybody to get out of the way of the swinging aluminum rail. Ritter recognized the other man in the jeep as Black Pedro, but the man didn't seem to be there to do business. Usually Pedro was the first on board with his stock of silk bandanas, parrots, and monkeys. It was a tangy afternoon, a fine day to be alive, with white shacks dotting the hills and the cathedral cross capturing the gleam of the sun at its zenith. Delete the cross and this backriver port might be Cadiz or Sagunto three thousand years ago, and the *Blythe* a Phoe-

nician trireme, anchored to call on the barbarians of Ultima
Thule to load the raw materials from those huge tin sheds.

Carr came up the gangplank with the company agents and
told Pedro to wait for him around the galley. There would be
errands for him in a few moments.

"I guess you're somewhat relieved to see me," Ritter
said.

They shook hands and Carr sniffed. "Don't flatter yourself. I never had any doubts you'd return. But it's good to see
you, anyway."

Carr waved back to Captain Erlander on the bridge. Ritter
pointed his thumb over his shoulder. "I've got your stuff in
my cabin, carpenter. Two heavy wooden crates." He extracted a letter from his shirt pocket. "And this is from your
friend, up in New York."

They moved out of the path of the stevedores dragging
rusty chains across the deck and unshackling the booms. Carr
pored over the five sheets of close, tortured script as Ritter
sat on the tarpaulin-covered hatch. "Y'know, your man,
Slavik, is a fairly good egg, carpenter. At first I thought he
was going to run me out of his office on sight because of my
denims and sweatshirt. But when I handed him your note, the
man went crazy. He hugged his nurse and told his receptionist to cancel all his appointments, they were closing up
shop for the day. And then we spent the rest of the afternoon
buying your stuff at these medical supply houses. He wanted
to hear all about you. I told him all I knew. But I omitted
about how you slugged me."

Carr agreed over the letter. "Yes, George is a very decent
fellow. I never appreciated him enough before."

"Yeah. He really gets around on that wooden leg. I'd have
never known you were such a big deal in the old country,
carpenter. Y'know, he insisted on buying me a shirt and
jacket and taking me to supper at Lindy's. He even promised
to fix me up with his nurse the next time I hit port. Anyway,
over the cheesecake, Slavik starts telling me how you were

130

supposed to be the up-and-coming brain man back in Central Europe. But he thought it was fine that you should want to stay here in Puerto Acero and help the natives, and all that crap, and he was glad that you'd finally gotten off the ships and he'd do what he could for you at the U.N. But he said he didn't think a man of your talents should be at this game.''

"That's very nice of George." Carr flipped a page.

"He said there were a lot of younger guys who should be doing what you're doing and that a man of your stature should be up in New York. That a place like Columbia would probably snatch you up.''

"Maybe.'' He had finished the letter and stuffed the sheets into the envelope. "Eventually.'' Carr looked at Ritter. "There's one other thing. He may have inadvertently mentioned my name.''

"Wolf Karol.''

Carr winced. The damage had been done. "As far as you're concerned, or this town, it's still Henry Carr. Right? I'll explain why, Jack. It's important to me.''

"Sure. Anything you say, carpenter. Oh yeah.'' Ritter's lips creased. "I saw another of our old buddies. Downriver. Guess who?''

"Who?''

"Piño. The Gallego.''

They chuckled and Ritter said: "Yeap. The Gallego really put on a show for us. A three-ring circus. You know that place where we come out of the delta onto the main channel? There was this smudge fire and we all ran over to the side and in the sand, in huge letters, was written, 'Hola F.B.I.' Up by the bend we came on the Gallego himself, with just these shorts on, in a canoe with Indian girls.''

Carr smiled, visualizing the Spaniard on the river. "How did he seem, Jack? I can't imagine him flourishing out there.''

"Pretty bad at that. His ribs were showing through his skin and he had this black muff hanging under his jaw. We threw

131

him everything we had—bottles, cigarettes, wooden boxes. I think I'll buy him a jug of tinto wine and lower it down to him in a basket if he's there when we go out tomorrow."

Carr motioned for Black Pedro and another boy to follow them and they drifted aft, toward Ritter's cabin, ducking under the wires and guidelines.

"I had to declare all those drugs and medicines in the manifest," Ritter said. "Captain Erlander was pissed off. He asked me whether I was going into the import-export business. Will we have any trouble getting them off the ship?"

"We shouldn't."

"How come?"

"There should be no difficulty. Custom's wife is due for a baby I'm to deliver and immigration's nephew has my cast on his arm. And Mr. Anderson, the AmCruz manager, has some corns he entrusts to my care, so they're all somewhat indebted to me."

"Sounds like you're in like Flynn around here, Doctor."

The stevedores obligingly told them to put their heavy load on a sling and used the rigging to lower the crates directly into the back seat of Carr's jeep. Ritter went down to the dock and helped Pedro secure the crates with a thick rope.

With the crates made fast, Carr jumped in the front seat while Ritter examined the insect-splattered windshield. "Where the hell did you get the wheels, Doc? I didn't know business was so good down here. Two months of pushing pills and the man has a car already."

"It isn't mine. AmCruz has only lent it to me." Carr patted him on the shoulder. "Don't be too envious yet. Wait till you see my cook and bottle washer. You're invited for dinner. I'll pick you up at six thirty."

Soledad served arroz à la marinera and Ritter had no qualms about wolfing down three helpings of the yellow rice, mussels, oysters, clams and shrimps, or easing their passage

132

with glasses of red wine. He did have problems in keeping his eyes off Soledad. Her blue silk blouse dominated the room and he was constantly forced to avert his eyes so as not to be caught gaping at her. In spite of the way she shrieked at his coarse jokes he could sense that she disliked him. Intensely. Why, he could not be sure. Perhaps because her man was laughing too heartily at anecdotes about Piño, Svenson, the crew of the *Blythe:* strangers to her.

They made an incongruous couple. Carr had his medical texts and Bubers and Unamunos in the unpainted bookcase and Soledad had her mending on the davenport and patched polkadot aprons hanging over the makeshift clothesline. But here they were, together, quite shacked up, and seemingly making a go of it.

The AmCruz Company was sponsoring Carr now. The jeep outside, much of the hand-me-down furniture and the glass medical cabinets in the front office bore the corporation's insignia on metal tags: crossed lightning bolt and smoke stack. Even the open chest of instruments, with its scalpels and scissors on terraced partitions of green felt, was stamped with gold embossed letters, "Courtesy of Am-Cruz."

Soledad complained that her "husband" made more money in his two days at the mine clinic than he did in his four days with the peasants, his operations, and trading his services for stupid arrows with the Indians. Carr told her to forget about it, but she went on to her final point—that her "esposo" was performing two-thousand-dollar operations at the government dispensary for a mere fifty cruceños. Or for nothing. The campesinos had heard about him and were coming from as far away as one hundred kilometers to have the blue sacs cut from their necks.

They did not switch to English until Soledad rose from the table to do the dishes. She left them with a plate of cheese, guava paste, crackers and a pot of coffee. Ritter noted that she had risen as if at some prearranged signal. She was

133

miffed and let them know it by slamming and banging around the pans in the kitchen sink.

Ritter lowered his voice. "Very nice, Dr. Carr. I drag a man to shore to show him the local ladies and come back two months later to find him 'dwelling' with the best-looking gal in town. That's progress."

"She's a nice girl. She has a temper, but Soledad's a nice girl."

Ritter filled their two snifters with Cognac. "And?"

"And . . . what?"

"And, Dr. Carr, to tell the truth, I'm still waiting, patiently, for some sort of explanation for all of our mysterious doings."

"You are?"

Ritter nodded. "I am. I'd say that you've had the basic use of about sixty days of my life, and I think I'm entitled to know what the hell is going on around here."

"I guess you are. I'll concede you that, Jack."

"Well. I'm glad we concur on that score. I've been mulling it over in my mind and you'll have to admit that this is all most odd. I head for shore with an English carpenter off a Norwegian freighter, get clobbered for babbling nonsense, and a few hours later the carpenter gives me two thousand bucks to buy up medical supplies in New York, where I learn that you are actually a noted Czech surgeon who has been playing hooky from the scalpel for many years. I return to find you *cohabiting* with a girl from Panama Street and still operating under an assumed name. Which leads me to the following question: what the fuck is going on around here?"

Carr removed the pipe from his teeth, amused by the description of events. "I guess you do rate some clarification. Especially since I'm going to ask you for the 'use' of another sixty days of your life. I'll tell you a story. A story you can record in that journal you keep. Do you prefer long stories or short stories, Jack?"

134

"Long stories. I think that's why I left Philadelphia originally. To get some long stories."

"Do you play chess?" Carr asked.

"Poorly."

Carr took his chess set from the table drawer and plunked it between them. He dumped two tribes of grotesque, lopsided pieces onto the battered board and chose the black for himself. The blacks were crudely sculpted blocks of ebony. The white army consisted of even more primitively carved chunks of mahogany. None of the pieces matched. There were bishops with lascivious leers, knights on lame horses, castles with pot bellies. The queens flaunted conical breasts and the kings were bestowed with codpieces stuffed in their breeches. Carr had received this chess set for the delivery of a seven-pound baby girl and Medina had been furious when he refused to let the treasure go.

They moved out quickly with their opening game and Carr did not speak again till he had confounded Ritter's standard Ruy Lopez alignment. "Does your family still live in the house where you were born, Jack?"

"No. My folks were living in an apartment."

"Born to an apartment. Do you know who your great-grandfather was?"

"Haven't the foggiest. My grandparents came from Allenstein. East Prussia. With everything mixed in."

Carr fortified his phalanx of pawns with an emaciated bishop. "That's very contemporary of you. An anonymous apartment building that has probably been demolished by now."

"I hope you're not going to come on with that old country versus raw America crap, Doctor."

"No. But I hope you'll realize that we cultivate different varieties of skepticism. With your background you'll view history as a gradually ascending curve, from the swamp up, while I see it as an undulating, deceptive wave, with abrupt

135

descents and slow recoveries. You no doubt have a reflexive sneer for yellowed Bibles, family heirlooms.''

''Not really. I'm a bit of a history bug.''

Carr eliminated Jack's knight, disposed to lose a bishop if it would clear the field for his phalanx. ''Fine. Then we'll commence in year thirteen ninety-one.''

''You *do* like to go back a way, don't you, Henry?''

''I'll start there because the chronicles of the Caro family of Toledo, Spain, dated from that year.''

''I can trace the Ritters back to nineteen five.''

''But we'll start with thirteen ninety-one because in the summer of that year the first Enrique Caro on record lost his life to an enraged mob. The usual circumstances: a fanatic clergy, cooperating with a debauched aristocracy—the nobles being quite diffident about paying their debts to Hebrew moneylenders—provoked the masses, superstitious peasants and the dregs from the urban slums. The usual charge—a ritual, sacrificial murder. The Hebrews were accused of celebrating a black mass, of carving up the body of a ten-year-old boy, drinking his blood for the wine, eating his flesh for the bread, while singing parodies of liturgical chants. It paints a lurid picture, doesn't it? Bearded Israelites dancing in gore-splattered caverns.''

''I wouldn't hang it in my living room.''

Carr castled. His castle now supported the formation. ''In Sevilla the mobs were led by one Ferran Martinez, and in Toledo, by one Padre Serrano, a converted Jew. The worshippers were dragged from their synagogue, the scrolls and ark and ten commandments heaped onto bonfires, and Dr. Enrique Caro came to reason with the exalted populace. He was, according to the diary, a distinguished physician, a familiar of the Court, and acquainted with many in the crowd. Caro exhorted them to desist, begged them to recall that Alfonso the Wise had been called the King of the Three Faiths. They stoned him, urinated on his corpse, and threw it onto the burning pyre.''

Ritter removed Carr's unhappy forward pawn and saw his own captured in retaliation. He moved for the queen with his knight.

"The Caros, to survive, became Anusim, forced converts under the surveillance of the Inquisition. Informers were encharged with scrutinizing their faces and instructed to report any grimaces, veiled ironies, the changing of sheets on Friday, signs of incredulity during religious ceremonies. In the year fourteen forty-one a José Caro was ordered to lower his trousers before the Holy Tribunal. His circumcision was taken for proof of apostasy and he was dismembered on the rack. The Caros, meanwhile, had constructed a stone regurgitorium in their wine cellar to vomit back the pork and other forbidden foods they were obliged to eat at their friends' banquets. For almost a century they prayed in secret. In subterranean passages. In caves. If you are an art lover, I could point out the hillside in El Greco's Toledo. Wolf Karol visited the site in nineteen thirty-six though it was subsequently obliterated during the Spanish Civil War.

"The next Enrique Caro was executed in fourteen eighty-nine. This time the charge was witchcraft. The family confessor of the Albas testified that he had boiled his instruments in hot water. Doctor Caro boiled his trephin, chisel, hammer and knives in water prior to opening a skull. And scrubbed his hands—three times. This stress on cleanliness was too reminiscent of pagan customs, Moorish baths. Since the patient survived the usually fatal trephination, the Holy Office concluded that malignant spirits had been invoked in the bubbling steam. After a protracted confinement, torture, and a forced confession, he and his sister were burned at the stake in an auto-da-fé in Burgos.

"So you see, Jack. Without a certificado de limpieza de sangre, a Certificate of Pure Blood, the Caros had no reason to vacillate when Ferdinand and Isabela issued the expulsion edict. Most of the Sephardim embarked in ships. They carried with them their 'caskets of gold,' and the Spanish language and poetry. The keys to their homes, a love for the country that had expelled and rejected them. Many of them did not reach their destinations, never saw land again. The captains chopped open their chests and caskets, gave their wives and daughters to the crew, and threw the men into the sea. The rest were strewn over the map of Europe: Constantinople, Amsterdam, Hamburg, Leghorn, Vienna, Bulgaria. Four centuries later many of the descendants of the Spanish Diaspora could still show you their keys, describe a fabled home in Córdoba or Salamanca. As the Karols of Prague still had the key to their villa in Toledo on March fifteenth, nineteen thirty-nine. But the Karols had become—as far as they might—excellent Germans or loyal Czechs . . .

"The next Caro to die violently was a Heinrich Karol. He was a physician serving with the Hussite forces and after the battle of Weisse Berg, in sixteen twenty, his body was thrown into a pit of burning oil, along with the other heretics. But a branch of the Karols survived. They lived in the same house in Prague for some four hundred years, through plagues, expulsions, and persecutions. They grew wealthy. Convenient marriages were arranged with girls brought from Janina and Bordeaux, girls with black hair and fat dowries. They never married the daughters of the Schneiders, the tailors from the Stare Mesto or Lichtenstein Houses, the cultureless Ashkenazim. Wolf's grandmother came from Salonika, crooned his lullabies in Greek and an archaic Spanish—the Ladino you corrected me for on the *Blythe,* Mr. Ritter . . . They grew prouder, if that were possible, proud of their dispensations. Others were confined to the Ghetto. They were exempted from curfews and exempted from wearing the distinctive hats. That would have compromised their distinguished clientele. They had been welcomed through the back door of all the golden palaces—the Czernin, the Hradcany, the Schwarzenburg, the Belvedere—sought after, usually at the last moment. Why? Three simple reasons. The fathers taught the sons. Two, they scrubbed themselves and their instruments, a radical innovation first suggested in the

Code of Hammurabi. Fewer of their patients died of infection. And the third? They were not permitted, fortunately, to enroll in the universities.

"Unable to attend the medical schools, they never learned that pus was laudible, never memorized Aristotle's ideas on the grasshopper, were involved in no theological disputations for their doctoral degrees. They could dedicate themselves to anatomy, not grammar; the examination of the object in itself, unencumbered by metaphysical considerations. They had no texts but the miserable, diseased bodies of the ghettos and with this, we come to the execution of the next Karol. This time, a Samuel. This time, a decapitation. Samuel Karol was writing a treatise on anatomy, purchasing cadavers from the diggers in the graveyard, and was apprehended, red-handed we might say, in his cellar. After a confession was tortured from him that this was a religious rite, he was beheaded in seventeen four."

Ritter replenished the snifters with the Remy Martin and they heard Soledad stirring in irritation, creaking the bedsprings and thumping a pillow. Carr held the bittersweet Cognac on his tongue and let it melt into an agreeable flame.

"The last violent death, in the annals of the Karols, till our modern age, occurred in seventeen ninety. The principal physicians of Vienna protested the incursions into their domain of Semites from Prague. But one of the ladies of the Court expressed a preference for her Dr. Hennie and he was summoned to attend her lying-in. Dr. Heinrich Karol was given a generous reward and was run down by a carriage and team of horses as he left the Hapsburg palace."

"That could very well have been an accident, couldn't it? But you would rather regard it as a murder."

"It may have been, Jack. Or no. It hardly matters now. Only to the last of the Mohicans. Your queen is in danger."

Ritter protected the queen with his ludicrous white knight. The defender was extinguished by a malevolent black knight, producing another "check."

"With no further depradations, with the advent of the

139

spirit of moderation and tolerance the Karols grew more haughty. They still did not mix with a Galitzian peasant or marry a son to the butcher's daughter from Slovakia. They became so arrogant, Mr. Ritter, as to emulate the Austrian aristocracy and maintain their personal rabbi as a family retainer, support their own small synagogue, their private poorhouse, import Sephardic mendicants from the Balkans or Vienna, so as to always have sufficient communicants for a service. When one died they brought in another, to maintain their synagogue a convenient two squares from the front door."

"Sounds like they had it made, Dr. Carr."

"Made? So made they forgot who and what they were. Which would bring us to the last Enrique Caro, a Professor Heinrich Karol, and his son, Wolf. When Wolf was thirteen his father conducted him on a grand tour of the Karol library, to teach him and explain the significance of each document, each book. There was a letter from Comenius, Czechoslovakia's greatest classical scholar, written from his exile in Oxford, written to Dr. David Karol, to inform his friend David that he had had to refuse the invitation to teach at the Harvard School in America because his wife feared seasickness and the feathered red savages. There were documents from the correspondence between Michael Karol and the Courts of Maria Theresa of Austria negotiating the return of the Jewish community to Prague and paying her an indemnification of two hundred and four thousand gulden. There were letters from Harriet Hess and a note from Polacky, thanking the Karols for endorsing his independence movement. A sonnet in Werfel's own hand, dedicated to Wolf's grandmother. A few bars of a round scribbled on a napkin by Mahler. Professor Karol impressed upon him the intrinsic meaning of each cherished object."

"Check," Ritter said. Carr smiled at the board.

"Czech, Mr. Ritter. And German and Sephardic. In the long run, a ghetto Jew. He loved too many things. The antithesis of Jahn and Arndt. His Folkdom was Europe. A man cannot love too many things with impunity. He cannot love Santa Teresa and Spinoza. He cannot read Judah Halevy with Wagner on the phonograph, find merit in Bismarck and merit in Marx. A degree of narrowness is in order, can save you, or the heart bursts, the mind snaps. As his did. We can fix the date: September thirtieth, nineteen thirty-eight. Professor Karol did not shave for the first time in forty years.

"On September twenty-eighth he was quoting Metternich to Wolf. 'England is the freest land, because the best disciplined.' The British Lion. Chamberlain will never desert us. And on September the thirtieth he refused to believe the newspapers. He came down to breakfast unshaved. It would be unusual for any man to break the iron habit of forty years but more so for Professor Karol. He was so meticulous in his ablutions, so vain about his presence. His friends had a story on him. He had been with the Czech Legion at Vladivostok, had deserted the Austro-Hungarian Army with his regiment, singing the 'Hej Slovani,' served with them during the Anabasis as they fought their way along the entire Trans-Siberian railway, fighting both the Bolsheviks and the Whites. And every day he shaved. On those freezing Siberian mornings he scraped at his chin with ice water and blunt razor. The soldiers in his regiment would ask if Dr. Karol had shaved today, as if the morale, the esprit of the regiment, balanced on the edge of his razor. At the National Assembly of the Provisional Government in nineteen eighteen, a delegate, a humorist, proposed that a special medal be struck in honor of Karol, as the only man who had shaved his way across the steppes, seven thousand kilometers, from the Volga to Vladivostok.''

"You're in check again, Dr. Carr. From the pawn.''

"A velvet-lined jewel box held the key to a villa in Toledo. German? In his youth he sang 'Next Year in Jerusalem.' His beard grew. The black bristles were ugly on his chin. But he continued his classes at the Medical

School until . . . it was November . . . he came home with blood trickling in his eyes. The students from the Law School had stoned him. Students of Law with rocks in their hands. Wolf bandaged his head and begged him to think of leaving, to think of the twins, Ruth and Naomi. He shook his head at Wolf's transgressions. He could not hear his son any more."

Ritter gulped down his Cognac.

"Professor Karol would have none of that. Wolf had wanted to emigrate for a long time, even before the riots and assassinations, and Henlein and the *Sudetendeutsche Heimatfront*. Do you know what his dream was? Wolf longed to emigrate to America. He would run his fingers over the map of the United States, spin the globe and stop at Iowa, or Montana. He saw himself teaching at a university with stolid, courteous students and nothing to intrude on his peace. He was going to explore and name a place for himself, not in the sky, not on land, but in the human mind. He would discover the location, the hiding place of evil. And amidst all those romantic landmarks—the Foramina of Monro, the Island of Reel, the Pons Varolii—a new name would shine. The Island of Karol.

"Professor Karol would have none of this. He sympathized with Wolf's desire to emigrate but said they must stay on till grandfather passed away. That gave Wolf another reason for hating his grandfather for the old man refused to die. "From his earliest childhood Wolf had despised the old man. Neither Wolf nor his father had been to the synagogue since Wolf's mother had died giving birth to the twins. But they maintained it—kept it for the old man, paid the rabbi's salary with a yearly donation, supported ten mendicants in the poorhouse. He loathed his grandfather's black and gray trousers and the way his watch was tucked into his vest. He winced at the red velvet bag for the prayer shawl and was humiliated when the guests averted their eyes as the old man shuffled through the room. Wolf shuddered with indignation when the lights were dimmed on Friday night and the dishes

142

were changed for Passover. But the old man hung on. He was a sickly sixty-five when Wolf was born and twenty-five years later was still trudging the two blocks every morning and evening on the chauffeur's arm. Wolf prayed for him to drop dead and be done with it.''

Ritter wanted to run from the house. If Carr did not cry soon, he was going to cry and they would end up sobbing like two infants.

"He refused to die to suit Wolf. The dim eyes followed his grandson reproachfully. Without a word. Mister Chamberlain returned to London. We would have Peace in Our Time, and old friends stopped calling . . . avoided us in the streets. Wolf did not blame them. His father's beard was down to his cravat and he looked demented. He couldn't hear me. Wolf shouted that they must leave the country for the sake of Ruth and Naomi, that he had no right to endanger them with this insanity. He coldly informed Wolf that his children might share his fate, whatever that might be.''

"Do you want to stop, Carr?''

"I screamed at him . . . 'Do you think you're too lofty for this century? Shall we eat our children while defending the walls of the Holy City?' Father replied that the timid might flee. If he did not stay after all he had said, after all his speeches, who would stay? He gave Wolf permission to depart for France, with the girls. He would remain with his father.''

"I asked you if you wanted to stop, Carr.''

"He was wrong about the cowards. Many who stayed were mice; paralyzed, hypnotized by the tinkling bell, the coming of the overpowering black cat, thrilled by their own helplessness. They were savoring their first strong emotion. Night had fallen. The beasts were coming in from the forest. And Professor Karol? Professor Karol had chosen martyrdom. He stroked his beard. He would march with dignity into the beast's mouth. Beasts who understand dignity?''

"Carr, I . . .''

Carr stared up at the ceiling. "Are the poets happy? They longed for a *Götterdämmerung*. They wanted fires to light the skies. An end to their false order. An end to the false gods." Carr looked down. "We come to March fifteenth, nineteen thirty-nine, when the German army entered Prague. Wolf's grandfather put on his cap to attend the evening service. Wolf watched him from his desk and could hear the tramp of boots on the streets, marching songs, the backfires of lorries, sirens. The staff and the chauffeur had fled. Searchlights beamed from Wenceslaus Square and the Wilson Monument was draped with swastikas. The old man grinned at Wolf maliciously. He was almost deaf and his mind was gone. In the last year he had been messing his trousers. There was no one to take him by the arm and lead him the two squares."

Ritter poured himself a tall slug from the bottle of Cognac and filled Carr's glass to the top.

"Professor Karol came down the stairs, his topcoat over his arm, and the old man waiting at the bottom smirked. A dry snicker came from my grandfather's throat. Wolf grabbed his father and said, 'I hope you're not planning on going out there.' Ruth and Naomi were crying on the landing and Wolf shouted up to them, 'Get back to your rooms! Back!'

"Professor Karol pushed Wolf aside. Gently. He took his father's arm. I shouted at him, 'Are you insane? Take him back to his room!'

"He brushed by me again. Gently. I shook him. I screamed at him. 'Do you have shit in your head? Are you senile? You don't believe? Look! Observe! Respect! Tolerate! But in this emergency your mind snaps. Your mind closes and you must lead this geriatric aberration off to hear his gibberish one more time before he drops dead. Do you think you're a martyr if you do go out there? You're a fool! Can you hear me? Can you hear me?'

"He shrugged my hands from his lapels and put on his topcoat. I slapped him across the mouth. I shouted, 'Can you hear me? You're murdering your daughters. I'll not mourn

144

you. I'll curse you.' He pushed me aside and I shoved him against the wall. I grabbed his coat and shook him. And as I shook him he just looked at me, no anger in his eyes . . .''

Ritter drew in on his Cruceño cigarette. He was helpless. Carr laid his head on the table, his fingers curling in his gray hair, and he remained in that position, motionless. A minute crawled by with the noisy clock making the only sound in the room. Ritter saw their reflection in the dull mirror. They both were dimmer, smaller in the glass. Ritter wondered why such vague creatures should be subjected to so much pain. They looked so inconsequential in the mirror, so nebulous.

Carr's left hand shot out abruptly, smacking the chess board, knocking pieces over. They rolled in small loops and then stopped.

Ritter slowly rearranged the pieces, sitting them upright and sliding them back to their previous positions. The drifts of used smoke hung heavily over the supper table.

Carr sat up again, hands locked behind his head. The man had aged ten years while his face rested on the table. Ritter averted his eyes and studied the chess board. He had lost the game, was hemmed in by an old-fashioned pawn drive. It seemed that on all levels he was beyond his depths with Carr. At least he had learned something tonight. For all of his *Weltschmerz,* he had always been a happy, lucky guy. There was simply nothing on his conscience. He had never been put to any kind of test and his life had not been spoiled and stained as this man's had.

"Take a drink, carpenter."

The advice was followed. Carr finished the entire goblet of Cognac in one long gulp. He wiped his mouth.

"You won't believe this but I never wished to do that. I've heard too many stories. I never wanted to be the refugee with his harrowing tale. I hope I didn't bore you too much."

"No. You've made me feel like a flippant shit, Doctor, picking open your old scabs."

"You've done me an enormous favor, Mr. Ritter. Though

I've done you none. It came as a relief to say that out loud, to let it break air for once and stink up the room."

"Enrique!"

Both were startled by a shout from behind the curtain.

"Enrique! Are you still up?"

"Yes," Carr called back. "I'm talking to the boy."

"It's too late," Soledad mumbled peevishly. "It's too late for talking. Come to bed."

Carr cracked his knuckles and nodded at the curtain. "My new executive director back there."

"It looks like you were kind of slaughtering me in our chess match, Henry."

They analyzed the positions. Ritter's slashing attack had gotten him exactly nowhere. Carr would pick up the queen with two more uncontestable moves. Ritter tipped over his king and Carr said, "I thought you put up a pretty good battle. We can have another go at it when you return."

"Return?"

"To hear the end of the story. And surely you'll want to learn about your part in it."

"Where do I have a part in it?"

"That you'd have to return for, to find out," Carr said.

"You know, you're a real bastard, Henry."

"I know. I use people without mercy. Though it's not totally necessary that you make another trip for me. It would help if you brought another crate of supplies from Slavik, but mostly I'm concerned about the communications. I could give you a letter to mail to him in New York, but the mayor here, Señor Mendoza, has given the post office instructions to let him have a look at all my incoming mail. The postmaster told me."

"Great country—"

"I realize it's a tremendous imposition, Jack."

Ritter toyed with the queen. He shrugged in resignation.

"All right, Doc. But only because I'm promoted to deck-hand this trip and it'll be better to pick up experience on the

Blythe instead of signing on a new ship raw. It would have hurt my pride too much to take another trip in the galley.''

Carr began returning the chess pieces to their box. "Congratulations on the promotion. Look at the brighter side of it, Jack. Doing me this favor will give you another chance to see Doctor Slavik's nurse.''

"That's a thought.''

"Enrique!'' Soledad was angry now, if the creaking bedsprings were any indication. "Tell the boy to go suck on a titty in La Zona and to let you come to bed.''

Ritter smiled. "That sounds like a fine idea, now that she mentions it. Lupe's waiting for me and if I don't show up soon she might think I'm not coming.''

Carr added a quick postscript to the letter he had prepared for Slavik and then slipped a thick stack of one hundred cruceño bills into the envelope. He slid it across the table and said, "Hold it for a second and I'll drive you down to Panama Street in the jeep.''

"Nah.'' Ritter folded the envelope tightly and tucked it into the pocket of his Levis. "You'd better stay here with Soledad. I hate to interfere with a man's love life.''

They shook hands out on the porch, and Carr gave the new deckhand a friendly punch on the shoulder. "If you see Piño going out, shout hello to him for me. We'll see you in about six or seven weeks then.''

"Seven or eight. We're hitting Charleston and a few other ports the next trip. Say goodnight to the little lady for me and take it easier, Doc.''

Carr lit up a cigarette and watched the American boy disappear around the curve of their winding path. The crunch of his shoes on the gravel grew fainter and faded in the darkness. It disturbed Carr that he had revealed himself to the boy that way, practically pushed the boy's face into Wolf Karol's chamber pot. He would not do so again.

Carr opened the screen door and found Soledad in the kitchen. She had slipped into her terrycloth bathrobe and was rinsing their coffee cups and ashtrays. His housekeeper could not bear to leave dirty dishes in her sink overnight. With her face cleansed of cosmetics, and the pink ribbon holding her pony tail, Soledad could pass for eighteen and not her thirty-three. Of course she had lied and told him twenty-eight, but he had chanced to see her driver's license when she took the test to use his jeep. He let his hands graze over her firm rump and she raised her cheek to accept his caress.

"You need your sleep, Enrique."

"We had a lot to talk about."

"Tomorrow you have to go early to the Indians," she reminded him with the tone of a tutor insisting on unfinished lessons.

"Don't be so discourteous to the boy next time. He's doing me a great favor."

She nudged him out of the way with her hip. "He'll get over it. Now come to bed. I woke up and I wanted you, and you weren't there. Tomorrow you have to go early to the Indians, and on Friday and Saturday to the mines, and on Sunday you're going to shoot Mister Emil."

Carr smiled at the brisk, dry fashion in which she said that, as if ticking off Emil were merely another item on his agenda.

"I told you I wasn't. Putting him out of his misery is about the last thing on my mind."

"Yes, you will, Enrique. He'll start talking his shit, and then he'll stand in front of you. You'll remember and you'll bring your rifle up and put a bullet square into his head. Lock the front door, Enrique."

7

Sunday dawn, sweet bells pealing, mothers hurrying reluctant broods along—girls in white bonnets, boys in drooping bow ties—up the dusty alleys to Padre Garibay's early mass. Few fathers were out. The men were burying their heads under pillows while the bells chimed in the unfinished cathedral on Plaza Paez. The devout waved at the English doctor in his familiar jeep and Bob, Emil's setter, barked at scrawny goats without fear of retaliation. A purebred trained for the hunt, he displayed the cockiness of the professional as the roosters and backyard pigs scattered from the jeep's path.

Arnstedt's face was hidden by dark glasses, pipe and pith helmet. Emil had little to say this morning. Before leaving La Loma he had mentioned another tiff with Bela, a quarrel about a shopping expedition to Concepción he did not approve of, and she again complained about the way he treated Klaus. Emil chewed at a large chunk of cornbread and sipped at his canteen of wine as they bounced along the upper river trail.

Once they entered the jungle shade, Bob was considerably chastened. The dog's purple tongue was stilled, his jaws shut. The jeep was carrying him into the deep bush and there were enemies in this forest that didn't fear him in the least.

The spider monkeys cheeped at him and coiled black snakes were clinging to the low-hanging branches. The jeep moved slowly and Bob became very quiet. Hoatzin birds and ahinga darters flitted by in the morning haze. The dog drew himself up to yelp at a scarlet-necked stork but faltered at the whiff of a distant cat.

Emil motioned to the left and Carr gassed the jeep up a steep grade. The sturdy vehicle hesitated at a rockstrewn crest but, with a crunch, pulled them up and over into a flat park. It was a caprice of nature. The overhead palms had fused to blot out the sun and the jungle floor ahead was smooth and as well groomed as a golf course. This stretch offered none of the snarled growth of the fluvial swamp below. The sun couldn't penetrate the roof of broad leaves and they sped along, over the dry loam toward the pajonal.

Reaching the high straw-colored grass they left the jeep and proceeded on foot. The dry season had come early and the stalks snapped with a flick of the hand. Emil predicted that with this dryness the springs at the mission would be crowded with game. Carr cursed quietly and slapped at his cheek. It had been bestial to bring the dog out here, into this puma and wild boar country. If they were sweltering in this tangled grass, the dog had to be a lot hotter. The pajonal rose above their helmets. Swarms of parched insects buzzed over them and pounced at their necks and arms.

The ruins nestled in a knuckle of sheer cliffs and seemed deceptively close once they had left the jeep. They had to cut through over a mile of savanna. Their Collins machetes hacked through the brittle grass and without commenting on it they noticed the sinister resistance. The trampled bushes rose immediately behind them, destroying all traces of the intrusion. The sun could attack them directly here in the open and the air hummed with an amniotic stickiness, sucked at their skins. Emil picked a persistent mosquito away from his lower lip. He squelched the insect between his thumb and middle finger. "Next you can read my chapter on Cruceño folklore and superstitions, Henry. It's still in rough form but you might be interested in browsing through it.''

"Very," Carr assured him.

Arnstedt slapped another mosquito from his wrist. "They employ, for instance, sprigs of mata de sabela over the doorway for good luck. *Aloe vera,* that is. And baths of palo-tal; the *Veronica scabra.* You must have observed the scapu-laries on the children's necks; the tooth of a crocodile. Or the tooth of a dog. Preferably a black dog. In many of their po-tions, they use peony seeds, the *Adenanthera pavorina.''*

"That should be harmless. Generally harmless.''

"Yes, my dear Henry, but if you plunge farther into the back country, they have many customs that are not quite so benign, practices almost African in their filthiness.''

"It's the same in the countryside throughout the world—'' Carr had to check himself. He was about to cite some of the practices of the Ruthenian peasants and then realized how in-appropriate a reference it would have been for an English physician reared in Gibraltar.

"It's the same, yes, the same, but some are more the same than others. I do not believe that our present-day German, or your English, agricultural laborers would still subject their children to urine baths. That's what they do back there, Henry. You go back one hundred, two hundred kilometers to the village of Alcalá, or Escorial, and they are still curing with vows to the Sacred Heart and La Candelaría. They use venom from the culebra bachaguera, snake venom with rum to purge the stomach. They still believe in the healing powers of wine, mudbaths, spider webs. Tobacco ashes to combat gangrene.''

"Why get so excited about it?'' asked Carr. "You seem to take it as a personal affront. If their backwardness bothers you so much, Emil, get your degrees validated and come over to help me at the dispensary . . .''

Arnstedt seemed not to hear. He ducked under the branches of a stunted orange tree and droned on, "I have this fully documented: Rosemary for colds. Verbena roots picked on Friday. They consider Friday to be ominous. Seven is mystical. Seven herbs dried for seven days in the sun. With prayers. But you must never cross prayers. I have this all written up . . .''

"You're a much broader man than I would ever hope to be, Emil. I'm intrigued by all these matters but I never seem to get around to them.''

Arnstedt shrugged and nicked a twig with his machete. "It's not breadth. One buries oneself in research here. You seek to extract some slight compensation from the barrenness.''

"Has it been barren for you? I'd say you're doing as well as the next man, Emil.''

They were tramping downhill now; they could advance without slashing at the grass but Arnstedt still hadn't sheathed his machete.

" 'Doing well?' I hardly think in those terms. You know something of my background. Not all of it. People like you and me, Henry, we can never 'do well.' If I've achieved anything, it's in the sense that I no longer waste time dwelling on the past. A man has won a great victory over himself when he orders the past.''

"That's odd. According to one of your most eminent philosophers, the superior man is the man with the longest memory.''

Arnstedt snorted. "Yes, the philosopher you're quoting died in an insane asylum. I try to think only of the future. My hopes, as commonplace as they may sound, center around my boys. Perhaps that's why I rail so against the Creoles. I shudder at the thought of having my sons absorbed in this farrago. Have you ever lost anyone dear to you, Henry?''

"Not lost. All my loved ones died of natural causes. And in their time. I guess I've been lucky that way.''

Emil looped his blade lazily at the wilting brown grass.

152

"Then you couldn't possibly understand what I feel for my boys. I, myself, am shocked by the depths of my affection. It was because—and you can well understand this—after the war, after we escaped, I considered myself through. My only thought was to live out my span, avoid the humiliation of a trial. As yours must have been, when you fled England. I had no illusions. I had no plans for a future." He chopped at another clump. "When Bela told me she was pregnant, after ten years of marriage, I took it as a painful hoax."

"You were in no mood for fatherhood," Carr prompted.

"It was much more than that," Emil said, irritated. "When William was born, I felt absolutely nothing for him. I regarded him as another problem."

The sun was higher now, aiming its full powers at their necks. Carr raised his collar. "Many fathers have no feeling for their newborn children. I'm told that it takes time."

"It was much more than a father's natural coolness. I thought it almost obscene that life should go on after all the slaughter I had witnessed. It was only after little Kirk was born that I began to view matters differently. Having had no children you couldn't possibly imagine how you can become absorbed in them, Henry. They become your only projection, your last sad hope of eternity. When we are callow, we see ourselves accomplishing splendid things, but circumstances and age . . . We live nearly half a century and find all our hopes are encompassed in two rough little chipmunks. Yet, in them I hope again."

They jumped over a fallen stump and Bob barked nervously. The stump was riddled with bloated termites. Carr examined his hunting partner. "You've become an optimist?"

"I have hopes," said Arnstedt, "for my sons. For my books. The books, I realize, will not be published in my lifetime. I have no illusions about that. But they are vital documents. Every Jew who can hold a pen will be scribbling

153

about Germany and the Jewish question. The world will need a counterbalance, the story from the other side.''

''I think you should write something about your service on the Russian front, Emil. I was always fascinated with that aspect of the war.''

Arnstedt ignored the suggestion. ''It was a long war. I saw service in several areas.''

''I'd be quite interested in that,'' Carr assured him.

''I'd imagine you would be.''

They heard the limestone springs as they climbed the low knoll Emil had indicated as their destination. Under the shade of an oak they spread their packs out, and Emil regaled Carr with more Cruceño legends as they ate their breakfasts. The sky was thick with game birds and there was no urgency to shoot. Emil explained that the birds and animals had come to regard these ruins as a sanctuary because the Indians from the river village, and even the civilized mestizos from the ranchos, simply would not venture near this mission. Three hundred years ago, it had been a flourishing plantation, worked by the baptized aborigines and administered by benevolent Jesuits as a self-contained theocracy. The mission was sacked during the revolution and the rebels, according to legend, beheaded the defenders and burned the priests' skulls on the altar. Now, the maiden aunts in Puerto Acero terrified children with bedtime stories of mutilated priests hovering over these charred walls, denied entrance to paradise and rebuffed at the gates of purgatory. This was their abode.

After the fruit, they unwrapped their broiled meat from the aluminum foil. Emil spiced his steak and then threw a pinch of the coarse-grained salt over his shoulder. ''It's the atmosphere that makes me do that,'' he told Carr. ''You feel as if the grass here were too green, the flowers, the orchids too brilliant. It's as if, after all these years, the massacre were still enriching the soil.''

''You're being a bit too morbid, Emil. Though it is rather

eerie. I never thought I could find brightness this lugubrious.''

"The brightness. Exactly! It is this light which terrifies the mestizos. The first time I came here I thought I had invaded a Gauguin canvas. I suddenly understood Gauguin, the horror in the sparkling colors. It stirred my interest in the myths of this region.''

Carr nibbled at the large green pickle Bela had placed in his bag. "You sound like you're well on your way to compiling an encyclopedia of Santa Cruz, Emil.''

Arnstedt used his tongue to eject the fibers lodged between his yellowing teeth. "Scholarship. Scholarship is the glory and curse of the Saxon mind. Consider only this one vast difference between our mode of thought and the Cruceño. The primary figure in their mythology is the Devil's wife and not the Devil, Henry. This stems from the Semitic imprint on the Hispanic soul, viewing the female and not the male as a primary source of evil. Vastly significant, no? Here, in Santa Cruz, she has three names—la Sayona, la Dientona, and la Llorona. But la Llorona is the most intriguing from our standpoint. She is the mother who murdered her own children and is condemned to wander in the shadows, shunned by all human beings, condemned to cry eternally at the sound of a child's laughter.''

Soledad was no prophetess. There was no danger of him picking up the Winchester and planting a bullet into this Señor Arnstedt. Emil Brenner was not yet ready. Sitting there and gnawing avidly at a succulent rib, tossing tidbits to Bob, he was just a happy dilettante with no memory. He was not yet dignified enough. He was writing a book of truth for the ages, eating well, managing a prosperous brothel, and sleeping with his beautiful whores. He was raising two sturdy sons and winning his chess series with his friend, the English doctor. A splendid autumn for a man's life.

Carr sensed his partner's eyes on him, the same intense

155

gaze he had detected at dinner the other evening. He took another sip of wine from his canteen and raised it in a silent toast to Emil Arnstedt.

It had been almost a quarter of a century since they had hunted together and Carr was impressed by the improvements in Emil's marksmanship. With every shot the Capuchin monkeys hurtled in consternation through the rafters of the blighted chapel. A cloud of black bats vomited through a fissure in the limestone cliff, their whirr exhuming a counterpoint to the shrill cawing of the birds.

Bob had cast off his gloom. The setter raced friskily with the joy of his job, retrieving the fallen crane and wild hare. The wildlife was so abundant at these springs that the slaughter could proceed without limits. Within seconds after every fusillade flocks of wild geese splattered the horizon and confused nutria scurried through the mission garden. Carr took his toll of the geese and regretted the transgressions of the youthful Wolf Karol. Wolf, the cosmopolitan, the would-be English sportsman, had delighted in this abomination, this mindless bloodiness. Wolf, in his stylish knickers, had been proud of his ability to outshoot his gentile friends, to kill with the best of them, and now Dr. Henry Carr could not be governed by piety and had to revel in this carnage, proving to Emil Arnstedt he was a proper gentleman. The pile of bloody fur and feathers at his feet was almost as high as Emil's bag. As Emil brought down a distant falcon, he evoked a cry of admiration, a shrill "Good shot!" The falcon plummeted to earth and Bob hustled off after the prize.

Arnstedt signaled an end to the morning's hunting by gratuitously obliterating a gargoyle on the refectory tower. The cluster of gargoyles was split into planes of mirth and tragedy and Emil's second bullet clipped away the nib of a conical nose, exploding it in a shower of powder. His next shot creased the foolscap and puffs of rotten mortar and decaying masonry

156

collapsed into the courtyard. The tingle of the fourth bullet seemed to hang in the viscous air as Carr and Arnstedt relaxed. Bob wandered into the roofless refectory and picked his way through the rubble. Carr stared at the dog, remembering the feeling of dawn on the sea. The dog was so incredibly alone there, life so small. It was so horrible to be specific in the midst of this profusion, this meaningless profusion of all these living things. Arnstedt was examining him.

"Something the matter, Emil?"

Arnstedt shrugged his shoulders.

"You had a very odd expression on your face," said Carr.

"Just thinking. It was a mistake to bring you here."

"Oh, come on now. I've enjoyed myself thoroughly. I was growing very stale in town."

Emil took a long pull from his canteen. "You have not enjoyed yourself, Henry. I feel your distaste for the shooting. I am very aware of your disapproval of me at times."

Carr laughed diffidently. "I wouldn't worry about it, Emil. I think you're a bit hypersensitive."

"I realize that you must think I'm a neurotic, Henry, constantly demanding reassurance of friendship, but the truth is—I've been a much happier man since you arrived in Puerto Acero. It's very difficult for any man, even a man who has lived a perfectly normal existence, to make friends at this stage, but for me, I . . ."

"Let's not get maudlin about it," Carr said crisply.

Emil Arnstedt tensed, and knocked over his canteen as he lunged for his rifle. Carr almost brought up the weapon across his lap in self-defense, but turning, he hid the gesture as he saw the puma on the cliff. It blazed in the sun, peering over the rim, jaw wide. A noise carried to them but the distance was too great to know whether it was a growl or rocks sliding. Emil grimaced at him, imploring the honor, and Carr lowered his rifle, conceding the shot. Arnstedt snapped the stock up to his shoulder and assumed the classic posture of the marksman. He would have to bring the puma down with one shot or it would be gone back into the rocks. The quarry was at least a hundred yards away, the angle difficult. The puma's tawny skin blended with the yellowish clay of the ledge. Bob was scurrying toward them, Emil fired, the puma shook with the boom—no ping or richochet. The puma was hit.

Emil's heavy boot smashed into Bob's ribs, almost curving the dog double before it could roll out of range of the second kick.

Arnstedt shook the rifle above his head like a spear and roared, "Bloody fucking animal. Bloody, fucking animal."

"I think you hit him anyway."

The shelf was empty. Arnstedt moaned, "You saw that magnificent beast, Henry. No one will ever believe me. That had to be the largest puma in the country. I ought to shoot this stupid dog."

"You wounded the puma. It might still be up there in the rocks."

"You're so calm. How can you stay so calm?" Emil shrieked, his voice cracking. "All right. Let's go and see."

Arnstedt broke into a trot. A few hundred yards beyond the mission wall the cliff curved gently into the meseta. There was a defined trail through the accumulated rockfall. Emil picked his way gingerly over the slabs of reddish slate and limestone. Carr jogged along behind him, amused, and wondered just how—if they brought down the puma—they would get it to the jeep. They would have to hack their way through the pajonal, attempt to drive the jeep all the way back here, and force their way out again. He was amused at himself for constantly worrying about logistical details, even during what were supposed to be exciting moments.

Bob was trailing behind them. The puma was in his nostrils and the dog wanted no more of this. Blood was dripping through his teeth and his squealing might be interpreted as pleas for them not to go on. Emil's kick had probably

158

cracked a few ribs. Arnstedt suddenly paused and held his rifle aloft, urging more speed. It was a grand moment for Emil Arnstedt. He was a fearless captain summoning his troops into the breach, the irate hunter in his tan field suit, cartridge belts and pith helmet.

They reached the crest and searched among the rocks and boulders. The puma could spring at them from any of these ledges. By some tacit accord they did not say a word. Carr closed his eyes under the glare of the naked sun. It was a superb day for it, but neither of them deserved so pure and noble a death. Not in the clear glare of this ridge. He had to cover Emil, protect his compañero, not let him be harmed in the flush of the hunt.

A mass of yellow clay stirred on the outcropping of chaparral over Arnstedt's head. It took shape, snarled, hurtled downward. For one second of beauty the great golden cat was endowed with the power of flight and Emil stretched out his arms to receive him. Arnstedt was down. Automatically, with nothing in his mind, Carr fired. The puma's head snapped and the echoes sang over the cliffs. Carr pulled again. The puma rolled away, slashing at the empty air.

His last shot, close up, was aimed at the magnificent green eyes, brilliant with their last gleam of defiance. He pulled. The bullet blew the puma's jaw away, splattered more blood over Emil's dusty boots. The report thundered back at him from the narrow crevices of raw rock.

A stupid puma that did not flee the echo of gunfire? They had been shooting for hours and the stupid animal had sought them out, posed on that ledge as if sculpted eons ago.

The arm of Emil's tan hunting jacket was in shreds, the pith helmet dented by the heavy paw, but it was the sight of the blood seeping through the shirt, spreading into a red splotch, that made Carr wince. He knelt down and quickly cut the shirt open. It took him some seconds to understand what had happened. His first shot had never gone astray—it had hit the puma. The bullet had torn through the animal and come out to pummel Emil smack in the chest. But the bullet might not have penetrated too deeply. The body of the cat should have reduced its impact. There was a chance if the bullet were removed within a reasonable period of time. Checking quietly, he found the pulse—an irregular heartbeat. But Emil had the dull patina of death on him. His facial muscles were totally relaxed so he looked simultaneously ancient and childlike.

Carr used his hunting knife to cut away the boots, cartridge belt, and jacket. If he were to carry his friend the two kilometers back to the jeep, he wanted as light a load as possible. He could leave Emil here, rush back to the jeep, try to bring it through, and return—or carry Brenner one way, through the high grass. Rotten either way.

He hoisted Emil over his shoulder and found him surprisingly light. He knew that he might regret that thought later on, hacking through the underbrush with his machete while the blood oozed from Emil's punctured chest. It was quite possible there would be no need to carry the burden all the way to the jeep.

Down below Bob was dying in the mission garden. The dog had curled into a ball of pain next to the pile of fallen game birds, twitching as the mosquitoes buzzed about his bloody maw and nostrils. Emil's kick had cracked his ribs for sure.

Carr lowered Arnstedt to the ground. Bob's hazel eyes were fixed on him, wide, expectant. He raised his machete, and with the splat, blood spurted over the grass. The hazel eyes on the severed head remained open. The flies and mosquitoes would have feasted and tormented him for hours.

Carr wiped the machete clean with strips of discarded aluminum foil. His hands were smeared and his sleeves flecked with blood from Emil's lacerations.

Grasping the machete with his left hand, he positioned Emil over his right shoulder. It had become very quiet by the springs. Carr turned and headed into the tall grass.

160

An hour later, deep in the pajonal, he was exhausted. It had been easy coming downhill but now he was paying a double price for the ascent. The afternoon was quickly brewing the ingredients for an idyllic sunset. Night might cover them before they even reached the dense brush. He glanced back over his shoulder at the mission and was chilled to see that it had taken on a sullen, malignant aspect in the shade of the cliffs and seemed to be spreading out its shadows to chase after them. He almost stumbled and wondered why they had shot so many birds at the springs. It would have been impossible to drag their burlap sacks of wild hare and birds through the tangled brush.

With a wide swing of the machete, he pushed on. His lungs hardened as they sucked in the sultry swamp air. They were not designed for these exertions. Each organ and system seemed to take on a distinct sublife, put forth its claim to his attention and voted for him to stop. He blinked the sweat from his eyes. His body was a treacherous physical plant to rely on. Ninety-five percent of energy went into restoration and maintenance. A meagre five percent, mixed with adrenalin, might be channeled into exertion, might be used to chop and hack and cut and slice through the lianas. And now he was lost. He could not admit he was lost, for then he might cry and that would divert needed energy, the tears accelerating the dehydration. He took the last swig of wine from the canteen and tossed it aside. He could pray but who should he pray to? No rational God would abet him in this hacking and swinging. In the night, under the huge mute sky, Emil's mind might slip away, filter out through his ear and be lost in the vacuum above. There was not even that. Just one solitary, lone spectre. If there were vampires, there might be angels. A devil would attest to the existence of God. But nothing.

He was crying anyway as he chopped through the vines. Perhaps he had been training himself for this ordeal. Impose order on the past. There had been no particular reason to get

161

on that ship in Fiume all those years ago. He could have chosen other means to search for Brenner. Now all those years at sea were no longer an accident, a waste, a loss. Now they took on meaning. He *had* been preparing. The young doctor in Prague could have never slung a man over his shoulder and ripped his way through this mat. The shattered wreck they discharged from the English hospital could not have carried Emil up this hill. Years of pressing the wall in his cell. Four years of pressing the wall to regain his strength. The waste and boredom and dreariness all became part of a logical plan, all so he could carry this heap back to an operating table. Unless Brenner were already released.

Night spread over them. The animal kingdom sang in a lower key. The inky cupola closed above and millions of cold stars were fleeing the curve of the earth. But the darkness did nothing to ameliorate the heat. His clothes seemed to squish with every slow swing of the machete. The years at sea had not been enough. Jacob labored twenty-one for love. Wolf had not served half as much for hatred. He could simply drop his load and sleep, awake in the morning with the first beams in the palms. Emil would be stiff by his side, the spirit gone.

He found a trail, or what seemed like a trail, and stumbled along in a daze. It was probably leading him away from the spot where they had left the jeep but he no longer cared. There had been no trail on the way in.

Carr sank to his knees and Arnstedt slumped into the dirt. There was still a pulse. Emil simply refused to die. This swine had greater resistance than a decathlon champion. It would be so much simpler if he died. Soledad would believe that he had acceded to her pleas. Mendoza would send his scruffy police out here tomorrow to recover the body and verify the existence of the dead puma on the cliff, and then he would nod gravely as he explained the circumstances. An inquiry, a report typed out, and the matter would be closed. The entire population would smirk as the story flowed from the cafés of Barrio Flores to the salons on

162

La Loma. It would all look quite tidy to them. Out of love for Soledad, the foreigner had ingratiated himself with the man who had caused her miscarriage, and had slain him in an unfortunate hunting accident. Mendoza would not want to pursue it much further. All very tidy. The pimps and thieves in La Zona would extol Dr. Enrique's cunning, and at the Nuevo Amanecer the black troubadour would compose verses, sing that the Englishman was macho, muy macho.

Carr stood up again and felt rusted. He positioned Arnstedt over his shoulder and staggered forward. He had been feeding off Brenner too long to let it end this inconclusively. There was no afterward without this load on his shoulder. He had too much invested in Emil. Could he go back to the ships? What for? Silly. Could he continue on as an English doctor? Silly. Could he return to civilization? Make money? Attend concerts?

He could no longer carry Emil. He dragged him along the ground by the wrist, tugging him through the clumps and thickets of angry thorns. He left the trail and plunged directly into the high grass again. He was lost. The trail was so much easier in the darkness, but some deeper instinct warned him that the trail would lead him nowhere.

He saw the glow in the darkness, the moon nestling in the jeep's windshield. With one last spurt of strength he hoisted Emil to his shoulders again and carried him the last hundred yards to the dry ridge where they had left the vehicle.

Arnstedt's eyes opened as his friend covered him with the khaki blanket. They glittered with amazement and then dropped shut. Carr found the canteen they had finished that morning and shook a few drops into his throat. It only increased his thirst. He rubbed the dirt from his wristwatch, the caked mud cracking open as he moved his forearms. The luminous dial said eight ten.

He had to drive slowly. The headlights penetrated only short yards in the dense gloom. His arms were itching and burning, the briers had minced his skin into a mat of raw

163

beef. With the buffeting Brenner was taking in the back of the jeep, it might all be in vain. Bela would look attractive in black. And she would dress little Kirk and little William in short black trousers, and black bow ties for the funeral.

It was Sunday night. Lopez would be on duty tonight. A pleasant fellow. By far the most promising of the trio. Lobos was sharper and faster but frittered away too many hours on the daily papers, ideological tracts. Lobos was charming and would undoubtedly end up as a senator in Concepción. He preferred Lopez. A good doctor was a narrow man. Unfortunately, Amalia, a stupid sow, would also be on duty tonight. He would have preferred Soledad to assist. Soledad was a dull student but she learned very well. He smiled in the darkness. It would also be nice to have a heart surgeon handy. He was about to enter territory he had not visited for fifteen years.

The headlights brightened the last curve, rose, dipped, and the town of Puerto Acero was spread out below him. He wanted to scoff at the warm feeling of familiarity that suffused him, but this dismal port was slowly conquering his heart. The moon was submerged in the depths of the river and burning on the cathedral cross over Plaza Paez. He saw the light in Los Olivos and thought of Soledad's rage if he managed to pull Emil through.

Five minutes later he braked in front of the government clinic and rushed into the lobby. Nurse Amalia—the one who objected most bitterly to Soledad's apprenticeship—was dozing on the sofa, dress up over her knees. The screen door slammed behind him and she awoke with a gasp of "Ay, Doctor."

Infuriatingly, she raised her hand to her mouth like the ingenue in an amateur theatrical production. "Dr. Enrique! You're covered with dirt and blood. Your face is scratched."

"Yes, Amalia, I am quite aware of it. Now I want you to wake up and move quickly and calmly. Is Dr. Lopez here?"

The woman clucked with fright and confusion. Carr could

164

sympathize with her better when he saw his reflection in the lobby mirror. The jaunty sportsman who had driven off this morning in crisp tans had returned in bloody shreds. The reddish blotches on his cheeks looked like Indian warpaint and his eyes were deep behind rings of dirt and fatigue.

"He's sleeping back there, Dr. Enrique."

"Excellent. Now listen. Señor Arnstedt has been wounded. A bullet in his chest. I am going to wake up Dr. Lopez and we are going to bring him in here and extract the bullet. I want you to cut away his clothes and, without jostling him, clean up his cuts. That you can do. Then get the operating room ready. Do you understand what I'm saying or are you still asleep?"

Amalia seemed on the verge of swooning and shifted her weight from foot to foot like an infant needing to urinate. "Did you understand me?" Carr snapped to shock her out of the daze.

"I believe I understand everything, Doctor."

"Good. And get the porter. Tell Ismael to drive to La Loma and bring back Señora Arnstedt. Tell him to say that Señor Arnstedt has been badly wounded and she should come at once."

Lopez responded more quickly. The boy, as soon as he recognized the intruder tugging at his shoulder, was on his feet, almost at attention, with that embarrassing respect they accorded him.

They stretched Emil onto the rolling table, and Amalia came to drag it away, struggling with the rusty, screeching wheels that refused to point in the right direction.

Carr heard himself soothing the flustered woman. "Just work steadily, Amalia. Clean him up, but don't shake him too hard. And bring some ammonia capsules. We don't want you to faint when we open his chest. Wait." He picked up a pad and pencil. "Give him injections of the antibiotics I note here."

He stripped naked in their makeshift washroom and Lopez

165

helped him to scrub off, sloshing away the dried squamous earth with a cruelly bristled brush. He soaped himself completely, stood under what passed for the shower, pulled the chain, and was hit by a deluge of cold water. Lopez swathed at the cuts on his face, neck and arms with a cheap, diluted alcohol that seared into him. An infection would probably hit him in a few days. That last swamp was a cloacal tank. He swathed on the peroxide and shivered with its stinging. His mind cleared.

Lopez was too discreet to venture a question. He was busying himself with his own antisepsis.

"It was a puma. It leaped on Arnstedt from above. It was all over him and I had to shoot. My shot tore right through the puma and hit Arnstedt in the chest."

"A most unfortunate mishap, Dr. Carr."

Dr. Lopez quickly slipped into his mask. Of course Lopez was willing to accept this rendition. Lopez would forgive Dr. Carr a half dozen Arnstedts.

Lopez was fastening his mask. Carr snapped on the rubber gloves. He was naked under the green smock and already beginning to sweat through it. That excitement was returning.

"Are you ready, Dr. Carr?" Lopez asked.

"Yes, but keep the ammonia tablets handy for me also. I'm very fatigued, Aurelio."

His stomach twisted in the brief moment it took to reach the operating room. It wasn't a fit place for removing a splinter. Not even an honest, back-alley abortionist would deign to scrape in this outhouse. This was what purported to be a hospital in a valley of fifty thousand souls, these unpainted wooden boards, crumbling plaster walls, slimy cabinets, all reeking of ammonia and bedpans. A wonderful country, Santa Cruz. They had a luxurious military hospital in Concepción. It looked fine on all the postcards.

Carr noted that Amalia compensated for her major deficiencies by minor excesses in her simpler tasks. Emil's chest was thoroughly scrubbed but she had spilled on so much

166

ethyl alcohol that the towels surrounding the bullet hole were soaked. There was no tincture of zephiran, Amalia complained. It was supposed to be in its spot on the shelf, where she always put it, but one of the other girls must have misplaced it. The other girls were always misplacing everything.

The instrument tray presented an interesting exercise in chaos. There was no reason or order governing use, distribution, sequence. No. He had been hasty again. He could detect a palpable effort to produce esthetically satisfying geometric patterns. The blood transfusion would have to go directly into the vein and Lopez would have to administer it. Amalia was going to be busy enough with her open drop ether. Distressing. Emil might suffer severe aftereffects during convalescence with this open drop ether on a cardiotomy, should there be any convalescence.

Yet the dispensary seemed to possess most of the instruments he might need, given the shipment from New York and donations from the AmCruz clinic at the mine: an ad hoc collection of Bethune forceps, Rienhoff rib approximators, Lebschesternum cutting knives, Duval forceps, Sarot needle holders, Coryllos rib shears, trocars, cannulas, mucosas. She had strapped Arnstedt to the table with two hemp ropes. Amalia was taking Emil's blood pressure, the other vital signs; and was being efficient for once. She smiled at Dr. Carr for encouragement and he nodded, blinking away the glare. This raw illumination was fatal. At a crucial juncture the four unshielded hundred-watt bulbs could well serve to blind him. Lopez was intent, concentrating, the technician fascinated only by technique, the faithfully followed standard, the radical deviation. Technique was all. The textbook. He commenced with Arnstedt in the dorsal decubitus position, using a left anterolateral thoracotomy incision, extending the neat round wound entrance sideways. What would Ruth and Naomi say of his attempting to save this man's life? They had called him Uncle Emil, always loved to go over to Uncle Emil's and Aunt Bela's house. What would the famous

167

six million say? It was already a cliché. An instant cliché. The human mind was incapable of conceiving of six million anything: six million pebbles, six million butterflies, six million cadavers. Impossible. The screen went blank at the effort. Fortunately, no threads or fragments of contaminated cloth seemed to have been driven in with the projectile. No need for plumbing about for scrap metal and snips of hunting jacket. Thank God for these modern bullets. With those old blunderbusses and rounds, whole wide khaki patches were driven in.

What was the betrayal of a few friends worth? The Israelis did not even classify the Brenners as war criminals. They would help, of course, to locate them, but the Brenners were insignificant. He was entering the chest cavity through the fifth intercostal space, and sectioned the fourth and fifth costal cartileges to provide a wider exposure. There was a chip fracture of the fourth rib. Pity, the whole rib would have to come out. It was in a worthy cause. Amalia's eyes widened as he positioned the rib shears. They made the nasty smacking noise of a meat cleaver on a wooden block. The nurse went green and Lopez nodded his assent, for whatever that was worth. How curious and frustrating that Emil should have survived being dragged along the jungle floor, and the bouncing in the jeep. A paradox. Professor Karol would have loved this. His father specialized in the paradox, and this situation was an interesting variation on the mad-sane matrix in Pirandello's *Henry IV*. If Henry Carr were sane, he would let Emil Arnstedt die and throw those last shovels of dirt over the past. If he were insane, he would do his best to pull his patient through.

Amalia's brown eyes again widened as he gently opened the Finochietto rib retractor wider, to establish a generous exposure for his operative field. In her honored years as a practical nurse she had not peered this deeply into the thorax. And she demanded attention; she had to impinge, oppress with her presence. He had no doubt that she regarded this as sacrilegious, and would probably faint when they pulled at the bullet. This had been forbidden territory up to sixty years ago, when Herr Rehn, with a simple, daring movement of the hand, took that vast leap into the unknown. Now every precocious student wanted to open the chest and give the heart a tickle.

There was the heart, once thought to be the seat of love, the repository of sentiments, now known to be a common mechanical pump. Emil Brenner's pericardium was distended and a royal violet in color. Emil Brenner's pericardial fat was stained with blood and precious drops of his blood were oozing into the thoracic cavity. But one discovered nothing new about Brenner by examining his heart. It was easier to know ten lands than one man.

Lopez was mobilizing the lung outward, covering the lung with wet pads—they should be warm, nobody to warm them—holding it in position with the malleable retractor. Lopez was such a pleasant fellow, a man of abnegation and dainty ligatures. When a Cruceño was admirable he was much more admirable than any other man, since the atmosphere in Santa Cruz was not conducive to personal integrity.

The opening in the pericardium was visible and the trajectory could be traced. Fat Amalia was swaying. Amalia must do something to let them know she was here. He wished again that Soledad was present. Soledad had the required single-mindedness and serenity, perhaps from waiting on a bed as mariner after mariner lowered his trousers. If Soledad were here he might tell her to remove her blouse so he could bend down and suck strength from her cork brown nipples. Lopez acknowledged his nod and injected five cubic centimeters of two percent procaine.

That was Dr. Henry Carr in the cracked overhead mirror. The crack divided him into two disjointed parts. With the green mask on, Dr. Carr was inscrutable. He was happy at this moment, always happy when he was working. He opened the pericardium medial to the phrenic nerve in an extension of ten centimeters and the edges were retracted with hemostats. The clots would have to be evacuated manually in this protracted quest for the bullet, the elusive bullet.

That was Bela waving from the small square window cut in the door. Ismael had certainly taken his time. Bela's wide-jawed, commanding face seemed huge, framed by the narrow window. As a loving wife she had not tarried to apply cosmetics, maybe a little dash of something under her deep gray eyes. She waved again, a gallant little flutter. Bela had come to take her seat in the gallery and wave him on.

Lopez motioned for her to move along with a decisive toss of his head. Good show, Lopez. He had not expected such spunk from the boy.

The clotted blood was removed, the bullet located. It was stuck in the myocardium, lodged in the wall of the left ventricle. Carr smiled behind his mask. He had been toyed with today at the ruins. The puma had served as a sandbag. Otherwise the bullet would have torn through Emil's heart and he would have been dead hours ago.

With each systole, tiny jets of blood were expelled from the laceration. As he had been anticipating, or was it merely dreary *déjà vu,* Amalia gasped as Lopez placed the forceps in his rubber glove. He engaged the bullet and their anesthetist was suddenly wobbling, her hazel eyes rolling above the green mask.

"Lopez, break open an ammonia capsule for Amalia. I don't want her fainting when I tug at this bullet."

"Sí como no, Doctor."

They paused as she quickly recovered with the ammonia fumes. She blinked her apologies with thick black lashes and Lopez returned to the instrument trays.

"Well, change your gloves, damn it, boy," Carr snapped. "Those ammonia capsules weren't sterilized."

Stung and hurt, Lopez hurried to obey the order. When he was again ready to assist, Carr pulled tenderly with the forceps. Even with the puma to take the brunt of the blow, the

170

Winchester had deposited its projectile with conviction. And Emil had a stubborn, recalcitrant heart.

Carr tugged again and Amalia's moan was muffled by her mask. Lopez also paled, stricken by the frantic extrasystoles and extreme irregularities in the cardiac action. His whole team might collapse on him.

"Lopez, I want you to hold it steady when I give you the nod. We can get it with one more tug."

Lopez responded, and Carr pulled again, the tension tightening his fingers. He was encountering resistance. At his nod, Lopez held the apex, and Amalia groaned. Carr felt it slipping. The bullet was out, naked and moist in his forceps.

Aurelio Lopez smiled triumphantly, his eyes crinkling over the mask. The extrasystoles had ceased immediately and Carr placed his finger over the laceration to temporarily quench the damage. A mattress suture would not suffice. Lopez introduced sulfathiazole into the cavity left by the bullet. They would control the bleeding by fashioning a pedicled graft over the anterior pericardium and the pericardial fat, suturing over the laceration.

Dr. Aurelio Lopez worked contentedly. He had read much about these operations, much about the work of Harkens and Brewster in World War II, and now he had participated in the removing of a foreign object from the heart. Doctors Lobos and Gomez would froth with envy when he told them tomorrow.

They finished closing the myocardium with four interrupted gut sutures and Lopez noted that Carr closed the pericardium around the drain to permit any blood or inflammatory fluids to escape and reduce the possibilities of tamponade. The operation would be quite successful and the patient would die.

Amalia yelped, the yelp of a cat with its tail stepped on—the heart had stopped beating, was at rest.

Emil was going to escape, slip irretrievably away. Carr thrust his hand into the crater again. His fingers would have

171

to generate a blood flow adequate to sustain life and thought. The ventricles had to be compressed suddenly and forcefully, sixty to eighty compressions per minute.

A small heart for a man this size. He had charged so bravely after the mountain lion. Perhaps he had nothing to fear. This heart could be manipulated with just one hand. Squeezed between the thumb and fingers of one rubber glove. With a sloshing sound. Transmitting the currents of blood up to this erudite brain. Amalia was on the verge of fainting again. They would soon run out of blood for Emil's transfusion and ammonia for Amalia.

Lopez wanted to inject epinephrine. At this point, anything.

Lopez injected it into the right ventricle and Carr squeezed. Emil, as a retired surgeon, would have been aware of these extraordinary efforts. The German University of Prague had once been an excellent school and the war gave first rate post-graduate training. Germany had contributed so much to medicine. Pagenstacher and Carl Ludwig. Joseph Hyrath and von Graafe. Langenbuch and Volkmann. Kocher and Rehn. Goetz and Dieffenbach. Koch and Sauerbruch. Von Helmholtz and Bilroth. Why Bilroth? Fuck Bilroth. And fuck Wagner. And fuck all their bloody ilk. Bilroth would have been at their side because they build superhighways, and are not entertained by gypsies. They have projections and plans for one thousand years. *O Deutschland, meine ferne Liebe . . . Gedenk ich diener, wenn ich fast . . .* composed one century too early.

Success. Life returns. The heart was functioning of its own accord again. Brenner's face was thin, drawn, had the pre-Raphaelite aura of the saintly recluse, the patina of withdrawal slowly tinging with color, the heart moving like a blowfish stranded on the beach. Emil wished to complete his unfinished business. Peel off the skin and the personality is shorn away. Emil wished to get back to his chapter seventeen. In which he explains everything. Everything.

172

Now it was all mechanical. Lopez was helping him prepare the drainage systems, using two types of water traps, a small catheter in the intercostal space. They closed the incision using interrupted silk. Technically, cosmetically, the night's work left much to be desired. Emil would have an unnecessarily ugly scar on his chest if he lived out the night, or the week. Still, there was a slight chance he might survive, return to his Club Moderno to give the customers his hearty welcome in seven languages.

It could not be known until later if there had been any damage to Emil's precious brain. By the clock on the wall the operation had lasted two hours and thirty-seven minutes. Carr's voice echoed strangely in his own ears as he gave instructions to Lopez on the post-operative care, and told the boy to call him in the lounge if there were any complications. He did not add that he no longer cared, was past caring—that the second his professional duties had ceased he had succumbed to all the exhaustion of his ordeal in the jungle.

Bela immediately rose as he came out of the operating room and headed down the hall to the bath. Fortunately, she was sensitive enough to say nothing. Her voice would have been intolerable at the moment and even the tapping of her high heels was agonizingly loud in his ears. With his weariness, every physical sensation was insupportable and he was annoyed at the exertion involved in pushing open the washroom door, kicking off his slippers, and tossing aside his bloody green smock. His torso and back were drenched with sweat and he saw her face tighten at the sight of the networks of cicatrices splaying his chest. That was true. Bela had never seen his scars before. Neither of them seemed to find it unnatural that he should stand naked in front of her.

He stood under the primitive shower, pulled the chain, and absorbed the shock of the cold deluge. He pulled the chain again and the water pounded him like a mallet on the skull. He was past weariness. In this state he could go on forever or dissolve into a heap on the damp concrete floor.

Bela helped him to dry off. She chaffed at his back and thighs with a rough towel, and had a cigarette ready for him as he slipped into borrowed gray pajamas. She placed the cigarette between his lips and he noticed the half moons of perspiration under her arms. She was wearing nothing under her cotton dress. This was fidelity. At Ismael's call she had hurried into an unbecoming frock and paced the dingy hospital hall for two hours. A sigh escaped her and she filled his nostrils with the saline richness of a sweltering mammal.

Without a word Bela followed him to the cramped lounge. She snapped the lock and then clicked the security latch. He wondered how much privacy she needed. She had tinted her hair a lighter shade of auburn and it made her look harsher, more aggressive. Such nonsense.

He collapsed into a folding chair and Bela approached, stood over him with her hands on her heavy hips. The weak lightbulb on the chain only accentuated the filth and disorder of the lounge, the card table crowded with Coca-Cola bottles, filled ashtrays, and munched apple cores. Ripped magazines were scattered over all the couch. He recognized that he had been remiss. It was not enough just to perform his small feats in the operating room. It was imperative to take this whole place in hand, order and clean up this entire mess.

He drew on the last of his cigarette and the night suddenly invaded him. The silence was swamped with the humming of the generator and the whimpers of patients in the adjacent ward. He heard the whirring of the overhead fan and the scratching of the insects on the screened windows.

"Are you all right now, Enrique?"

"Strange that you should ask about me . . . first. Emil's the one that's in a bad way."

"Ismael told me a very confused story. Something about a puma, and your shooting him."

"That's not entirely accurate. A wounded puma leaped on Emil and I fired. Perhaps I should have fired my first shot in the air to frighten him off. Instead, my bullet traveled the entire length of the puma and hit Emil directly in the heart. I just removed the bullet from the wall of his heart.''

"He'll live?'' The question expressed disappointment.

"Possibly. The operation was, technically, successful. But he's very weak. And there's the possibility of brain damage. I had to massage his heart. We'll see. I'll be spending the night here in case there's any worsening in his condition.''

"Why, Enrique?''

"An accident. And stupidity on my part. I could have shot in the air and maybe the puma might have scattered.''

Bela sank to her knees in front of him and took his hand. "I meant why did you try to save him? Why didn't you just let him die?''

"Bela?''

"Don't Bela me. You know what I feel for you. You've seen me longing for you, and you turn away.''

She kissed his hand and he was too tired and confused to resist.

"I still don't think—''

"You never think anything, Enrique. You live with a whore in a shack on the hill, and you waste yourself on these worthless people. A man like you. We could escape from here. I've despised that man for so long.''

"I'd still have a responsibility to—''

"You have a responsibility, Enrique—to us. This is nothing now. I've wanted to leave Emil since the day I married. We could leave this horrible place. We could have so much together, Enrique.''

"Perhaps, but . . .''

"But?'' They had both risen. Bela placed her warm palm over his mouth. Then she took her hand away and brought his lips down to her open lips. This lascivious hag was intent on raping him. She was shivering and trembling against him, grinding her hips against his groin like a dancehall girl. Her fingers were kneading the nape of his neck. She had snapped the latch beforehand, was planning ahead on this. Were it not

175

so ludicrous, were he not so exhausted, he might knock her down, kick her, kick her in the stomach and the skull.

She pushed him away and strode to the door. He thought it was to leave, but she snapped off the lightbulb and, spinning around, with a wrenching abruptness she reached for the hem of her dress and pulled it over her head, flung it aside as the moon poured in through the screened windows over her naked flesh. She was smiling broadly. The last time he had seen Bela like this, she had been a pinched, neurotic virgin, regarding his intrusion as a painful defilement, sobbing into her pillow at her loss of purity. Tonight she was gross with desire, her breasts heavy.

The moon was her ally, coating her coarse strength with dull luster as she swept the magazines from the couch. She beckoned. Her massive thighs opened to receive him and she groaned, "Enrique," as he entered her, her head rolling loosely until her teeth clamped into his shoulder.

It was monstrous, that his organ could respond to hatred, that he could press forward into this moist pit, make love to this same woman over the chasm of time, his second woman after years of exile from their pleasures, stare down at her face and glinting green eyes, her teeth and tongue on his mouth again. A few feet away, behind a flimsy wall partition, a man was dying and he could hear Lopez and Amalia conversing out in the hallway. At any moment they might rap to announce that Emil was gone. Bela pulled him down against her cheek and her tongue lashed into his ear, drinking at his brain.

He was suddenly in control of himself again, could float while this heaving cow pounded at his loins, scratched his back, tightened her tubes to suck in love. She was enormously alive because there was a mace between her legs to liberate her from a despised husband. Bela had no past, no memory. She had become a ripe and rotten tropical fruit, and Henry Carr her demon lover. So he could hold in abeyance the impulse to pound his fists into her ribs, smash her against

176

the wall, clamp fingers into her throat. This writhing animal would not remember a friend, an ex-lover at her door, two little girls crying in the vestibule, sirens, boots, lorries. His member could grow harder at the softness of her belly and the obscene promises she whispered, but his hands would not yet lock into her throat. That would come. One day he would whisper into her warm ear, "Hello, Bela. How are you, Bela? This is Wolf. Do you remember me, Bela? You've become quite a passionate woman."

Pussy willows. The shops were closed, markets empty, the streetcars resting in their sheds. Only a few flower vendors had opened their stalls to toss bouquets at the occupying army. Naomi and Ruth went to the corner in the morning and returned with pussy willows. The last things Wolf saw as he ran from the house were the sprigs of willows in a green vase.

8

"Today we go to the Ayacaras, no? The Ayacaras are more docile than the Guyananas, Dr. Enrique. Three years ago the Guyananas killed a trader. They hacked him to death with machetes because he sold them defective rifles. At least, that's what everybody tells you. Nobody knows for sure. They only know that he went to their village and never came back. He was a Turk or a Lebanese or something."

Pedro Alfarez continued to talk while the sputtering outboard motor coughed and gasped. Carr could hardly hear a word of his helper's chatter but he felt obliged to nod at what seemed appropriate intervals. The broad river stretched before them, the placid surface seeded with mossy tree trunks bound for the delta. It was a pellucid morning and the trees on both banks delineated a spacious green highway. For all immediate preoccupations this could be a penny swanboat on the municipal pond and not a fragile outboard on a rushing Amazonian river.

Carr nodded again at his helper. Alfarez reveled in his role as captain of this small craft. The black scoundrel had even filched a yachtsman's cap, tilted at a jaunty angle for these expeditions. Pedro, broad-shouldered and white-maned, would make a memorable Othello with the proper training and this English doctor . . . a passable Ahashaverus, or the Mad Scientist. The Mad Scientist was highly indebted to the AmCruz Company. AmCruz was converting him into a film star. For the presentation of the jeep, Jerry Anderson had merely brought around the photographer from *La Tribuna*, but for this motorboat they extracted a full hour of posing with elaborate equipment and asked him to deliver the text of the accompanying narration: "The granting of this craft, which Dr. Henry Carr utilizes to head into the wilds and extend the benefits of modern medicine to the Indians of the rapidly disappearing Ayacara tribe, is but another manifestation of the public spirit of the AmCruz Corporation and its desire for the closest possible cooperation with the communities of the Cumaná Development District." The technicolor film featured scenes of the clinic and recreation center at the mine and the elementary school at the workers' housing project. Dr. Carr entered for the finale, in stylish white jacket and tan pith helmet. Drs. Lopez, Lobos, and Gomez were also furnished with starched white jackets. As the cameras ground, they busied themselves giving smallpox shots to a line of the healthiest and most attractive children of Barrio Flores, paid one cruceño apiece for their time as extras. Soledad had also heightened the undying enmity of the practical nurses by being the only woman asked to participate in the production. She was triumphantly gorgeous in a snug blue uniform and irritated the director by smiling directly at the camera. He had not, however, hesitated to focus on her knees as she stepped into the boat. Later, over a drink at the Club Lido, Anderson used the confidential tone usually reserved for imparting the fact that the woman with the tray of canapés is an easy mark. "Y'know, Henry, we're extremely satisfied with your work. Everyone in our outfit is highly pleased with you. I'd say that you've made a lot of friends around here."

"I'm quite glad to hear that, Jerry, but why don't you make your pleasure patent? Fatten my pay or give me another day's work up at the mine."

Anderson snickered. His yellow mustache twitched with the exertion. "Y'know, I thought you'd say that. You're a funny guy, Carr. I'd personally like to raise your pay, but you know how these things are. We had to hire you as a local and put you on at the local rate, and if I tried to pull a fast one and switched you onto our rolls, I'd have hell to pay with the union boys. And Dr. Baker's contract's got another year to run. Maybe when he goes. Baker ain't too happy down here. Maybe. I can't guarantee anything. But I can tell you this. I did write another letter about you to our Houston office and I want to tell you that Russell Bennet was interested. Old Russ Bennet himself."

Anderson formed the words "Russell Bennet" as if they were some potent invocation that would multiply loaves or part the Red Sea. He reached out to nudge Carr's forearm for no apparent reason. "Russ is comin' down here in a few months to look things over and he intimated that he'd like to meet you, Henry. And with a livewire like Russ, that could make for all kinds of action. I wrote them what Lopez said. Lopez said what you did to pull old Emil through was sheer magic."

"Not really. There are many surgeons who do it routinely."

"Maybe so up there, but not in this town, Doc. They tell me that old Emil's up and around already. Not doing too much but he's out of bed. And they're swearing you're a witch doctor. That nurse, Amalia, goes around telling everybody you almost yanked his heart right out of his chest to tear the bullet loose, and Lopez backs her up right down the line."

"Amalia's not a very reliable witness. She was faint at the time."

"Still in all. If I ever get a bullet in my heart, I'll drop around for you to pick it out for me, Henry."

"Good. The next time you have one in there you come over and we'll see what we can do for you."

Anderson shook his head over his Bourbon and gingerale.

The Texan engineer was crusty, narrow and drank too much, but he had good instincts. And his imperfections could be overlooked. He had donated this boat to the English expatriate, a vessel to carry him to the diseased, dying, and decimated Ayacaras.

Pedro was calling to him again, cupping his hands around his mouth. He would have to move aft and listen to his helper's opinions. His self-styled handyman had the strength of a bull elephant and more gossip than the neighborhood yachna.

"Everybody says we shouldn't do this, Dr. Enrique. Everybody says we should not molest the Indians. Everybody says they can take care of themselves without our interference."

Laughter would have been discourteous. "Who is everybody, Pedro? Is that 'everybody' at the Nuevo Amanecer or 'everybody' on the benches in Plaza Paez or 'everybody' at the Club Montparnasse?"

"No. It's everybody. Everybody in the city. And Dr. Apolinario and Dr. Mendicuti too. They all say that the Indians are naturally strong and can resist the jungle fevers without our medicines."

"What the devil do they know about the Indians? They see them from the airplane window when they fly to Concepción, or from the deck of the mainship when it goes to San Martín."

"But that's what everybody says," Pedro insisted.

Carr wiped away the spray moistening his cheeks and lips. "Well, the next time you're all discussing tropical medicine at the Club Moderno, tell 'everybody' to shove it. How old are you, Alfarez?"

Pedro shrugged. "Who knows? I'm supposed to be between forty-five and fifty somewhere, but the girls tell me I'm still young, Doctor."

"A ripe old forty-five. And the average life span in Puerto

181

Acero is around forty, and among the Ayacaras I'd judge it to be around twenty-seven. So they're obviously not holding up too well."

Pedro thrust out his lower lip. He was undaunted. He hunched his shoulders. "Perhaps. But everybody says you should spend more time at Los Olivos. You already go two days to the clinic at the mines and we come down here one day a week to the Indians, so you don't give enough attention to the people of Puerto Acero. And they all say you don't make enough money from the Indians, either."

"Since when is 'everybody' so concerned with my bank account?"

Pedro shook his head like an old grannie, grieving over the present generation. "Everybody in Puerto Acero talks about everybody else. What they all say is that you don't make much money at Los Olivos and you don't charge enough for your operations and then you can't make much money with the Indians. And maybe one day an Indian will die by accident and they'll shoot you with an arrow."

"Not likely, Pedro. Not likely. I'd say that the Ayacara village is safer than Panama Street. And these trips are profitable. One day with the Ayacaras is more profitable than four days at my office. Medina gives me more for a few arrows and parrots than for a whole truckload of vegetables and chickens. He promised me twenty cruceños for every parrot we would bring him."

"Twenty cruceños!" Pedro roared in anger. "That bastard! He sells them for one hundred. Twenty cruceños? You must demand sixty, Dr. Enrique. Why don't you let me do the bargaining for you? You are a man of letters and do not know how to handle these lowly matters. I am a man of the roads and streets and can easily get down to Medina's low level."

Pedro had made this offer several times, but Carr hadn't given it any serious consideration. This morning he saw advantages in letting Pedro syphon off a bit of the proceeds. He

182

had been acting too much like a fanatic, like a miser, growing desperate as his goal seemed to recede in the distance. By letting Pedro take over he could avoid those demeaning squabbles with the Turk, those arguments over the plumpness of a duck or the freshness of a sack of beans.

"Done, Pedro. I'll make you my financial agent on this. You seem to know the market better than I do. Today we'll have to ask Fulgencio for flutes and drums. Medina says he's having a big run on flutes."

"Fulgencio will get them for us. Don Fulgencio is a strange bird, isn't he, Doctor? How could he go back to his village after living so many years in Concepción? I couldn't. After television and radios, and autos and films . . . to live in a hut in the jungle again. But maybe he came back to be chief. In the capital he only washed dishes but here he is chief."

Pedro rambled on about the job situation in Puerto Acero, where everybody applied for jobs as maitre d' and nobody applied for a job as busboy, and Carr let him babble. His mind was elsewhere—on the way he had plunged into the affairs of his adopted community, his address before the Ladies' Auxiliary of the Good Shepherd of San Martín in the Blue Salon of the Ateneo. The ladies marveled at the foreigner's eloquent Spanish as they fanned themselves, and, behind cupped hands, exchanged sly comments on how well the Englishman was looking, filling out on Soledad's cooking. The ladies seemed to agree with him when he stated that it was presumptuous of him to intrude on their canasta party, and they seemed unmoved as he described the wretched conditions of life on La Colina, as if they were unaware of them. They only perked up when he suggested that microbes respected no zoning regulations and epidemics ignored surnames and social status. If a child fell sick on La Colina it was no distant tragedy, for that illness endangered their own children. La Colina needed more modern outhouses. The flies of Puerto Acero found it to be only a short flight from the unmentionable droppings of La Colina to the meats and vegetables on the dinner tables of La Loma. And the subterranean currents that flowed under those ranchitos carried contaminated water and intestinal parasites to their own artesian wells. The ladies shuddered.

Feeling a close kinship to Belavignus, he brought out sketches for cheap, hygienically sealed latrines. This would be no mere charity campaign. What they invested in outhouses for their unfortunate neighbors, they themselves would save in medical bills over the next ten years. The city also required a modern incinerator. It was only a quick hop for the bugs from the pest-ridden garbage dumps on the edge of town to their own spotless kitchens. He held up sketches for a practical concrete incinerator, such as those gracing urban areas of similar size in the most advanced nations of the globe.

He was accorded an ovation. Then he remained on the stage and observed the admirable exercise of democracy in action. The ladies voted to postpone their canasta and to discuss the latrines and incinerator. They voted to organize a subscription campaign and hold a charity bazaar raffle. They nominated a committee to consult with Padre Garibay on how to organize the shiftless and unemployed of La Colina to help themselves. And they passed a resolution aimed to bring pressure upon Jefe Mendoza to allocate public funds. They were going to be modern women in a modern society for the well-being of their children.

Prodded by the powerful Ladies Club, Mendoza acted with exemplary alacrity, authorizing a preliminary feasibility study, and three days later awarded the contract to his brother-in-law's construction firm. Dr. Enrique Carr was named special voluntary consultant on public works.

But was he capable of doing it? Kirk and William Arnstedt, accompanied by their tutor, Klaus, came to visit him at the construction site. They were out for their afternoon stroll and it was a scene from a pastoral: the sensitive tutor clutching his slim volume of Verlaine, and scolding his two charges for their rowdiness. The boys scampered about in blue sailor suits and white caps, red anchors sewn on their sleeves. William, the older, was much the quicker of the two, and it was William who came to chat with him under the shade of the acacia trees.

"Do you speak the German language, Dr. Carr?"

"Just a little, William. I had to learn a few poems by rote when I was in school. When I was about your age. There was a time when I could recite 'Zwei Grenadieren.' "

The boy, with his pink translucent skin, spoke with the gravity of a mature man. He frowned and said, "We had that poem in our anthology, Dr. Carr, but my father told Klaus to cut the page out. He said it was an evil poem about bad men who fought for our enemy, Napoleon."

Klaus blanched helplessly at the Englishman and Carr waved it off, indicating that it did not matter.

"Maybe they fought for Napoleon, Guillermo, but it can still be a good poem. As the years slip by all of the quarrels and causes are forgotten and we are left with a residue of pure and noble sentiments."

Kirk blew his whistle at a centipede. He was a rough, sturdy boy, with high cheekbones and narrow eyes; he looked Asiatic, as if a Tartar had stayed far from the Main Horde and left his traces in Prague. Kirk was bored by the conversation and crawled after the centipede, blowing his whistle at it.

William Arnstedt rose to his knees and yanked out a loose tuft of grass. "Why are they digging that hole and building that building?"

"It's going to be an incinerator," Carr explained, "for burning trash and rubbish. So the garbage doesn't contaminate the city."

William did a somersault and then recovered his fallen cap. Naomi and Ruth had been almost this age—bright, inquiring minds; healthy, pink-cheeked.

"My father says you're a great man, Dr. Carr. And my

185

mother, too. She says we should grow up to be like you."

"That's very kind of them. Both of them."

Klaus took William's hand. "We're bothering you, Doctor. I'd better take the children away and leave you in peace."

"No, I don't mind. They're both fine boys and William here has a sharp mind. How are your studies coming along, Klaus?"

"I'm fairly confident. I should be able to take the orals in Concepción in the fall."

"I suppose you'll be glad to be getting out of Puerto Acero, won't you?"

Klaus smiled ruefully. He gazed across the river and seemed to be seeing the capital, four hundred kilometers away. "I don't mind admitting that, Dr. Carr. They've been kind to me, but I'll be happy when I get out of that house. It can be a small hell when they start arguing."

"Yes. It's a pity they get along so poorly . . ."

An hour up the Río Blanco took them fifty thousand years into the past. The tributary narrowed. The fronds and palms overhead almost touched, blocking out the sun. Don Fulgencio was their only link with this age.

The Río Blanco widened again into a sun-splashed lake, and they saw the Ayacara canoes on the far beach. The Ayacaras were waving and they could make out Fulgencio, in his rags, signaling with his straw hat to guide them in. Fulgencio, the subchief and interpreter, was the only man among the Ayacaras who spoke Spanish. He still wore ragged, khaki trousers, a straw hat and a silver medallion, the symbols of his sojourn in the city.

"There they go," Pedro shouted over the motor.

There they were, and there were precious few of them. They blended with the underbrush, not more than eighty in all. Klaus had said that the Ayacaras once numbered in the

thousands and fought major battles with the Spanish conquistadores. Contact with the white man, chicken pox, smallpox,
mumps, measles, bronchitis, ascaris and the common cold
had reduced them to this woebegone bunch. At least the yaws
were gone. A sailor had brought in yaws from Haiti and it
had been endemic among them. One shot of penicillin per
capita and it had cleared up.

Fulgencio came wading out to help them drag the boat up
to the dry sand. The toothless headman was grinning with
gray and blue gums. "Saludos, Señor Doctor. Saludos. Some
of my people were beginning to murmur. They said you
would not come again."

"I thought you Indians were supposed to be stoics, Don
Fulgencio, and here you protest because I arrive one day late.
How have you been, old one?"

The Ayacara children surrounded Pedro and tore off his
cap. His black skin fascinated the coppery Ayacaras and his
fuzzy white head was an endless source of joy. The straight-
haired Ayacara children delighted in rubbing their palms over
his bristling, woolly head and he goodnaturedly submitted to
all their pranks.

"How did the malaria pills hold out, Don Fulgencio? Did
they last the week or were they gone the first day?"

"They lasted two or three days, Señor Doctor. I tried to
protect them, even slept on the sack. But we have no locks
on our huts. Every time I left my hut they would sneak in and
gobble them down like caramels. They like the taste, Señor
Doctor."

The greetings dragged on as the children scratched at Pedro's scalp and the women nuzzled him amiably and then ran
to peek at him from behind the trees. The nuzzling was innocent and incited no jealousy among their men. Fulgencio
helped Carr set up their card table and two folding chairs next
to his thatched hut and Pedro finally broke away from his ad-
mirers and busied himself unpacking the tarpaulin bag of
supplies. Alfarez fancied himself in the role of assisting phy-

187

sician. On their last trip he had slipped the stethoscope around his neck and went about fondling the breasts of the fourteen-year-old girls until Fulgencio yelled at him. It would have meant the bloody end of both of them, since the Ayacaras had a taboo against fornicating with outsiders. It was a wise provision. The taboo had spared them the gonorrhea and syphilis so prevalent in town.

Fulgencio shoved and pushed at his people, tried to cajole or force them into a semblance of a line so that none would be skipped and all would receive their inoculations. Unfortunately for order and public health, the concept of a "line" did not exist in this aboriginal cosmos. Fulgencio could only manage to herd them in giggling packs up to the card table, where Pedro jabbed them in the arms, legs, and buttocks. They tittered at the needle's prick, perhaps because no fears had been instilled in them, or perhaps because their masculine puberty rites featured a test in which they were sewn into cotton togas with hundreds of starved wasps. A few of the boys were returning for the same injection, to demonstrate to their friends that it had not hurt. There was much that might be done for these Ayacaras and yet nothing could be done for them.

Carr spread another white sheet over the card table. Today was oral hygiene day. He prepared the first injection of Novocaine and the Ayacaras were bumping each other gaily, disputing the number one spot. The Santa Cruz National Association of Odontologists might frown on these activities, but it wasn't likely that any dentist would be coming up this tributary for some time yet.

He tapped at the jaw of his first patient, a lithe and hairless stripling who would never reach manhood. The boy opened wide, dispelling another myth of the South Seas. His mouth was a sewer. The needle entered his inflamed gums but the boy would not jerk or flinch, not while his friends were watching. Carr called for the next boy. He had to use these assembly line methods. An X-ray machine would have prob-

188

ably ordained five times as many extractions as he was permitting himself. As it was, he could delude himself into believing that he was rendering effective aid by removing the empirically putrescent.

Fulgencio was frantically chasing away all those who had already received Pedro's shots but wanted more. Carr fought a gnawing depression. There was not one single Ayacara in this hamlet who might be termed healthy. The hunters plucked their eyebrows and lashes to "sharpen their aim" for spear fishing, and many suffered from conjunctivitis. All had had their bouts with backwater fever. All of them had the bulging belly, the sign of endemic malaria—a hypertrophied spleen. A simple chest cold with those immense spleens and they were gone. The naked eye calculated that thirty among them were tubercular. X-rays would up that figure.

The teeth were easily wrenched from the putrid gums, removed much more easily than the bullet had left Emil's heart. Henry Carr cursed Rousseau for lack of anyone better to curse during the long, hot afternoon. His *Complete Works* had borne the imprint of three noble savages on the binding: a powerful warrior, his stately mate and their splendid offspring. He wished Rousseau had devoted more time to chess or peered into a few of these vile mouths before propagating his nonsense on the glories of primitive men.

By sunset he was rubbing and chaffing at his wrist. He had extracted sixty or so foul, brown teeth. On his next trip the Ayacaras could look forward to losing another hundred. Fulgencio was also ragged from running after the boys, who had snatched the infected teeth from the bucket and invented the game of tossing them in the air and catching them in their mouths.

The fires were lit for the evening meal. Gray smoke, with the agreeable aroma of cooking fish, rose into the pink dusk. The Ayacaras insisted that their visitors eat with them. Carr would have preferred avoiding the ordeal, remembering that the last dinner had cost him two days in bed. But he could

189

never insult his friends so brazenly. He joined the chief's circle and squatted on his haunches next to Fulgencio while Alfarez did business on the beach. Pedro distributed knives, bullets, mirrors and red Chinese fans to his customers and collected arrows, bead necklaces, parrots and bamboo flutes in return.

Carr detected an elementary protocol in the seating arrangements. The more important elders gathered themselves to his right and the lower echelon slipped off to his left. Fulgencio translated what little they had to say to him from Ayacara into Spanish, but they obviously did not believe in spoiling good food with conversation. They played host by pushing more and more of the boiled fish, mashed bananas, mangoes, and gourds of beer at him, beaming jovially and pointing out the choicer tidbits.

Talk did not begin until dessert. The old men sucked noisily on stalks of sugar cane and smoked rolled tobacco leaves, blew the harsh smoke in each other's faces and roared at the huge joke. Fulgencio rolled a specially selected leaf, lit it, puffed, and passed it to Carr while the old men laughed and scoffed at Pedro for not being able to produce a whistle on their flutes.

"They asked me to ask you whether you liked our food, Señor Doctor."

"Tell them for me, Don Fulgencio, that I find it very savory. But the fish is a little too piquant. Very spicy. Hot."

Fulgencio repeated something in Ayacara three times and the old men bellowed. They thought it was hilarious. Carr frowned in jest. This could hardly be called a faithful interpreter or whatever he had said had gained much in the translation. Fulgencio turned to him again. "They say that they want to give you something valuable, Señor Doctor. A gift. They say that they want to give you something that all white men want, but will never obtain from us. Only you."

"Tell them I'm very grateful, Don Fulgencio."

Fulgencio repeated that for him in Ayacara and the elders

190

nodded gravely. The supreme tribunal was concurring in a momentous decision. They mumbled and pushed a basket toward him. The stick and straw basket shook and trembled as if a bird or animal were fluttering inside.

"Take it please, Señor Doctor. It's yours. But please don't lift the lid too high or they'll jump out."

Carr peeked through the lid. There were two brilliant blue macaws in the basket. The elders gaped at him expectantly and he smiled back with all of the appreciation he could muster. Suddenly the blue macaws shrieked, startling him, and he snapped the lid down. Everyone in the circle roared at his consternation and he joined in the laughter.

"These are very valuable in Puerto Acero," Fulgencio explained when the laughing stopped. "Many years ago there were many blue macaws by the river, Señor Doctor. But now they are very rare. You can go three years without seeing macaws as beautiful as these."

"Tell them that these blue macaws will be one of my most cherished possessions, and that every time they screech I will think fondly of my good friends, the Ayacaras."

Fulgencio must have translated that well because the elders grinned broadly, revealing the gaps between their sparse teeth. Then Fulgencio embellished it as he continued on for five more minutes.

As Pedro packed their equipment for departure, Carr drew Fulgencio aside and they went behind the rocks to smoke one last leaf of raw tobacco. Fulgencio sensed that an important matter was to be discussed. He had the direct and absorbing eyes that served a superior intellect. Under other circumstances, in another age, this fullblood could have been a king, instead of helping to preside over the demise of his tiny nation. He might have been another Tupac Amaru.

"Tell me, please, Don Fulgencio. How long were you in the city?"

"I lived in Puerto Acero for three years, Señor Doctor. And then I lived in Concepción for thirteen."

"Would you tell me why you left your people? You are the only Ayacara who has ever left this village and gone to live with the whites."

The gnarled and wrinkled chief let the sand sift through his fingers. "I saw the ships float by on the Río Verde, Señor Doctor. And I wanted to go with them."

"But you came back. May I ask why you came back to this village?"

Fulgencio looked up at the sky. The pink and orange glow would soon be blotted from the horizon and they would have to light the lamp on the motorboat. "I was growing old in Concepción, Señor Doctor. And I did not want to die in the city. I saw many men die in the city and it was always bad. The ambulance would take them away and nobody cared. People made jokes and they laughed at the ambulance. That hurt me very much."

"And here? Here it would be better?"

Fulgencio smiled at the question. "Here it will be much better, Doctor. Here they will place my body on a new hammock and they will put everything that is mine inside the hut. They will put my rifle and my flutes and my clothes under me, and they will burn my hut. No one will keep anything that is mine for fear that my spirit will come back to torment them. You know what would happen in the ciry, Señor Doctor? In the building I lived in, men, the best friends, would kill each other to get my shoes or even my shirt. They would pull out knives and fight each other while my body was still warm. Here, while I burn, the women will cry and pull their hair for me. Hunters will come from other villages to cry and mourn. That is much better than dying in the city."

"No one could dispute you in that, Don Fulgencio. But may I ask you other questions? I need your help."

"I am at your disposal."

Carr pointed his thumb over his shoulder, in the general direction of the capital. "When you were in the city, when you

192

were in Concepción, did you ever go to a doctor, to a hospital?''

Fulgencio traced a small circle in the sand. "During one period. For three years I scrubbed floors in a clinic and I saw many doctors there.''

"Good. And were most of them good men? Did most of them work hard to cure the sick?''

"Most of them worked hard to cure the sick and were good men. Some of them charged too much money, but most of them were good men.''

Carr accepted the last few puffs on the rolled leaf. The sweet, shrill flutes were whistling all about them now and drums were being tapped. The Ayacaras would have music and then sleep. "Now. Suppose you met a doctor who did not work to cure? A doctor who killed? Suppose you met a doctor who put men in a refrigerator to test how long they might endure the cold before dying? What would you do to such a man?''

Fulgencio shrugged and smiled at the relative ease with which the question might be answered. "A man like that should be killed, Señor Doctor. He should be beaten to death.''

"Why, Don Fulgencio? Your people die so young, of fevers, of malaria. They have committed no crime. Why should that man endure no more pain than the innocent?''

"I do not know the answer.''

"No one knows, Fulgencio. But I want you to ponder my question. I want you to think about it and we'll talk more when I return next week.''

"I will try to think of a reply, Señor Doctor.''

A start had been made. Carr pushed himself up and brushed the sand from his trousers. "I have one more question. Do you believe that the Ayacaras are my lifelong friends? Could I rely on them to do me a great favor if I continued to come here?''

193

"We are your loyal friends, Doctor. We would do anything you asked of us."

"Good, Fulgencio. Good." They walked toward the beach and the headman pocketed the pack of cigarettes Carr placed in his hand. He patted them affectionately and said, "These are about the only things I miss."

"I'll bring you a carton next week." Carr suddenly covered his eyes with his hand; paralyzed with an intense sadness. He could see it clearly—these huts with no fires, insects swarming over bleached bones, the last of them dying with no one to gather his possessions under him and kindle the fire. He stood straight and dropped his hand before Fulgencio noticed. "Please try and ration out all the pills, as I told you, Don Fulgencio."

Pedro Alfarez had to engage in more horseplay with the children before the Ayacaras would release them. Then the young men pushed their boat through the rocky shallows and waved until they were lost from sight on the dark river. It made a lovely picture, looking back: azure smoke rising from campfires into the deeper blue of the night, the trilling of low-pitched flutes, natives gamboling on the sands. Already they would be crowding around Fulgencio to get their share of the pills. And they were doomed. Spraying the village might help to slow the downward cycle. Periodic visits by medical teams. But they were doomed. In twenty years there would be only fifty Ayacaras and in the next generation thirty, and the next fifteen. And then the Ayacaras would join in line behind the Atlantans, the Etruscans, the Siboneys and all the lost tribes of the past. He had a special affinity for the lost, the last. He would do everything he could for them while working toward his own goals.

The return trip down the Río Blanco and then up the Río Verde to Puerto Acero always seemed ten times as long as the morning journey. Pedro broke out a bottle of aguardiente and held the course with his elbow as he conducted a heated monologue on the profits from the sale of each item and gift.

Medina should pay at least twenty cruceños for the carved bone flute. They might demand two cruceños for the arrows and ten for the strings of beads. Medina was a tight man. Medina was harder to deal with than the Jews and Polacos in Concepción. But Dr. Carr must not sell the blue macaws to that rapacious Turk. A genuine blue macaw sold for five hundred dollars. The Yanquis at the mine might even offer seven hundred for the rare bird.

Pedro lifted the lid and shrieked into the basket, imitating the birds' shrill squawks; then he endeavored to teach them a few obscenities. "Mierda!" he shouted. "Coño! Verga maricón!" But the macaws were not apt students; they only screeched back at him. Pedro nudged the basket out of the way with his foot and took a long swig from his bottle. He wiped his mouth off on his sleeve. "Those birds are beautiful but they are very stupid, Dr. Enrique. If you want to train them you have to start them young."

"That's true for anything, Pedro."

Carr thought of William and Kirk in their blue sailor suits and white caps, the red anchors on their sleeves. He wondered whether Emil had instructed Klaus to snip other poems from that anthology. Possibly "Nachtgedanken"—"And since I left the homeland . . . the grave has claimed many, many a friend . . . those I loved, I count the toll, and count them with a bleeding soul . . . And count I must and as I count, my torment and their numbers mount . . . I feel their dead bodies heave upon my chest . . . Thank God! They leave."

But they do not leave. That was not a fit poem for children. It had also been written a century too early. Tonight, under this sky, he was timeless.

The diesel cranes could be heard for miles before they reached the final bend in the river and saw the lights of Puerto Acero climbing into the hills. There were two ore carriers in port, being loaded. With each scoop of ore a swirl of red dust drifted over the waters to the far shore. The floodlights on the AmCruz sheds glowed on the river as the boat puttered by the fishermen's quay and docked at the smallcraft wharf. Sailors were already staggering back from La Zona while others were just starting out for the evening. The guards and stevedores waved to Dr. Enrique and his helper, Pedro.

Carr drove Alfarez to Panama Street and dropped him off at the Club Montparnasse. Pedro still had a full night ahead of him. He would be wandering from bar to bar with his flash camera, snapping photos of the drunken seamen and their tarts. Alfarez would of course lie to the bouncers and bartenders and tell them that he had crept off this afternoon with one of the fourteen-year-old Ayacara girls.

The lights were off in Los Olivos and the screen door unlocked. Carr was amused to find himself slipping out of his shoes like any common drunk returning from a spree, closing the screen door quietly, placing his box of flutes and arrows on the table. He left the basket with the macaws in the kitchen and tiptoed back to the sleeping alcove. Soledad had kicked her sheets aside. With her hands clasped under her cheek, she looked like a child dozed off in the midst of prayers. She was much less striking and much more appealing in these moments.

Out in the dark kitchen the macaws squirmed in their basket. Soledad rolled over. Her eyes fluttered open, and then she stared directly at him.

"Enrique."

"I didn't mean to wake you."

"Is it late?"

"Not very. I had to pull a lot of teeth. And the Ayacaras insisted I stay for dinner."

She tucked the mosquito net aside and then lay back, folding her hands behind her head. "Or was it because you went into the bushes with one of their women?"

196

"That's not even funny, chula. Besides which, it would be too dangerous. The Ayacara have a strong taboo. They don't fornicate outside the family."

"Pedro Alfarez tells everybody that he has two women every time he goes there with you."

"Of course. And everybody knows that Pedro is the biggest liar in town. The Ayacaras feel very strongly about their prohibition. They'd stick a spear in any man who toyed with their women."

Soledad was awake and alert now. He extended her his cigarette, but she pushed his hand away. "You'd be crazy enough to do it anyway, Enrique. I really think you're crazy. Everyone is still talking about you. Arnstedt was dead and you brought him back to life. His heart stopped and you rubbed it and made it beat again. The old peasant women say you must be a sorcerer."

"So? I told you I didn't want him dead. Anybody can kill a man. That takes no skill whatsoever."

"Yes. Your plan is to go on and on and on and torture me and keep me here as a slave."

He stretched out next to her and blew a thick cloud of smoke into the mosquito net. "Well, I'm sure that if conditions here become too unbearable you can always get a room at the Club Lido. Or Arnstedt might even give you your old room back at the Moderno."

She pinched his wrist. "Don't be cruel, Enrique. I love you and I don't want to go back to that, and that's why I can't stand what you're doing. You don't really want him dead. You want to sit here and play with the idea like a little boy playing with his tool."

"I didn't know I was so transparent, and that you were such a profound student of human nature. Everyday you surprise me with new attainments and graces." He said that coldly. If he did not furnish scathing replies to her absurd outbursts she would ask him if he weren't feeling well.

"I just want to live a normal life, Enrique. I don't even

197

care about Arnstedt any more. He was dead and, as far as I am concerned, he's still dead. I only want us to go away, to Concepción.''

''Eventually.''

After an angry pause she said, ''Let me bring my children here.''

Carr closed his eyes. He saw Koch locking his wife out of the cellar, Tolstoy fleeing through the snow to die in peace in a train station. ''I thought you said you did not wish to bring your children to Puerto Acero because the other children would taunt them, and tease them about your career.''

''They'd soon get over it, Enrique. Their mothers would teach them to shut up. There are not too many women in this city who can point a finger at me and get away with it. Half the hags in La Colina were once in La Zona and half the women in Barrio Flores still aren't legally married. What could they say when you marry me, Enrique? And I could tell you stories about the ladies on La Loma. And their men. Especially their sons and husbands. If Jefe Mendoza ever gets difficult with you, tell him that I'll tell the whole world what his kneepads are for.''

''Soledad, please.''

''Please shit, Enrique. I'm tired of waiting for you. I want my children with me.''

''Later.''

''Later shit. Do you know what I'll do if you don't do something soon? I'll go to Arnstedt's home and I'll say, 'Arnstedt! I have something to tell you. Enrique's really a Jew. His face was changed by an operation in the war but he's really a Jew who knew you in Europe and he's planning to do something horrible to you.' ''

''That doesn't sound too wise, chula. I don't see what benefit you'd derive from that. You'd never get to Concepción that way. The only thing you'd get from that would be Arnstedt sending Ezequiel Cardenas around here to shoot me. And probably you, too.''

"I don't care any more. I'll do it anyway unless you make your move soon."

That last came without too much conviction. Soledad still seethed but the low rumblings promised no further eruptions. He reached over to press out his cigarette in the ashtray and she grabbed his arm. A small struggle ensued—she wanted the last puff and exerted all of her woman's strength to pull his wrist back as he relinquished the butt into the ashtray. Soledad snarled, but, glancing down, saw that the tussle had excited him. Without a word she abruptly threw her leg over him and, with a simple motion, submerged his member in her loins. Her breasts were heavy on his chest as she crouched over him like a panther hoarding food. She laughed. It was a cunning, alien sound, from another world, from a woman whose anger always led to this.

They moved together with the ease of lovers who are with each other often and want no surprises. He took his pleasure slowly so his hands could glide over her, from softness to firmness. His Soledad had a lovely back. His fingers could start at the tender nape, touch the strength through the firm dorsal curves, softness in her ample bottom, and coiled strength again in her hard thighs. This was surely God's wisest device, this truce where every wretch could feel like a king.

Henry Carr seemed to be in his estrus season. It was Soledad who had done this for him. After those barren years when the thought of touching a woman made him ill, he was avid for her, could not get enough of her. But he did not want these trances to deter him. His mind still fondled revenge even as they made love, even as she twisted over him and mixed her passion with technical expertise.

Soledad had accused him of being a happy man. Perhaps that was true. He had never acted with such purpose in normal times, over twenty years ago. If those could be called normal times. That misanthropic young man had become a veritable dynamo just when his energy should have begun to taper off. He dined in many homes. He was the motive force behind the construction of a municipal incinerator. He thrived and lived intensely, for he had an ambitious project. Surely that was an ambitious project: to create and administer a proper hell.

He kissed this woman who had made him a man again, and hoped that nature was not trying to buy him off so cheaply, with pleasure.

9

Jack Ritter advanced his rook and trusted that Carr would not rely on his standard strategy of trading merely to simplify structure. He had already been defeated twice and a clean sweep seemed imminent. This Carr had a truly devious mind. He always seemed to be down on pieces and then magically pulled a checkmate out of his left ear.

"I believe that's the game," Carr said.

"How so?"

"Two forced moves. I sacrifice my queen, which you must take, and then move my rook to that column, and you have no place to go."

Ritter studied the board and then glanced up. "You are a sneaky bastard, Henry."

Carr poured him more coffee. "So Dr. Slavik's adorable nurse did not yield to your importunate lunges?"

"To a degree. We wrestled all over her couch for two torrid hours and then, when I finally divested her of blouse and bra, she started whimpering and informed me that she was engaged to be married. To some intern."

"A fortunate intern to have such a faithful sweetheart. And you, as a well brought up boy, did not press the issue further.

How about my friend, Dr. Slavik? Still exuding as much brio as ever?''

"You read his letter, Henry. But he didn't sound too encouraging when we went out to dinner. He said he'd been to the U.N. and all these foundations about getting you a mobile unit, and that he'd sent in proposals to about fifty different agencies but everything was snarled in red tape. It could be years before anything came of it.''

Carr shrugged. "It's no longer quite that urgent, Jack. And I don't believe I'll be needing you to make any more trips. I'm safely established now and can order what I need from Concepción.''

They began setting up pieces for a fourth game and Ritter said, "I can't say I'm too sorry to hear that. It hasn't been that onerous. But I'm getting fed up with the *Blythe*.''

Behind the flimsy partition, Soledad twisted in bed and muttered. A pillow was smacked, sheets kicked. The two men smiled at the Chinese screen that hid the sleeping alcove.

Ritter turned back to the chessboard. "And you don't owe me anything, Doc. I'm no scavenger and it's too painful for you to go over your past. I don't ever again want to see a man looking like you did that last time.''

"Too much abnegation, Mr. Ritter. A deplorable excess of nobility. I believe in strict accounts. I used your time and services and I owe you the rest of the story. Right up to the point where you enter the picture and become a major figure.''

Ritter blinked at him. "How the hell do I become a major figure?''

Carr advanced his queen's pawn. "We'll go back to the fifteenth and bring ourselves up to this evening.''

"Not if it's going to tear you up, carpenter.''

"I've become quite serene lately," Carr said quietly. He sat back. "Wolf, on the fifteenth, if you recall, had just slapped his father, sought to prevent him from escorting his

202

grandfather to the synagogue. Five minutes later both were dead on the streets. Wolf was to learn later that it was Prague-born local extremists, our neighbors, who kicked them to death. Hitler, you see, had promised a 'decent' occupation, appointed a 'decent' protector. One Baron Von Neurath. Hitler was so kind as to present President Hacha's daughter with a box of chocolates when they went to Berlin to sign over the rest of our Republic. Wolf, of course, knew nothing about these matters at this time. His concern was to get his sisters to a safe place.''

The two blue macaws fluttered in their cage.

''We'll try the attack,'' Ritter said, moving a knight.

''Bad move. Wolf was fulminating about treachery and cowardice. The English and French had attempted to buy a shoddy peace from the bad-mannered Bismarcks with our borders and fortifications, and now Hitler sat in Hradcany Castle. Our brothers, the Slovaks, had established a Nazi puppet state. Hitler stood on our President's balcony and gazed over our fairy-tale city, our baroque architecture, our one hundred spires, Saint Vitus' Cathedral. Wolf and his sisters ran past the famous Apostle's Clock. Can you imagine what it's like to run in terror through your own city, Mr. Ritter? When the familiar no longer supports you? Nothing is ever to be familiar again. They were running toward the Mala Strana or, more exactly, a quaint side street off the Golden Lane, the home of Wolf's oldest and closest friend . . . a Dr. Emil Brenner.''

''Check, from my rook,'' Ritter said.

''That would lose you the game in six moves. Try the pawn. They had been inseparable. Competitors in school for honors, they had sewn their wild oats together and Brenner had married one of Wolf's girls, Bela. So with troops goose-stepping down the Prikope and Vaclovski Namestri, what more logical refuge for his sisters than the home of his closest friend? Too logical. He pounded frantically on Brenner's door. Even at that moment Wolf had the objectivity to view the banality of his predicament, the humiliation of pounding on a friend's door. Lights were on in the front room and the curtains drawn. Banally enough, 'Der Rosenkavalier' was on the phonograph. The girls were crying and Wolf kicked at the door. The volume was turned up inside and Wolf kicked harder, incredulous, and despising himself. Eventually, Dr. Brenner answered the door. He seemed surprised to discover Wolf and the girls out there. He apologized and explained that he had not heard the knocking because the music was so loud.''

"I gather that he wasn't too happy to see you all.''

"He was not overly happy, Mr. Ritter. Brenner told me to come in, and Bela was right behind him, drying her hands on her apron. He told her to dash upstairs and prepare a room for the girls. The Brenners exchanged a quick glance. Wolf saw the exchange. It was some prearranged signal but he did not attach sufficient importance to it. Which is not true, either. He did attach importance to it, but willed himself to ignore it. Brenner sent the girls to the kitchen and told them to help themselves to the food on the stove. Wolf blurted out what had happened. His father, his grandfather—''

"And the man told you to get out?''

Carr took Ritter's pawn. "No. Not quite. He expressed shock. Horror. This was a crime against humanity. Express promises had been made that such excesses would not take place. But then had it not been irrational of Dr. Karol to go to the synagogue on this day, on all days of the year? Had not Dr. Karol advocated the withering away of Judaism and all other faiths? He had not instructed his children in the doctrines of any religion whatsoever, and then he blindly leaps into the lion's den. Did that not border on insanity? Wolf said yes.''

"Do you still think it was, Carr?''

"I still don't know—I've never resolved that question. But I assure you, I have given many hours to considering it. I do know, however, that several minutes later there was another knock on the door, and this time Brenner responded without hesitation; this time a crisp German captain and five soldiers politely entered. Frau Brenner had gone upstairs to call the new authorities.''

Ritter stared at him, and Carr smiled. "So drearily revolting, isn't it, Mr. Ritter? The captain was a patient man. He waited while Brenner harangued Wolf. The girls were crying in the vestibule as young Dr. Brenner relieved himself: This was exactly like a Jew! To let a friendship cool as his reputation grew, and then crawl around demanding aid in a crisis. Were old friends to be remembered only in a crisis? This was precisely like a Jew, to run off to Spain to fight for the Communists and not expect political repercussions. And how many times had he begged Wolf to warn his father to stop his provocative acts? And this was exactly like a Jew, to be aloof when his reputation was burgeoning and then come sniveling around on the day of reckoning.

"Wolf listened with a pervading sense of divorcement, as though he had been expecting this tirade, as if he had heard this speech many times before—in different centuries, in different lands. In Portugal, in Russia, France. He could hardly feel much animosity toward Emil. Poor Emil was merely acting out his part. Life had assigned him a wretched role and he could not rise above himself. Wolf pitied him.

"Emil ranted until the dapper captain intervened. The captain said this was all very well, very fine, instructive, and he would like to hear more. But there were urgent matters to be attended to.''

Ritter shifted in his chair as he reached for the bottle of Cognac. "Did Wolf ever see this Bela again?"

"Briefly. She was standing at the top of the stairs as they led him out. He looked up and saw the hem of her skirt and the lace of her pink slip. Wolf and the twins were taken to a gymnasium that had been converted into a detention center, and three days later they were herded into a boxcar, destined for a concentration camp. Please don't wince so openly, Jack.''

"I wasn't wincing."

"You were wincing," Carr said without resentment. "But you have my full permission to wince. The world is sick of hearing of those concentration camps, sick of being prodded and reminded. We are irritated by the refugee, the survivor, because he perpetually reminds us of the inconceivable. He has not had the good grace to die with the rest and form part of the comfortably shocking statistic. He is alive and carries the stench of evil about with him. He has been touched by evil and the stench lingers, so we wish to avoid him. I've seen this inevitable antipathy develop toward the refugee, toward the Russians that fled the Bolsheviks, the Armenians and Greeks that fled the Turkish massacres, the Republicans fleeing Franco. At first they elicit a sympathetic reaction. One is shaken by their accounts of tortures and executions, and then the subject palls. A reaction sets in. You become bored by their incessant recapitulation of obsolete atrocities. You wish to be about your business, and this derelict has nothing else to dwell on but the daughter or brother he has lost. In self-defense you begin to notice his personal defects—a trait, a mannerism, bad breath—anything to restore him to your limited frame of reference, your safe and blood-less plane. And the dwarf in you says, let me out. Because you are engaged with today, which this man can never be. He is obsessed by murders decades old. So, if he is proud, he shuts up."

"Look. Everybody knows . . ."

Carr suppressed a smile. "Everybody knows? Everybody knows what? I felt that same antipathy when the refu-gees began to pour in from Germany in 1935. Their grief and rage were so impotent. I just wanted them to shut up and stop repeating and repeating. And we do well to repress the mem-ory of those camps. If we thought about them too much no politician could prattle about progress and the cleric would lose his Providence. The world would stop and we would all sit there and think. But don't worry, Jack. I'm not going to regale you with any atrocity stories. You see, Wolf never reached the camps. There was an accident, a train derailment, and several hundred prisoners escaped. Wolf among them. I will spare you the grand adventure story of the trek across Germany to Switzerland. The hair-raising episodes meant nothing because I felt cursed with my luck. I should have died in the accident, but instead, like some heaven-blessed zombie, I made it to safety while men much more desirous of living were tracked down in the forest by dogs. I felt cursed, protected by a cloak that shielded me from all harm while those I loved were slaughtered around me. It all became a dream. I reached France just in time for the war and served as a field doctor with a Polish unit, until the French collapsed and I was evacuated with the British at Dunkirk.''

''You just weren't supposed to get it, Doc.''

''Not at the time. Mine was coming. First I became a paragon of all virtues. During the Blitz, it must be admitted, I felt certain qualms about providing my excellent services to the British. I became a glutton for work, but there was an ambivalence in my attitude. When the ambulances poured their cargo into the operating room, I could congratulate myself and think, 'You see, Doctor Karol. You see how dedicated your son is now? He is no longer a cold snake. Everyone praises him and tells him he must rest, tells him he is running himself into the ground.' And simultaneously, I wished to ask the bodies on the tables . . . had they cheered Chamberlain? Had they approved of Munich . . . these hawkers of democracy? But my need to impress a dead father and sisters, to make some restitution, was stronger than my resentment toward the unknown bodies.

''In spite of this, I was still not a serious man. After a year or so in London, I was able to go dancing with sympathetic

English nurses, project myself as the embittered exile. I could sniff modestly when the Janes and Annes murmured in my ear that I was working too hard, should relax more, could not win the war by myself. And, after a year or two, in the late hours of the evening I was able to tell those Janes and Marys the story of a father's martyrdom, make the big confession, call upon their sympathy as a prelude to seduction."

Carr studied his distorted reflection in the Cognac goblet.

"You know, Doc. You make these appalling demands on yourself. Don't you think you had a right to some consolation after what you'd been through?"

"Thank you. A very benevolent attitude. And you're quite right. A young man needs his consolations. And he will use what he has to get it. Medals, scars, shame, or his guilt. I wallowed in my guilt and I used it. So I was relieved when history finally punished me. Victory was almost in sight, but Hitler still had his last gasp. He unleashed the V-2 rockets. I remember ducking into a shelter with my nurse, feeling not the slightest fear. I was immune, of course. I had been inoculated against all further disasters. I wore a protective mantle because my future was all laid out for me. The rockets were falling but I was impervious. I was destined to ride into Prague with pretty girls throwing flowers at our tank. I was going to find the Brenners and shoot them both. And I was going to build a memorial to my father on the banks of the Moldau. And wallow in my survivor's guilt for the rest of my life. So nothing could touch me, naturally.

"A child, a girl, was crying in the bomb shelter, and my nurse and I went over to reassure her. She had run from her house with a music box that played Brahms' 'Lullaby.' I was winding it up for her when we had a direct hit. The explosion blew several of the gears and springs into my chest and face."

"It sounds very much as though you had more than your ration, Dr. Carr."

"It came as a relief, to be shattered that way. I had finally paid the price. Can you understand, Jack, that it is a relief to be smashed and have no further responsibilities? The English exceeded themselves with the mess extracted from the rubble. I was approached as a group project. Surgeons vied for the opportunity to participate and keep this thing alive. Some three years and thirty-five operations later, I was released, with this improved face and a more or less functioning body, though enough parts were removed to stock a pathology laboratory."

Ritter nodded. "That's about what I thought when I first saw you, Henry. I took you for a man who'd been through a cement mixer and then taken up weight-lifting for therapy."

"A very apt description. Though actually I never did lift weights. I built my body back up by pushing at the walls of my cell. You see, when I was released from the English rest home and returned to Czechoslovakia, in forty-eight, I arrived just in time for the coup. Masaryk, our voice over the BBC during the war, had just been defenestrated—thrown out of the window of the Czernin Palace. And I was an unwelcome stranger in my own country. I wandered around the streets of Prague, staring at the reflection of my unfamiliar face in shop windows, passing my old home, a clubhouse for the Communist Youth League, and after about a week as a tourist in my native city, I was picked up at the Hotel Esplanade and taken to the Pankrac prison. The new regime believed that I had sojourned too long in the West, and that I had returned as an agent."

"But they finally released you. Otherwise, you wouldn't be here."

"They released me almost four years later, my friend. And at the intercession of a Russian. He had come to Pankrac to assist in the interrogation of another prisoner and he remembered me from a field hospital in Spain. He was now a general and recalled with gratitude that I had saved both his legs at

Teruel. One week later I was released from Pankrac and told to leave the country, to go somewhere and make a new life for myself. In Tasmania or somewhere.''

"And here you are," Ritter said.

"More or less." Carr moved, sacrificing a knight for a pawn. "More or less. Because an American messboy wanted to philosophize about the meaning of life with an English carpenter."

"That still doesn't explain why you picked this shithole to sign off the *Blythe*. Or why you slugged me when we came out of the Club Moderno."

Carr chuckled sardonically and said, "I slugged you, Mr. Ritter, because you are a bird of ill omen. You forced my hand. For years I had been searching for my old friends, the Brenners. I was in contact with Israeli organizations and several offices based in Vienna. I had been all over our wonderful world, following leads they gave me, and had information that the people I was searching for might be here in Puerto Acero. No one else was interested in the Brenners. Betraying old friends is not classified a war crime."

"Hold it up a second, Henry. When I met you, you weren't searching for anybody. You were holed up on the *Blythe,* and not getting off that ship at all."

"That's quite true. I was afraid. I was afraid to check out the lead. Because I was afraid of what I'd do when I found them. Every time the *Blythe* docked here, I was in an agony of vacillation. And then you barged into my cabin with all of your lah-dee-dah about the Club Moderno and the Danubio Azul. That was it. As the saying goes, I had to either shit or get off the pot."

Ritter closed his eyes. "And the proprietor of the Club Moderno is your Mister Brenner."

"Yes."

Ritter nodded. "But that still doesn't make sense. I was at the Club Moderno this afternoon and Lupe told me how you had saved her boss's life."

210

"Naturally. I don't want him dead yet."

It took a moment for all the implications to sink in. Finally Ritter murmured, "Good Lord . . . me and my big mouth."

"Don't go taking on any gratuitous guilt feelings, Mr. Ritter. You were an unwitting lever, a lever to get me off my duff."

"From what you've told me, the man deserves anything he might get, but I can't figure out why you haven't done it."

"I'll write you when, how and why it happens, Jack. That much I owe you. Right now I'm beginning to feel too much like Scheherazade, so we'll talk about something else."

They finished the game of chess, with Carr winning, and began another. Ritter had already said goodbye to Lupe that afternoon, told her he would not be returning to Puerto Acero. Lupe had spoiled their parting in the end by asking him for a twenty-dollar "loan." She needed it for a new pair of shoes. He gave her the money and wished she had not reverted to whoredom at the very last. Apparently nothing was allowed to be too perfect in this life. Jack Ritter sighed at his minor league sorrows.

It was past two in the morning and Carr was just shaking Ritter's hand and wishing him luck in getting a ship to Europe when there was a knock on the cottage door. The doctor stiffened. A caller at Los Olivos at this late hour might mean many things, most of them unpleasant. Outside might be a campesino to explain that his wife's pains were coming regularly now, or a dishwasher from La Zona with the news of a sailor with a knife in his guts, or a waif from La Colina to whisper that grandfather was spitting blood on the pillow again.

Carr opened the front door and was taken aback by the grinning apparition on his porch. The filthy scarecrow under the light was shirtless and otherwise covered by torn khaki trousers, a mud-splattered jacket, and on his feet toeless

211

boots. He was clutching a duffel bag. Straw and dust clung to his matted beard. Ritter was the first to recognize the grinning skeleton.

"Piño!"

"Coño!" the Gallego roared. "Enrique! You didn't even recognize me!"

Cackling, he dropped his bag through the front door and wrapped his arms around Carr's back, pounded him in a fierce abrazo. Then Ritter received an abrazo, but before anyone could speak Piño shouted, "Hold it, Enrique. Don't say a word. I have a joke and if you say one word, I'll forget it. It's a great joke about doctors. It seems that this buxom, good-looking mother takes her skinny son for an examination, and the doctor checks the boy over and says, 'Madam, your boy has rheumatic fever, tuberculosis, ulcers, a hernia, two cancers, diabetes, and dandruff. Madam, would you please take your clothes off and spread yourself out on my sofa?' And she says, 'But, doctor, it's my son who's the sick one.' And he says, 'I know. But instead of repairing that piece of shit, I'd rather give you an entirely new model.' "

Piño was glowering at them expectantly. They both shook their heads and Carr said, "You look terrible, hombre. What have you done to yourself?"

"Sit down before you fall down," Ritter told the wild-eyed Gallego. "I've never seen anybody in as bad a shape as you are."

The Gallego did not have to be asked twice. He brushed Ritter aside, threw his leg over a chair at the dinner table, and sat down firmly. Carr nodded his assent and the Gallego, grinning dementedly, grabbed a bowl of cold arroz con pollo and yanked out a plump chicken leg. His teeth sank into the meat and they sat down flanking him. Carr filled a wine glass as Piño's teeth worked like a hungry shark's cutting their way through fat tuna. He stuffed a chunk of white bread in with the chicken and mumbled "Caballeros!" with his mouth filled and his cheeks puffed. "What a magnificent time. Passion! Mnngh!'' He blew a kiss at the ceiling. "Fire. Mnngh!'' He blew another kiss. "Love!'' A third kiss. "A hot little criolla in a cozy shack. Caballeros! Just caressing Rosalia produced a second-degree burn on the palm. The only problem was, my ass itched all the time I was out there. The next time I go into the jungle I'll be sure and take along a case of toilet paper.''

"Did you just get in?'' Ritter asked.

Piño shoveled the yellow rice into his mouth with the wooden serving spoon. "No, hombre! I've been walking for days. My paradise ended with a loud fart. Six long days ago I was sleeping in the morning and all of a sudden I see this big Indian in the doorway, holding this transistor radio and these dolls, and these bundles, and he says, 'Who are you?' And I say to him, 'Who are you?' And he says, 'This is my hut. These are my children. That's my woman!' ''

Piño shoved another huge mouthful of rice into the lump he was already chewing and wiped his cheek off with his wrist. He smiled brightly. "So this Indian, he goes for his knife, and I went for the machete on the wall while Rosalia screamed and all the children shouted and ducked in the corner. Then we manuevered and circled, until I was at the door. I stepped outside and he didn't come after me. He was too busy beating Rosalia.''

"You're lucky they didn't kill you,'' Ritter said.

"Oh, the Indians are more reasonable than we are, F.B.I. I spoke with the man that afternoon and he told me how he had been working in San Martín, holding down two jobs to save money, and I told him how Rosalia had sworn she was abandoned. The other men from the village were there and they told me to get out; they would not kill me.''

Carr shook his head sadly at the emaciated, shivering Spaniard. "You'd better let me look you over after you've finishing eating, Rodolfo. From the light in your eyes I'd say you've brought in twenty bugs and fevers with you.''

"It feels like fifty, Enrique. I have a temperature of three

213

hundred and eighteen degrees. And today the *Blythe* sailed by and I waved and I waved, but nobody saw me in the bushes. And I said to myself, 'Coño! I must get to Puerto Acero and see whether my great friend, F.B.I., is still aboard. And see what happened to my great compañero, Enrique Carr. Then these fishermen picked me up and brought me to the docks. I went to Panama Street and I asked these bums in a bar if any of them had ever heard of an English sailor called Henry Carr. And everybody looks at me as if I'm crazy and they say, 'Who has not heard of Dr. Carr, you idiot? Dr. Enrique is the great surgeon. Everybody knows he lives in Los Olivos!' Coño, Enrique. A doctor! You're famous. And then this man grabs me. The owner of the club. And he starts asking me about you—what I knew about you. And I told him that you were the best man on our ship and how I convinced you to return to the land and take up medicine again. And then these bums tell me you're living with Soledad. Soledad! Hoo hoo hoo! How do you like that, F.B.I.? Enrique, you sly devil, you. It's these quiet ones you have to watch out for. Who would have thought it? Enrique and Soledad.''

Ritter turned. Soledad had pushed the curtain aside. Her hair was in pigtails, a lumpy robe covering her white chemise. She glared at them.

''Who is making all the noise out here?''

The obvious culprit stood up. Piño held out his arms to her. ''Soledad! Just as lovely as ever. Even more lovely now that Enrique is reforming you. If you didn't belong to Enrique, I'd throw myself at your feet.''

Soledad looked fixedly at Carr. ''Who is this filthy clown?''

''Be nice to him.'' Carr said. ''Piño's an old shipmate of mine.''

''Soledá, Soledá,'' the Gallego pouted. ''You don't remember me?''

''Should I?''

214

"Of course, Soledá. I went to the Club Moderno all the time. Just to see you. But you were always busy."

She pulled the folds of her robe closer together so he would stop gaping at her chemise. "You and twenty thousand other sea rats, hombre."

"Yes! But I'm something special. Everybody always remembers me wherever I go. Don't they, F.B.I.? And I'm one of your best friends, Soledá. It was I who reminded your husband, Enrique, that he was a doctor. Right, Enrique? Right? You remember that night we went to the Club Moderno together? When we were walking? It was I who reminded you. You took my advice and decided to get off the ships. Right, Enrique?"

Carr nodded. Piño sat down and finished off some flan. Only salad remained on the table. He knocked the chess pieces over as he reached for the bowl of lettuce and was too busy munching to notice the three glancing at one another.

Piño stuffed the lettuce into his mouth with his fingers. He grinned up at them. "And tonight Enrique's going to let me sleep on the floor, and tomorrow I'll look for a job. I could probably get back on the *Blythe,* but why? I've seen enough of the ocean. I think I'll try to get a job as bartender in La Zona. I can mix great cocktails. Things you never even heard of. Maybe at the Club Moderno. Then, Soledad, I can try to save your girl friend Aurora. Do you think you could introduce me to her formally? I mean, I've slept with Aurora but I've never met her socially. She's too nice a girl to continue at that trade. There are going to be a lot of changes made now that I'm back in town."

The Gallego returned to his attack on the chicken remnants, sucking noisily on the bones, and then, in the sudden silence, a puzzled expression creased his face as he saw the way they were staring at him.

10

Florencio Negrón was brooding on the high wooden steps of the Nuevo Amanecer. His cuarto was out of tune, but he didn't feel like tuning it. He grumbled in his darkness, and the wood felt dead in his hands. Why bother? Nobody came to the pulpería these nights to listen to a blind troubadour. They came to the pulpería for the yah yah records on the jukebox or they turned on the popular station from Concepción. Boogiewoogie, swing, rock, desperation, consolation, miss, kiss, eyes, pura mierda, pure shit. He was Florencio Negrón, singer of ballads, and in the better days, thirty or forty years ago, the hunters and traders had stamped their feet while he recited and then loaded his straw hat with solid silver coins. Now the stupid snotnoses came in for the screeching.

Morales had helped bury the traditional "romances." Dictator Morales had decreed that all Cruceño stations must feature at least fifty percent nationally inspired compositions, and for all those years the people had suffered from those artificially composed "folk songs" that had the rhythm but nothing of the soul. Since the downfall of Morales no one would listen to the real verses and the powerful ballads from the days of the Castilians.

216

It was too late for Florencio Negrón. There was that one chance, so many years ago, when the professors came with the recording machine and made him sing for three straight hours, sing every song, every snatch, every ballad he knew. "Florencio!" they exclaimed. "You are a national treasure, a living monument! Your mind is a sacred urn holding the patrimony of the Cruceño race. We will play this on the National Radio Hour and you will become a famous man. Scholars will come from great universities to study your ballads as historical documents. Record companies will pay large advances for the exclusive rights to your songs. Agents will wish to sign you for contracts for the night clubs of New York, Río, Paris, where you will interpret our ethnic lore."

He waited. Five months he waited. Six months. Seven months. Everyone in Puerto Acero knew about it and talked. Florencio Negrón, the shoeless guitarist from the Nuevo Amanecer, was destined to be a famous entertainer. Then the letter came from the Institute of Folklore. Padre Garibay read it for him: "We again wish to thank you for your invaluable cooperation. Your contribution has been deposited in the National Archives of the Central University Library, and registered under your name. Unfortunately, the commercial application is extremely limited."

Nothing else. He became the clown of Puerto Acero. The parasites from La Zona and the loafers from the benches in Plaza Paez called to him, "Hey, blind one! When are you leaving for Paris, blind one? When does your ship leave for New York, Caruso? When does your big check arrive, star? Didn't they send you money for shoes yet?"

They were again featuring the old songs on the "Hour of the People" program, but it was a terrible farce. He had never heard a real singer use only one ball, or sing those made-up lyrics and use an electrical guitar, sometimes even a piano!

They had no respect for traditions. There were forms that should never be touched. The ballad must be sung with one

217

cuatro, with a steady strum, in a strong natural voice, and none of this fancy, tricky shit. Dr. Enrique had sung the ballads one night. That had been a great night. They clapped and stamped their feet on the wooden boards and he smacked the cuatro as Dr. Enrique sang. Dr. Enrique said he had learned "Branca Fro" at Gibraltar and he knew verses even older than the verses of Santa Cruz, verses from the days before Colón discovered America. It gave old Florencio a chill to hear a stranger sing their songs with those ancient words, words from the days of *El Cid* and *Rolando* and the *Seven Brothers of Lara*. From the days of the Moors. Dr. Enrique taught him those older verses and had the deep tones of a gypsy as they sang together that night.

The worm-ridden beams had almost collapsed from the tumult and applause. Dr. Enrique promised he would return and sing again those verses, older and stronger than the verses of Santa Cruz. They would again enjoy great nights, like those foot-stomping, hand-clapping nights from long ago.

Bela Arnstedt, in the twin bed next to her husband's, dreamed of slipping across the room and placing a pillow over Emil's face. She could not wait until Thursday afternoon, when Enrique would visit her at the Danubio Azul.

Jefe Civil Virgilio Mendoza, in his palatial villa on La Loma, was brushing his teeth. He decided that his gold teeth would have to go, be replaced by a natural-color inlay. If he were destined to serve in grander arenas, destined to be elected to the Chamber of Deputies, it was imperative to arrive in Concepción with a modern, confident smile. Gold teeth were too rustic, too reminiscent of the provinces, and Remberto Davila said that gold teeth produced a glare on the television screen.

A chat with the Englishman was in order. Dr. Carr seemed to be doing quite well for himself these days. He would explain to Carr that administrative costs had devoured the major part of their original bond over this year and another five hundred dollars might be required—to shore up the bond—in case of an emergency.

At the Club Moderno Jerry Anderson slouched in the rear booth and signaled for another Scotch. He eyed Lupe and wondered whether he should take her back to the rooms. His old lady was going to accuse him anyway of arriving late because he'd knocked off a piece. He was too old for this country. This fucking country was O.K. for a guy in his twenties or thirties but a drag for an old married man. Next month he would lay it on the line to Russ Bennet. He would corner him and say, "Mister Bennet, sir. I don't wish to complain. Far from it—AmCruz has been damn good to me. But I figure I've been out here in the boondocks long enough. There have to be a lot of bright young boys with the company that'd give their left nut for my spot out here and I figure that with my intimate knowledge of field operations, I could be a pretty useful man at the home office in Houston. And I don't want to drag in my personal problems, sir, but my old lady has been giving me a tin ear about getting out of here. She says she wants the kids going to school up in the States, and doesn't want them growing up talking no Texmex."

Rodolfo Piñedo served Anderson his drink and returned to his position behind the cash register. The Gallego straightened his bow tie and composed himself. He knew it was his turn to rinse the beer glasses but he decided to let the other barmen and waiters perform that chore. It was more on their level.

For a Tuesday night it was slow. He had never imagined tending bar in a brothel could be so boring. All work was boring. Even dangerous work. Painting bridges and helping

219

the dynamite engineers had both been boring jobs. One day somebody falls or gets crushed by a boulder and for two days everybody jabbers about it and takes safety measures and then it goes back to the same old routine.

Ezequiel Cardenas, the bouncer, was glaring at him and Rodolfo Piñedo sniffed at his new enemy. He knew he was resented. The other employees envied him because he had his job through the intercessions of Dr. Enrique Carr; and Señor Arnstedt, the proprietor, treated him like a privileged character. Spiteful gnats. They could all kiss his ass. It was crap all over, from the B-girls in Antwerp to a slut like Rosalia, out in the jungle, who could shack up with him while her husband was away, holding down two jobs in San Martín. Crap all over.

Once in a very great while he saw something that was not crap. Usually, when the surface was scratched, out oozed the worms. It was discovered that the hero went home and put on silk panties, or that the priest was fondling himself behind the screen. But what Enrique was doing was beautiful. And Rodolfo Piñedo could take credit for that. It was all right for a useless bum like Piño to chip rust on a forgotten ship because nobody cared what a clown did. But a man of science, a man with a great gift, had an obligation to the world.

Puerto Acero should be grateful to him for guiding Enrique back to his duties, but instead these dregs—Cardenas and all these perverts on Panama Street—hated him. They were jealous because he was occasionally invited to Los Olivos for supper and because, when Enrique needed the cottage painted or the roof fixed, he called upon Piño. But mostly because of Soledad. When Soledad went shopping, it was Piño she asked along to carry packages. It was sweet to desire Soledad in this manner, to desire her ferociously and yet never try to touch because she belonged to his great friend. There was something beautiful between them. Soledad knew that he wanted her and knew he would never touch her. Maybe he could ask her to talk to Aurora. Soledad could at least intercede for him.

Henry Carr was sweltering on damp sheets and listening to the fluttering of his blue macaws. It was impossible to sleep. He was vacillating between irritation and boredom while Emil recuperated so slowly. It was easy to see why the youngbloods like Gomez and Lopez and Lobos were determined to get out, were already packing up to take the plane when their terms expired in March. If it were not for AmCruz and the Indians he would be hard put to buy razor blades, let alone acquire costly facilities. The poor paid him with prestige. He could not stroll down Avenida Reforma without being dragged into a pulpería for a cup of chica. Room was immediately made for Dr. Enrique and his Soledad. Obviously, there was a cosmic plot to buy him off, appease him. For months he had been led by the nose down the path of righteousness for His Name's sake. The woeful poor. The scrawny chickens they gave him for helping ease another soul into this world could not begin to pay for the Ergotrates and Demerol he left in their shacks.

There were ironic barbs in his plight, if he chose to notice them. Wolf Karol was doing exactly what he swore he would never do—patching up the miserable. It left him with nothing, only the stench of hovels in his nostrils. A child was born and seven slept next to that child, dirty bodies bartering their diseases. He did what he could but there was no need for so much of this. The misery might be alleviated and they would not be lined up at his door with their worms, lice, scabies, chancres, rotten intestinal tracts. Yet if they were not there, if they were all magically and suddenly transformed into prosperous burghers, with stout wives and robust children, autos, bonds, and fraternal clubs, proudly proclaiming their ideals and principles, what would happen if he, in need, appeared at their doors? They only inspired pity because they had no doors to knock on.

Some days he simply forgot why he was here in Puerto Acero. He went to the Arnstedts for dinner and, instead of being concerned that Emil should discover his true identity, he had the much more mundane fear of the husband learning about his affair. They had lost count in their chess series and now played for the mere pleasure, without the tension of competition.

It was Emil who insisted on shocking him back to reality. Emil reading passages from his grand opus on Germany and the Jewish Question. Emil mentioning the camps again, and finally confessing that, after being wounded on the Russian front, he had been sent back for rear line duty and duty at Belsen. It was Emil who exhumed Wolf Karol from his grave. The week before he had felt his heart clutch as Emil turned to him on the patio and said, "It's uncanny."

"What's uncanny?"

"The resemblance you bear to an old friend of mine. Sometimes I turn around and I could swear that you are he, sitting there. Other times you don't resemble him at all. Bela's often made the same comment. She says you often remind her of Wolf."

"Wolf?"

"Wolf Karol. I've mentioned him to you before. My comrade of university days."

"Yes. I remember you quoting some of his theories."

"It's so strange. I've only had two friends in my entire life and you're both so much alike."

"That's not so strange. We think we change over the years but we actually don't. You're attracted to the same type of person."

"But you have none of his arrogance, Henry. Wolf was a renegade Jew. And if one considers the Jew to be arrogant, then their intellectual renegades, their apostates, can be supercilious beyond bearing. In that sense they resemble ex-Communists."

"I've never thought of it that way, but now that you've pointed it out it seems a fair analogy."

"You remind me of him, Henry, but purged of his cruelty. He utilized his virtues to inflict pain. How can I explain it? I was an excitable young man and I basked in his calmness. He

222

possessed this quality, a skepticism that spared him all my agonies. I'd attempt to goad him into arguments about the existence of God, or I'd attack the Church, or the Marxist menace, and he would shrug me off in a manner that was too disarming even to be condescending, as if he were born a thousand years old, with all of such questions resolved in his mind. Once I tried to please him. I spent days organizing my thoughts. And than I gave him my thesis on anti-Semitism: that it sprang from the rebellion of the hairy, anal, sensual white race against the strictures and hideous demands of the Jewish heresy—the Christian faith. I was sure that he would appreciate this but he merely shrugged, as if this had been considered ages ago, and dismissed as inadequate.''

"I'd agree that your friend sounds like a bastard, Emil."

"But it was never blatant. He used his correctness like another man uses a lash. And what I could not abide in him was that grace, that posture, that pose of eternity."

"Are you sure the man had all this, Emil? We're prone to build up our old friends in our minds. Give them too much. Especially after many years have gone by."

Arnstedt's voice came as if from beyond a thick wall, from a sealed chamber.

"I took a terrible vengeance on the man, Henry. Someday I'll tell you about that. My side of it. I've spent many years thinking about him and I've often wondered how much of what I did was caused by his influence. You can't really escape the major influences over your life, and he helped to shape and form me as much as my own parents did. And I had to cast him out. I apologize for nothing. When one extirpates a cancer considerable benign flesh may be cut away; and though the man I am today would not do what I did then, I will not beat my breast and beg forgiveness from anyone. I contemplate the misery that the Jew has brought upon this world and I shudder, Henry. The renegade Jew has been the architect of our despair. The Western world now struggles to escape the thralls of three erroneous interpretations, three dis-

223

torted visions of man, all thrust upon us by Jewish apostates—the Christian, the Marxist, the Freudian. I categorically reject all three. Man is . . ."

Henry Carr tossed in his bed. Emil's strident voice fading in his mind. 'Man is.' Who was Emil to pontificate in those terms? Man is a sleepy creature, too limited and trivial for his power. The sweep of his history is hardly worth the package in a baby's diapers.

Carr slept. It was a brittle trance, a cancellation of the time he loathed and feared. Soledad was by his side and yet far away. He was frozen in a ferrous cast, limbs stiff, a body that would not leave a true imprint on the sand.

Four guerrilleros galloped down the margin of the AmCruz railroad tracks leading a fifth, riderless horse. Along the route they were seen by the brakeman and switchman at La Corona Real depot. But as these railroad men were all traditionally radical-socialists—which in Santa Cruz meant to the left of the stodgy Communist Party—none was about to telegraph ahead to Internal Security Headquarters to report that saboteurs were in the vicinity, probably to dynamite the railway bridge.

They dealt their hands of poker and treinta-uno and fought the night's heat with pitchers of beer from an iced keg. Their shouts became louder and the laughter more hysterical as each demonstrated to his compañeros that he could not care less. The more pensive waited apprehensively for the reverberations of a blast down the tracks, and others thought about the sermon Padre Garibay might deliver on Sunday. They did not want this. Damage to the railway would mean a disruption in their lives, problems, changes. And yet they were ashamed, or afraid, to stand up in front of their compañeros and argue in favor of calling company headquarters or the police.

The guerrilleros reached La Colina shortly after two. It

was Pedro Alfarez who spotted them leading their horses under the railway trestle. Alfarez could not even think of calling the police. There was not one single telephone on La Colina, not a telephone in the entire huge sprawl of shacks and cardboard huts. Pedro returned to his shack and whispered to his oldest son to run down to Plaza Paez and inform the security forces that a band of infiltrators was heading in the direction of Los Olivos. Then he retrieved his own pearl-handled thirty-eight from under his pillow, told his woman to shut up, and went from shack to shack, recruiting all the neighbors with weapons. Practically every hut in La Colina had its shotgun or revolver. The roof might leak but every home on this hill had its television set and firearm.

Carr was awakened by the snorting of his blue macaws. They protested as the screen door screeched open and the arc of a flashlight curved across the room. The curtain shielding the bed was thrust aside. Soledad would have screamed but the burliest of the three intruders raised his rifle and she buried her face against Carr's chest. The youngest, their apparent leader, pushed his subordinate's rifle away. Imperfect teeth flashed, the smile of a nervous boy covering his inexperience with theatrics.

"Good evening. You are Dr. Carr, I believe, sir."

Carr rubbed at his eyes. This was too ridiculous.

"It's past my office hours, young man."

"We're sorry to have disturbed you at this hour, sir, but our movements are necessarily clandestine."

"They're the guerrilleros," Soledad whispered. The three revolutionaries could not take their eyes off the curve of her hip under the white bedsheet.

"Thank you for not calling us bandits," the boy said with an impudent click of the heels. "The reactionary press chooses to refer to us as such. Dr. Carr, I am Captain Londoño of the Revolutionary United Front of Workers, Peasants and

225

Intellectuals. My comrades are Sergeant Torres and Sergeant Tovar. Outside, we have Sergeant Monroy standing guard.''

''Mucho gusto,'' Carr heard himself answering with the same assinine jocularity. His mind continued to insist that this was preposterous, but the rifles lowered at him were quite substantial.

''We have been ordered by our colonel to escort you to our encampment in the hills, where your talents may serve the progressive forces of the nation. We will give you five minutes to pack your personal belongings and instruments. Your woman may accompany you, if you so desire. My men will turn their backs as she dresses.''

''Very kind of you.''

Carr threw the sheet aside and stepped out of bed. Sergeant Torres covered him with his M-1. Their horses were hitched to the porch rail but none of his neighbors would be disturbed by their scuffling. If they bothered to peer through their windows they would believe Dr. Enrique was being carried off to another emergency in the countryside.

''It would be a great boon to our movement,'' Captain Londoño said, ''if a man of your stature and reputation were to join us voluntarily, Doctor.''

Carr lit up a cigarette. ''Some other time, young man. Meanwhile, you have my permission to use my name on your letterheads.''

''Why all this bullshit?'' Sergeant Tovar snarled. ''Padilla told us to bring him in, not waltz with him.''

''Right. Tell him to move his ass or we'll move it for him.''

Carr applied another match to his cigarette and in the dim light studied his captors. They wore makeshift uniforms: blue denim trousers, red shirts, cartridge belts, black berets. This seemed to be the usual trio composed to conduct revolution—one self-styled intellectual and two apes.

''I'm very sorry, Doctor,'' Captain Londoño said apologetically, ''but you're coming with us, voluntarily or not.''

226

"Return in a few months, gentlemen. We'll discuss the matter then."

"Enrique!" Soledad pleaded. "Don't answer them that way. They're not playing. They'll kill you."

Captain Londoño winced and brought his fingers to his lips, imploring her to lower her voice. He turned to Carr.

"Doctor, we salute you for the humanitarian spirit which impels you to dedicate yourself to the oppressed masses of Puerto Acero, but you are politically naïve. Your individual efforts are little more than bourgeois romanticism. Santa Cruz needs basic reforms—the eradication of our feudal autocracy and the creation of an entirely new structure. With your admirable efforts to alleviate the misery of the workers, you are merely shoring up the corrupt regime with palliatives and actually delaying the day of reckoning."

"Muchacho," Carr said slowly. "If you are compelled to make a speech at three in the morning, why don't you stand on a bench in Plaza Paez and not requisition my bedroom for that purpose?"

"Surely you're not with the Mendozas?" Captain Londoño said vehemently.

"Of course I am. I love him. He's a stupid, incompetent man and my life would be much grimmer with you at his desk. Now get your stupid asses out of here and leave me in peace."

Soledad tugged at his arm and begged, "Enrique, stop it. Don't talk to them like that."

Sergeant Tovar raised his weapon. "I'll cut both you imbeciles down if you don't lower your goddam voices."

There was an abrupt flurry out on the porch. The horses bucked and tugged at the rail, sending a tremor through the entire cottage, and then there were frantic footsteps and a shrill yell from the sentry outside. "We're surrounded! The damn place is surrounded!"

Carr pushed Soledad to the floor and dove toward the heavy kitchen cupboard. As he rolled over, Sergeant Tovar pumped a round directly into his stomach. It was like being slammed by a battering ram, the pain exploding through his body. With clouding eyes, suddenly widened with horror, he watched Sergeant Tovar drive his rifle butt down on Soledad's face and kick her in the spine.

Bullets were tearing through the cottage, ricocheting off the stone fireplace, and Carr writhed at the electric claw tearing through his entrails. The sounds grew dimmer, indistinguishable, the bark of automatic weapons, horses screaming in agony, glass shattering, and then an explosion shook the house, plaster raining down on his face, bursts and licks of flames near him, and the pain eased as darkness blotted out his mind.

Part Three

11

Jefe Civil Mendoza flipped the sheet over and temporarily lost his place. After a second of nervous searching he recovered his composure and resumed his speech:

"The savage beasts peer through the jungle thickets as our noble and industrious workers extract the rich veins of red ore from the dangerous bowels of our eternal mountains. They erect soaring smokestacks over the modern factories which furnish the expanding families of Puerto Acero with the appliances and material comforts required by a spiritually oriented, religious, stable and cultured society."

Two factors were working against Mendoza. His unctious voice, which grated on the common ear, and the south wind that swept across the turf of the athletic field and whipped swirls of dust over the crowd assembled in Yankee Stadium. They had come to pay homage to Dr. Enrique Carr and celebrate the arrival of the mobile operating unit.

Jerry Anderson squirmed with impatience. Anderson, representing the AmCruz Corporation, had presented the trailer with little more than a five-minute speech in a broadly accented, grammatically atrocious Oklahoman Spanish and then sat there perplexed while Padre Mateo Garibay followed with a twenty-minute mellifluous paean to the benefits of interhemispheric cooperation before conceding the microphone to Mendoza, who had now been ranting for half an hour on the future of Santa Cruz, the beauty of its women, its rapid progress under his party and the perils of neo-colonialism. An occasional reference was made to the reason for this gathering—the white trailer. Otherwise Anderson was wondering how this had become so complicated. AmCruz was donating the operating room directly to Dr. Henry Carr, but the Church, the government and every damn charitable, social, musical, and business organization in town had horned in on the party.

Jefe Mendoza took a sip of water with great deliberation.

"Our dear Dr. Enrique is from England, which we once called Perfidious Albion, and which once sought to conquer us, but whose martial expedition we drove from our shores in the glorious Battle of the Port in 1805, but with whom we now maintain amicable relations. The AmCruz Corporation is one of these ubiquitous American 'Trusts' which under the judicious legislation of our Foreign Investments Act and the close scrutiny of our Ministry of Development, has finally begun to act almost correctly within our national boundaries . . ."

The other sufferers on the platform exchanged glances, counseling patience. Soledad took Carr's hand and Bela and Emil smiled at him wanly, conveying that they too were wearying of Mendoza's prolixity but that these were the lands of lavish orations and nothing might be done about it. Afterward would come the parade. Carr was to sit in Anderson's convertible, preceding the white trailer, and all would march to the blessing at the Cathedral. This ceremony gave the people a chance to turn out, wear their uniforms, tramp down the Avenida Reforma to music. There were many uniforms in the crowd: olive drab, khaki, green, and navy blue of the Army, Navy, Air Force, Marines, Coast Guard, and Police of Santa Cruz, boyscout and girlscout outfits, and the volunteer firemen's band had devised its own gaudy trappings

232

of electric blue jackets with silver buttons and white crossed belts with glistening hussar's helmets.

Carr gazed up at the pauper's cemetery overlooking the athletic field. It seemed so long ago that an English carpenter had sat on that stone wall and courted Soledad as the mourners shrieked and tore their cheeks over Alma's grave. Now poor Pedro Alfarez was up there too, behind the stone fence, one of three from La Colina who had died in the shootout with the guerrilleros. Alfarez would have thrived on this ceremony, probably set up a souvenir stand by the main entrance to sell photos of his associate, Dr. Carr.

Soledad saw where he was looking, sensed his thoughts and squeezed his hand. It had taken courage for her to come to this ceremony today. Her scar was almost healed but she had insisted on combing her hair, endearingly, in the sultry Veronica Lake style that covered half her face. It took him back to the nurses he had dated in England. But she should flaunt that scar instead of hiding it, he thought. The scar was her ticket to respectability. The good women forgave her now, erased her past, imagined that she was no longer beguiling when, in reality, she was much more of a menace with that slash on her cheek. Marred, imperfect, she penetrated deeper into a man's mind.

There were still people waving to him from the stands, trying to gain his attention. During his recovery they had smothered him with gifts and affection. These simple people had touched him more than he cared to admit. The silly women of the Ateneo Ladies Club had taken charge, sending over their maids to give them both round-the-clock service. The workmen, the carpenters and plasterers, had repaired the cottage gratis and wanted to discuss the construction details, suggest fifty possibilities as to design and colors. He could not tell them his surroundings meant nothing, that he could not care less about such things. The campesinos had arrived in an endless procession with baskets of fruit, homemade pastries, and roasted chickens, and it had been Piño who administered all those offerings. Piño had been there every day, as tender as a woman, so he could not tell the dense Gallego that his incessant chatter was irritating beyond all endurance. They all needed their myths. The idea was firmly ingrained among the destitute of La Colina—Dr. Enrique had almost let himself be beaten to death rather than be taken away from his people.

Remberto Davila, with his editorial knack for synopsis, had summed up the situation. Davila, slightly drunk, had sat on a stool by his hospital bed, finishing off a bottle of Scotch sent over by Mustafa Medina, of all people.

"Now you are lovable and available," he said. "Before you were too distant and perfect for us. You did too much for everybody and allowed us nothing. Now we can appreciate you because you're helpless and in pain. Everybody takes pride in their response to your helplessness. They ostentatiously vie with one another to demonstrate the depths of their humanity. We have now sacrificed to have you with us. Pedro Alfarez and two other of our people dead, three more wounded. Your neighbors on the hill will speak about the battle of Los Olivos for many years to come. I venture to predict that within five years the Battle will have assumed epic proportions. Our noted liars will swear that they were in the thick of the crossfire, carried on though wounded, performed deeds of incredible heroism . . ."

Jefe Mendoza was having more troubles. The breeze attacked the remainder of his speech and the sheets almost blew away. Even the natural elements were rebelling against his pollution of the atmosphere. Henry Carr jerked his head up. He had been close to dozing. It would not be proper for the honored to catnap in the limelight.

Mendoza glanced over his shoulder at Anderson.

"None will quibble about the good will of the AmCruz Trust in donating this operating room to our grand city. But had not the powerful trusts and monopolies, the manipulators of Wall Street and the magnates of London, exploited our resources mercilessly, we should be able to provide our own hospitals, our own roads, our own sewers, our own infrastructure. Now, after centuries of ruthless extraction of our riches, they have the moral obligation to aid us so that we may have what we would have had had they not used us as mere sources of raw material, hewers of wood and drawers of water. A moral obligation to . . ."

The crowd in the wooden stands resolutely refused to applaud his speech. The workers of Barrio Flores and the poor of La Colina were vociferously anti-American and usually aroused easily by demagogues, but even they sensed the poor taste in using this forum to villify the donor. Fortunately, Jerry Anderson did not understand enough Spanish to suspect that he was being attacked. Anderson merely smiled every time he heard AmCruz mentioned. The other dignitaries on the platform—the regents from the Ateneo, Padre Garibay, Remberto Davila, Judge Pratt and the Chief of Police—were embarrassed but could do nothing.

Carr wondered what Russell Bennet would have done in this situation. Bennet spoke Spanish fluently and a man as volatile as the Texan financier might have ordered this show stopped and given instructions to scuttle the trailer. The tycoon had spent less than eight hours in Puerto Acero and the town was still recovering. He had arrived from San Martín in a helicopter, the first seen in this region; and then flew up to the mine, where he drew hearty cheers from the ostensibly radical miners with the announcement that there would be no production cutbacks and AmCruz was going to need every ounce of ore it could get, meaning lots of overtime and Christmas bonuses for all.

In another guise Bennet had charmed Soledad with his "Miss Soledad," and hat tipping and arcane gallantries. He was profuse with regrets and apologies. Of course he would much rather take his lunch with a "beautiful little lady like Miss Soledad" but this luncheon was "exclusivamente para los muchachos." He felt guilty about robbing her of her "husband" for a while, but a serious parley was to be forth-coming and she didn't want to hear all those profanities any-way.

The luncheon took place in the plush private salon of the Club Montparnasse and the serious conversation did not com-mence until after the third cup of coffee and all the AmCruz executives except Jerry Anderson had excused themselves. Bennet, a man of many parts, at first chose to assume the protective coloration of a blustering simpleton. He thrust a cigar at the doctor. "Henry! You don't mind me calling you Henry, do you?"

"That's my name, Mr. Bennet."

"None of this Mr. Bennet crap, Henry. Everybody calls me Russ to my face and Lord knows what the hell they call me behind my back. And Henry, I don't mind telling you, or I do mind telling you, that when I got Jerry's, here, letter about what happened to you and Miss Soledad, something very unusual happened. I've acquired a reputation over the years for being an 'A' number one son of a bitch. But when I read that letter about you and Miss Soledad getting pistol-whipped by those bastards and how all the women and peas-ants were lining up in front of your house and praying for you to get well, a funny thing happened. You may not be-lieve this but I broke out crying. I am not kidding you. I broke out crying right there in that big fat office of mine. It's been a damn long time since I cried, sir. Not since my youngest daughter passed on. But there they were, rolling down my cheeks. My secretary came in and I damn near scared her out of her pink bloomers shouting for her to shut the door."

"I'm very touched that you were touched, Mister Ben— Russell."

"I couldn't help it, Henry. I started thinking about all of our ball-less wonders up in Washington, and I got mad. Re-ally mad. And I said to myself, here are all these useless loudmouths trying to run the show and fouling it up every

236

which way and here is this man down there, dedicating himself, giving of himself, and what does it profit him? He gets a bullet in his guts and weeks of agony in bed. So the first thing I did, I called in my secretary and I dictated a letter for our finance department instructing them to make up your back pay retroactively as a regular employee of the firm, and not as a local.''

"That was extremely kind of you, Bennet. But it wasn't really necessary.''

"Necessary, my ass, Henry, if you'll pardon the strong language. AmCruz is my outfit, or it is not my outfit, and I'm sick to death of taking advice from men who basically hope I die in the county poorhouse. Y'know, I wanted to be a doctor at one time.''

Carr smiled. "That's all right, Russell. I wanted to be a financier at one time. I read Dreiser and wanted to be a tycoon.''

"I'm not kidding you, Henry. My old man was a doctor. The first graduated doctor born in Jim Benson County, Texas. It almost tore him apart when I said I wasn't going on to college. But when I graduated high school I said to him, 'Dad, there are clodhoppers running this circus who couldn't pick their nose without a roadmap. I'm going where the money is.' ''

"I gather that you've made some.''

Bennet grinned. "In a manner of speaking, Henry. I figure that I owe around forty million dollars.''

"Owe?''

The grin grew wider. "Why hell yes, Henry. Any shithead can feather a little nest. It takes a rare talent to rack up forty million dollars in debts and outstanding notes.''

Bennet and Anderson roared at this, rattling the table, and Carr could not help recalling the chiefs in the Ayacara village, blowing the tobacco smoke in one another's faces and slapping their sides with glee. Bennet raised his hand. "Why sure, Henry. When you owe that much money nobody'll

237

touch you. They're afraid to topple you, afraid they'll get paid off at two cents on the dollar.''

"You'd think he'd raise my salary at that rate,'' Anderson inserted.

"But seriously, Henry,'' Bennet cut off any further discussion of Anderson's salary. "I'd have made a pisspoor doctor. Sometimes I start congratulating myself as a great humanitarian when I count up all the lives I've saved by not going into medicine. But I like to keep my finger in it. I send two deserving boys from Jim Benson County over to the University at Austin every year and the only thing I ask from them is that they write me a letter every semester to tell me how they're progressing.''

"That's good, Bennet. That's very nice. It must be nice when a man can do what he does best and nothing derails his life.''

Bennet dissented. He reached for the bottle of Jack Daniels. "I'm still too envious of a man like you, Henry. If I were on my deathbed—and I do think about death—I'm sure that there would be a crowd around my home all right. They'd be crowding at my door and trample each other in the rush. A whole slew of accountants, ex-wives, and probate lawyers and cousins and fifty agents from the Internal Revenue Service. That's why my blood still boils when I think of all our ball-less wonders up in Washington trying to come to terms with these Commies while they're down here stomping on your head. I did a little checking on you, Henry. You never went to Edinburgh. Where did you study?''

"I'm afraid I can't tell you, Russell.''

"That's good enough. I've got a lot of boys working in my office with five degrees and they ain't worth the powder to blast them off their asses. Now I've got another question. Are you thinking of marrying Miss Soledad? She seems like a fine girl.''

"I'm afraid that's also none of your business, Russell.''

238

"Also good enough. But one thing I did set up. You're going to be our regular company doctor next year, when Baker's contract expires. You can pick your own assistant and keep your office here in town."

"Good. I already have him picked. Lopez. A very competent young man. I'd say he was more naturally gifted than I am."

"Lopez?" Bennet said dubiously.

"Yes. Very jolly, likes people and likes to cut things open."

Bennet leaned forward. He hesitated. "There's one other matter, Henry. And this is sort of embarrassing. I'm almost afraid to ask you. Are you a bird fancier?"

Carr stared at him. "Well, I don't go out to observe them in the morning if that's what you mean."

"No, it isn't. I don't want you to get the idea that I'm some crass Texan trying to flash a checkbook and buy one of your most cherished possessions. I'm talking about those birds of yours. Those blue macaws. They're about the finest I've ever seen. I'd like to know where you got them."

"The Ayacaras. The Indians I occasionally visit."

Bennet gulped down a straight shot of the whiskey and reddened. "Jerry, here, wrote me about that too. Are you very attached to them birds, Henry?"

"Not too attached. Soledad is."

"Well, I mention it because I sort of keep a small private zoo in Houston. Nothing too ostentatious. People have exaggerated about it and try to paint me as some kind of nut. A few chimps. A few cats. Coupla' birds. Nothing overboard. People got nothin better to do than jabber about their neighbor and then some smart-aleck reporter tried to picture me as some kind of nature boy wandering around in my own Garden of Eden. I'd really love to get my hands on your macaws, Henry. I intend to donate my private zoo to the city when I pass on but, meanwhile, I'd say I spend some of my

239

finest hours out there, among my chimps and birds. I wouldn't want you to think of me as a brassy bastard trying to swap money for something you love, but what would you take for those macaws?''

"Forty thousand dollars, more or less, Russell. Probably more.''

Anderson thought this was hilarious. He was going to open his mouth to laugh when he suddenly realized there'd been no levity in the physician's response. His merriment receded into an uncomfortable wheeze. Bennet had not been deceived. A somber grin crossed his face, as though a trick card had fallen from his sleeve. "That's just your initial asking price, right? Now we can start haggling.''

"No haggling. They're yours for forty thousand, Russell. Or, better said, a mobile operating unit. This town needs one. You can put your name on it with an inscribed golden plaque. With 'Texas' on it.''

"That's still a pretty damn stiff price for two birds, Henry.''

Carr flattened his lips as though it were beneath consideration. "I should think that a man like yourself, who owes forty million dollars, wouldn't haggle over such a nominal sum for philanthropy. You should be able to pull that out of your petty cash till, Bennet. I can write you a letter once a year and tell you about my progress.''

The Texan eyed him. Bennet was enjoying this. He was enjoying it too much to readily commit himself. "I'd have to talk this over with some of my professors at my foundation, Henry, and see whether they could fit this request into the budget. They get an awful lot of proposals.''

"I'd imagine that you ran your own company and your own foundation. Why would you have to ask your hired professors how to spend your money? I'd imagine they're all essentially public service type people who'd love to see you in that poorhouse you mentioned.''

240

Jerry Anderson blanched. No one in his recollection ever used this detached, cynical tone on Russell Bennet. Yet he seemed to be amused. He quenched his cigar butt in the coffee cup. "You're a hard-nosed man, Dr. Henry Carr."

"Not necessarily, Bennet. It would be mutually beneficial. I'd pay you back every cent over the standard price for macaws out of deductions from my salary and services to your employees. Plus interest. This town needs one of those trailers and you're the sport to supply it. Just by unscrewing your fountain pen and signing a check. Think about it. Am-Cruz has a bad reputation to live down. Look what it could do for your corporate image."

Bennet hooked his thumbs into his belt. "Cut out the bull-shit, Henry. I'll have to check on this. But I will tell you this, sir. If you ever get fed up with the medicine racket, I've a spot for you as manager of my sales department. You could ride herd on my bright young drones. Two lousy little birds for forty thousand dollars?"

"I didn't fix any price. It could be more than that. Just send the trailer, Bennet."

"Don't rub it in, Henry. But if we do work it out, tell Miss Soledad that I'll send her a modest little gift to sweeten her loss, too. A modest gift? I'll have to go on an austerity program if I shell out forty thousand bucks for two measly birds. Are you sure you haven't got a bit of the Hebrew in you, Carr?"

"There have been rumors about a maternal grandmother."

"It's been a rare privilege, Henry Carr. A rare privilege."

"Call me Hank."

Emil was tapping him on the elbow. Dr. Apolinario and the Police Chief were also nodding at Carr in commiseration. This pressing heat had carried him off and he had been doz-ing, reliving the afternoon in the salon of the Club Montparnasse, Bennet's Mexican silver ring, the Americans planting cigarette butts in their mashed potatoes till they looked like pillboxes surrounded by moats of gravy.

Carr smiled as he recalled Bennet's discomfiture. One of the occupational hazards of being a millionaire was running into aggressive solicitors. Yet even the most abstruse mystic must keep his eye on the main chance, maintain his contact with the real world.

Emil Arnstedt had his eyes on Henry Carr's face as the doctor lit Bela's cigarette. Arnstedt wondered whether his friend was gloating, if that expression had to do with furtive meetings and cuckoldry. Bela was blooming like a tainted avocado. She had taken on the sheen of forcefed poultry. Bela had cause to be grateful. This was her Indian summer, before the onset of menopause, with all of the pollens and seeds furnished by his fast friend, this Englishman. But now he must think forbidden thoughts. He must ask this question about his crony and chess partner. The indecision had gone on too long. Was that man over there . . . Wolf Karol? Wonderful! A leap. An act of courage. No gray areas here. He would die one day or he would not die. There was a supernatural or there was nothing beyond this life. Bela was sleeping with Carr (Wolf?) or she was not sleeping with Carr (Wolf?). Henry was Wolf Karol or he was not Wolf Karol. He could not be one quarter or one half Wolf Karol.

You may no longer vacillate, study his mannerisms, torture yourself as you have been since the first evening he entered your house.

It is totally illogical. Wolf would have never saved you, extracted a bullet from Emil Brenner's heart. Point two: not even plastic surgery, and this Carr has undergone plastic surgery, could so alter a man. Point three: if he were Wolf he would have attempted to kill you long ago.

Now you are trapped in a labyrinth of your own design. You have studied his every gesture, his gait, the way he lights his pipe, his skillful fingers, and you are sure it is

242

Wolf, unless your memory is playing tricks and you are merely recalling Henry's characteristics from a few months ago. But that day hunting at the ruins, the way he held his rifle, it was Wolf, Wolf in his English knickers. Except why would he then carry you all the way through the pajonal and save your life in an operation.

It would be ridiculous to ask point blank. Carr would look at you as if you were insane. And if you did not ask him, if you ordered Ezequiel to stab him in an alley, that would end this tension. Another insane idea. If he is not Wolf Karol then you would be ordering Ezequiel Cardenas to stab your best friend. What a perfect revenge for Wolf. He would triumph after all these years in the grave, unbalancing your mind, causing you to murder the only friend of your mature life.

Wolf has triumphed anyway. You always concede him the right of rebuttal. You're always conducting these dialogues with a dead man. Wolf would say this and Wolf would say that. The man has done you an inconceivable amount of damage. You have had to stare into the face of every man who entered the Club Moderno. He has isolated you entirely. Against all logic, sense, reason, you fear your only friend, the only man with whom you have been able to speak in all these years. That was entirely his fault. Wolf had no right to knock at the door. It was definitely an imposition.

There was a pause and Mendoza cleared his throat.

"A year and a half ago, my fellow citizens, when Dr. Enrique, as we call him, entered my offices, his papers were not yet in order. We all know his story. Due to a personal tragedy he has spent many years at sea, wandering this earth. But I looked into his eyes and I immediately perceived that this was a good man, a man with a great heart, a heart that had been moved by the beauty of our city and the warmth of our people. He asked permission to stay here, to work, and

243

live among us. What could I do? I could have been an unimaginative bureaucrat, your typical government official in his haughty tower, removed from the urgent needs of his people, and I might have thrown up my hands and said—sorry, we must await approval from Concepción, an approval that may take many months. But I regard myself as a man of the people, close to your needs, and I said to Dr. Enrique—Dr. Enrique, we are a proud people: a people who work, love, suffer . . .''

In the upper stands, under the corrugated iron roof, Rudolfo Piñedo attempted to graze his hand over Aurora Valverde's knee. She flicked his hand away and he playfully kissed the spot she had touched. It was small solace for all the bullshit he had to listen to.

Mendoza held up the last sheet of his discourse. The crowd tittered. Even the insensitive Jefe Civil was forced to grin broadly with the admission that he had been somewhat long-winded. His voice rose for the finale:

"Dr. Enrique carried a seed in his heart, a seed of science and love, a hybrid cross of the red rose of Jericho and the holy white rose of Lima. He searched the globe for a place where it might bloom and flourish, and it was here, among us, that he planted that seed which has given forth such mighty fruits. Not the least of which we see before us—this white trailer of hope wherein he and his colleagues will bring the blessings of modern technology to our ill and infirm. My brother Cruceños, emotion has carried me away. I have spoken too long and I will keep him from you no longer. Our Dr. Enrique Carr.''

Carr tried to take Soledad's hand as he rose but she extricated it and he had to stand alone. He had wanted her by his side, to share the ovation. That would have added the final gloss to her new aura of respectability, rammed her down their throats. It was achieved anyway. After this appearance on the podium, with all of the community factotums, her status was assured.

As the clapping and cheering finally subsided, Carr turned around and winked at Jerry Anderson. The brass section of the volunteer band blared an outrageously flat fanfare and some women were still waving bonnets and handkerchiefs. Emil Arnstedt smiled wanly as Carr unfolded his single sheet of paper.

12

Und so bin ich allein. Du aber, uber den Wolken. Vater des Vaterlands, machtiger Aether! Und du. Erd' und Licht! Ihr einegen drei, die Walten und Lieben.

Carr dropped his match into the open gutter and reminded himself that something should be done about these sewers. A few more years in Puerto Acero and he might announce his candidacy for mayor, promise sweeping reforms.

Und so bin ich allein.

He had sworn not to use that contaminated language, and he was musing, dreaming, more in German lately in moments of tedium. Nothing could be escaped or discarded. It all returned to the backwash, slipped back under the door.

Mr. Ritter wrote from Copenhagen. He enjoyed the Tivoli, was fascinated by the Ripperbahn, wished to inquire how the "project" was unfolding.

He could inform Mr. Ritter that Dr. Carr's affair with la señora Arnstedt had bogged down into a provincial once a week routine. He lunched every Thursday afternoon at the Danubio Azul at which time the restaurant closed for two hours. The cooks and waitresses were gone, and Bela Arnstedt took her favorite customer back to her office. They had become extremely efficient at their liaison, and the time devoted to the formality of conversation had almost shrunk to zero. Bela immediately pulled her dress over her head, lowered her bloomers and covered the sofa with her broad hips, springs groaning as she received him. An hour of thrashing about and then they would be dressed and back inside the closed restaurant, where passerbys on the street could observe them enjoying a discreet coffee and cigarette. Of course, they were deceiving no one, least of all the help. But last week the good wife had demanded a "definition" of their relationship.

"I want more than this, Enrique."

"You only close on Thursday afternoons."

"That's not what I meant and you know it. I never thought I could feel like this again."

"We're sexually compatible?"

"Stop it, Enrique. It's so much more than that. The physical part has been wonderful but we can have so much more than that."

"Neither of us is free, Bela."

"We can be. In two weeks I'm going to Concepción on a shopping trip. Alone. You can invent some reason to fly to Concepción. I'll have withdrawn my savings from our safe deposit box and we'll have more than enough for a new start. In Mexico. Or maybe Miami."

"You make it sound more like an ultimatum than an invitation."

"I can't stand living with him any more, Enrique. He enters the room and my skin crawls. I was cynical at first. I thought I could enjoy you, lightly, as I've enjoyed other men and nothing would come of it, but it's become so much more than that. You're my last chance for a life, Enrique. After all these years of waste. You won't regret it."

"And William and Kirk?"

"Emil loves them very much. I think he should be left with something."

She touched his wrist. On his last trip to the Ayacaras he

247

had picked up a poison he would administer to her three days from now, one that would afford her a very slow, agonizing death, giving him enough time to render explanations.

Carr sat down to rest on the park bench in Plaza Paez and wondered what else he might write Mr. Ritter: that preparations for the carnival were in their final stages, the temperature was thirty-one degrees Centigrade, old Florencio still plucked his cuatro in front of the Nuevo Amanecer, and Soledad was balking now that everything would come to fruition in three days.

The city would not sleep tonight. The women were up sewing and mending costumes for the Lenten Carnival. Carnival from *carnelevare*—to take away the flesh. The overhead arc lamps were glowing in Plaza Paez and over in Yankee Stadium the volunteer clubs would work until dawn, constructing floats for the parade. It was strange that in the Northern Hemisphere Latins were reputed to be slothful. It was merely a matter of priorities. They channeled their energies into spectacles instead of producing dreary consumer products. On this steaming night those shirtless carpenters would labor until the first light building papier-mâché Venus di Milos and dragons for the procession down Avenida Reforma.

"Good evening, Doctor."

Carr glanced up. "Good evening, Rodrigo. How's the wife?"

"All puffed up again." Rodrigo's hand suggested a rising mound. "You know how it is."

"That's number nine.?"

"Ten."

"Shooting for an even dozen, chico?"

Rodrigo chuckled and waved in parting. Carr took out a cigarette and shook his head. Most children in Barrio Flores were conceived at five in the morning. The ore train came in from the mines, engine whistle blowing as it passed the brewery, and the men stirred in their darkened shacks. The infants and children were asleep behind their curtains so a man could finally take his pleasure with maybe the noise of the old, coughing their lungs out, as the only disturbance.

The volunteers were suspending wires of red, yellow and blue bulbs from lamp post to lamp post and across the plaza to the windows of the cathedral and the Municipal Center. They chattered and argued and he could not begrudge them their gaiety. He was weary of being Wolf Karol. There had been other options. When his ship touched Haifa in 1955, he thought of staying on, joining the experiment. And rejected the idea. The Israelis were such cocky creatures they hardly seemed Jewish. More like Australians. And a Jew was as boring as the next man when cast as a cabinet minister, tractor driver, or a postman. Emil was quite right. A Jew only possessed interest as a victim, a catalyst in moral evolution, a laboratory sample in metaphysics. It was too easy to remain in Israel and run around in tan shorts among the orange groves. That was for others.

"Evening, Dr. Enrique."

Carr looked up. "Good evening, Paco."

"What disguise are you going to wear for the Carnival?"

"I think I'm going to attend disguised as a doctor."

Paco roared with laughter and said, "That's very good. I've got to tell everybody that. Dr. Enrique will be disguised as a physician. That's very good. Hasta luego."

"Hasta luego, Paco."

Or perhaps he might go disguised as a seaman. He had spent eight years masquerading as a seaman, taking long walks in obscure ports. Talara, Boma, Kuwait—looking into every café, tapping strangers on the shoulder, marching kilometers down a back road in the Congo because he heard that a tall German was operating a *manga-manga* in the next village.

There were German colonies in Río Grande do Sul, southern Chile, and Argentina. It became a calling, a trade: searching for the Brenners. At sea he read, wallowed in

249

books on inquisitions, pogroms, expulsions, luxuriating in two thousand years of persecution. Monotonous chronicles of suffering in nation after nation, the charges repeated ad nauseum; the Jew was avaricious, aggressive, treacherous. Only one accusation struck him as totally implausible, one accusation tinged with the strangeness of eternity.

"A very pretty night, Doctor."

Carr nodded amiably. "Yes, pretty enough, Eduardo. Not a cloud in sight."

"How are you feeling? Do you still get any pains from your stomach wounds?"

"They're healing nicely."

"And Señora Soledad? Is she feeling better?"

"Much better thank you, Eduardo."

"We're happy to hear you're both feeling better. My respects to Soledad, Doctor."

"Thank you, Eduardo. My respects to your wife."

Specimens might be found for all the other charges. The tailor with his obnoxious mannerisms was on the street corner, the financier in his counting room—but where was the ritual murderer? He existed in the folklore of every nation, the legendary fiend reveling in gory ceremonies, parodies of the mass, using the blood and flesh of Christian children for the bread and wine. How many men by rack and fire had been tortured into confessing to the blood rite? Even the Nazis had felt the need to mount an exhibition in Prague, proof positive of the blood guilt.

In the silence of his cabin it occurred to Wolf that just once, if only once, among man's dramas and ceremonies, the sacrificial murder should take place, stylishly.

Once that vision crystallized in his mind, he could no longer search for Brenner. He averted his eyes or walked quickly ahead if he heard German spoken. He received the tip from Vienna that the couple he was looking for might well be in Santa Cruz, and he signed on the *Blythe,* sailed up the Río Verde, and, at the last, could not bring himself to leave the ship to verify the information. Not for six trips. Like a classical neurotic he fled reality, the possibility of realization. Others thought him so calm as he sat there.

So, Mr. Ritter, things will come to a head in three days. On Carnival night the Arnstedts are invited to the Carrs for dinner. Where they will be properly entertained. Bela will be given a potion prepared for her by the Ayacaras and Emil drugged and carried to the adjacent white trailer, where he will be castrated, blinded, and have his hands and feet amputated. His stump will be transported to the Ayacara village, where we have prepared a proper facility to receive him. Don Fulgencio will attend to Emil during the week and a voice shall visit Dr. Brenner every Sabbath. I only demand the three years that Wolf Karol lay immobilized on English hospital beds. He does not owe me the four years in a Communist prison cell—that we write off to history. But we demand a strict accounting for those three years of unrelieved pain. And we demand two children in compensation for Ruth and Naomi. There is, of course, no need to harm Kirk and William. It is enough that Emil believe his sons are dead, that I have stuffed them into the municipal incinerator. No need to touch the boys. Emil must only believe this, envision in his darkness the smoke rising from the concrete blocks on the hill. Soledad and I may even adopt the orphaned boys and give them a decent upbringing.

We are concerned here with ultimate values, Mr. Ritter. On those Saturday visits we will read Emil's manuscripts with him, discuss his theories and their application, observe whether he changes any of his views about national glory, Lebensraum, sacrificial lambs, cancerous cells.

And who will be blamed for these mysterious disappearances? In this case the Communists make excellent scapegoats. The following morning Soledad will dash down Avenida Reforma, disheveled, shouting to the revelers that the guerrilleros returned, kidnapped Dr. Carr and the Arnstedts, and left a message tacked to the door, demanding a large ransom. In two weeks, after Emil's stump is accommodated in its new lodgings, and any postoperative complications attended to, the English doctor will dramatically reappear in Puerto Acero to explain that he had escaped and that the Arnstedts are dead. If all goes well, God willing.

Carr saw Dr. Aurelio Lopez approaching; he would have preferred his solitude but could not be discourteous to his young friend.

"All alone tonight, Enrique?"

"Just relaxing a bit. Sit down and join me for a while."

Lopez promptly accepted and slumped down on the park bench. "I'm glad I ran into you. I really did have something I wanted to discuss with you."

"No serious problem, I hope."

"Yes and no. I wrote my family about your kind invitation to be your assistant at the AmCruz clinic next year, and they were adamantly opposed. You know the reputation Puerto Acero has of being one big brothel. My father practically ordered me to return to Concepción and open a practice in the capital."

"That's a shame. I want you out at the mine with me next year. And certainly Concepción doesn't need any more doctors. The city is crawling with them. A man of your talents is needed out here. And twenty more like you."

"That's what I was wondering, Dr. Enrique. If you could do me a very great favor . . . If you could write a letter to my father and explain that to him. He thinks I'd like to stay on here because during my student days I was such a skirt-chaser and that I'm running to La Zona every night. The old man doesn't realize just how dreary Panama Street can be. And that I'm truly sincere in my desire to collaborate with you. That I can learn more with you than I possibly could in graduate school."

"Do you really think my writing your parents would do any good? You're a man now, Aurelio. Twenty-four."

"Not to them. And not in Santa Cruz. But it would help.

Your reputation has spread all the way to Concepción. Remberto Davila was telling some other journalists about you, and one of them wrote a feature article in the metropolitan daily about your services to the Indians.''

Carr winced and closed his eyes. About the last thing he needed at this juncture was publicity. Or a lot of snooping journalists investigating his humanitarian endeavors.

"I'll write your letter, Aurelio, but I think I'm going to practice a little blackmail too. I'm going to need your help for the Carnival.''

"I am on duty that night. What masks will you and Soledad be wearing?''

"That's the thing. We don't plan on joining in the festivities too much. We're having a few friends over and are planning a quiet evening at home.''

"Very sensible, Enrique. I've been to the last two Carnivals here and they can be incredibly messy.''

"Well, I was wondering whether you could do me this one great favor? Just for one night I would like not to be disturbed. I know it's an imposition. You'll probably have a lot on you hands with thirty thousand drunks running about the streets. Did it get pretty bad last year?''

Lopez grimaced eloquently. "Bad? Four dead. About fifty cases of heat prostration. Lots of stab wounds. And one boy blinded by a firecracker.''

"Ooof,'' Carr murmured. "You might really need my help at the clinic.''

"I'll handle everything myself, Henry. Personally. You deserve some time to yourself.''

Carr patted him on the back and said, "You'll have my eternal gratitude. And now I'd better be going if we're to start work at seven tomorrow. Soledad raises a storm when I get in this late.''

Carr headed down the diagonal walk toward Avenida Reforma. He lit up a cigarette and found it strange that he should have grown accustomed to the local brand. And the

Estrella de Luxe was a lot cheaper than the imported American cigarettes.

As he reached the curb a taxi bumped around the corner. It stopped in his path. The driver was Antonio Sanchez, father of nine. Antonio poked his head out the window and said, "May I drive you home, Dr. Enrique?"

"No thanks, Antonio. I'd rather walk."

"I mean gratis. Business is slow and I've got nothing better to do."

"That's very kind of you, but I'd still prefer to walk. My greetings to your wife."

"Hokay. Respects to Soledad."

Antonio shrugged, drove off, and Carr smiled at the perplexed expression that had crossed the man's face. Sanchez could not imagine someone of substance preferring to walk. These kindnesses only happened in small towns. Once he had disliked small towns. In another life Wolf Karol told a girl named Bela that he needed the pressure of millions around him to remain alert, alive, competitive.

The lights along Avenida Reforma were too raw for the empty hours of night. Millions of mosquitoes swarmed under the lamps. Carr sensed that an auto was following him, slowly and deliberately creeping up on him. It was hovering thirty yards back.

All of the shops were closed for the evening, heavy metal screens rolled down over the front windows. The merchandise was safe. That was the telltale sign of a poor country, the metal shutters and corrugated iron curtains pulled down over glass, keeping out the many poor with their many bricks.

He thought of turning down the side street at the next corner but the back alley would be even more dangerous. Four blocks ahead the Café Juno at the corner of Reforma and Bolívar was still open. Its electric sign flashed in the darkness. Davila would be there. Four blocks.

He glanced back. That was Arnstedt's big American car behind him. Ezequiel Cardenas was at the wheel. Another man in the rear seat.

The auto was speeding up. The last sound he might ever hear could be the crack of a pistol.

"Henry. Is that you?"

Emil Arnstedt had rolled down his rear window. His face was sallow, blue eyes small above puffy white cheeks. Arnstedt had gained an unhealthy amount of weight during his convalescence.

"Well, you gave me quite a start, Emil. I thought it might be some hoodlums about to attack me."

Arnstedt let the door swing open. "No, please. I know we shouldn't have crept up on you that way but I wanted to make sure it was you. Get in. We'll take you home."

The door was open. He had no choice.

"Muy buenas, Doctor," Cardenas mumbled.

"Muy buenas, Ezequiel."

Arnstedt squirmed over and Carr moved in and closed the door. The vehicle started forward smoothly, as if the click of the latch had automatically set it into motion. Emil's chauffeur had truly massive shoulders. They seemed to extend across two thirds of the front seat.

"Drive down past the docks," Arnstedt said. "I want a few minutes to speak to Dr. Enrique."

Ezequiel nodded an assent. Carr rolled down the window to lessen the odor of the chauffeur's cologne. They turned off Avenida Reforma and bumped over the ruts. There were no more lights. They had been seen by no one.

"We drove by Los Olivos, Henry, and Soledad said you were out. She said you were probably strolling in the Plaza so we drove about searching for you."

"Anything special on your mind?"

"I was worried about our dinner party the evening of the Carnival. I hope Soledad isn't putting herself out too much. I mean, she doesn't have a maid or cook and I wouldn't want her to ruin her entire day in the kitchen if she'd prefer to enjoy the street dancing.''

Carr tugged at the ashtray in his armrest. It would not open. And probably neither would the car doors if he tried to leap out. "I don't think we have to worry about that, Emil. I think she's planning on a simple roast. Lamb or something.''

Arnstedt was silent for a moment. After the few seconds of reflection he said, ''What I meant was, if it would be too much trouble for her, we could have you for dinner at our home again.''

"I wouldn't think of it. We've accepted your hospitality at least ten times now and you've never been to Los Olivos with Bela.''

"My only concern was for Soledad. It's senseless for her to miss the Carnival when we have two overpaid cooks.''

Carr shook his head. "I think she'd be most disappointed. She's been looking forward to this for quite some time. Soledad's a sensitive girl and might assume that you didn't want to come.''

"No, no,'' Arnstedt protested. "You know it's nothing like that. I was only worried about her.''

"Then let's hear no more about it. We'll be expecting you around nine.''

Arnstedt reached forward and touched his chauffeur on the shoulder. "You can park up there, Ezequiel. And then go take a walk and smoke a cigarette for a while.''

The Zambo glanced back at them. "Sí como no, jefe.''

Ezequiel backed onto the rickety wharf assigned to the poorer fishermen and yanked on the emergency brake. As the Zambo opened the driver's door to step out, the entire vehicle seemed to rise an inch, relieved of his enormous weight. His heavy tread made a loud clopping sound on the loose boards as he walked down the wharf. The river currents were lapping under them, swirling around the green, rotten pilings. Carr drew on his cigarette and the sudden glow lit the auto, illuminating Emil's sallow face. He wondered if Ezequiel were down there preparing some chains and rocks.

"Another matter, Henry. It might have waited until morning but I was tossing so wretchedly in bed that I had to come and see you."

There were no lights in the AmCruz offices. Usually they were lit for the charwomen and janitors. A few weak lights shone on the fishing boats and the ore carrier tied up at pier three. If he could break away he could outdistance the lumbering Zambo, rouse the watchman on the ship. They would not shoot him with witnesses around.

"Henry?"

"Oh, sorry," said Carr, stirring. "It must have been pressing for you to get out of bed."

"While I was recuperating I began to review many things I had not thought about for years. An idea came to me. An idle idea. I brushed it away, but lately it returns. I began to think. I was so close to death, in fact dead, and you brought me back. Maybe I have ten, twenty years left to me. Maybe only a day. But I wanted to make the best use of that time."

"That's only natural. People who've had so close a brush generally start taking things more seriously."

Arnstedt turned to him and earnestness suffused his posture. "It came to me—the club, the restaurant, they practically run themselves. Bela doesn't need me at the Danubio Azul and I only have to drop in a few hours a night to make sure my bartenders aren't cheating me blind."

"You're beginning to feel superfluous."

"Something like that. I have a vast amount of free time facing me. I once thought I could devote it to writing but lately I've seemed to run dry. I seem to have said what I had to say and there is nothing left in me after seven thousand pages."

Ezequiel was returning, slowly making his way back. Carr tensed, ready to move. "Then I guess it's time to give up, Emil."

"It came to me—I was wondering whether you could use me around the clinic. I know I've been away for a long time but so had you. I could return slowly. I'd have to do a lot of reading. Catch up with the times. They've made marvelous advances over the last fifteen years, haven't they? Remarkable advances. But I'm still basically a well-grounded scientist. And there's certainly a need here. You can't deny that there's a need. I could drop around and break back in slowly."

Carr relaxed in the darkness. He wondered whether this man actually believed he could get off that cheaply, achieve redemption with a hobby. He tossed his cigarette into the river and it fizzled out in the black water. "I think it sounds like a splendid idea, Emil."

13

Soon after the Carnival procession along Avenida Reforma dissolved into a hectic welter of quarrels, and the ramming of floats began in the open fields behind Yankee Stadium, all public order broke down. The San Martinos of Puerto Acero—notorious for their exuberance and tempers and capacity for alcohol—set about the real business of the celebration: drinking, dancing, lechery, revenge and cuckoldry. Liberated by imported Scotch, the rotund merchants from Avenida Bolívar pranced among the spectators, emboldened by their masks, recalling that though they no longer possessed the dashing silhouettes of cavalry captains they might still be the Marqués de Bradomín, the least pernicious of Don Juans—ugly, Catholic, and sentimental. They pinched the bottoms of the girls whose escorts were not too large and, giggling, slipped away into the milling crowds. The oppressed husbands of Barrio Flores, faithful and frustrated, remembered better, wilder days. Stimulated by the sun, chicha and beer, protected by crêpe helmets over their faces, they searched out the women they had been eyeing all year long, grabbed them around the waist and danced them over the sticky asphalt, delighted that their work-weary legs could shuffle in time to the compelling twang of the cuatros and the frenetically pummeled bongos.

As in Carnivals past, the drinking commenced long before the late afternoon parade and many among the disgruntled populace greeted Jefe Mendoza, on the lead float, with drunken catcalls. Mendoza, refulgent in purple robes and a red sash, doffed his golden turban to his constituency. The whistling became shriller over the raucous glissandos of the Municipal Brass Band. His supporters, on the payroll of the P.N.R., felt obliged to dash across Avenida Reforma, through the marching formations, and to punish the demonstrators. This first altercation of the day erupted on the stoop in front of Anastasio's pharmacy. Several of the banners suspended over the crossing were torn down and Inspector Gonzalez's two police cars arrived with whirring sirens and flashing lights. They quickly broke up the incipient riot and carried the three more gravely wounded to the dispensary. Many of the oldtimers commented on this and agreed that the trouble was starting much earlier than usual. The violence usually began around sundown.

Well behind schedule, the floats paused in Plaza Paez, where a wooden tower had been constructed for the research team from the National Institute of Folklore and the cameramen feverishly trying to capture the scope of the seething Carnival, a celebration as yet uncontaminated by the tourist commercialism of the lenten festivals in the capital. Elias Alcazar, Director of the Institute, instructed his crew of photographers to concentrate on the more colorful costumes, so his assistants spread out among the celebrants. The San Martinos in the more evocative disguises were too busy dancing to pose, while the clods with unimaginative trappings wanted to monopolize the footage and would not get out of the way. Another team of researchers, North American professors from a California university, mixed with the antic mobs. The professors had strapped tape recorders on wheeled tray tables which they pushed from band to band to procure for their archives the clashing dissonances of the cincos, tambourines, creole harps, bandolas, flutes, cachos and accordions, all mixing with the drums. They struggled through the crowd with their carts, but could not get a clear shot at any of the quartets nor isolate them for effective recording. Their samplings were blurred, smeared flurries of noise. A treasure was being lost, a treasure in joropos and merengues, mambos and guasas, boleros and decimas, rumbas, corridos. . . . The San Martinos danced in the cacophonous pandemonium. The musicologists could not make them pause and perform for their tape libraries.

As the last of the golden floats wound past the statue of San Martín, another howl went up from the rabble. Dr. Mendicuti's oldest and ugliest daughter was ensconced on her swan throne as the Queen of Carnival and surrounded by her court of dowdy princesses, the daughters of the privileged of La Loma. Most of the crowd was displeased about the twenty-eight-year-old spinster, with the spotty complexion, presiding over their joy. Anyone with eyes could pick out fifty prettier girls along the sidewalks. The hissing and whistles rang out as Queen Maria Elena waved her wand over her unruly subjects. The Regents of the Ateneo were shocked by this vileness and murmured among themselves on the reviewing stand. The dregs of La Colina were becoming more disrespectful every year. Judge Arnulfo Pratt admonished the mob with his ivory-knobbed cane and was answered by a volley of firecrackers.

There was an irritating lull in the antic swirl as Padre Mateo Garibay led the Procession of the Niño down Avenida Bolívar. The tiny beatific element of the community reaffirmed the essentially holy nature of the Festival, trudging behind the floats with gaudily painted cribs holding plaster-of-Paris images of the Christ child and ceramic crosses adorned with azaleas and pink roses. The wooden saints from the hillside chapels were held on high. The devoted, in their lugubrious black suits and lace mantillas, dragged their chil-

261

dren along and temporarily dimmed the sun. They chastened the throngs with reminders of unpaid debts, promises broken, crypts, the dangers of venereal disease and tomorrow's splitting headache, until they circled past the reviewing stand and entered the Cathedral, where Garibay blessed the cribs and the figurines of San Ramón and San Benito.

A young boy sank to the pavement with an epileptic seizure in front of Medina's emporium. He died before the ambulance could reach him. The vehicle was occupied elsewhere. There had already been two knifings on Panama Street and the dispensary was filled to capacity, with Amalia and the other nurses setting up cots in the halls to handle the heat prostration cases pouring in. To worsen matters, Doctor Lobos announced this was his free afternoon and he was leaving to join the festivities.

In the patio of his villa, Emil Arnstedt fidgeted nervously with the damp bandana he used to cover his face during afternoon naps. He had slept soundly in the fold of his canvas hammock and woke with his pajamas soaked by perspiration. He wondered whether he was making proper use of his time. Raising his head to peer over the hammock's side, he observed that Bela had pressed the fountain button for spray. Her toes were curling in enjoyment of the clash between the sun rays and the soothing mist. Her youthful figure on the beach towel filled him with a sense of oppression. It was a responsibility he had grown weary of many years ago. Bela was such a soft creature, like a voracious pudding. Even the sauces she spread over her avocados were too creamy. Once, long ago, he had been capable of making that flesh tremble. That was a memory of a memory now, and not even a fond one. There had been too many humiliations since then.

He watched her prop two cushions under her neck to preserve the carefully lacquered upsweep of hair and smooth the oil over her broad shoulders and bosom, both to be displayed

262

by the low white dress she had chosen to wear this evening. She was dedicating her entire day to preening like a cat, relaxing so she could be lovely, radiant, for the Carrs. A futile endeavor. Time was against her. Not even with that scar to distort Soledad's beauty was Bela able to compete with the whore.

From the very beginning they had been an incongruous couple: the slow-moving, athletic Bela and her high-strung intellectual. He had believed that she would continue to respect his mind—always a mistake with women. Now she was seeking a change and this was quite unfair. There were bonds. It was absurd of her to conceive of an entirely new existence after what they had been through together.

"What time is it?" Bela called out.

"About six or so, mi vida."

"Could you wake me at eight thirty, please, Emil?"

"Of course. Have a nice nap."

"It's difficult to sleep with all that racket rising from the town. The din is even worse than last season."

"I know. Try anyway. Just close your eyes and let the music carry you off. You know how we are with Henry. Once we get started talking, we could be up all night."

He covered his face again with the moist bandana; and through this screen was able to view the red sun low on the horizon. There would be revelry till dawn. After fifteen years in this town he still did not dare walk the streets during Carnival, not with all the populace wearing masks—waiters he had fired, whores he had turned out of the Club for growing too fat or old, enemies from the past. He could take up the point with Henry this evening: the question of continuity.

It was over anyway. All those sterile arguments. There were just a few more points he wanted to make to Henry. The question of the progressive diminishment of human life, of the individual, under the statistical crush of a burgeoning population. There was a period, eons ago, when the death of one man, one woman, might deny humanity grand and invaluable genetic qualities. But today, with three billion bipeds crawling over the face of the earth, with all of the infinite permutations and varieties, what did the loss of one man, one child, mean to the species? As the earth grew more crowded, each individual became increasingly isolated, meant less. The loss of ten, a hundred million, meant nothing to the species. A repugnant yet incontrovertible fact.

What would Wolf say to that one? Wolf abhorred Hegel, rejected all claims on the individual; the State, the Fatherland, was a convenient fabrication, a myth manipulated by politicians.

Emil was tired of the dialectic. He felt as if ejected from a maelstrom. He could only gaze up at the blank sky and ask—was that the life of Emil Brenner? No, impossible. Emil Brenner was going to be a fine, upright man. Some disease had infected his clean, shining spirit. But he could still be purified and purged and restored to the core of his being. He could be restored to his essence.

Henry was a man who understood such matters. Henry was foul and corrupt enough to be obsessed by the same concerns. Around them a meaningless confusion of idiots, yet they had enjoyed such a grand year together. Henry had not only saved his life this year but had also given it dimension and meaning.

Emil Arnstedt tossed the damp bandana aside and reached for his water glass on the stucco rail. He could, of course, call Carr, tell Henry he was ill, would not be able to make it this evening. And yet that would be so silly, so extremely silly.

The team of American researchers had finally made a profitable strike. At the Nuevo Amanecer pulpería, far enough away from the racket of the main thoroughfares, they had discovered the troubadour, Florencio Negrón and surrounded him with tray tables and tape recorders. The microphones, held near his mouth, did not annoy the blind artist. Adelberto, his grandson, started off by charging the Gringos five cruceños a song but, observing their enthusiastic reaction, raised the price to seven and eventually ten. Florencio might exhaust his entire repertoire that evening, but at ten cruceños a ballad, el trovero was not going to let these wealthy imbeciles get away. Florencio began to sing ballads no one had ever heard before. The regulars hid their amusement behind their hands, suspecting that the old black was inventing instant folklore.

After sunset the fevered tempo of the Carnival rose in pitch. The task force of musicologists, ethnologists, anthropologists, sociologists, cameramen and historians from the National Folklore Institute filtered through the mobs with their flash and movie cameras, recorders and notebooks, and finally recognized the impossibility of capturing the frenzied dynamism of this spectacle. Ten years ago Puerto Acero had been a moribund jungle outpost. Since the mines had opened the poor had swarmed in from all corners of the Republic: swarthy miners from the cordillera, tough llaneros from the savanna, aborigines from the delta, and blacks from the coast and the island of Costilla. They had arrived with their dances, guitars, masks, and were all on kaleidoscopic display tonight.

Director Alcazar noted in his folder that there was a great deal of repetition of costumes. The most popular figures were Death, with black cape and cardboard sickle, the Skeleton, with luminous white bones and a rubber-skull mask, Judas Iscariot, with beaked nose and a scraggly red beard, medieval knights, Madame de Pompadours, evil witches, Sleeping Beauties, Cinderellas, Chinese bandits, Bluebeards, Blackamoors, Arabian sheiks, red devils, Pagliaccis, Spanish pirates, Napoleons, Cleopatras, and Maria Magdalenas. One or two months' wages many of these celebrants had spent for their costumes. The children, resplendent as Narcissus, Cupids, redskins, cowboys and imps, would not eat for several days after they gorged tonight.

The fireworks began early, a volley of green flares gyrating in erratic orbits over the river. The soldiers manning the antique cannon on La Colina responded immediately with a roaring salvo that shook the ground with such force that the Cathedral bells pealed—one low penetrating note that lingered and caused many of the superstitious in the crowds to quickly cross themselves. Twenty more rockets thundered into the dusk over the Plaza. They exploded to form the letters P.N.R. in streaking red prisms, and Jefe Civil Mendoza, on the dignitaries platform, winked at a disapproving Remberto Davila. The opposition parties would not overly appreciate this fine little touch.

Rocket after rocket soared into the lavender mists. At the Club Moderno Rodolfo Piñedo held his hands over his ears. Lately, every time he attempted to enjoy himself his stomach became upset and his temple throbbed. A few piddly drinks, a few empanadas with hot sauce, and he was ready to crawl into the corner and curl into a suffering ball. Once, not that long ago, he had been infamous at all the ferias in Spain. People said he had to be Andaluz and not a Gallego. Night after night he could go, pissing wine into his mouth from the bota, clicking his heads, outroaring any Gypsy in a cante jondo, sleep for a few hours and be fresh for the races again.

He dipped his hands into the dirty dishwater and felt himself lucky to be working this shift. Otherwise he still might be downtown playing an ass. This morning he had been the public fool. He was stronger than any of these young local punks, but his agility and coordination were not the same any more. The donkey knocked him over in the donkey race but the deep humiliation had come from the bulls. Nobody believed him when he said he'd won first prize at the Feria de Cadiz, and several ferias in Mexico, for lasting longest on the bull. And today the beast tossed him with one tricky buck.

The whores from the Club Lido mocked him and Gloria shouted, "Hey, Gauchupin! We thought you Spanish were all supposed to be machos. My grandmother could have lasted longer on that bull." And he shouted back, "Your grandmother would have tamed that bull from below." Gloria chased him and made him slip in the mud again.

A hell of a way for a man to end up—as the laughing stock of a foreign city. The girls had been so pretty on Avenida Reforma this morning, roses and ivory combs in their black curls, their breasts swelling in their blouses, and when they lifted their skirts to dance, he could see the wicked red-flowered slips. But when he drew near them their fathers and brothers stiffened like bulldogs. Everybody knew who Piñedo was. He was the barman at the Club Moderno and served colored tea to the whores.

It was odd that the only person in this city who treated him with proper respect was the best man in Puerto Acero. Enrique had stopped to chat with him directly in front of the reviewing stand, right in front of all the big shots, Mendoza and Judge Pratt. Enrique did not care about the mud on his trousers, just patted him on the shoulder, and Soledad let him kiss her good cheek. Then they walked off, across the Plaza, the way a man should proceed down the street in his mature years. Distinguished. In a fine white suit and a broad hat, with a beautiful woman on his arm, a woman with a bottom like Soledad's, and all the urchins running after him, begging for pennies, the men saying, "Qubo, Doctor? Como le va, Doctor?"

Respect. Dignity. Position.

With the spluttering firecrackers the sky over Puerto Acero had fused into an unearthly nocturnal rainbow, blending tints and tones never seen on any human canvas, colors that might have been torn from the bowels of the planet after a devastating volcanic eruption. Soledad Cumare was still panting from

267

the steep climb up to the capilla of San Benito. Glancing quickly around her, she hid behind the hillside grotto, assured herself that no one was peeking from the bushes, drew up her skirts, and yanked and tugged her girdle down to the ankles. With another ferret-eyed check of her privacy, she stepped out of the garment, kicked it up into her hands, squashed it into a ball and stuffed it into her handbag. It was only then that she groaned in relief and scratched at her liberated flesh. Lupe said it and Lupe knew what she was talking about: the girdle was invented by a maricón who wanted revenge on women.

Soledad deposited herself on the worn rock facing the capillita and squirmed until the stone's configurations adjusted to her contours. She brought out her compact to examine her disarray. Her lipstick was smudged. She pouted archly at the reflection in the tiny mirror, pushed a tuft of hair aside to examine the deep scar, and then hid it again. With her thick black hair over one eye, she looked like Veronica Lake, Enrique said. He was such a prudish, strange man. This morning he refused to let her wear the blue silk Chinese brocade with the slit up the side, saying she was no longer on the market and could not advertise her legs. She argued with him, but she liked his jealousy. It would be nice if the child she had in her belly looked like Enrique. He was a handsome man, though that was not his real face. She hope to God their children would not have big noses like the Polacos with their stalls on Avenida Bolívar. Those Jews arrived with nothing in their pockets and within five years they owned all the shops downtown and drove fancy cars and sent their children to school in the United States.

Her decision was made. She had given Enrique ample time to kill Arnstedt and, if he were so set on it now, he could do it himself. Besides, he might lose respect for her if she aided him. She was a woman, a mother, and she would not curse the child in her loins by participating in the horrible deed he was planning. This was a fever Enrique had in his brain and, if they could get through this one night, he might recover and realize how mad he had been. She had her own way of taking care of Arnstedt—Piño. The Gallego was crazy for her. The idiot would obey any order she gave him.

The music was much better from up here. Down there it was jumbled and here it was mysterious, like the sound of waves splashing on rocks with bells. And the people in Plaza Paez looked like thousands of puppets and rag dolls shaking on a tray. Her prayers and spells might be effective with these Chesterfield cigarettes. Doña Eusebia said that the Spirit of Tobacco was called by seven specially selected leaves, dried for seven days and rolled seven times. But the San Benito had been blessed in the Cathedral this morning, which might impart to it enough potency to compensate for the weak tobacco.

She decided to use six cigarettes, strip them down, and place them in San Benito's bowl, light a seventh cigarette, and blow the smoke over San Benito and the memorial candles. The Ronson lighter might also dilute the spell. Doña Eusebia had said that only the enchanted flints could awaken the dormant Spirit. But the Spirit should understand that this was an emergency. If she blew the hot smoke over San Benito and the candles, the Spirit would whisper instructions in her ear.

Soledad fingered the tobacco and spit into the bowl seven times. She kneaded the mass until it had a soggy consistency and put the seventh cigarette between her lips, letting the smoke smart her eyes until they teared. If the Spirit saw her bitter tears, he would surely respond more quickly. Her hands clasped in prayer and she intoned with all the gravity of a high priestess:

"I offer and bestow the smoke of this tobacco to the judgment, soul, will, life and five senses of Enrique Carr. I offer this and invoke the triumphant spirits that they may destroy all obstacles which prevent Enrique Carr from being mine. To the tortured spirit that he may torture Enrique's brain. To the desperate spirit that Enrique may despair for me. If he is sleeping, let him dream only of me. If he speaks, may he hear my voice. May his enemies be impaled on tridents and thrust into the flames. Saint John of the Four Winds, imprison Carr within my walls. I implore the Virgin of the Withered Flower to snap the wings of his heart so that he may feel no pleasure nor emotion with another. Spirit of the Weeping Mother make Carr weep for me. This we beg from the Four Condemned, the Damned, the Lost, and the Five Diabolical Cherubim. Amen.''

She repeated the invocation seven times and added seven more cigarettes. The candle flames grew brighter. The Spirit was heeding her. The smoke was swirling around San Benito and drifting out over Puerto Acero. It was rising up to the gray clouds, up to the pink and blue haze of the fireworks. She had cast her spell and the Spirit would heed her, if the rockets did not interfere.

Dr. Aurelio Lopez had impressed himself with his newly discovered faculty for driving subordinates to greater exertions. He had always envisioned himself as a meek and passive type. Capable, of course, but essentially the assistant, a number two man, and he was pleased to discover these administrative abilities, and freshly sprouted fangs. All day long, as case after case poured in, he had harried his overworked and flustered nurses with artful bursts of temper and then rewarded them with encouraging winks and smiles, and the girls had performed well for him. With one phone call to the chief of police, he had Lobos brought back in a squad car. And Lobos was inside now, infuriated, still cursing under his breath, but doing his job. Best of all, today the stricken and wounded on the cots had treated Dr. Lopez with the same deference they usually reserved for Dr. Carr.

With everything temporarily under control, he granted

270

himself five minutes for a smoke on the front porch of the clinic. The rockets were bursting into creamy pink puffs over the river and he was saddened by this insane extravagance. His clinic had such pitiable facilities and only the Lord and the supplier knew how much Mendoza was throwing away on this puerile spectacle.

Sighing in his discontent, Lopez noted that of all of the cottages on Dr. Carr's hill, only Los Olivos was lit up. The observation produced a curious twinge. He hoped that Dr. Carr had his guests tonight. The entire city was celebrating, paganly, and the darkened hills looked abandoned, with just the candles burning in the primitive chapels and the lamp on Los Olivos.

The same sensation of emptiness had touched him on his last steamer trip down the river to San Martín. He had stepped out on deck on a moonless, starless night and shuddered at the lonely points of light in the dark jungle, the kerosene lamps from distant shacks and ranchitos. How brave those settlers had to be. Life was too short and tragic to spend it so far away from other human beings. He had wondered how they dared to turn their backs and lose themselves in that huge, black night.

Wolf Caro had finished his preparation. The table was set and the good goblets polished. Soledad had sworn she would be back by seven and it was past eight; however, he wasn't surprised. It would be silly to grow angry at a natural phenomenon. From the very beginning of this enterprise, without facing or admitting it, he had sensed that, at the last, Soledad would fail him. Prescience—this ability to perpetually foresee how people would react, and invariably fail him. He was no Jungian, though perhaps Emil was correct, and Wolf Caro was born ancient, with a mind seared by the memory of events he had never experienced.

271

Caro sat down at the dinner table and he was alone. The wall to his left was still decorated with all the get well cards that Soledad refused to let him cut down. The elementary school had sent them thirty selected works of art done in crayon: blues, reds, greens, blacks, many with lurid drawings of operations in progress, Dr. Carr and Soledad bending over rigid bodies, the white-jacketed surgeon and nurse cutting into a chest with blood spurting to the four winds. The girls bordered their cards with red roses, curlicues and yellow dandelions, while the boys were more clinical, a few malicious and acute observers drawing Soledad with voluptuous dimensions, straining against a white smock.

He should thank those guerrilleros for depositing that bullet in his stomach and reacquainting him with pain. And reminding him that a life was never over until it was over, that there was always time for fresh afflictions. A bullet in the stomach was such a sharp reminder of those commonplaces. He had writhed in agony for weeks and Emil had come to sit by his bed. So solicitious, dear Emil, assuring him that he shared that pain, had witnessed so much suffering on the Russian front. Twenty million dead in the snow.

It was better to be alone now. He had been wrong from the start. Soledad had no place at this ceremony. She was down in the Plaza, dancing, alive. What could she know of slaughters long past by streams now dry, and the injustices of forgotten cities? This rite was for the Caros, and for all those falsely accused and tortured into confessing that they had committed sacrificial murders, for the thousands in unmarked graves. So let their spirits rise, flock to him, and join him tonight, fill the unoccupied chairs at this table with their presence, crack the unleavened bread with him, and sip from these metal goblets. Let them come from English moors and Russian steppes, the barren expanses of Castille and Polish forests, wherever they had been stretched on racks and flogged into false avowals to satisfy the ignorance and bestiality of their loving Christian neighbors. They were welcome

272

at this table tonight, to share his bitters and unleavened bread, and then might rest easier in those graves.

Caro opened the *Book of Prayers,* studied the ancient letters thousands of years old, so familiar and so alien, and read aloud.

"For my danger is in my hand, and now we sin before Thee. Let them not laugh at our fall but turn their device upon themselves as we make him an example that hath begun this against us . . .

"And give me boldness, O King of Nations and Lord of Powers. Give me eloquent speech in my mouth before the lion. For I abhor all signs of high estate and I have not greatly esteemed the King's feast. Neither has thy servant joy since the day I was brought here to this present. But You, above all, hear the voice of the forlorn and will deliver me from fear."

The Passover would come early this year. His father was dead and he had complete discretion to invent his own calendar and observances. The table was set with four silver cups of wine, a white radish, a boiled egg, a salad of chopped apples and nuts, a plate of crackers, and the shankbone of a lamb. He raised his first cup of wine and spoke in the silence:

"Such corruption of ritual and custom. My father is not here to impose adherence to the sacred dates and the lunar calendar. All order is gone from the universe. Yet even in this vacuum there should be more joy. More joy at this table. Look at those empty chairs. I should have a wife here, bright sons, and Ruth and Naomi should be here with husbands, crying infants rattling the cups and dishes. And in that chair, at the head of the table, my father—the man I slapped a few minutes before his death—presiding over this ritual of grace and deliverance. He would be over eighty now, a venerable man, and his mind would still be sharp, surprising us with his wit. But I am here alone and may conduct this service as I see fit. I am the last of my line. And after four thousand years, I hold the last service.

273

"Praised art thou, O Lord our God, King of the Universe, who has sanctified us by thy commandments, and has permitted us to kindle the Festival Lights. Alive and unscathed.

"Praised art thou, O Lord our God, King of the Universe, who has kept us alive and sustained us, and brought us to this season.

"Let us praise God and thank him for all the blessings of the life that is gone. For life, health and strength. For home, love and friendship. For the discipline of our trials and temptations. For the happiness of our success and prosperity. May this day be a memorial for your departure from Germany. He has chosen you for his service.

"Praised art thou, O Lord our God, Ruler of the World, who hast created the fruit of the wine so that the drunken swine below may vomit in the gutter, stagger home to beat their women and deny food to their children.

"Caro! Caro! This is not the season for bitterness but joy. The Angel of Death passed over your home and spared you. He definitely spared you and you celebrate the deliverance. Sip your wine and toast the Angel of Death. Eat your cracker. Lo! This was the bread of affliction which your fathers ate in one hundred lands. Let all who are hungry come and partake. Let all who are in need come and celebrate. May it be His will to redeem us from all afflictions and servitudes. Next year at this time may our house be free.

"Why is this night different from all other nights of the year? Because tonight you will amputate Emil Brenner's limbs and pluck out his eyes.

"Why on this night do we eat especially bitter herbs? You do not find them particularly bitter.

"On all other nights we eat without special festivities. Why, on this night do we hold this service? We hold this service that the false may become true. For the murdered, tortured, and humiliated.

"How much more then are we to be grateful unto the Lord for the manifold favors he has bestowed upon us. He brought you out of Germany, divided the English Channel for you, permitted you to cross to dry land, sustained you for twenty years in the desert, granted this Sabbath, led you to Puerto Acero, granted you this trailer and has sent you many prophets of Truth so that you may once again believe and be a holy man seeking to perfect the World under the Kingdom of the Almighty, in Truth and in Righteousness.

"This very night, which we, a happy generation, celebrate so calmly and joyfully and safely in our habitation, was often converted into a night of anxiety and suffering for our people in former times.

"In former times? There was only the present, which dwelled side by side with every moment of the past and future."

Caro turned the page and smiled at words he had not read since former times. He opened his mouth, and sang lustily. "Hah, Godyaw. Hah, Godyaw. Hah, Godyaw. Then came the Holy One, blest be He, and destroyed the Angel of Death, that slew the butcher, that killed the ox, that drank the water, that quenched the fire, that burned the rod, that beat the dog, that bit the cat, that ate the lamb my father brought, an only lamb. Hah Godyaw. Hah Godyaw."

A whistling in his ears now. The symphony of a shell by the ocean, or the wind tearing through a distant gorge. His tears had stained the tablecloth and he was no longer Wolf Karol or Henry Carr, or any of those fictions forged by time and place. He was empty and complete, devoid of memory, turned to stone before he became human again.

A fist formed involuntarily and shot up to strike his face. He laughed at the quaintness of the gesture. Had he actually just struck his own cheek? He had imagined himself to be incapable of such atavistic twitches—a modern liberated man—and suddenly recognized the dimensions of that arrogance. He was a Caro, the Caros had thousands of years of breast-beating behind them. One should be here to guide him. Wolf was breaking all the rules with no elder to correct him on the

275

forms. He had become thick with wine when tonight was for lightness and joy. Solemnity and joy.

Grief would stain this occasion. After a cold shower he could sit outside on the porch and await his guests, enjoy the music rising from the plaza. Tonight, through the window, with the rockets bursting over the river, Puerto Acero glowed like a town from some ancient Levantine fable.

Rosa Maria had been flipping her skirts up and exposing her girdle to the patrons in the Coney Island Bar. The bartender grabbed her by the scruff of the neck and rushed her through the swinging doors into the arms of the cavaliers and buccaneers who were gyrating to the Brazilian samba emanating from the Club Zanzibar. The Pirate pushed Rose Maria to the Cavalry Officer. He twirled her into the embrace of King Neptune, who bit her on the neck. She broke away, into the clutches of the Red Death. Red Death tore at her blouse, ripped at her black brassière. They smacked her on the hips and thighs until she screamed and ran into the arms of the purple Skeleton. Rosa Maria sank her teeth into his white, hairy wrist and broke free. She escaped into the narrow alley, knocking over the ashcans and garbage cans behind her to block her pursuers. The Red Death and Amadis de Gaula chased after her. They slipped over the wet cobblestones and broken glass and finally cornered her beside the rain barrel. Red Death clamped his forearms across her throat, tripped her over his knee, and dragged her to the ground. He rested his weight on her torso and pulled her skirts up. She tried to drive her knees into his groin as his hands grappled with the tight band of her elastic girdle. With the elbow digging into her throat she was going black, falling into darkness. She relaxed to let them do it. But the Red Death had drunk too much today. With a groan of rage he began to punch and slap her face.

Police Sergeant Gregorio Urquiza saw this clumsy assault

from the street. He extracted his revolver from his holster and fired a warning shot into the air.

Amadis de Gaula and the Red Death ignored the shot and continued clawing at Rosa Maria. Urquiza took aim and fired his second shot into the water barrel. The bullet smashed the rotten wood frame and a cataract of stagnant water spilled over the three on the ground. The Red Death and Amadis de Gaula rolled away quickly. They got to their knees and scampered down the alley as they saw Urquiza coming for them. Rosa Maria raised her head and let the water splash over her bruised eyes.

Soledad had stiffened with the two shots and quickly pushed her way through the swinging doors of the Club Moderno. Lupe Varona, seated at the corner table, was so startled that she almost knocked over her glass of cheap champagne. It had been so long since Soledad's brawl with Señor Emil.

Lupe rose from her chair to run to Soledad but the sailor she had been plying for drinks grabbed her wrist and forced her to sit down again. Other girls at the tables broke away from their partners and immediately convened near the bar to discuss this sensational arrival. Within an hour everyone in town would know Soledad Cumare had visited the Club Moderno.

Aurora Valverde and Ezequiel Cardenas were occupying a side booth and the bouncer acknowledged this event with a broad wink. "Take a look, mi vida. Perhaps our little Soledad has grown weary of the English and playing nurse. Maybe she wants her old room back."

"No," said Aurora. "Maybe to look for Señor Arnstedt. She has a lot she could tell Señor Arnstedt. About certain things."

"Like what?" Ezequiel asked.

"Don't play the fool for me, Zambo. You know perfectly

277

well what I'm talking about. The lustrous pair of horns your master wears. Placed on him by his best friend, our dear Dr. Enrique.''

''You know about that, eh?''

''You think there's anybody who doesn't? The head nurse at the clinic has told everybody that Dr. Enrique has more than his lunch at the Danubio Azul on Thursdays. Bela gives her cooks and waitresses two hours free and off. A tightwad bitch like Bela wouldn't give her employees time off unless something fishy was going on.''

Ezequiel shrugged tolerantly. ''I wouldn't mind two hours on top of the Alemana myself. She's one of those rare women who need it. A whore like you, you take on ten men a night, but if they didn't pay you, you'd never touch another. A cow like la Bela, if she didn't have a cock all the time, she'd be stuffing bananas and carrots up there.''

Both Aurora and Ezequiel observed the consternation in Piñedo's face as he came out of the bathroom and spotted Soledad in the side booth. His head snapped back as if physically struck. He quickly wiped his hands on his apron and signaled to the other bartender to cover his station. The Gallego hurried toward her with contradictory sentiments struggling for precedence in him: pride that Soledad should be crooking her finger at him in front of all these dregs and concern that she was hurting her reputation.

''Soledad,'' he whispered, ''you shouldn't—''

''I was employed in this place for five years, so let's not pretend I lost my virginity coming through the door. Piño, sit down. I have to talk to you.''

''Is anything wrong with Enrique?''

She gestured impatiently. ''Just sit down, hombre.''

He obeyed and they sensed every eye in the hall on them. The Carnival music from the street clashed with the tired revolutions of the overhead fans and the irregular flashing of the neon sign over the beer keg.

Bartolomeo arched his brows and Piño signaled to him for

two Scotch and sodas. The Gallego turned and tapped at his temple. "You look pale, Soledad. Are you ill? I have this terrible headache. All these drums and racket. They say it will last till dawn, and my shift in this shithole lasts till five in the morning."

Soledad rummaged through her purse for a cigarette. She checked under her crumpled girdle, then remembered she had used her last on the hill. She accepted one of Piño's and began without preambles as he lit it.

"You once said you would do anything for me, Rodolfo."

"Yes. I said that. I told you that if you asked me I would place my hand down on the railroad tracks and let a locomotive crush it. For you or Enrique."

"Did you really mean that? Or were you just talking, Rodolfo?"

"I mean it, chica. Every word of it."

"Talk is so cheap, Rodolfo. All you men are bullshitters. I've heard so many men tell me what they would do if, if, if—" She abruptly pulled the tuft of black hair covering her eye aside and flaunted her bad cheek at him. "Am I too ugly now with this scar, Rodolfo? Does it disfigure me too much?"

He glanced around quickly, nervously, aware of how their every move was being studied by fifty big mouths.

"You're still the most beautiful woman in Puerto Acero, Soledad. I wish I could take your scar for you, approach and kiss your scar away."

The pointed tip of her shoe touched his calf under the table. "You still desire me, Rodolfo?"

"Too much."

"How much?"

He withdrew from her touch. "Stop this, Soledad. This is no good."

"You could have me. You could have me, Rodolfo."

"Stop this," the Gallego pleaded.

"You would have to do something for me. A very great

279

favor. Yet it would not be for me. It would be for Enrique. Not for me. Then you could have me, all of me. As you want me.''

"I don't want to hear any more of this," the Gallego said.

"You'd have to kill Señor Arnstedt. For Enrique. Tonight. Right now."

"For Enrique?" Piño spluttered incredulously. "Arnstedt? You're crazy. Arnstedt is his great comrade. They're always talking together and playing chess at the Ateneo. Enrique even saved his life once, with a miracle.''

They were silent for a moment as Bartolomeo served their drinks and then Soledad rasped, "That's all you know, Rodolfo. He saved him so he could torture him. There's so much you don't know. Enrique and Arnstedt were friends in Europe but Arnstedt couldn't recognize him because Enrique was hit by a bomb at the end of the war and had many operations on his face. You think Enrique's such a saint. He has this worm in his brain. If he can survive tonight he may be all right. Arnstedt was responsible for the death of his two little sisters and all Enrique has been doing in this city is preparing his revenge. Enrique is a Jew and Arnstedt was a Nazi. That's why he's here in Puerto Acero.''

Piño sat back and grimaced in disgust. He almost laughed. "You're crazy, Soledad. You're fabricating all this. Because Arnstedt hit you once and made you lose a baby.''

"Am I? Why do you think Enrique has been training me for all this time? To help him tonight. We're supposed to drug and tie up Bela, carry Arnstedt to the trailer. Enrique's going to slit out his eyes and cut off his balls.''

He blinked at Soledad. "I'm supposed to believe this? You've been drinking absinthe or smoking marijuana. This is the worst crap I've ever heard.''

"I wish it were, Rodolfo." Her voice had risen and the customers were turning about, straining to hear what was being said. Soledad stared them down and leaned toward Piño again, pressing against her dress to let him see as much

280

as possible. "I wish it were. But what do you think it has all been for? All of his trips to the Indians? The trailer? He has been carrying provisions to the Ayacara village and he has a cabin prepared there with a bed, and medicines, and antibiotics, and tanks for clean water. The Indians will be waiting in canoes by the docks tonight. To collect Bela and Arnstedt."

Piño coughed with derision. "You have a fertile imagination, chica. You should write stories for the radio. I'm supposed to believe this fantastic story about a man like Enrique?"

"If you don't believe me, come to the trailer at midnight. He'll be operating on Arnstedt. You can pull open the door and see for yourself."

The Gallego lit another cigarette. His hands were shaking. He took a quick gulp. "This is just a trick, no, Soledad?" He grinned to encourage her. "You're pulling my leg?"

Soledad sipped her Scotch and returned the glass to the table with a loud clink. "No, Rodolfo. Unless you do something quickly, something terrible will happen."

"Me? Why me?" He pressed his thumb against his chest. "Why do I come in? This doesn't concern me."

She stroked his wrist and he flinched at her touch. "You said you'd do anything for me. And it wouldn't be difficult. You could take the pistol from behind the cash register and ask Bartolomeo to take over for an hour, and hide near Los Olivos and shoot Arnstedt when he arrives. And then you could throw the pistol into the river. They might arrest you but they would never convict you. They might not even investigate closely. Nobody likes Arnstedt in this town."

Piño smiled directly into her eyes. "You like to use men, don't you, Soledad? You think that we're all suckers for a pair of big tits. I'm just a stupid puppet that's supposed to dance when you crack the whip?"

"If I use you, I pay you, Gallego."

"How much?"

"I said I'd reward you, Rodolfo. You've always desired me. I saw the way you hungered for me when I was in the hospital. If you do this for me you can have me three times. Not three pieces but three complete nights. And I'll do whatever you want me to do. I can be very wonderful when I want to, Rodolfo."

"Three different nights?"

"Three." She was going to caress his calf again but he nudged her away.

"And is Enrique supposed to know this, Señora?"

"Of course not. This will be strictly between us. You'll never regret it. I can be very warm with a man. It will be our shared secret. But we're doing it for Enrique."

The Gallego looked away, down at the sawdust on the floor. "I'll have to meditate on this, Señora. It's a grave matter."

"How can you? We have so little time."

"I said I'd need to think about it. Now get out of here and stop disgracing your man." The Gallego's neck was flushing red. He wanted to slap Soledad across the mouth and kiss her. "Get out of here before I rip open your dress and drag you out on the dance floor and shout that you're a bitch! You've told me fifty times how much you miss your children and how much you want to bring your children from Cali. Meanwhile you're offering me three nights' worth of your ass to kill a man. Why do you want to bring your boys here—to pimp for you?"

"You'd be my first customer, chiquito. You'd pay fifty cruceños to kiss my ass."

"Go home, Soledad! Go home with your three nights."

She pushed herself up from the booth. "All right. I was mistaken. I thought you were a man. I was mistaken. Adiós, maricón."

"Adiós, angelita. Honey drips from your tongue."

Not one customer in the Club Moderno missed the exchange of insults. They watched as Soledad stormed by the drunks at the bar, scraped a chair aside and shouldered two blearly-eyed dancers out of the way. She was seething. Every inch of her flounced and shook with her broad, rapid strides. Soledad pushed through the swinging doors and was immediately swallowed up by the furious cadence of the street.

They looked back at the rear booth and the Gallego's face was drained and flat, his eyes devoid of light.

A minute went by before Piño snatched a bottle of rum off the tray of a passing waitress. His glass clicked loudly against the bottle as he filled it to the rim. Watching him, all of the girls and customers were prepared for a moment of melodrama. The Gallego took a long gulp of straight rum and snickered at what had just transpired. These women always imagine they are so clever, and Soledad was not particularly clever. She had used an entirely incorrect approach on a man like Rodolfo Piñedo. He was too old to be handled by a little snip like Soledad. She had used the wrong technique entirely, failed to accord him the proper respect. Why had she not approached him to say, "Piño, you are a tough and violent man, you were in the army and in jail, and you know how to use weapons and how to manage these affairs. Enrique has a madness in his brains but you can stop him, Piño. Because you are a fine, hard man, and our friend." But no. She had to be clever, use tactics on him straight from the shithouse. It has to be a business transaction—kill a man for three nights of pussy.

Perhaps she was being shrewder than he thought. If he did it, he would be captured and she would never have to pay off. Very shrewd. Enrique had a job to do. Good for Enrique. Let him chop the swine to pieces, if that was his fancy. He, Rodolfo Piñedo, might have helped Soledad if she had chosen to handle him properly. He had killed before—no big thing. If she knew anything about Gallegos she would have asked this strictly as a favor, and strictly on behalf of his friend. Then, afterward, she could have dropped around to give him his proper reward. With her stupidity, she had created a dilemma that now made it impossible for him to help Enrique. So to hell with Soledad. And to hell with his great friend, the doctor. One should never interfere with these personal affairs. He intended to slice up Arnstedt? Beautiful. It took education and breeding to devise such splendid plans. As for Rodolfo Piñedo, he was a simpler type. Tomorrow he would catch the next ship out of this shithole.

The stevedores were drinking in the yard behind Medina's Emporium, their backs against the brick wall. They were splitting their last jug. Overhead spluttering rockets exploded into brilliant spinning comets and falling stars, before they crackled into red and azure puffs.

They passed the jug from mouth to mouth, trying to be fair, and wiped off the lip before passing it on. One orchestra was still performing in the plaza. The Cuban mambo sounded tinny at this distance, as if played on children's instruments. The public Carnival was ending. The plutocrats were beginning their masked balls on La Loma, and the nice girls would be at family dances and parties in Barrio Flores, protected by their fathers and brothers. Only whores were left in La Zona, all wearing plastic noses and red hats.

They passed the jug and they were not happy. They were alone out here with crippled beggars from Avenida Bolívar and the smelly ragpickers selecting their supper from the garbage cans.

Guido unzipped his trousers and pissed on the stacks of discarded newspapers. He scowled. There was not enough piss in his bladder for all these newspapers. The shed adjoined the rear office of the Emporium. All of the stevedores in his dormitory owed trader Medina money. The fat Turk had come off a steamboat thirty years ago with a bundle of bloomers to sell and now he owned half the town. Guido

Herrera struck a wooden match and glanced at his compañeros for support. They nodded and he spilled the last few
drops of liquor over the dirty newspapers. He dropped the
match, but the flame did not take. The others saw what the
game was and joined in, tossing matches on the boxes of cotton wrappings and trash. Soon the papers were burning
strongly, curling into black wisps, climbing the dry boards.
Guido hurled his jug of chica through the window. Fanned
through the opening, the flames touched the gauze curtains
inside, and reached the sheaves of invoices on Medina's
desk. The stevedores turned and ran down the alley toward
the avenue, shouting like children released early from school.

Caro saw the smoke from his window. He was naked except for the towel around his waist and had just dropped his
empty bird cage into the wastecan. His blue macaws were up
in Houston tonight, in Russell Bennet's modest zoo, and their
original donor, Don Fulgencio, was waiting with three other
Ayacaras in a canoe across the river. He did not want to
disappoint them nor disappoint himself. The reparations offered were inadequate. Emil wished to get off so cheaply—a
bit of social service. A few hours each day of tinkering
around the public clinic.

The arguments came so easily. This afternoon he had felt
himself faltering and despised his weakness. But he worked,
meticulously disinfecting every surface in the white trailer,
sterilizing every instrument, adjusting the cyclopropane unit.
How easy it was to be humane, good, sane. It took no skill
whatsoever, nor character, to follow the natural bent. This
other was hard, the darkness cold. The scale of justice had
broken so long ago and he was but one tiny weight, trying to
tip it back to equilibrium. It was a great responsibility he was
accepting—to become the incarnation of a legend. Divine
providence, should such an institution exist, must surely note

this temerity. Why had no telegram arrived advising him against this course of action? Or must it adhere to its policy of silence and nonintervention in human affairs?

The other option was too easy, those pleasant little musings as he puttered around the shop this afternoon, the happy craftsman polishing up his tools, secure in his vocation, sheltered and sustained by an identity. How treacherous the mind was, to suddenly and insidiously relax, furnish those moments of serenity on such a day, wooing him with subtle flattery. So convenient, sanity whispering that it was the better part of humanity to recede into this sentimental fiction created by the good people of Puerto Acero. Sanity deployed all of its enticements. Why honor Emil Brenner by elevating so squalid a figure to the status of sacrifice, sanity whispered, trying snobbery. Why not proclaim Enrique Carr a better man than Wolf Karol and close all the ledgers?

Caro dressed slowly in fresh tans, hid the table setting beneath a linen cloth and then went out to the porch with a pitcher of cool wine and the case containing his fine German binoculars. He studied the conflagration through his field glasses. He was not displeased to discover that the fire seemed to come from Medina's Emporium. The municipal fire engine, intended mostly to quell riots, had arrived. But water pressure was so low that the power hoses could quell neither riots nor fires. The feeble trickle could hardly challenge the powerful flames feeding on Medina's tins of kerosene, bottles of Scotch, and bolts of yarn and cotton.

The destruction inspired mixed sympathy. An ugly building was being obliterated for a single moment of beauty. The soaring flames shimmered in the depths of the river and the rocketeers, perversely, continued to launch their missiles into the haze, where they exploded into talisman roses.

He observed, through his binoculars, that not many people were helping at the Emporium. A few volunteers seemed to be scurrying about with buckets of water from the taps in surrounding stores while the poor, who owed Medina money, had gathered to enjoy his woe. He spotted Medina dashing around in the crowd, slapping the laughing children, grabbing men by the shirt, obviously begging them to get buckets and join the battle.

Caro put down his binoculars and sipped at his wine. He wanted the full scope of this fire and not the precise, microscopic details. The distant smoke mixed with the brightness of the rockets and he concluded that all carnivals, rites, and celebrations should end with fire and wine. Emil would also understand that. They both had loved Wagner. Their tastes were so very much alike. Emil, of course, was too small to pick up the bill for this century, to pay the entire check, so Emil should feel privileged to have been chosen for this ritual, honored at the opportunity to become an element of myth. He was sure Emil would appreciate this, once it was explained to his stump at the Ayacara village.

The rockets stopped.

A taxi was winding up the dirt road leading to his cottage. He frowned as he watched the vehicle take the dangerous curves with suicidal aplomb. There had to be many casualties from the fire, with the fools and looters dashing into the flames to grab merchandise, beams collapsing on their heads, smoke and ashes blowing into their lungs. Tonight he was not available for looters stricken by smoke-inhalation.

The driver of the taxi was Antonio Sanchez, his favorite.

"Dr. Enrique. You must come," Antonio shouted. "There's been a shooting."

"To the clinic?"

"No. The Club Moderno."

"I thought you were coming about the fire," Carr said and sensed the ridiculousness of that statement as it came out of his mouth.

"No. Dr. Lopez sent me. There's been a shooting with several dead. Your friend, Señor Arnstedt, shot some men."

Carr dashed into the cottage for his bag and then jumped from the porch with one bound. They were off with a neck-wrenching jerk before he could even close the car door, as Antonio plunged them over the ruts, the chickens scattering.

It took them less than five minutes to reach Avenida Bolívar, but there Sanchez honked his horn to no avail at the crowds blocking their way. Every car in Puerto Acero was out tonight. Sanchez poked his head out the window and shouted, "Get out of the way, you cretins. It's Dr. Enrique. Let us through. It's Dr. Enrique."

The crowds were still streaming toward the fire, which had spread to other shops on the block. The taxi was trapped. With each spray of the hose a huge cloud of acrid smoke burst from the charred walls of the gutted building. Carr smacked Antonio on the shoulder in way of gratitude and jumped out of the taxi. He could get to the Club Moderno faster on foot. He pushed his way through the revelers and ran toward the Plaza. It was too hot. The sweat poured down his chest. He was too old to run.

The Plaza was empty except for a few lost souls wandering around in the low-lying smoke, and drunks sprawled on the grass asleep. The reviewing stand was empty, orchestra pit empty, the ribbons and banners blowing loosely from the tarnished statues. The benches were overturned, the strings of tinted lightbulbs dangling from the lamp posts, the walks littered with torn flags, ruptured balloons, discarded masks. A mongrel spotted him and came yipping across the street, snapped at his heels as he took the shortcut through the municipal building courtyard. Two more blocks to run. Henry Carr was too old to be panting like this, running down back alleys, too old to have anything more happen to alter him, too tired for another change, for this confusion.

The crowd in front of the Club Moderno let him through with murmurs of "Dr. Enrique, Dr. Enrique." A guitar lay in the gutter, the frets cracked, the wire strings curling crazily. Lobos and Gomez were easing Piño onto a stretcher and Padre Garibay was kneeling over someone in the bar. The trunk to the police car was open. Two pairs of shoes stuck out at odd angles. Inspector Gonzalez had Lupe by the shoulders and they were surrounded by the girls from the Club Moderno and the bars along the street. Lupe was both hysterical and dramatic for her large audience—clowns, devils, pirates, dukes, milkmaids, kittens, all with their masks off, costumes drooping and faces drawn.

Lopez nodded, and pointed to the stretcher bearing Klaus. "Arnstedt's nephew is past hope, Dr. Enrique. The bartender has superficial bullet wounds in the shoulder and left thigh."

The crowd protested as Gonzalez slapped Lupe across the mouth. He shook her by the shoulders and shouted, "I told you to stop sniveling and tell us what happened, idiot."

She tried to hide her face in her hands, but Gonzalez twisted her wrists. "Talk before I really give you one."

More spectators were arriving. The fire at the Emporium was under control and many who had heard about the shooting at the Moderno were streaming down Panama Street.

"Tell him, Lupe," Aurora half shouted. "Arnstedt came to talk to you."

"I didn't do anything," Lupe whimpered.

"Nobody said you did anything," Gonzalez snapped. "We only want to know what happened. You were talking to him when the shooting started."

Lupe dabbed her nose with a rumpled napkin. Between sobs she managed to get out, "I don't know. He came in. He came in with his nephew. They came to my table, and Señor Arnstedt asked me how I was. And I said all right. Then he introduced me to his nephew and said his name was Klaus, and that from now on, whenever Klaus came here, I was to give him a good time. So I asked who was to pay for this good time, and Señor Arnstedt said that from now on my

289

room rent would be cut in half. And that I was to go with Klaus even if he was not here because he might be going away on a long trip and there might be a new manager."

"I heard that part of it," Aurora said. "Every word she says is true."

"But then, all of a sudden, Ezequiel shouted, "Watch out!" The barman had taken the revolver from behind the cash register and was aiming at Señor Emil. And Ezequiel shoved Señor Emil and the bullet hit Klaus."

"And Klaus fell down," Aurora said. "Piño ducked behind the bar and Ezequiel and Señor Emil both pulled out pistols and Ezequiel fired and his shot hit the mirror behind the bar."

"The mirror broke," Lupe said excitedly, "and knocked all the bottles over, and we were all screaming and jumping for the floor."

Carr listened. Their babbling roared in his ears. He wanted to lose consciousness or vanish from the earth but he was forced to hear them.

"Everybody was shouting and crawling behind the tables. But Piño fired and struck Ezequiel and Señor Arnstedt fired twice." "But Piño fired again and Señor Emil ran through the swinging doors." "Everybody was running on the street or was flattened against the walls." "Except for Florencio, the blind man. Florencio was in the middle of the street." "He was holding his cuatro over his heart and didn't know which way to run." "Everybody was shouting at him, 'This way, Florencio. No! No! This way, Florencio.' And Florencio ran a few steps this way and a few steps that way but he didn't know which way to go with everybody shouting at him." "Then Señor Arnstedt grabbed Florencio and held him in front as a shield and Florencio dropped his cuatro." "But Piño had grabbed Ezequiel's pistol and kept coming at Arnstedt, walking down the middle of the street." "And Señor Emil kept backing away," Aurora said, "Holding Florencio in front of him." "Señor Emil shot Piño again, in the leg, and Piño fell to his knees.'' ''Then Florencio broke away and everybody was calling, 'This way, Florencio! No! This way.' '' ''But Florencio was confused, and he was crawling around on his knees, looking for his cuatro.'' ''And Señor Emil didn't know what he was doing and he shot Florencio.'' ''And then the bartender shot Arnstedt. Arnstedt fell down and the bartender crawled forward and shot him one more time, in the head.''

Part Four

Part Four

14

All in all, I had not done too badly. I thought things were going to be worse, but my view from the balcony at the Concepción Hilton afforded me a more balanced perspective on these last fourteen years. Concepción was mushrooming, a neo-Los Angeles being superimposed on what was originally a shoddy version of Madrid. I could draw these comparisons now because I had seen the world. Mr. J. Ritter was a highly paid consultant, a renowned proposal writer in the burgeoning health–education complex, commuting three times a week between Washington and New York. As the old saying about the Quakers went, I had started out to do good, and was doing well.

Not that well. Otherwise I would have felt more comfortable on this hotel terrace, watching the cars stream down the wide freeways and the cranes lifting the beams to the skeletons of the skyscrapers, soaring so high they were almost on the same plane as the shacks barnacling the surrounding hills. I had never suffered from vertigo. Fourteen years ago ordinary seaman Ritter had scampered up masts like a monkey and now, as a married man, the father of three daughters, and a respected educator, I was unable to approach a balcony railing and gaze down at the traffic on Avenida Revolución, seventeen stories below.

Uncle Burt had surprised me on the flight down. After harping for two hours on the details of our business, irritating me with all the repetition, he abruptly switched subjects and said, "I guess this trip is sort of a sentimental journey for you, Jack."

"How so?"

"Well. Were you not down here before, when you were a young buck?"

"Not Concepción. Never to the capital. I'll be as much of a tourist here as you."

"You went up the Río Verde, though. I remember your mother, God rest her soul, showing me some postcards."

"Strange you should remember things like that. I never knew you followed my career that closely, Burton."

"Oh, I always knew what you were up to. You've always been my favorite nephew."

"Strange, you've never been my favorite uncle."

"I'll make it easy on you. For the next week or so, think of me as your employer. We'll get along better."

He ordered me another drink from the Pan-Am stewardess and after she served our Bourbons with extra bags of peanuts, he turned to me and said, "Your mother was always worried about you but I never was. You were such a wild kid. I was always the one who assured her that you would eventually straighten out—once you got the sea out of your system. And I think events have borne me out. You've carved out a pretty nice niche for yourself down in Washington."

"That's what they say."

"You've got complaints? Tough. Everybody's got complaints," my uncle assured me.

"They sure do."

Behind me, in the suite, the bed was covered with memos and estimates, and all the dry Xeroxed chaff that made the wheels of international commerce spin. This was actually not my line. Business had always bored me, but Burt offered two hundred a day and expenses for my interpreting services, plus discretion. There would be one week of conferences, luncheons and meetings dealing with a new garment factory to rise in the outskirts of Concepción. Two Congressmen had to receive their sealed brown envelopes, and a colonel was being set up as straw man in order to comply with the law requiring Cruceño citizens as major partners in all foreign investments. The deal had its seamy side but I preferred to focus on the positive aspects. Eighty women would get jobs as seamstresses and, though the wages might be sweat shop level, any job was better than no job in a country as poor as Santa Cruz. After a dozen years in Washington I generally had no trouble finding a justification for any activity that benefitted me.

There was one manila folder on the bed, containing personal correspondence, and one old and yellowed letter I would have to read again in honor of my return to Santa Cruz.

I pushed the sliding glass door aside and stretched out amid the litter of translations and blueprints on my bed. Before taking Piñedo's letter from the folder I poured myself a tall glass of Bourbon.

Esteemed F.B.I.

Hello!!! Before I forget I better tell you the latest joke. Jesu Blanco, the prisoner in row seven, had a good joke for us. Blanco really knows how to tell a joke. He is here for murdering the flower vendor who was visiting his girl friend. He has thirty years like me. Here is the joke.

This Gringo expert is (he says Gringo but he really likes Americans because he worked on a fruit boat and got good money) this expert is visiting a small jail in this Central American Republic and the director of the jail is taking him on a tour of the facilities when—from nowhere—they hear these horrible screams. Aaaargh! Eeeegh! Ooooieaye! And the Gringo expert says—what is that, señor? And the director of the prison says—We are electrocuting an assassin, Mr. Jones. He was a very evil hombre. He knifed six men. And the American expert says—but why all the screams? An electrocution is very simple. In the United States we merely pull the switch and the condemned man is fried crisp. They hear more moans. Augh! Ooogh! Ulugh! And the director shrugs and says—yes, Mr. Jones. But when our generators are not working in the power plant and our electricians are out on strike, then we have to do the electrocution by candle light.

Jesu Blanco has a knack for telling jokes. We all laughed. I thank you from the bottom of my heart, F.B.I., for the twenty dollars you sent me in your last letter. The only problem is that I never received them. The only way that I know that you sent them is because Ángel Duran, the night guard on our row, told me there were twenty dollars in the last letter you sent me but that Tiburcio Rey, the captain on the block, opened the letter and took the twenty dollars out before giving me your letter. Ángel Duran has mailed this letter for me and he says that if you want to send me any more money, you should send it to him and he will deduct only ten percent and surely give me the rest.

I ask you for this money because I only need this money for Aurora because Enrique still sends money to the canteen for my special food and cigarettes. Some of the whoresons in my block gripe because we always have Estrella de Luxe cigarettes and get special food in my cell because Enrique sends money for my special diet, and me and my friends always get beefsteaks. But that is purely envy and none of my friends gripe. Enrique could not come this month because Soledad is due. He said last time that she looked fat enough to drop quintuplets. Soledad has not come with him for the last four months because she said that the long trip on the river in the steamboat was too hot and tiring for her and she was afraid that one of the bad prisoners would give the baby in her belly the evil eye or that the baby might be born marked with the shadow of the bar cells.

Enrique said that he would come next month when Soledad was out of bed and on the last visit I asked him why he did not get out of Puerto Acero. He said that he must stay in Puerto Acero as long as I am in this prison and I told him that he was crazy because I have the maximum sentence and that means that he must spend another twenty-eight years in Puerto Acero. I told him that if he really wants to do something for me he should go to Concepción and become a big rich surgeon and then he could make so much money that he could pay a big bribe to get me out of here. Surgeons can make a lot more money in the big city than in a small town.

Only sometimes I think I don't want to get out of this cell. I start thinking about how I accidentally killed that boy and how I helped to kill old Florencio and the tears come to my eyes and I want to commit suicide. I did not care about the Zambo and Arnstedt. I am glad I got them. But I remember the boy and Florencio and I want to twist my shirt from the rafters and hang myself. But before I hang myself I would like to have one more woman. I have written a letter to Aurora and Aurora has answered me that she is willing to take the steamer here and spend a night in my cell if I pay all of her expenses. I would ask Enrique for the money but I don't like to molest him with these matters and I don't want him to know about this. I have calculated a reasonable budget for her trip and you can review my figures and see whether you think my budget is reasonable:

$5.00   for chief of cell block, Tiburcio Rey

$4.00   one dollar for each cellmate so they sleep on floor in another cell that night

$7.00   round-trip steamer ticket for Aurora

$3.00   her meals on steamer

$2.00   a little gift for Aurora

$20.00   for money Aurora loses in 2 nights away from club

$1.00   flowers for Aurora

$4.00   for our special supper in cell

$5.00   ten percent for Ángel Duran

$4.00   miscellaneous

$55.00 (fifty-five) American dollars. (No checks because it is very difficult to cash a check here drawn on a foreign bank.)

I could ask Enrique for the fifty-five dollars and he would surely give them to me but I don't want him to know that later I am going to hang myself. He has not been well lately. He is very pale and he has lost a lot of weight and he is working too hard. I don't want him to find out that after Aurora comes to see me I will hang myself so I turn to you for the money for you are my good friend. I asked Soledad the last time but she said I was crazy, so now I rely on you, F.B.I. Fifty-five dollars is really not that much money because you are on a United States ship and it is very easy to earn big money on a United States ship.

300

Remember all the free meals I got you and all the money I saved for you when we were on Atlantic Avenue in Brooklyn. My respects to your mother and your brother and all your family and friends.

Sincerely,
Rodolfo Piñedo #71738

Penitenciaría Estatal de San Martín
Ciudad San Martín, Edo. San Martín
Republica de Santa Cruz

There had been no thank you note for those sixty dollars and it took me three letters of inquiry to ascertain that Rodolfo Piñedo had, indeed, managed to strangle himself with his own shirt. So for many years I have had to wonder whether I was responsible there, too; whether Piño might have decided to live if I had refused to send him that money. We do like to drag our chains around with us.

There were immediate duties. I scribbled out a postcard to the wife and girls. The wife appreciated these little gestures. She had kindly packed a book in my valise. A book club selection, an alternate. The wife was a soft touch for subscriptions.

I stretched out on the bed. The weekend loomed as an appalling dose of time. I dialed Burton's room and he said, "You want to go downstairs and knock a few back?"

"Not exactly. I was thinking about a little trip inland. By myself—"

"Leaving me here alone?" he protested. "Is that what I hired you for at two hundred bucks a day?"

"I didn't think you hired me to hold your hand. Our first business meeting isn't until Monday."

"You're on the payroll though."

"Fine. Knock me off the payroll for two days. No problem."

"No need to get testy about it. I guess I can get in some golf with the Colonel over the weekend. He speaks enough English for social purposes. Just make sure you're back by Monday morning when we have the meeting with the Congressman."

"You're very kind, Uncle. *Ciao.*"

Another phone call to the front desk revealed that there was now daily plane service between Concepción and Puerto Acero. Two hours later I was looking through the window of a 707 and sipping at a Scotch and soda just handed me by a good-looking Cruceña stewardess. I checked. The women had finally learned to shave their legs in this country. My flight was booked with prosperous tourists loaded down with bundles and packages, and there was a contingent of European engineers—Italians—browsing through folders marked "Río Verde Development Plan." The wide river was to our left. I searched unsuccessfully for the spot where Piño had stripped naked on the deck and tossed his clothes to the Indian girl in the canoe. Impossible of course. It was just a wild and boundless jungle below us, and we were too high to establish any landmarks.

Progress had hit Puerto Acero. A boxlike glass and steel airport graced the environs, and construction equipment lined the road all the way into town. My limousine chauffeur demanded the equivalent of twelve dollars for the trip and immediately reduced the fare to eight when I disputed the price in Spanish. I told him to take the twelve and use the difference to give me a half hour tour of the city.

It was difficult reconciling the new skyline—the skyscrapers and bustling suburban sprawl—with my memories of a muddy, grubby port. Except for the shacks on the hills, the damn place looked like Fort Lauderdale. The corner of Bolívar and Reforma was dominated by three skyscrapers: a twelve-story government building, the eleven-story headquarters of the AmCruz Corporation, and a glass front commercial center. Avenida Reforma now boasted a Sears, supermarket, laundromat, cafeterias, parking meters, and no parking space. The chauffeur proudly informed me that the population had just passed the one hundred thousand mark, and that a new two-hundred-bed hospital opened last year.

Checking in at the new Hotel Continental I ignored the bellboy's sneer at the fifty-cent tip he received for carting my one overnight bag. He showed me how the television set worked, advised me that it was still not safe to drink the tap water, and mentioned prostitution was now "theoretically" illegal, that all of the old brothels on Panama Street had been demolished and replaced by stores but, if I so desired a woman would knock at my door at eleven p.m. for thirty dollars for a short time or sixty dollars for all night long.

After showering and changing shirts, I called the new hospital. Twenty minutes were consumed as one receptionist and two secretaries interviewed me before I was finally put through to the Director, Dr. Aurelio Lopez. The gentleman was quite reticent until I glibly explained that I was a journalist representing *The Reader's Digest,* and was planning a feature article on Henry Carr and other doctors who had done notable work in the region. Lopez then said he had been one of Enrique Carr's closest associates and would be delighted to collaborate on the project. Moreover, he would bring along Remberto Davila, editor ex-meritus of *La Tribuna,* who had also been closely connected with Dr. Enrique.

We dined that evening at the Villa Sorrento, formerly known as the Danubio Azul. I confessed, with a certain embarrassment, that I had used a ruse to get them there, that I had known Dr. Carr and Rodolfo Piñedo personally, and my true interest was in finding out what had happened to them. Both Davila and Lopez found my subterfuge to be amusing and were more than glad to open up. They well remembered the incident at the Moderno and the principals involved. So much had changed, Davila assured me. Carr's two old adversaries, Dr. Apolinario and Dr. Mendicuti, had both died peacefully in their sleep. Jerry Anderson had been promoted

303

to the home office in Houston and, for the last ten years, the local managers of the AmCruz holdings had been Cruceño citizens, and much harsher administrators than the Gringos, Davila inserted. About Aurora Valverde or Lupe Varona they could tell me nothing. No one ever knew where retired prostitutes went.

It had gone badly for Mustafa Medina. After he built a modern, three-story department store over the ruins of his emporium, Sears had set up a branch store and put him out of business. Padre Garibay? Poor Padre Garibay had left with a team of doctors and missionaries to minister to the Indians in the Darién peninsula, and had contracted amoebic dysentery. He was convalescing in the sanatorium of the Sisters of Mercy in Panama but was not expected to linger on much longer.

Davila smiled when I mentioned Jefe Mendoza's name. Mendoza had been elected to the Chamber of Deputies in 1962, and had fled the country after the coup of 1966. At last word Mendoza was in exile in Miami, Florida, and employed as a used-car salesman. Lopez added that groups of medical technicians and doctors now visited the Ayacaras periodically but had never been able to gain the confidence of the Indians. The Ayacaras still remembered Dr. Carr and asked when he would return.

Unfortunately, they could supply me with few details on Carr's present whereabouts. Henry Carr had spent six memorable years among them, and then disappeared as abruptly as he had arrived. There was still a movement afoot, Davila explained, to change the name of the recently opened Hospital Pelayo to the Hospital Enrique Carr. He was one of the leaders of the movement, had published several editorials to that effect, but it would be difficult to achieve. There was little public support for the change, since over sixty percent of the population were recent arrivals who had poured in since the aluminum smelters had opened, and it was only the oldtimers who still talked about Dr. Enrique.

Carr's sight had begun to go, Lopez said. A glaucoma that responded to no treatment. One morning he and Soledad and the children were gone, with just a note tacked on the door. One person had received an occasional letter from Carr but she now resided in Concepción. La Señora Bela Arnstedt operated a restaurant on the Avenida 14 de Mayo called the Hotel de Vienna. Bela Arnstedt might know. They had been very close in the years after her husband's death and Carr had taken a great interest in the education of the Arnstedt children. He had often been seen strolling in the hills with the boys.

I thanked Lopez and Davila for their troubles and would not hear of letting them pay the bill. We went to the Club Lido afterwards for a few more drinks and discussed politics. There was general agreement among us that economic and social progress in Santz Cruz was being retarded by the unstable political situation.

The next morning I took the ten o'clock flight for Concepción and, on Sunday evening, went to the Hotel de Vienna for dinner. It was an elegant establishment, tastefully designed around the motif of a green house, with exotic lanterns, sculptured shrubbery, and windmills and waterfalls in the garden. The menus were printed in Spanish, English and French, and I calculated that the cheapest entrée was equivalent to a maid's weekly wages. In spite of all my cynicism I was still a knee-jerk liberal, which meant that I enjoyed the good life while ill at ease. Two blond young men in tuxedos were hustling about as maitre d's, and I surmised that they were William and Kirk Arnstedt.

I ordered the grilled Argentinian shortribs, a Chilean Pinot Noir and asked my waiter if it were possible to speak with the proprietress. To my surprise, he noted my booth number on a list. Apparently there was a whole waiting line of people who wished to see Bela Arnstedt.

The explanation arrived along with my coffee and dessert. An enormously stout woman, wearing flowing gypsy skirts

305

and a blue silk turban, swished toward me in red harem slippers and peasant blouse, dangling golden earrings and a gaudy array of bracelets, beads and pearls. She jingled with every step and sounded like an entire caravan breaking camp. With her incredible girth, she seemed to belong to a different species. One hand held a long cigarette holder and the other a crystal ball. The proprietress of the Hotel de Vienna smiled down at me.

"You wished your fortune told, young man?"

"I suppose so, Señora. I hadn't thought of it that way. Is that your specialty?"

"Our fee is thirty-five cruceños, or five dollars, but since you've had a full dinner we can reduce that to four."

She slipped into my booth and shifted her great weight until she was directly in front of me. Our knees touched. Bela Arnstedt took my hand and flattened out the palm. She peered at the lines, and then arched her lashes at me coyly.

"You're an American?"

"Is that in my palm?"

"It's in your general demeanor. And your cravat. And your eyes. You have extremely strong and delicate fingers. Do you play a stringed instrument? The cello?" She pushed up my cuff to examine my wrist.

"I once played the classical guitar but I don't have much time to practice any more."

"Your palm is very intriguing. Such conflicts. You once worked with your hands and now you work with your mind. I see discontent and a burning desire for accomplishments."

"Very profound, Señora. Like a Chinese fortune cookie."

Our knees brushed again. It was ridiculous, and touched with an unfathomable silliness, but sex had entered the picture. This ample lady, with a good two decades on me, was exuding her musk—almost daring me to reach across the table and cup those ponderous sacs.

"You're going to be very successful and very unhappy, Mr.—"

306

"Ritter. Jack Ritter."

"You believe in nothing, Mr. Ritter. Neither the stars nor the daily newspapers."

"That could apply to just about anyone these days."

She stared at my palm again. "No. It goes deeper than that. There are enigmatic breaks in your lifeline, complex interruptions. You have been scorched by some terrible experience."

"That's not really true, Señora. My life has been a bed of roses. I can't even recall missing a meal."

"Would you care to know about your future, Mr. Ritter?" she said, looking up. "You resist and make it difficult for me to practice my art, but you're still paying me to learn of your future."

"No. It would be more useful if you told me more about my past. I'm trying to get in touch with an old friend of mine, a mutual friends of ours. Dr. Henry Carr. If you recall him."

Señora Bela Arnstedt laughed harshly, almost as if I had told her a risqué story. "So? You knew Enrique? And where did you know him from?"

I resisted the temptation to say Prague.

"We sailed together. We were shipmates on the *Blythe*, right up until he signed off in Puerto Acero. We communicated regularly for a while, but I've sort of lost contact with him over the years."

She motioned for service and I lit Bela Arnstedt's cigarette with the violet candle that had illuminated my dinner. For one flickering second, I penetrated the disguise of age and saw this mound of flesh as the beautiful woman she must have been in Prague thirty-odd years ago. It was an eerie sensation to know this much about a stranger, to know that she wore a pink slip with lace on March fifteenth, nineteen thirty-nine, was playing "Der Rosenkavalier" on her gramophone, and had made a phone call that sent two young girls to their doom.

"Since I'm down here on business I thought I'd try to get in touch with him, Señora. It's been a long time.

Eros had fled our table. My gypsy fortune teller answered me crisply. "That would be extremely difficult, Mr. Ritter. Henry's gone quite native, you know. Unless you like to travel by mule, you'd have a devil of a time reaching him."

Under other circumstances, another evening, I might have laughed at the hilarious pseudo-British colonialisms creeping into her style. But not tonight.

"Well, if you could just supply me with the name of the town, Señora. My business here will be concluded in about five days and I thought I'd drop by and see him afterward."

"It is a bit much to get there," she assured me in a brittle tone. "He's living in the village of Alcala, about two hundred kilometers inland from Puerto Acero. With no roads. Just a dirt track out there."

"Is he still practicing medicine?"

My hostess smiled. "In a sense, I gather. The Indians around Alcala regard him as a witch doctor, and they go to him. And he apparently treats the other peasants who come to him. But I rather think it's that woman who supports him these days. He wasn't well, you know, and his eyes were going bad. Soledad runs a small pulpería and from what I hear, Henry doesn't do much more than sit on the front step and sing. He's begun to fancy himself as a singer, of all things. And breed! They have four children besides Soledad's brood."

"That's great."

"Do you think so, Mr. Ritter? A man of Henry's caliber throwing himself away like that?"

"Yep. That's lovely."

The woman was nauseating. She also managed a nauseating garden restaurant. The parking lot outside was filled with Mercedes and Buicks, and the maitre d's were struggling to contain the lines behind red velvet rails. This Bela was too unscathed; I was moved by a malicious impulse. I rose.

She looked up with a contemptuous smile. "Since you're a friend of Henry's, we'll forego the fee for the palm reading. And you didn't let me tell your future, anyway."

I took a twenty from my wallet and slipped it under the ashtray. It covered the drinks, dinner, palm reading and tip.

"Oh, you finished it, in your fashion. Thank you. You've been a great help, Señora Brenner."

I allowed myself a few seconds to enjoy the way her features dissolved and her face darkened with shock. Glancing back from the lobby, I saw her struggling to shift her bulk around the booth, to rise and follow me, but she was too fat for the effort.

It had been a small knife. And not mine to plunge. A traveling American businessman had no right to drop in like a visitor from another planet, mention the foetus buried in the back yard. But then, this life was basically such a one-sided affair, matching off enormous defeats with small triumphs, that at times I could content myself with these minor points.

I walked down Avenida 14 de Mayo toward the Hilton. Lovers were strolling hand in hand after the spring shower. The forecast for Monday was clear skies. In the future I would be more tolerant of my own foibles. I was approaching forty and had done little damage to other human beings so far.

At the end of the week I would take Burt's check and send it off to some charity. I had to go through with these conferences because Burt and I had a contract, but I did not need the money. It was a small gesture, tokenism at best, but I wanted to feel clean next week when I went out to Alcalá. I wanted to appear clean before that blind man who sang on the steps of the pulpería. I had a few questions for him. It was possible to learn so much about time and yourself, define space and time, when old friends met again.